HELL FLYERS

STARSHIP JERICHO
BOOK 1

TOBY NEIGHBORS

Hell Flyers (Starship Renegade series book 1)

Copyright © 2025 by Toby Neighbors

All rights reserved.

ISBN: 978-1-968189-04-4 eBook

978-1-968189-05-1 print

Mythic Adventure Publishing, LLC

Idaho, USA

Freedom is never voluntarily given by the oppressor:
It must be demanded by the oppressed.

MARTIN LUTHER KING, JR.

CHAPTER 1

"DUMP POWER TO THE DEFLECTORS," Commander Justin Kase, callsign Hard Case, ordered. "We're in gravity now."

"Express elevator to hell, going down!" Animal cackled. Lieutenant Phillip Van Dice liked to talk when he flew. The joke was old, but one of his favorites.

"Spread out. Double your stern deflector screens," Commander Kase told his six-ship squad. They were a tight group making a standard planetary invasion run. Their old fighters were loaded with new Arodoni tech, including energy shields that could deflect laser fire. "Save your power for the climb out."

The darkness of space around them shifted to the faint glow of the planet's upper atmosphere. The squad cut their engines and let the planet's gravity pull them down. Around them, laser fire from the surface began to flash like bolts of lightning in reverse.

They spun around, twisting and zigging and zagging to make it hard for the computer-automated defense cannons to track them. Hard Case didn't need to tell his people what to do. They were all good flyers—the best of the best in his opinion - and even though they had only been together a short time, they were gelling as a team faster than Kase had hoped for.

"Fighters are scrambling," Lieutenant Lynn Jasmin, callsign Indigo, reported.

"Time?" Kase asked.

"Four minutes until they're close enough to engage," Indigo replied.

"That's enough time for one run," Lieutenant Blake Stone, callsign Bishop, said.

"Make it count, people," Kase said. "Looks like we'll only get one bite from the apple. What's the ETA on that troop carrier?"

"The *Pegasus* is nine minutes out," Lieutenant Lucy Sky, callsign Diamond, replied. "On course for planetary entry as planned."

"Let's make sure she has a clear path to the LZ," Kase said.

"Time to clear the road!" Animal declared.

The squad was in standard fast attack ships. The wrench spinners called them Chimera's because they were multi-purpose vessels. New alien tech, specifically, enhanced power cells, gave the ships enough energy to utilize deflector screens and laser cannons. But the main ordinance of the ships was missiles and bombs that could be attached to the wings and fired at targets on the ground or in the air. The ships could also fight in space, although that environment required a completely different set of aviation skills. Commander Kase was one of the few flyers who could handle both. His new squad also had fighter training in atmosphere and hard vacuum. Fortunately, there hadn't been much need for their skills in the Sol system, but all that was about to change.

"Move to attack speed," Kase said, throttling up his engine. "Activate targeting radar."

Below the squad was a set of defensive installations on a mountain ridge that spread out over ten miles. They were protecting a nuclear processing facility that was built underground. It could have been nuked from space, but the Brass wanted confirmation of kills and acquisition of fissionable materials. That would be done by the jarheads on the *Pegasus,* which was following the squad down. The job of the fighters was to make sure the troop carrier wasn't shot down before the Marines could do their part.

"Target acquired," Indigo said. "Permission to engage."

"Permission granted. Fire at will."

"Delta one," the reports came in as the aviators fired their air-to-ground missiles. "Delta two."

Twelve missiles shot ahead of the flyers and seconds later detonated on the laser cannons that had been firing at them. Not all of the weapons were destroyed, but several were completely disabled. The others were shrouded in smoke and debris from the missile attacks, their targeting systems unable to locate the SDF ships racing over their location.

On Commander Kase' HUD, information popped up. There were radar warnings of incoming ships, and the satellite data on the result of their attack run.

"Four batteries down," the Commander remarked. "Two are still operational."

"We can circle back," Bishop suggested.

"Not before those fighters arrive," Diamond said. "We don't even know if the last two defensive units can hit a target."

"Have to assume they can," the Commander said. "Animal, Indigo, circle back. Diamond, Bishop, Aspen, you're with me. Spread out and target incoming fighters. Missiles first. Don't waste laser power if you don't have to."

Power was the new fuel. The fast attack fighter ships had once relied on liquid fuel for both the hard vacuum and atmospheric operations. Yet eighteen months ago everything changed. SDF personnel returned to the Sol system with an alien vessel called the *Independence*. It carried massive amounts of technical data from a race called the Arodoni. Since then, humanity had been in a race to see what they could do with that technology and the Space Defense Force was at the head of that sprint. One of the changes was the swap from liquid fuel to fully rechargeable battery power. Commander Justin Kase had been educated on the change and trained with the new tech, but he didn't trust it yet.

Lasers had always been major power drains. They still were to a certain degree, although the new alien technology had made the weapons on the Chimeras more efficient. Kase still didn't like the idea of using lasers in combat. It just seemed careless to him, especially when the goal was to climb back up into orbit instead of landing on the ground. Breaking free of a planet's gravity was also a huge power drain. That necessity never left the Commander's mind.

"Plenty of targets," Lieutenant Lynn Jasmin, callsign Aspen, said. "That's a full air wing of defenders."

"Makes it hard to miss," Animal declared.

"Those are conventional fighters," Commander Kase said. "Your missiles have the advantage."

It was true. Conventional fighters still used bullets and some missiles. The ordnance on the Chimera's had greater range. His targeting computer was busy locking onto the enemy ships.

"Delta three," Aspen said as she fired at the incoming ships. "Delta four."

Their air-to-air missiles had longer range and more sophisticated tracking hardware than the air-to-ground ordinance. The targeting computer locked onto an enemy ship, conveyed that data to the rocket, which steered after the aircraft until it impacted the ship or ran out of fuel. They had smaller warheads, but great fuel capacity and better aerodynamics than their larger cousins, which utilized gravity as much as propellant to reach their targets. Plus, the targets on the ground moved a lot less than those in the air.

The dogfight never really materialized. Four Chimeras, each launching four air-to-air missiles, took out over half of the defending ships. The rest were recalled. They turned and hit their afterburners to race away from the invading ships just as the *Pegasus* appeared above them.

"Hell Flyers, this is Pegasus actual. Are we clear for landing?"

Commander Kase checked the satellite info on the defensive batteries. It should have them all disabled. The pilots on the *Pegasus* had the same information, but they wanted confirmation from the fighters.

"All clear, *Pegasus*. You can begin your landing. We'll stick around and make sure nothing unwarranted pops up."

"Copy that. LZ is clear. *Pegasus* is inbound for landing."

"Hell Flyers, assume defensive formation. Let's walk the *Pegasus* to school."

"Copy that," Aspen said as she moved into position just off the Commander's starboard wing.

The rest of the squadron paired up. Animal with Indigo and Bishop with Diamond. It was a standard formation as they spread out and circled the landing area. Their perimeter was fifteen miles around the LZ, adding the radar on their aircraft to the one on the SDF ship in orbit above them. The computers were synced together and formed one radar picture that covered nearly seven hundred miles on the planet and in the air above the ground. If anything penetrated that invisible box, the pilots and officers on the command ship would know it almost instantly.

But nothing else came around. Once the *Pegasus* was safely on the ground, the squad of fast attack ships were recalled to the command vessel in space. Hard Case was pleased to see that the climb back into orbit used less than half of the remaining power in the new battery banks on his all-electric ship.

After landing, he disembarked, only not from a fast attack ship, but from a flight simulator. He looked around. There were a dozen spherical pods on the Lunar training station. Commander Kase and his new squad, the Hell Flyers, had been training on the new tech for over a week. And soon, he knew, they would be called into action. What type of action, or where, was a mystery. Everyone in the SDF knew something was afoot, but no one had any specifics. Commander Kase had been recalled to the Lunar training facility two weeks previously, and given orders to form a squad for multi-environment air combat. Since then, he and his team had flown simulator missions and waited for their assignment to come through.

"Hey, Commander," Animal said as he wiped the sweat that had formed on his face from the goggles he wore in the simulator. "How long are we going to play video games?"

"Yeah," Indigo agreed. "This is getting tiresome."

"You find combat tiresome?" Hard Case asked.

"When there's no real threat," Bishop said. "It gets tedious."

"There has to be some news, right?" Aspen asked.

"If that's the case, no one has shared it with me. When I know, you'll know. That's all I can promise."

"It may be a new Space Defense Force, but it seems like the same old system to me," Diamond said.

"Let's get some grub and see what's on the net," Aspen said.

The squad of highly trained - and understandably bored - pilots set off in the direction of the Lunar facility. Hard Case couldn't blame them. They were fighter pilots but they had been training on missions that were almost too easy. It didn't make sense. Worse still, he had no answers for them. All he could do was wait and keep running the simulations. Eventually, new orders would come down. Until then, they would all have to be patient. That was a virtue that didn't come naturally to a bunch of flyers who were trained to push everything to its limits and beyond.

CHAPTER 2

THEY WERE ALMOST BACK HOME, but the Sol system was feeling less and less like home to Captain Darius. He was the senior officer on board the Arodoni-built ship, *Renegade*. In many ways, he was his own master. His superiors in the SDF no longer had the standing to give him orders. Not because of pride or ambition on Darius' part, but because their focus was limited to the Sol system. As long as Darius kept the alien war ships at bay, they gave him a very long leash, as well as enough personnel to outfit the *Renegade*.

She was a very advanced ship, maybe the most advanced vessel in the galaxy. Almost completely automated, she had space for a crew of three thousand. Currently, she carried exactly two thousand souls and most of those were researchers and support personnel. The ship was almost completely automated. Darius had run her with less than a hundred people, and even fought in combat with that few. But since clearing the Sol system of the Imperium warships eighteen months prior, there had been no shortage of volunteers. About a quarter of their current crew was alien. That's the way Darius liked it. Humanity was new to the Galaxy and still had a lot to learn. Having a diverse crew allowed him access to various points of view that helped fill out the picture of what was really going on in the galaxy.

The 'brass' weren't interested in what the *Renegade* did, as long she brought back spoils. Darius knew the tech from the Arodoni ship was more technological knowledge than the entire human race could master in ten lifetimes, but that didn't mean the people in charge of things, namely the Space Defense Force, didn't want more. At every system where an inhabited planet existed, the natives wanted to send a representative to the Sol system. Darius was keenly aware that humanity's militant nature made them unique. Every other species that had a history of warfare had been defeated and eventually wiped out by the Ashi. They were a militant race of towering, powerful beings who had conquered the known galaxy thousands of years ago. They encouraged both slavery and genocide. Until the crew of the SDF ship *Jericho* had left the Sol system a few years before, the Ashi had gone uncontested in recent millenia.

The *Jericho* was a ship built by the SDF but using information from a foreign entity. Unknown to the builders, the *Jericho* was capable of interstellar flight using the network of hyperspace routes that were revealed to Darius and his crew by the same foreign entity that designed the ship. Yet, the *Jericho* wasn't merely a trans system vessel. It was also the core to the Arodoni vessel *Renegade.* Along with a unique power conversion apparatus that the *Jericho's* Marine platoon recovered on an extinct planet called Lawash, the screw shaped *Jericho* fit into the *Renegade* to provide power to the much larger Arodoni ship.

The *Renegade* was over seven kilometers long and four kilometers wide. It was shaped like a fish with an open mouth, and a collar around the head. The upper head portion was the command center of the ship. It contained all the ship's controls, as well as meeting spaces and berths for the officers. Unlike most military ships, the best berths on the *Renegade* were apartment-style cabins that overlooked the large, green space that stretched five kilometers long, and three wide, in the center of the alien vessel. The space contained open fields, trees, shrubs and running streams. There were also floating platforms that were covered with exotic flora. There were even animals, herds of small cattle that were harvested to provide sustenance to the crew. There were birds and insects that flew in the wide open space above the park. And all around this incredible green space were cabins with balconies on several levels.

But there was a lot more to the ship than just flight controls and green spaces. There was a large commercial area with everything from warehouses to storefronts. Volunteers had come aboard and opened stores, restaurants, clubs and entertainment venues. Not just for the humans, there were also alien eateries and shops that sold goods from various parts of the galaxy.

Along with the commercial section of the ship was a highly advanced manufacturing center that contained both a refinery and the means to make nearly anything a person could think of. Raw materials were captured via artificial gravity beams, hauled into the open mouth section of the alien ship, broken down into usable materials, from rare minerals to water. Those materials were then used to create whatever was needed on the massive ship. Unlike a human vessel, things rarely broke down on the Arodoni ship. When they did, automated drones fixed the issue almost immediately. There were drones that cleaned the ship, others that tended the green space which the crew called the Park. There were drones that harvested animals and crops from the Park and stocked the galleys and restaurants on the ship.

And in the rear of the ship were huge workshops, laboratories and classrooms. The spaces were stocked with chemicals, minerals and substances from across the galaxy. No one knew much about the Arodoni, including why they had abandoned this fantastic ship or what they had done with it before they disappeared. But it seemed likely that researchers among their kind had carried out experiments in the workshops and laboratories.

The ship had a powerful supercomputer, but not Artificial Intelligence. In its memory banks were vast stores of data about the ship, its technology, the hyperspace lanes that connected the galaxy together, and knowledge on a wide variety of scientific fields. That information was open to the crew and had been copied and delivered to the beings on every inhabited planet the *Renegade* had visited. And yet, somehow, the people in positions of authority in the Sol system wanted more. So, Darius delivered it to them in the form of ambassadors who shared the history of their race, their native planet and the Galactic Imperium.

"What's our status?" Darius asked.

"Two hours and twelve minutes until we leave hyperspace in the Sol system," Lieutenant Jacee Bertoli said from the navigation console.

"Very good. Let me know if anything changes," Darius said, getting up from his captain's chair on the Bridge. "Lieutenant Stanislaus, you have the con."

"Aye, Captain, I have the con," Alex Stanislaus, the chief engineer, said.

Darius looked around. He had veterans and rookies on his staff, but they were all good officers. The Bridge of the *Renegade* had been remade. The padded benches used by the Arodoni were replaced with human chairs fabricated in the manufacturing plant below them. The holographic displays were tuned to be ideal for human sight. Above them, the transparent canopy that stretched over the Bridge showed the colorful swarms of light in hyperspace. Darius didn't quite understand the physics of the extra-dimensional travel, but he understood there were lanes that stretched between the star systems and allowed interstellar ships to travel through the corridors traversing huge distances in a very short amount of time. They had never experienced any sort of trouble in hyperspace, but Darius was a cautious commander. The safety of his crew, and the vessel they operated, was always on his mind.

He left the Bridge in capable hands and went down one level. His quarters were on Kappa, as was the Officer's Wardroom. It was a simple space, occupied mostly by a long table. In the back was a buffet-style cabinet with food warmers. Alex Stanislaus' engineers had been busy after they discovered and took control of the alien ship. Most of the areas in the command section were modernized, or humanized, depending on how one looked at them. Not all of the officers on the ship were humans, but most were. And so, most of the appliances and conveniences had been made for them.

Opposite the buffet counter was another set of cabinets that contained beverages. There was a cooler with a transparent door for cold drinks and a variety of machines to make hot drinks as well. Darius preferred plain drip coffee, and he was pleased to find a pot was already brewed. Captain Zeke Darius wasn't the only officer who preferred plain, black coffee to the fancier versions.

When Darius stepped into the Wardroom, Marine Corps Major

Remmy Steel rose to his feet. It wasn't necessary. The two men were friends as well as colleagues, but the Marines were sticklers for discipline, and the Major was a perfect example.

"At ease, Remmy," Darius said. "How's the coffee?"

Remmy Steel sat back down and placed his hands on his mug. "Good," he said.

Darius knew his Marine commander was not a man of many words. So, he nodded, and poured himself a cup.

"How is everything in grunt country?" Darius asked, referring to the section of the ship where the Marines carried out their training, and kept their weapons of war.

"Fine, sir," Remmy said.

"Are we losing a lot this cycle?"

"About half," Remmy said. "None of the Spec Ops personnel though. And we have one returning commando."

"Sergeant McManus?"

"Yes, sir," Remmy said. "He's decided to stay."

"Is that wise?"

"I know him pretty well. He's certainly worth taking a chance on."

"Very good," Darius said, sipping his coffee. It was good. Not too fresh, not too old and strong enough for his taste. "I always get nervous going back home."

"Expecting trouble?"

"It's hard not to think we're going to get surprised by some power-hungry new Admiral who thinks we should all be replaced."

Remmy just gave a low chuckle. He was not the kind of man Darius would want to cross. The Major didn't project hostility; in fact, he was just the opposite. He projected cool and calm, even in a crisis. The idea that someone would try to force him to leave the *Renegade* was unthinkable.

Darius thought that every crew member on the Arodoni ship deserved the highest citation the SDF could award, but Major Remmy Steel actually had been awarded the Medal of Honor. That fact alone put him on par with every officer on board. It was customary for all officers, no matter their rank, to salute winners of the Medal of Honor. Yet Remmy never insisted on the perks his accomplishments had earned him. He saw himself more as an NCO, which is what he had been until the *Renegade* had left the Sol system after the Battle of Saturn. When Darius reorganized the volunteers that remained and prepared to take on new crew members, Darius had insisted that Remmy take command of the Marines on board, elevating him in rank to Major.

The alien ship had become their home. It wasn't just because it offered so many amenities to what a person could afford back on Earth. It was because they had made it their home, through sweat, blood, improvements and sacrifices. They had fought in the ship and fought to defend the ship. They had traveled the galaxy in the *Renegade* and it only seemed right that they be allowed to continue their mission, which was to free as many systems as possible from the tyranny of the Galactic Imperium. But Darius was still just a Captain, and his superiors could try to change the arrangement. Darius didn't want that kind of hassle. He wouldn't give up command, partly because he loved it, but mostly because no one else in the entire fleet was qualified. They didn't know the ship or the nuances of the galaxy. He was the ranking officer who had ever left the Sol system. Eventually that would change. The SDF was building ships capable of traversing the hyperspace lanes. There were worlds waiting to be discovered and colonized by the ever-growing human population. New breakthroughs were rampant due to the Arodoni data brought to the Sol system and that included terraforming. Mars had already begun a vast, soil rejuvenation program and was seeing rapid growth in flora that was transforming the Red Planet's atmosphere.

But the threat that he might be given orders he didn't agree with hung over Captain Darius like a black cloud whenever they returned to the Sol system.

"Will you tell them your plans?"

"Already have," Darius said. "I send regular reports through the hyperspace portals, but I haven't heard back if they'll supply what we need."

"It can be done with drones," Remmy said.

"Maybe," Darius said. "But I'd like to have every resource at my disposal before we go back into the core systems."

Remmy didn't argue. He gave a nod of solidarity and sipped his coffee. Since the battle of Saturn that had sent what remained of the

Imperium fleet running back to the core systems, they had gone into that sector of space only once. It was unlike anywhere they had been before. Every system around the core had defensive systems, from automated laser batteries to garrisons of Ashi fighters. Going back was dangerous, but to break the Imperium's hold on the galaxy, they needed to be defeated and the power stripped away. The *Renegade* couldn't do that without putting herself at risk. Darius' plan was bold, although he believed it was necessary, both to free the planets in a thousand star systems, but - maybe most importantly - to neutralize the Ashi threat to humanity.

"Don't worry, sir. The whole ship is behind you," Remmy said. "We'll get what we need."

The Major stood up. His movements were smooth, despite the flecks of gray in his buzzed hair. He didn't seem tired, or nervous despite the fact that he too could be recalled by the Brass back in the Sol system. The entire crew could be rotated off the grand Arodoni ship. That was the way of things in the SDF. Darius knew that if such an order was given, there would be a revolt on the *Renegade*. They would be forced out of the Sol system to keep from fighting their own people. It would mean never going back to the system they still called home. Perhaps, Darius thought, it would be for the best. But maybe not yet. Maybe they would give him what he needed and let him do what had to be done for the good of the galaxy. He would know soon enough. They all would.

CHAPTER 3

REMMY WALKED from the Command section of the ship and took the gravity lift down to Epsilon deck. He came out into the wide concourse where a variety of businesses and shops were located, along with the Administration offices. It was always a busy section of the ship, but he didn't mind. Remmy could remember when there were so few people on board the *Renegade* that most of the storefronts and business spaces were empty and dark.

The Concourse was sleek with polished floors, chrome and diamond accents that reflected light which poured in from the various businesses. It reminded Remmy of a shopping mall, only mixed among the stores, restaurants, and entertainment venues were businesses owned by aliens from different planets. He passed the lounge where the handful of Dudonus aliens recreated. It was filled with artifacts from their culture, which had been scattered across the galaxy when the Dudonus were categorized as a slave race by the Imperium.

He passed an eatery for the Casians on board. They were large-bodied, pachyderms with six legs who ate leafy greens for every meal. When they weren't busy in the drone command, they were either lounging in the Park or eating at the alien-run cafeteria.

There were others, some exotic, some so plain they seemed boring in comparison. Among all the voices of the people he passed, music from some of the storefronts was added. It made for a merry space, cheerful and - at times - exuberant. Remmy preferred the peace of the Wardroom to most of the places in the Concourse, but he did enjoy walking the various levels and looking at all the incredible goods that were for sale or experiences waiting to be tried. At times he thought that if he ever retired, perhaps he could start a little business some-where in the Concourse and live out his days on the magnificent ship.

Eventually, he left the Concourse and entered the Park. There were other ways to reach Grunt Country but none that compared to walking Epsilon deck and seeing all the sights. To go from the bustling Concourse, into the wide open expanse and tranquility of the Park was almost therapeutic. He strolled along a small stream. It was impos-sible not to wonder at the beauty and genius of how the ship's water was treated on the *Renegade*. The same water that was used for washing and drinking was used to water the vast green space, and sent running along the many streams that gurgled over rocks and tumbled off elevated platforms.

He couldn't help but compare it to the water on a standard SDF vessel, which was cleaned using desalinators and harsh chemicals, then kept in plastic containers. It was an acquired taste that Remmy didn't miss in the least. Nothing like the fresh, almost sweet tasting water on board the *Renegade*.

The clean water, fresh air, open spaces and luxurious accommoda-tions were part of why he, and so many others onboard the alien ship, loved it so much. But it wasn't just the amenities that made Remmy think of the ship as his home. That was different, deeper and more difficult to define than just preferences. It was the first place that felt permanent to Remmy. Most human ships and space stations were vessels that required constant maintenance and left a person feeling that they should be scrapped very soon. But the *Renegade* had been in existence for hundreds of years. No one knew how old it was. It had been abandoned by the Arodoni for several centuries before it was discovered by the crew of the SDF ship, *Jericho*. That alone made it older than the Inner System Coalition government at Sol. It was impossible to know how long the Arodoni had it before the ship was abandoned. The automated maintenance droids kept the entire ship looking brand new.

Remmy and his small band of Marines had fought a running battle on the ship. From the Flight Deck, or Hangar C, the Ashi had come on board to take possession of the vessel, only to find a determined group of Marines waiting to disuade them of that notion. It had been a difficult fight and had caused a lot of damage in the Park and Concourse specifically. But within two weeks, there wasn't a sign of that battle. The scorch marks were gone, the shattered glass replaced, the burns and disturbed soil in the park groomed until a person would never know anything violent had ever happened there.

The first structure along his path was what appeared to be a gazebo made of alien wood and covered with growing vines. It was open to the park on one side, but instead of a place to sit or a table where friends might gather for a meal, there was an open pit. Remmy walked up to the opening and looked down. It was clear. He stepped out into empty space, felt his stomach flip inside him, and slowly floated up to the ceiling of the structure.

It was one of several gravity lifts. Some went from Alpha deck all the way up to Lambda. The one Remmy was using just connected the lower decks. He reached up, pushed himself away from the ceiling and floated down.

Grunt Country occupied most of Alpha and Beta decks above Hangar A, which had been converted to use by the Marines. The *Renegade* had three massive hangars. Hangar B was the flight deck, what a person would think of as a standard hangar on a spaceship. It was large enough that most SDF military vessels could land inside. But it was used mostly by transports and shuttlecraft. Over half of the deck space on Hanger B was empty and ready for ships that might come and go.

Hanger C was the drone hangar. It was filled front to back, side to side, and top to bottom with autonomous vehicles. Some were big enough to be used as drop ships and could fly in hard vacuum as well as in atmosphere. They were surrounded by smaller military drones, some for use in space, others for use in atmospheric operations. They were controlled by operators in the *Renegade*. The Casians mainly, but there was a host of human drone operators too. They weren't called pilots even though the flight controls were very similar. But the drones could do things no human pilot could pull off. They were smaller than standard craft, some only as big as a dinner plate. Most carried high explosives, and the drones were considered expendable. The *Renegade's* manufacturing plant could build them relatively quickly and there were over a thousand stored in Hangar C just waiting to be used.

There were two Marine platoons on the alien ship and a third special operations platoon. Each group had its own lounge area. The Spec Op lounge also doubled as a Ready Room where their weapons and armor were kept ready for action. There was space on the ship for separate rooms, but the Commandos preferred to keep their weapons close to hand. Remmy wasn't surprised when he walked in and saw several of the Special Forces Marines cleaning their weapons.

"Officer on deck!" someone shouted when they saw Remmy and everyone leapt to their feet, stiffening to attention.

"As you were," Remmy said calmly.

He waited just inside the doorway, looking around as the Marines settled back into their routines. After a few moments, he walked up to the biggest man in the room and waited until Hugo McManus looked up.

"Settling in okay, Sergeant?" Remmy asked.

"Yes, sir," Hugo said, glancing around. "It's good to be back."

"You don't miss Libertine?"

Hugo paused for a minute, thinking about the question. Remmy didn't rush him. Hugo was a unique person. Most people were prone to say what they thought you wanted to hear. Hugo was more direct and less socially adept. He was, to Remmy, an acquired taste. He was also a fearless combat veteran and one of the few people that Remmy absolutely trusted by his side in a fight.

"Some things," Hugo said.

"Lieutenant McPherson and I want you to have chow with us when you're ready to talk about how things went down on Libertine."

"Yes, sir. I will."

"Good man." Remmy held out his hand and Hugo took it.

The other Marines were watching. There weren't many Marines who commanded the Major's respect the way Hugo did. It made them curious.

Not far from the Spec Ops Ready Room was the Marine Corps

officers' admin space. Each one had an office that was partly for work, partly for rest. Remmy rarely used his. He was the ranking Marine officer on board and part of the Senior Officers group, which meant he had to spend most of his time in the Command section of the ship. He ignored his own doorway and went instead to Lieutenant Laila McPherson's office, where he knocked.

"Enter," Laila called.

Remmy palmed the control pad and stepped inside the office as the door slid to the side. Laila was at her desk looking at a list of names. Remmy waited until the door closed, then walked around behind her desk and began massaging her shoulders.

"Oh, you have no idea how good that feels," Laila said.

"I can imagine," he replied. "Why are you stressed?"

"Why are you not?" she exclaimed. "We're almost to the Sol system."

"And?"

"And besides the fact that we're losing an entire platoon of Marines with no assurances they'll be replaced, we could be reassigned. You know that's a possibility, right?"

"I know they might try," Remmy said.

"And if they ordered you to report to a new assignment?"

"I'm an officer now," he said slowly. "I suppose I would just resign."

"That's another thing," Laila said. "My enlistment period is up."

"You're an officer now, not an NCO."

"Says you," she remarked. "We were given field promotions. Back in Sol, I'm just a Staff Sergeant whose term of enlistment is up."

"I doubt that's how anyone else thinks of it."

"Easy for you to say. You're a hero with the medals to prove it. You can practically pick your assignments. The rest of us have to go where we're told."

"In that case, I'm your CO, and any reassignment would have to go through me. I would refuse such orders."

She stood up, turned to face him, and smiled.

"You know just the right thing to say."

They kissed. It was more than shipboard romance. Remmy and Laila had broken the unspoken rules on their long cruise out to Saturn in the *Jericho*. When given a chance, neither hesitated to stay on the *Renegade* and stay with one another. During their downtime, they shared a plush apartment on Lambda deck that overlooked the Park.

"How's Hugo doing?" Remmy asked when Laila sat back down.

"Fine so far. I've got him on the Spec Op team. Lieutenant Brasas is rotating off the ship and hasn't been working them hard. No sims, just PT and weapons. Hugo has no problem with that, you know."

"I do. I told him we want to talk with him."

"You think he will?"

"Talk about what happened on Libertine? I think so. He trusts us."

"Has he said what happened to Rip down there?"

"Not to me," I said.

"What if the brass wants to debrief him?"

"I thought about that. There was a human with him. A former slave who claims she was abducted from Earth as a child."

"That's a chilling thought."

"Indeed. She'll have a hell of a story, I imagine. The brass can get whatever they need from her, I suppose."

"You would fight to keep him on board?"

"Yes."

"You don't worry, he's not fit."

"I can't think of anyone more fit."

"Remmy, he disobeyed orders and sacrificed himself. Some might say he has a death wish."

It was true. When the *Renegade* was racing back to the Sol system before the battle of Saturn, Captain Darius had asked Remmy to stay behind and deal with the ships that were trying to intercept them. It was a suicide mission since none of the Marines were pilots with combat experience. Hugo had taken the MECH and used its powerful missiles to chase down the Ashi corvettes. He should have died in orbit around Libertine, but Corporal Albert "Rip" Van Winkle had absconded with a shuttle. The two of them were listed as MIA, and when the *Renegade* returned to the Libertine system, only Hugo and a handful of refugees were there. Rip was not among them.

"He made a selfless decision," Remmy said. "I wouldn't be here if he hadn't done it."

Remmy would never have ordered another person into a situation with no hope of rescue. He had been planning to take the MECH, but Hugo beat him to it.

"He's a complicated person, but not dangerous. Not to us, at any rate."

"That's your call," Laila said. "I'm glad he's okay, but he might create waves on the Spec Op team."

"If that happens, I'll deal with it," Remmy said. "Let's rally the troops and make sure those who are leaving have everything squared away."

"Yes, sir," Laila said.

They headed toward the door, but then Remmy stopped and turned to face her again.

"You don't want to rotate off, do you?"

"No," Laila said.

"You're not just staying for me, are you?"

"Don't be a wiseacre. You know this is our home."

"That's how I feel, but sometimes I fear that I'm keeping you here against your will."

That made Laila laugh out loud. "You are the man of my dreams, Major Steel," she said, leaning close. "You've given me the adventure of a lifetime, not to mention a position of authority that was completely out of reach."

"That's not true. You could have gone to officer's school."

"Sure. And pigs could fly."

"I'm serious."

"So am I, Remmy. I want to be here. I want to be with you. One doesn't negate the other."

Remmy breathed a little easier and he kissed her again. They were right where they needed to be. He couldn't be happier.

CHAPTER 4

HARD CASE WALKED into the meeting room. It was one of the original domes that had been built on the moon decades earlier. The interior had obviously changed many times and it was currently a briefing room with wide windows that showed Earth and the ring of satellites in orbit around her. Commander Justin Case was always captivated by the sight of Earth from space. He had been born in the slums of the Eastern American megalopolis. Growing up, it was rare to see the sky. He could look up between the towering buildings that crowded the narrow streets and see a pall of smog. Only on the rarest of occasions could he actually see blue sky above him ... or stars for that matter.

When he was a teenager, they climbed the stairs of their building to reach the rooftop in the hopes of seeing what lay beyond Earth. His entire life, the dream of traveling to the stars was a possibility, but until recently, leaving the inner part of the solar system had yet to be accomplished. That all changed with the *Jericho*. The debate over the actions of the *Jericho*, who disappeared from the Sol system on her very first cruise, was legendary. Some people called the crew heroes, others called them traitors. Some people said the ship had launched an interstellar war and some alien ships had appeared once, but that was

over a year ago and, to his knowledge, the massive alien ship supposedly crewed by the members of the *Jericho* had disappeared shortly
after.

But Justin had made it to outer space. He was no longer trapped in
the filth that lined the old city streets. He was no longer blinded by
smog and buildings so tall and tight they blocked out the sun. He
could see it all, the beauty and the danger.

"Commander, if you could wait one more moment," a Lieutenant
working the controls by a small screen on the opposite side of the room
from the window said.

"Of course," Commander Kase said.

He grasped one wrist with his other hand behind his back and
stood with his feet apart, gazing out the window. Soon, another man
entered. His name was Commander Mathias Elder, callsign Legend.
Justin couldn't stand the man. Every flyer was extremely confident,
but Legend was insufferable.

The look on Legend's face made it obvious that he felt the same
about Hard Case. Neither man spoke, but Legend walked past his
peer and stood by the table where the lieutenant was busy on his
computer.

"Commander Elder, to see Admiral Paulson."

"The Admiral will be in soon," the lieutenant said. "If you could
please wait along with Commander Kase."

"I'll wait here," Legend said, as if standing by the desk somehow
made him more important.

Fortunately, the Admiral appeared almost immediately after
Mathias Elder, and Kase snapped to attention.

"At ease, Commander," Wendy Paulson said. "Thank you both for
coming."

"It was my pleasure," Legend said.

Hard Case remained silent. He figured it was best not to say more
than he had to with the SDF brass. Maybe he was finally going to find
out why he had been ordered to Luna and given a squad to train.

"You've both been called here because an opportunity has arisen,"
Admiral Paulson said. "You've both heard of the *Renegade*, no doubt."

"Alien ship, supposedly crewed by a rogue captain," Legend said.

Hard Case's heart was beating faster. They hadn't been training to fight a large ship in space. He doubted they were going to be attacking the *Renegade*, but it was possible they might join her.

"It is an alien-built vessel," Admiral Paulson said. "And I need not remind either of you that it is a highly classified ship. If either of you shares what I'm going to tell you next, you will be court-martialed. I will personally see to it that you die in prison for treason. Is that clear?"

"Yes, ma'am," Hard Case immediately.

"I'm familiar with the regulation," Legend said. "And I have top-secret clearance."

There was a look on the Admiral's face that told him she thought as much of Mathias Elder as Hard Case did.

"Very well. The *Renegade* is returning. Her Captain, a highly decorated naval officer, is Zeke Darius. I believe you both know him."

That was true. Hard Case and Legend had both been on the *Sargon* fresh out of flight school. Captain Darius had been a Commander then, second in command. There were times when both pilots had overstepped their bounds and been confronted by Darius. But Hard Case had respect for him. Zeke Darius was tough, but fair, and from all reports a good Captain to serve under.

Legend didn't say anything, and Justin knew that meant he didn't have the same respect for the ship's Captain that Hard Case did.

"He has requested two squadrons of fast attack craft," Admiral Paulson went on. "Not just average flyers, but the very best the SDF has to offer. Are you those flyers, Commander?"

"Yes, ma'am," Hard Case said immediately.

"I'm the best there is," Legend said.

"So I hear," Admiral Paulson said. "The truth is, we really have no idea what Captain Darius is dealing with, but his mandate is to keep whatever forces might threaten the Sol system from ever getting close. And in the last year and a half, our scientists have made great strides in propulsion and aerospace engineering. Soon, we will be able to expand beyond the Sol system, setting up colonies on various worlds not yet discovered. I say that to emphasize how important the SDF's mission of keeping humanity safe is becoming. We will soon be players on the Galactic stage and the *Renegade* is currently our only presence outside the system. Anything done as part of that crew will be highly classified. You can't talk about it. You can't even tell your family that you'll be on the *Renegade*. And, for that purpose, SDF regulations require that you have a choice in such an assignment."

"We're being assigned to the *Renegade*?" Legend asked.

"That is the assignment. New fighters on an alien ship, doing God knows what outside the solar system."

"I'm in," Hard Case said.

"I'm not sure how I feel about a rogue ship," Legend said before the Admiral could respond to me. "There's no oversight on the *Renegade*. No chain of command?"

"The chain of command is intact," Admiral Paulson said. "But you won't have anyone to run to if things don't go your way, Captain."

Hard Case knew that Legend had contacts. He was from a wealthy family with political connections. In fact, if the rumors were true, he had gone around his commanding officers to get the assignments he wanted. It wouldn't surprise Hard Case if that was true and the Admiral certainly seemed to be implying something along those lines.

"It's preposterous," Legend said. "What if Darius orders us to do something we don't agree with?"

"You will follow orders, whether it be from the captain of the *Renegade* or whoever you are serving under," Admiral Paulson said. "This is a once-in-a-lifetime opportunity, gentlemen. You both have very talented squadrons, and there is no doubt that whatever you are needed for, it is important."

"And dangerous," Legend said.

Hard Case felt no need to contribute to the conversation. To be part of whatever was going on with the alien-built ship was what Hard Case had always dreamed of. Missions would take place outside the Sol system and that was good enough for him.

"Frankly, with your reputation, Commander Elder, I would have thought you would jump at the chance for action."

"No one can match my flying, Admiral, in or out of the Sol system. There is no doubt about that. But I'm not sure I agree with a single ship having free rein to do whatever its commander thinks best. Surely, more oversight is needed with Captain Darius."

"Captain Darius will be remembered as the most important commander in the history of the SDF. His decisions were outside the norm, but he and his crew were responsible for boosting our knowledge by hundreds, if not thousands of years. Do you understand that? I know much about his work is classified, but make no mistake, Captain, the work being done on the *Renegade* is, for lack of a better word, legendary."

Justin Kase was a disciplined man, but he almost cracked up laughing. He remained quiet, but his face gave away his mirth at the Admiral's remark. When she glanced over at him, there was just the faintest hint of a smile at the corners of her mouth as well.

"I suppose it's the best choice for my career," Mathias said. "I agree. Will I be in charge of the air group?"

"You and Commander Kase will be of equal rank and authority under the ship's command structure," Admiral Paulson said. "I will leave it to you both to share the opportunity with your flyers, but anyone who isn't on board will be immediately reassigned. Tell them as little as possible."

"There's really not much to tell," Legend said.

"As any classified matter should be. You are both to report to the shuttle bay at 0600 hours with your squads."

"What about our ships?"

"They will be delivered to the *Renegade*. Good luck, gentlemen. I wish you both well."

"Thank you, Admiral," Hard Case said, snapping to attention and saluting.

"Luck is for hacks," Legend said as he walked away.

Hard Case didn't watch him go. There was no need. Protocols like salutes weren't mandated, but rather a sign of respect among officers. It seemed like Mathias Elder had little if any respect for the people around him. He was wealthy and thought of himself as important. In Justin's mind, the combination of entitlement and privilege was enough to ruin a person.

Admiral Paulson watched Legend for just a few seconds, then returned Hard Case's salute.

"I wish I was going with you," she said.

"Why don't you?"

"We don't all have the connections to pick our assignments," she said, glancing at Legend again as he left the room. "My place is here."

"Thank you, Admiral."

"Make us proud, Commander."

He nodded and hurried to tell his squad.

CHAPTER 5

THEY HAD ARRIVED in the Sol system, and Hugo McManus stood outside the apartment that had been assigned to Zaya Wright. She was leaving, he was staying; in his mind, that left nothing for them to say. But he wished he could think of something that might ease their parting. It was breaking his heart, but he was unaccustomed to thinking about things in such ways. He understood the pain, just not how to deal with it.

"That's it," she said. "Kind of sad, I guess."

"Why?" Hugo asked.

"I am a grown woman," she said. "It feels like I should have more belongings than what fits in a single bag."

"I could have gotten you more," Hugo suggested. "Perhaps if we hurry—"

"No," she said, holding up a hand. "You've done enough."

He was surprised to find that his banking information was still active, and he had been earning his regular salary during the nearly eighteen months he had been on Libertine. The *Renegade* didn't have access to the SDF banking network, so the ship created its own digital currency. He had an equivalent amount of money on the ship as he had at home. And so, he had used some of the money to get Zaya new clothes and useful items such as a hairbrush and handbag.

Still, despite their life together on Libertine, it was soon clear that those bonds wouldn't last once they returned to civilization. Hugo's biggest fear had been that she didn't care for him. They had been the only two humans on Libertine, and it was lack of options that made their relationship work. With the arrival of new options, Zaya had pulled away.

"I'll walk you to the hangar," he suggested.

"You don't have to," she said.

"I want to," he replied.

They left the apartment, which had a nice view across the immaculate lawn of the Park. She had never been on a ship like the *Renegade*. Not that she had been on a lot of ships. She had been on a few, but they were slave ships, and the last was an Ashi battleship. Neither was meant to be luxurious. And on each she had been a slave. No one cared about the comfort of a slave. It was still difficult for her to accept that Hugo wasn't merely pretending to care about her. And why should he? They were no longer the only people around. There were more people than she had ever been around before. Most were humans, and that seemed incredibly strange to her. Since being abducted from Earth as a child, she had been in the minority of every group she had been in.

They left the opulent apartment. It was nothing more than a couple of rooms, but everything about it glistened and shone, from the windows overlooking the Park, to the facilities in the bathroom. It seemed incredibly strange to have robots doing everything that she had been forced to do all her life. They were tireless and unfazed by the lowliest of tasks. It seemed so much more efficient to her than living slaves. It also seemed strangely obscene for some reason she couldn't identify.

When they reached the gravity lift that led down to the hangar with neither of them speaking a word, she stopped him.

"Hugo, I think it's best if I go on from here by myself."

"Why?"

Her voice quavered with emotion. "Because, it's hard to say goodbye."

"I know," he replied softly. "I wish it didn't have to be."

It was her turn to be confused. She didn't know if he was saying he wished they didn't have to leave one another, or if he just didn't want it to be painful.

"I have to go," she said. "The authorities have a lot of questions for me."

"They'll make sure you have everything you need," he said.

"I guess. When you come back... I mean, if you come back, look me up, okay?"

He nodded, but didn't say anything. She leaned forward, kissed his smooth cheek. That was a nice change from before, his ability to shave every single day. He looked to her in that moment like a mash-up of a mythic hero and a sad little boy.

She had never been more beautiful to him. Zaya had a scar across one cheek, and another over the opposite eye, but her hair was brushed until it shined in the light from high above the Park's green space. And she wore a dress over black tights that made her look feminine. He wanted to reach out and grab hold of her. He wanted to pull her into a tight embrace and never let go, but she had been forced to do someone else's will all her life. And he was determined to give her freedom, even if she used it to leave him.

"Bye, Hugo," she said, stepping into the gravity lift and pushing herself down. He stood, watching her go. She got smaller and smaller, then at the bottom, stepped through the door and out of sight. She had never even looked back.

It felt to Hugo McManus, combat veteran, Special Forces commando, like he had just been dealt a wound that would never heal.

Down on Alpha level, Zaya stepped through the portal and then dropped to her knees and sobbed.

In the Command section of the Arodoni ship, Captain Darius came out of the first of what would be many meetings. He had gone through the list of beings flying from the *Renegade* to the new SDF transfer station between Saturn and Jupiter. It was a plain, bare bones facility, but it utilized the new gravity technology that had been brought to humanity by the *Independence*. That and so much more was part of the technology gained by the adventures of the SDF *Jericho*. Leaving the Sol system shortly after making contact with the alien artifact who called herself GIGI had been a huge gamble. But it had paid off for the entire human race, and much of the galaxy as well.

Darius had ordered copies of the Arodoni databanks to be copied and shared. That information was greater than anything the Imperium had, and would level the playing field. Not that every system would use the technology to build defenses, but they could if they wanted to, and that, he guessed, would make a difference in the long run.

He walked from his cabin back up to the Bridge to check on things. His second in command, Lieutenant Pete Best, was in command of the ship. They were on approach to the holding area just twenty kilometers from the transfer station. Other ships were moving in the area, but none as big as the *Renegade*. A few fast-moving ships that utilized Arodoni tech had been constructed to run between the transfer station and the inner system. Two were docked to the station.

"How we looking, Pete?" Darius asked.

"A-okay, Captain," Lieutenant Best said. "Just bringing the *Renegade* to a static position."

"Very good. Are we facing the portal?"

"We will be," Pete said. "Scopes are clear. All radar scans show nothing out of the ordinary."

"Just two weeks and we're back to work," Darius said. "Make sure you log some downtime."

"Will do, Captain. Thank you, sir."

Darius left the Bridge and went back down to his cabin. It was a lavish space compared with what he was accustomed to on SDF vessels. His quarters had a big central space with both office and formal sitting area. His crew had dutifully created a pair of matched sitting chairs and a sofa. There was a mini-bar with some liquor in crystal decanters and a small drip coffee maker. A high-resolution holo-projector sprang up from the floor near the sitting area, and another smaller version served as a monitor for his computer on the wide desk.

Another room contained his personal living quarters, with a round bed which had been the style of the Arodoni and adapted by the humans on the ship. It had a wide set of cubbies which served as his closet. And his bath facilities were spacious. In total, it was the nicest quarters Darius had ever lived in, either on ship or on land.

He poured himself a cup of coffee, then settled into his desk. There was a lot of work to do. Supplies needed to be restocked. Not that the *Renegade* couldn't supply everything they needed, from power to victuals, to new uniforms, and weapons. But the ship was also home to well over a hundred vendors. None of the shop owners, restaurateurs or club proprietors were service members. Most were former SDF enlisted members, but a few were just adventurous entrepreneurs, and most needed supplies from vendors in the Sol system. Many were also using the resources of the ship, but some crew members wanted things they were used to. Sodas, prepackaged snacks, and unique food items, especially spices and herbs, needed to be delivered to the ship.

The biggest need was human personnel. Some of the crew simply weren't accustomed to long cruises. A six-month tour on the *Renegade* was all they could handle before needing to get back to familiar surroundings. Others were put off by combat ... and the *Renegade* had seen battles. In most systems, there was at least one Imperium ship. Sometimes as many as three were stationed near the inhabited planets or moons. In each one, the *Renegade* had deployed her powerful laser cannons and blasted the Imperium ships to atoms. Oftentimes, this was followed by a Marine deployment to the planet where the Imperium officials were rounded up and turned over to the natives. Sometimes, there was violence involved in rounding up the beings who were in charge of the Imperium government. Occasionally there were encounters with slave traders. It was a lot to wrestle with, both mentally and physically, depending on a crew member's area of responsibility.

The *Renegade* had liberated over fifty systems, and it was just the proverbial tip of the iceberg. Darius knew they needed to do more. They needed to hit the enemy where it hurt, in the galactic core. But to do that, they needed a full complement of ships at their disposal. The *Renegade* could sit back and pick off the Ashi battleships, but to get past planetary defenses and land Marines on the surface of the core worlds would require ace pilots in hybrid fighters that weren't like other ships. Darius had made the request for the pilots and he was about to find out if they were coming or not.

CHAPTER 6

"THE *RENEGADE*? CAN YOU BELIEVE IT?" Animal asked. "This is so epic."

"It might not be a cool as you think," Aspen warned.

"Yeah, an alien ship," Bishop pointed out. "That might be weird."

"How long?" Diamond asked Hard Case.

"Unknown," he replied. Commander Justin Kase had been fully briefed on the *Renegade*, although over seventy percent of the information about the alien ship was redacted. He did know a few things. "Her last few cruises have been about six months."

"That's a long time," Indigo pointed out. "I don't think I've ever had a relationship that lasted that long."

"You love 'em and leave 'em, Indigo?"

"Get out before you get hurt, that's my motto," she replied.

It wasn't surprising. As Ace aviators, they were in high demand. The SDF moved them around frequently and few civilians could understand, much less keep up, with their fast-paced lifestyle.

"You think we'll make a six-month cruise?" Bishop asked. "I might go crazy in one place for that long."

"We'll have to wait and see," Hard Case told them.

They were on a fast-moving ship, one of the new System Runners.

And they weren't the only passengers on board. The vessel was packed with people. The pilots were SDF, but they didn't actually do much flying. The ship's autopilot did most of the work. Even docking was done by a gravity beam that pulled them perfectly into place. It was not the kind of assignment that Hard Case or any of the flyers in his squad would have been happy with.

But he couldn't complain about the time it took to reach the transfer station. Only a twenty-two-hour flight from Ares, just past Mars, to the transfer station between Jupiter and Saturn. It was a marvel. As was the basic layout of the ship. It was, for all intents and purposes, a barge, just a simple platform with a cabin for passengers, and a cargo hold. Never before had any of his squad been on a ship with artificial gravity. It was so much better than the regular ships that had to spin, creating centrifugal force to mimic gravity. He was used to everything being slightly curved and feeling a sense of motion that could at times be nauseating. The fast mover was like stepping onto a planet. It felt normal and looked normal, but in space, things were so rarely normal that the ordinary ship was extraordinary.

"You think the *Renegade* is like this?" Animal asked. "You know, flat and normal."

It had been what Hard Case was wondering too. "Must be," he said. "That's where the tech for artificial gravity came from."

"I thought the *Independence* brought the technology," Bishop said.

"It did, but that ship's crew, and the advanced technology, came from the *Renegade*."

"How's that?" Indigo asked.

Hard Case shrugged. "That's all I know. Most of the information in my briefing packet was redacted."

"Everything we're doing is top secret then?" Aspen asked. "That probably means it isn't legal."

"Who's to say what's legal and what isn't?" Diamond spoke up. "We're leaving everything we know behind. Aliens may do things that we find abhorrent, and what we think of as just, they may consider criminal. We have to have open minds about everything the moment we step onto that ship."

They were talking about something top-secret. Everything about the *Renegade*, her crew and her mission was classified. Anywhere else in the system, they would have been out of line talking about it, but on the fast-moving transport, every passenger was going to join the crew of the mysterious ship. They were all thinking the same things and wondering about the same possibilities.

Suddenly, the pilot's voice sounded over the speakers in the passenger cabin. "Attention passengers, we are on approach to the Mid-System Transfer Station. Please gather your belongings and prepare to disembark."

Hard Case stood up. His rucksack with everything he owned in the world was in a compartment under his seat. He retrieved it and stretched his back. The flight had been so smooth he had little trouble sleeping. He had even been able to go into the lavatory and freshen up. Like the rest of his squad, Hard Case was ready to get to the *Renegade*. He was curious about the ship and, more specifically, their new mission.

But first, they would need to change ships at the transfer station.

"I can't believe how different this is," Aspen said. "It's like riding a train instead of a flight."

"Even the docking sequence," Indigo added. "I've never heard of passengers being allowed to move about while a ship is moving into port."

"It's a shining new world, people," Animal said. "Just think, we're here to take advantage of it."

"Well, make sure you don't do anything you shouldn't," Hard Case warned him. "I'll not tolerate my squad making trouble."

"Rules are meant to be bent, Captain," Animal replied.

"We rise above," Bishop said.

"You know that's right," Animal said loudly.

"Just, take a breath," Hard Case warned. "The time for hard charging will come. First, let's find our place."

They were officers and had the privilege of being the first off the ship. The transfer station was essentially an enormous warehouse in space. It was gloomy, with bright lights hanging high overhead, and dark shadows surrounding huge pallets of goods that were stacked and wrapped in thick plastic. The far side of the building, which was how

Hard Case thought about the transfer station, was divided into rows with goods stacked up almost to the ceiling, which was forty feet high.

They came out of the ship and into a typical military administration area. There were desks and automated kiosks. Above them, a second floor undoubtedly held offices and berths for the personnel working at the station. Hard Case saw what looked like forklifts moving cargo around. They worked fast and he marveled at the sight of them. It was no different than a warehouse on Earth, yet it was hovering deep in space.

Windows high up on the walls showed stars that were bright and clear. They were closer to Saturn than Jupiter, but far enough from the ringed planet that it looked to be the size of a coin through the high windows.

"This is incredible," Diamond said.

"And a little sad," Aspen remarked.

"I wouldn't want to be stationed here," Indigo added.

"Work is work," Bishop said. "Let him labor doing honest work with his own hands, so that he may have something to share with anyone in need, Ephesians 4:28."

"No sermons," Animal said. "We're here to have a *good* time, remember."

"Wisdom calls aloud in the street, in the markets she raises her voice," Bishop quoted the proverb from memory.

"Let's just get processed," Hard Case said. We're only here for a bit, then we move on to the *Renegade*."

"How do you feel about that, Bishop?" Animal asked. "Renegades break the rules, they don't follow 'em."

"We'll see," Bishop replied.

They stepped toward the desk where a logistics Staff Sergeant waited to process their orders through the system.

Above them, in a tiny room with only a pair of metal folding chairs and a bank of hidden cameras, Zaya waited. She had already lost track of the time since coming on board the transfer station. What she knew for sure was that she had been escorted to a tiny room with a bunk that folded down from the wall. It was big enough to stand up in, and there weren't exactly bars on the door, but it still felt like a prison cell to her.

She had been allowed to shower once during her stay, and while she had been questioned about her life as a galactic slave, those sessions never lasted long. Her military handlers were interested in things she had no experience with. She had been on an Ashi battleship, but she couldn't give them much in the way of details. She didn't have knowledge of engineering terms that would have allowed her to give them the kinds of salient information that would have made her a valued asset. Instead, she spent most of her time waiting.

When the door to her interrogation cell, officially a debriefing room, opened and a woman in coveralls stepped in, Zaya knew something had changed. The woman held a flat device with a screen on it. Zaya had vague recollections of her parents having small, handheld devices that could make calls and send messages. She had played games on the devices, but she didn't remember much about them. Her handlers always carried their devices, which were larger and must have had instructions on them. Occasionally, when she was being asked questions, they wrote on the screen, although she had very little information to share. She had been a slave. She knew about the hyperspace network, yet nothing specific about it. She knew the names of a few different alien races, but nothing more. The feeling that she was worthless grew with each interview. No one had prepared her for the flood of emotions she would feel being back in the Sol system.

"We've run a search," the woman in coveralls said. "Unfortunately, your parents passed away nearly twenty years ago."

That was shocking news, but Zaya hadn't known how she would deal with meeting her parents again. As a child, she had been terrified of the visitors that came into her bedroom at night. When she told her parents, they assumed she was having bad dreams. No one believed her and, more to the point, her parents failed to protect her. How was she supposed to look them in the eye after thirty years of terror? Her life had been thirty years of hard, degrading labor, with no hope of rescue or escape. Part of her wanted to see them, to confront them and prove that she hadn't been making up stories to get out of her bedtime. On the other hand, she didn't know what she would say. They had been dead to her for decades and she had never expected to see them again. She had even forgotten what they looked like.

"Okay," was all Zaya managed to say.

"Social Services has programs you can take advantage of," the woman in coveralls said. "Here is a pass that will allow you transportation through the Solar system for the next month. There are work programs on Mars, and new opportunities on Titan that look very promising."

"Work programs?" Zaya asked.

"Yes, and you've been given a green level immigration card, with full work privileges across the board."

"I don't understand," Zaya said.

"Basically, you can legally work any job that will take you on," she said, as if she were revealing the grand prize at a game show. "Nothing's off limits."

"I can go home?"

"I'm afraid there's no home for you. But this is a wonderful chance to start over. You can make whatever kind of life you want."

"On Earth?"

Finally, the fake smile on the woman's face faltered and, for a brief instance, Zaya saw actual emotion. It was part compassion, part resentment.

"Earth isn't all that people make it out to be. Crowded and very, very expensive. You'll need to save for a while before you can afford to visit Earth."

"I can't go back?"

"You can, eventually, if that's what you want. But the real opportunities are out here. Like I said, Mars, Titan, there's even talk of new worlds opening up within a few years."

"Oh," was all Zaya could manage to say.

"I'm sorry there isn't more I can do for you," the woman in coveralls said. She was nothing like the military officers who had questioned Zaya for the last three days. The woman seemed more practical, and less demanding than the others. "But hang onto that pass. It's worth a lot of money. And Social Services can help with housing and food until you get on your feet."

"You're from Social Services?"

"No, I'm a Sergeant in the Space Defense Force. There is a transport leaving this transfer station soon. It will take you to the inner system and, from there, you can go where you like. Just remember to check in with Social Services wherever you choose to go; they'll help you."

"Okay," Zaya said, but she felt as though the ground had disappeared from under her.

Uncertainty and fear were her constant companions. The only time she had ever felt differently was with Hugo. He was confident, strong and capable. When she had been with him, she felt safe, but even then there were times when he disappeared for days at a time, leaving her to wonder if he would ever come back. She wished that things were different. What she had wanted was for him to go with her, even though she couldn't tell him that. It was difficult being honest when her feelings were so strong. That was one of the things she loved about Hugo; he never tried to pry her feelings out of her. They could be silent and comfortable in that space. Just being close to him was enough for her, but every time they got close, not just physically close but emotionally close, all her fears reared up. It was like she was carried away from the one thing she really wanted most.

The woman led Zaya to a desk, where another soldier in coveralls took her picture and created an ID card for her. She got the ID, the transport pass and a meal voucher. Beyond that, she was on her own. That realization was shocking to Zaya. She was surrounded by people, but she had never felt more alone.

There were lines of people and big flashing signs that Zaya couldn't read. Whatever she had learned before being abducted by aliens as a six-year-old old she had completely forgotten. She could read the Imperium language, although not very well. But human language was foreign to her. She was forced to ask about everything. Eventually, she ended up at a table with a tray of food. The transport back to the inner-system wasn't leaving for another nine hours. The one meal would have to last her until then. It was mostly processed protein and she forced it down. Better to eat bad food than to go hungry. She had lived on fortified protein most of her life, yet it seemed strangely different than food on the base. The meals she had eaten on the *Renegade* had been exquisite. Real food was incredibly tantalizing and she suddenly wished she could get back to it.

"You mind if I sit?" a short, balding man asked.

Zaya was seated at a table surrounded by people she didn't know.

There weren't many empty places. She nodded at the balding man and noticed that he had kind eyes. Someone from her distant past had kind eyes, but she couldn't remember who.

"Thanks, this place is a madhouse," the man said. "And the food, good Lord, don't get me started."

"It's not good," Zaya said softly.

"That's the understatement of the year. I don't know how I did it for twenty years. My name is Ethan."

"Zaya."

"Haven't seen you around here before. You're a civie?"

"A what?"

"A civilian," he said.

"I don't know what that is," Zaya said.

"You know, non-military."

"Oh, yes, that's right. I'm not military."

"You headed out on the *Renegade* then? That's a sweet ship and I don't mind saying it. We've never built nothing like that, I can tell you."

Zaya shook her head.

"You okay?" Ethan asked.

Zaya had been hit by a wave of emotions. She suddenly felt like she needed to get back to the *Renegade*, back to Hugo. But he didn't want her. He hadn't fought to keep her. Of course, she had to leave. The authorities thought she had valuable information. But she didn't. Now she felt adrift with no place to go and no one who cared. The emotions were hard to control and she could feel the tears in her eyes threatening to overflow.

"Look, I didn't mean to pry," Ethan continued. "I just, well, it's a habit. I'm in the people business, you know, and I sometimes get a little nosy. I'm sorry."

Zaya shook her head. "It isn't you."

For several moments, they studied their food as if it were important. Neither of them was in too big a hurry to eat any of it. Finally, Zaya spoke up.

"I'm just not sure where I'm going," she said.

"How's that? Do you have legal status?"

Zaya nodded and showed Ethan her ID.

"Well, that's perfect," he said. "You can do anything you want with a green level work permit. Anything you're qualified for, I suppose. Do you mind if I ask you a question or two? I might be able to help."

"Sure," Zaya said.

Ethan was moving things around on his tray with his fork, but rarely putting any of the food into his mouth.

"What kind of work are you looking to do?"

"I don't know," she said. "I like to fix things."

"Okay, now we're getting somewhere. What kind of things do you fix?"

Zaya shrugged. "Whatever I can get my hands on."

"Yeah, that's a fantastic skill. I know some people who could use you. Or, what I mean is, they could use someone with your skills to help them in their business. Where do you want to go?"

Zaya could only think of one place she wanted to go, and that was back to the *Renegade*. She knew people were working on the alien ship who weren't in the military, but she had no idea how to connect with them, or if they might take her on.

"I... well..." She was afraid to say it out loud. He would probably tell her it was impossible. He might even laugh in her face.

"Look, my job is helping people who need employees. I've got contacts all over. Normally, I don't come this far out, but a friend of mine needed a favor. I'll be on the first transport back to the inner system and there are lots of jobs that way. I also know a few people who haven't gotten all the help they need on the *Renegade*. But that's a pretty big commitment. You wouldn't be able to leave for at least six months and you have to sign a safety waiver."

"I will," she said, unable to keep the hope from showing on her face.

"You want to work on the *Renegade*?"

"Yes, I'll do whatever job they need me to do."

"Alright, yeah, that's good work. Let me see, have you ever waited tables?"

"Do mean serving food?" He nodded, and Zaya said, "Yes."

"Alright, once we finish eating, I'll introduce you to some people. With your access level, there's no reason they shouldn't take you on."

He seemed satisfied that he had been able to help her. Even though she didn't notice it, he looked over her shoulder and gave a curt nod to the woman in coveralls who had been watching since Ethan sat down across from Zaya. Satisfied her charge was in good hands, the woman in coveralls went about her business and Zaya felt a glimmer of hope for the first time since saying goodbye to Hugo.

CHAPTER 7

"LIEUTENANT ERIK HANSON, reporting for duty, sir!" the tall, blonde officer said.

Remmy thought he looked young and, while eager, the Major couldn't help but wish the Corps had sent someone with more experience. They were face to face on the flight deck. Hanson had just gotten off the shuttle from the transfer station and was followed by a few other enlisted Marines.

"Welcome aboard," Remmy said. He liked to meet his officers as soon as they stepped onto the ship. "This will not be like any cruise you've ever been on, Lieutenant. What experience do you have?"

He could have just scanned Hanson's military ID with his data pad. The info would have popped up and he could read the list of assignments and after-action reports. But he preferred to hear from his officers first. Their official record could be studied later. Remmy had been the same way with NCOs when he was just an enlisted man himself. Better to hear what he wanted from the people he was working with. That way, he got more than just information; he got a feel for the person too.

"Two cruises, one combat drop. Didn't see any action though. I just completed Spec Ops training, Major. I'm ready to serve, sir."

"I'm sure you are," Remmy said. But in the back of his mind, he felt a strong sense of caution. Captain Darius had bold plans and the Marines were key players. They would see combat without a doubt, and fighting the Ashi wasn't like anything humans could imagine.

"You'll be serving under First Lieutenant McPherson," Remmy said. "She's the real deal and highly experienced. This is not a typical SDF cruise, Lieutenant. It's not a matter of if you see combat, but when and how much. My sense is we're about to get dropped into a highly contested space and we'll have to fight for every inch of it. Are you ready for that?"

"Yes, sir. I was born for this, Major. I'm ready."

"Very good. Sergeant McManus will take you to your berth and then give you the layout of grunt country. You've probably heard rumors about the *Renegade*. It's a big ship, and there's a lot to see and do, but we are gearing up for heavy action. Don't get carried away by your surroundings. I expect my Spec Ops officers to be the first in, last out, and leading by example. Is that clear, Lieutenant?"

"Yes, sir!"

"Very good. Sergeant, take him up to his berth."

"Yes, sir," Hugo replied. "Follow me, Lieutenant."

Remmy watched them go. It was obvious to Remmy that Hugo was struggling with something, but he had returned to Marine discipline flawlessly. The Spec Op platoon was in transition, with a few members rotating out, including the CO. Remmy wanted to promote Hugo, and felt that if anyone deserved it, the big Sergeant who had survived on Libertine for nearly a year and a half alone, certainly did. But, Hugo was also a risk. He had never been one for teamwork, preferring to charge ahead and fight with abandon. What Remmy needed was strong leadership that could hold a platoon together, no matter what they faced.

Time would tell if Hugo was what Remmy needed or if the big Sergeant was going to flame out. He had tapped Hugo to introduce the new LT around because he needed them to bond. A good leader would see the potential in Hugo and, hopefully, find a bond. Otherwise, the big sergeant would be a loose cannon that could jeopardize a mission.

His internal musing over his Spec Op platoon was interrupted as two familiar faces stepped off the shuttle and glanced around.

"Welcome back," Remmy said. He wasn't much of a welcoming committee, but the Captain had asked him personally and he was not the kind of Marine who told his CO "no".

"Good to be back," Commander Henry Nash said. "Feels like coming home."

"The neighborhood got busy though," Lieutenant Vivian Ramos said.

"Wait until you see the concourse," Remmy said.

"I'm actually pretty excited to see this place with a full crew," Nash said, "the way it was meant to be."

"I'll just be glad for a hot shower and some decent food," Vivian replied. "You look good, Major. It seems that officer life suits you."

"I can't complain," Remmy said, walking the pair of senior officers toward the gravity lift. "But we aren't going for a walk in the park, if you take my meaning."

"Captain Darius has big plans, is that it?" Vivian asked.

"Some might say audacious," Remmy said.

"You disagree with him?" Nash asked.

"No, sir," Remmy said. "I think it's the right move and now's the right time. But that doesn't mean it will be easy."

"Out of the frying pan and into the fire," Nash said.

"Well, I've been in the pan too long," Vivian said. "I wanted to go back, and I'm glad I was able to see my family, but serving on a standard SDF ship after being on the *Renegade* is torture."

"I heard Commander Lee got her first ship," Remmy said.

"The *Venice*," Nash said. "It's relatively new."

"Not new enough for my taste," Vivian said. "This is it for me. I'll stay on the *Renegade* until they kick me off and then I'll resign my commission."

Remmy reached the top of the gravity lift first. He bounced off the ceiling and into regular gravity without problems. Turning, he held out a hand for Vivian, who took it and let him pull her onto the floor of the pavilion that covered the gravity lift. Henry landed beside her, and both of them took a second as the increase of gravity pulled down on them.

"That, I haven't missed," Vivian said.

"You get used to it," Remmy reminded her.

"But not this," Henry said, sweeping one arm toward the Park. "This never gets old."

"There's nothing like it," Vivian agreed. "A little slice of paradise."

They took their time. And there was plenty to see. Somehow, the automated system that kept tabs on the Park had noted the increase in crew and allowed, or somehow prompted, the herd animals to reproduce faster. Big herds were moving slowly near the pavilion. Some were near a stream, drinking the clear water. Others grazed on the rich, green grass. And around the Park, people and aliens could be seen on the balconies of the apartments that overlooked the park. It was, in Remmy's mind, like a vacation scene.

"I hope there are some apartments left for senior officers," Vivian said.

Remmy nodded. He understood the appeal. His berth in the Command center was better than any he had ever had in his military career before coming on board the *Renegade*, but there was nothing like a view over the Park.

"I guess we'll find out," Nash said.

They made their way back to the Grand Concourse and the pair marveled at the changes. What had once been dark storefronts and empty corridors were now bustling and bright. They took the gravity lift around to Lambda, the highest level, and went straight to the Bridge. Only Captain Darius wasn't there. Lieutenant Pete Best had the con.

"Welcome back," Pete said with enthusiasm. "Captain Darius had a meeting to attend. He said to let you get settled and he'll see you at dinner this evening."

"Everything looks the same," Vivian said.

"Or better. They made improvements to the seating in here," Nash pointed out.

"But nothing looks worn," Vivian said. "Even after a year and a half, it still looks brand new."

They went down to their cabins and Remmy left them there. They weren't new crew members; they had been on the *Renegade* before. It might take them a while to acclimate again, and catch up on the changes, but Remmy had no doubt they were professionals. In his own cabin, he went to the desk. It was smaller, not a full office space like Captain Darius enjoyed in his berth. But it allowed him to stay connected to the ship's network. His duty as the senior Marine officer involved making reports, and ensuring that the fighting men and women on board the ship had whatever they needed. It was still more administrative than he liked, but the post gave him the authority to help plan combat missions with Captain Darius. The two of them had become close over the last eighteen months. Remmy was the Captain's sounding board, pushing back at times and encouraging him at others.

He checked the manifest. Only a third of their new Marines had boarded. That was fine. He preferred that they come in waves. Soon, he would have them all training hard and preparing for what lay ahead. The ultimate test of humanity's skill in martial combat was about to be thrust onto the shoulders of seventy-five Marines. Remmy hoped they would rise to the challenge. Otherwise, the future of the human race was in serious doubt.

CHAPTER 8

"NO, Admiral, we won't be careless," Darius said. "Every member of my crew knows there is no help coming for us if we fail."

"Good luck then," Admiral Paulson said. "I'll leave you to it. Two squadrons of fighter jocks are a lot for any ship, even one as big as the *Renegade*."

"We'll find a way to make it all work," Darius said.

He was excited. A year of preparation and planning had gone into his new mission. The Brass trusted him or, at least, were willing to let him do what he wanted, as long as they continued making break-throughs that lined their pockets. It was a cynical view of his superiors, but there was no other way of explaining it. Maybe they just didn't want to fight him for control of the *Renegade*. It was possible they didn't really understand the power of the Arodoni ship. It was, as far as Captain Darius knew, the most powerful vessel in the galaxy. The Arodoni power converters turned dark matter into copious amounts of usable, clean energy that not only powered the massive ship, but also the four monstrous laser cannons. There were hints that the ship was capable of destroying entire star systems. That was something Darius didn't want to think about.

"Keep us informed, Captain," Paulson said. "And good luck."

Her image was as clear as if she were sitting across his desk from him. But it faded away as she ended the video call. Darius glanced at his schedule. He had one more call to make before he could take his customary walk through the ship. Not that he could tour the entire ship in the short amount of time he had. But he could make it as far as the Park and back if he stayed on the upper level and the exercise did him good. He did his best thinking when his body was in motion. And there were still a lot of details to tie down.

He reached over and pressed the transmit button on his desktop comlink. "Ensign Jones, how are the Wardroom preparations going?"

"Fine, Captain," the junior officer replied immediately. "Everything is ready. The culinary team is working on the menu you requested, and the materials you wanted loaded up in the holo-projector are ready. I tested it all myself, Captain."

"Very good, Jones. I appreciate it."

"My pleasure, Captain. Anything you need, I'm here for you, sir."

Darius tapped the comlink again and then looked at the computer icons floating over the physical top of his desk. He reached out and tapped one that brought up the video conferencing options. A list of names and ranks, or political offices, appeared in the air above his desk. He reached out and stuck his finger on the name O'Dell, Connor, Secretary of Development. It was a new office, and one that enjoyed a great deal of power since it gave the Secretary control over the alien technology that had been brought to the Sol system by the *Independence*. Darius took a deep breath. He wasn't looking forward to the call.

The list of names disappeared, and in their place a strange face blinked at him. "Oh, alright, I guess that's working... Captain Darius. I see you."

For a moment, Darius was flummoxed by the fact that someone in charge of technological development seemed to have never used a video call before.

"I believe Secretary O'Dell is expecting my call," Darius said.

"Yes, you are on the schedule. Unfortunately, he is still tied up in a meeting. Can we put this on hold until he returns? Thank you."

The hologram froze before Darius could reply. Not that he could argue the point. If Connor O'Dell wasn't available, Darius had no choice but to wait. He got up and fixed himself the last of his coffee. There was no need to worry about the call going through while he was away from his desk. The alien technology followed him. The hologram of whoever he was speaking with would turn to face him even if he paced back and forth or made laps around his desk.

There was just one more element that was needed for his plan to work. It was a long shot, but Darius had to make the request. He had written a lengthy memo over a month earlier and sent it back to the Sol system through the hyperspace network. All he needed now was the official yes, or no, from the man in charge. Unfortunately, Captain Darius didn't have the best relationship with Connor O'Dell. He had been a scientific advisor on the *Jericho's* mission to retrieve the alien artifact and O'Dell had been diametrically opposed to Darius taking the *Jericho* out of the system. But with their communications cut off, and the threat of the Galactic Imperium revealed to him, Darius did what he thought was best. That had taken them to a variety of star systems and eventually to the *Renegade*. When officers and crew members volunteered to take the *Independence* from the Libertine system back to Sol to deliver the Arodoni technology, O'Dell had jumped at the chance. And, it seemed, he leveraged his unique experiences into a very sought-after post on the Inner-System government. Businesses and political figures were lined up to see him and petition the Development arm of the government to grant them access to the massive amounts of alien technology. In that regard, Darius was just one of many to approach the Secretary, but his request was undoubtedly strange.

Darius was pacing when the hologram unfroze, and the odd man looked up at Darius. "The Secretary will see you now," he said in a patronizing tone.

"Thank you," Darius replied. He hated politics, but it was a necessary evil when the *Renegade* was in the Sol system.

The hologram changed and showed a large image of Connor O'Dell. He looked the same, perhaps a little more gray at his temples, but otherwise the scientist was unchanged.

"Captain Zeke Darius," Connor said. "It's been a while."

"Yes," Darius said. "You look well, Mr. O'Dell."

"I am well. But extremely busy, as I'm sure you are. How can I help you?"

"You got my memo regarding the GIGI?"

"I'm sure someone in my office did. We get thousands of requests every single day. There simply isn't enough manpower to go through them all. What was it you requested? I assume you still have access to the Arodoni tech."

"Yes, but I am about to embark on a very ambitious mission. I would like to have the Galactic Information and Guidance Instrument on board for this cruise."

"GIGI is an alien artifact that is under intense study by some of the best minds in the Solar system, Captain. I can't just send it to you."

"I know what I'm asking is big, Mr. Secretary. But so are the stakes here. You know that as well as anyone."

"I know that you and the crew of the *Renegade* are playing with fire. I've made that abundantly clear to the President. I think we would be much better off decommissioning the *Renegade* and reverse engineering her tech. Or, at the very least, keeping her in system for security reasons, but it seems I am in the minority."

"You have to see that fighting the Imperium on their turf is better than bringing the fight home."

"That is one theory. But to my way of thinking, you are simply poking the bear. One ship cannot wage war with a galactic empire. We should be sending diplomats to forge a peace agreement with the Imperium, not fighting a war we can't win."

"I know your point of view, Connor," Darius said, ignoring the way the Secretary's eyes narrowed at the use of his first name. "But I can fight a war with GIGI. She can control hundreds of drones with perfect coordination. No one else can do that, not even the Ashi. Please, Connor, I wouldn't ask if the need wasn't great."

"I'll have to check with the department overseeing the Artifact. If it's possible, I'll give the go-ahead, but I can't make you any promises."

"Your best efforts are good enough for me," Darius said. "Thank you, Mr. Secretary."

Connor nodded, but didn't say anything before signing off. Darius stretched his back. There was no way of knowing what Connor's answer would be. He would just have to proceed as if he didn't have GIGI. If they were lucky, that would change; if not, they would just have to make do. Either way, he had a job to do and no bureaucrat was going to stop him.

CHAPTER 9

ZAYA FOLLOWED Ethan to where a pair of men were unloading equipment. She didn't know a lot about what she was seeing, but it seemed the goods were some type of food delivery device.

"Saul, how are you, old friend?" Ethan said in a loud voice.

"Busy! What do you need, Ethan?" one of the men said.

He was younger than Zaya had expected. A strong-looking man in his mid twenties, with broad shoulders and dark stubble on his square chin. She could even make out a dimple below his bottom lip.

"I need nothing. I'm here to help you."

"I've heard that before. It always ends up costing me something," the man with the dimple said as he turned and looked first at Ethan, then Zaya.

"Not this time," Ethan said. "Someone else is footing my bill and I think I have something you'll want."

Zaya was beginning to get nervous. Ethan was talking about her like she was a commodity. She didn't know much about human behavior; she had been around so few of her own kind through her life ... but she understood slavery. Zaya was not willing to give up her freedom again. Hugo had shown her it was better to die free than live as a slave and she would never return to her old life. But she had also been told that humans had given up slavery a long time ago. So, she gave the balding Ethan a chance to finish what he was saying.

"I don't have time," Saul said. "I've got to get this equipment onto the *Renegade* as soon as possible."

"Then let us help you," Ethan said. "Saul, meet Zaya Wright. She has a green level ID."

Saul looked at Zaya again, studying her. It was uncomfortable, but she forced herself not to flinch or turn away.

"What do I need her for?"

"To help you run the brewery. She's looking for work and she's good at fixing things."

"Looks like you've had a rough go," Saul said directly to Zaya.

"I'm not looking for a handout," she replied. "I can work."

"Do you really have a green level ID?"

She pulled it out of a pocket and showed it to him.

"How'd you get this?" he asked. "You bribe an official somewhere?"

"No," Zaya said. "But, I've got a past."

"Don't we all." Ethan said with a chuckle.

"What's that suppose to mean? I don't work with ex-cons."

"It's not that kind of past," Ethan said.

"I was taken, as a child," Zaya said. "Forced into slavery. There's nothing for me here. I'm looking for a place to be useful."

Saul was clearly not convinced she was telling the truth. Maybe he had heard about the slave trade in the wider galaxy, maybe not. It didn't matter to Zaya. She just needed to convince him to take a chance with her.

"Do you know what this is?" he held up a copper vat.

"No," Zaya admitted. "But I'm a fast learner."

"What do you know about distilling liquor and brewing spirits?"

"Nothing," Zaya admitted. "But I know my way around engines, power supplies, repulsers, and just about anything mechanical."

"We work long hours here," Saul said. "This ain't no pleasure cruise. I run a pub on the *Renegade* for just one reason - access to the alien grains. I'm going to create a new brew that will make me a very rich man one day. And, to support my passion, I run a successful pub on the *Renegade*. So, when we aren't dabbling with new brews, we're hustling drinks to thirsty sailors and wiping down tables. It's fast paced, hard work. I've got four employees, two tend bar, two run drinks. I could use a third, but you'll have to do your share and then some. I need someone who'll free me up to work on the new brew. If that's you, then welcome aboard. If not, I understand."

"How much does it pay?" Ethan asked.

"That doesn't matter," Zaya said.

"It's the only thing that matters," Ethan said.

"I thought you said someone else was footing your bill, headhunter."

"Sometimes, I help people in need just out of the goodness of my heart, you know," Ethan said, but it was unconvincing. "Let's just say I owed Staff Sergeant Magal a favor, and now I don't."

"Good," Saul said. "I pay minimum rate for service hours and cover your berth plus one meal a day. If you're as handy as you say you are, then we can negotiate for extra duties. But you've got to prove yourself. Taking you on will put me right on the razor's edge of viability."

"I don't want to put you out," Zaya said.

"You aren't, but the point is, I'm not running the pub to make money. I run it to pay for what I need until I get what I want."

"She can probably help you," Ethan said. "My gut tells me she knows a lot about alien grains."

"That true?" Saul asked.

"I know some," she said. "But not about brewing."

"You really were a slave?"

Zaya nodded. It wasn't something she liked talking about. Her slave masters were cruel and abusive. She hadn't known any other way until Hugo shot down the ship she served on. Over time, he proved that not everyone was hateful and out to get whatever they could from the people around them.

"Alright, give me that ID. I'll have to register you with the Employment Authority, and get you on the *Renegade* manifest. As long as there are not issues with either one of those, you're in. Welcome to the team, Zaya."

He held out a hand and she shook it. It gave her a surprisingly good feeling. Not because Saul was young and handsome, but because for the first time in her life she felt like an adult. She had made a deal and given her word. It was her decision and she was taking control of her life. That meant something after so many years without any agency over what she did, where she went and what she could do.

"My work here is done," Ethan said. "Good luck, Zaya. Saul's a decent fellow. No matter what people say about him."

The last phrase was for Saul, not Zaya, and both men laughed.

"Go ahead and help Lester get this gear loaded," Saul said. "I'll be back soon and we'll get you squared away onboard."

"Thank you," Zaya said.

She bent down and picked up the copper vat. It was heavy, but she was strong. Saul watched her heft the copper implement, nodded approvingly and set off with Ethan.

"Lester," the other man said, extending a hand.

"Zaya," she replied, shaking his hand after she put the vat onto a cargo cart.

"Glad to have you," he said. He was a little older than she was, with hooded eyes and red cheeks. "Don't let Saul fool you. Our little pub is a popular place. We made out good in tips."

"That's good to hear," she said.

Together, they went to work moving the distillation equipment from the shipping pallet onto the cart where it would be hauled onto the ship. Zaya had never been paid for her work before. It felt good to know she was doing something that would earn her a living. Most of all, she was relieved to know that she was going back to the *Renegade*. There was no way to know how Hugo would feel about it, yet she was anxious to find out. After three days of being grilled by interrogators and feeling worthless in the process, she was relieved to have found a place where she could belong. The *Renegade* would be home, at least for now, and she felt really good about that.

CHAPTER 10

COMMANDER JUSTIN KASE led his squad of 'ace' pilots off the shuttle and onto the *Renegade*. They had seen the huge ship from the shuttle's windows, but it wasn't until they stepped onto the flight deck that they really began to get a feel for the alien ship's enormity.

"Would you look at this?" Animal said.

Bishop made a low-pitched whistle.

"It's enormous," Aspen said.

"And so..." Indigo began, searching for the right word.

"Pristine," Diamond said.

"It looks brand new," Indigo said. "What is this floor, some kind of marble or something?"

"It's one piece," Bishop said, "Look, it goes right up the wall, like it was carved from one massive stone."

"That's impossible," Animal said.

"I'm just saying, that's what it looks like, brother," Bishop said.

"Alright, let's just hold it together. It's a ship, okay? A fancy, big ship, that's all," Hard Case said. "Let's find our berths and get settled in."

"Commander Kase," A young, female officer said, crossing the hangar straight toward him. "I'm Lieutenant Bertoli. Welcome aboard."

"Thank you, Lieutenant. We're glad to be here," Justin replied.

"If you and your squad will follow me, I'll show you to your quarters," Bertoli said. "This is the flight deck, one of three hangers on the *Renegade*."

"Three?" Animal asked.

"Are they all this big?" Aspen asked.

"All three are the same," Jacee Bertoli said. "Two klicks wide, by one kilometer deep."

"That's insane," Animal said.

"Will we be using all three hangars?" Hard Case asked.

"No, just the flight deck. Hangar C is the drone hanger."

"Drones?" Animal asked with a note of derision in his voice. "Who flies those?"

"The Casians are the main drone operators, but we have human crewmen who operate them depending on the need."

"What are Casians?" Indigo asked.

Jacee pointed across the deck where a pair of pachyderms with six legs were helping to move a large piece of equipment.

"There," Bertoli explained. "From the planet Casa in the Casasil system. It's one of the first places we took on the Ashi in battle on the *Renegade*."

That caused the squad of ace pilots to fall silent. They were great flyers, but none had fought in a real combat zone. They had - at most - run cover for the laser SDF ships and played chicken a time or two with rogue groups who managed to get their hands on an aircraft. Nothing had come of their engagements; no one in the squad had even fired on an enemy target outside of simulators.

Jacee Bertoli led them out of the hangar and into a corridor. It was made of the same, polished material as the deck in the hangar. And there didn't appear to be a speck of dirt anywhere on the ship.

"How do you keep the ship looking so new?" Aspen asked.

"We don't," Bertoli replied. "The ship has an automated maintenance system that cleans up after us. You'll see droids moving about from time to time, although they mainly work through the night hours."

"A self-cleaning ship," Hard Case said. "Why haven't we thought of that before?"

"Thinking of something, and engineering it to work, are two different things," Bishop said.

"Amen to that," Animal replied. "But this ship is cherry. How old is it?"

"Five hundred years old that we know of," Bertoli said. "Probably much older."

Once again, the squad was speechless. They passed a wide open room with rows of thickly padded seats covered in what looked like leather.

"This will be your mission briefing room," she said. "It's been reserved for the fighter squadrons."

"Are there more than us on board?" Diamond asked.

Hard Case knew the answer to that, but he hadn't told his squad. Not that they couldn't take the competition, but he didn't want to put negative thoughts into their minds concerning the other flyers.

"Your squad is one of two," Jacee said.

They passed another room with large, egg-shaped flight simulators. One of the compartments was open and Hard Case could see the flight controls.

"This is your training room. You've also got a lounge and Offices on Beta deck," Bertoli said, pointing up. "This way to the gravity lift."

"I've been on many ships smaller than all this," Animal said. "I've never seen an SDF vessel with this much space. I mean, just this hallway alone is wide enough for five people to walk shoulder to shoulder."

"The Arodoni built the *Renegade* to be spacious, I suppose," Bertoli said.

"What do we know about them?" Hard Case asked.

"Almost nothing," Jacee admitted. "There is a statue of one in the fountain outside the Admin Center in the Grand Concourse."

"Wait," Animal said. "This ship has a fountain?"

Jacee smiled. Hard Case noticed that it was a pleasant smile.

"It's got a lot more than that, Lieutenant Vin Dice."

"Call me Animal," he said with some pride. "Everyone does."

"Animal? That's your callsign?"

"It's because of the way I party," Animal said.

"It's because he eats like one," Indigo said.

"Smells like one?" Diamond added.

"Acts like one," Aspen remarked.

"Guilty on all counts, but I fly like one too, right, Commander?"

"Let's just focus on the new ship, shall we?" Hard Case said.

Bertoli took the hint as they neared what appeared to be a large ventilation shaft. It rose through several floors from what they could see.

"This is the gravity lift. As you know, the *Renegade* utilizes artificial gravity, but in certain areas there is no gravity, allowing crew members to traverse the multiple decks."

She stepped into the shaft and with a small kick went gliding upward, turning as she went so that she was facing the squad. And something inside of Hard Case clicked into place. For just a moment, no one said anything and Justin wished that the moment would last forever. Lieutenant Jacee Bertoli looked like an angel, at least to Hard Case's way of thinking.

"Are you kidding me? Zero gravity? Yes! Let's go!" Animal shouted. He stepped forward and as he started to rise up, he threw himself forward into a spin. "Yaaaaahooooooo!"

The others followed quickly. The only thing better than flying a spacecraft with a huge engine and bigger guns was flying through zero gravity. Hard Case followed but he didn't do any stunts. Instead, he just kicked off the floor and kept his eyes on Jacee Bertoli.

When they got off the lift, their minds were completely blown by the Park. To his knowledge, no ship had successfully mastered hydroponics, much less created an entire green space completely with animals, birds, and insects. They were all completely speechless.

"The Park is maintained by the ship's robotic systems," Jacee explained. "Herd animals help maintain the grasses, as well as fertilizing the soil. They're also part of the ship's victuals, with animals harvested for food on an ongoing basis."

"No way," Indigo said.

"Fresh meat?" Bishop asked. "We get real food on this ship?"

"As real as it gets," Bertoli continued. "The water in the streams is part of the ship's hydro cycle."

"We drink water from these streams?" Aspen asked.

"Not directly, but the simulated rainfall and the streams are part of the water recycling system. It's a very natural way to clean water."

They spent a full ten minutes just watching the moving platforms and the birds flitting through the trees. The air was warm and there was a light wind. The sheer size of the Park was hard to grasp. It was bigger than the parks he had visited as a child in the Eastern Megalopolis that spread up and down the East coast of the North American continent. It was one massive city and there were beautifully manicured parks in the more upscale locations, but none were even close to the massive size of the Park on the *Renegade*. Additionally, it wasn't just the length and breadth of the park that took his breath away. It was the towering open sky above. Hard Case had never seen anything like it, or even imagined it.

"I'll take you to your berths now. You're all on Kappa level," Bertoli said. "This way."

They each had an apartment on the next-to-highest floor. They weren't huge, but compared to berths on most space ships and space stations, they were massive. Each one consisted of a living space, a bedroom and bathroom facilities. The beds were round, which was the only odd thing about them. The furniture was human in both the living area and on the balconies, which overlooked the park. Jacee showed them the controls that transformed the big walls of windows. With the press of a button, the windows could be made to block all light. They also doubled as video screens.

"You mean we live here?" Bishop asked. "This place would cost a million credits on Earth without the view."

"It's awesome!" Animal declared.

"Meals are provided in the Mess Hall, or you can buy from vendors in the Grand Concourse," Jacee continued. "The facilities in your berth are more for storing and rewarming foods, not really cooking."

"I may never leave," Indigo said.

"A lot of us feel that way," Jacee said.

"Do you have an apartment here?" Hard Case asked her.

"No, my berth is in the Command section."

"Oh," he said, trying not to let his disappointment show.

"If you'd like, I'll give you a quick tour of the Grand Course, then I

have orders to escort Commander Kase to the Ready Room for an officer's meeting."

"Straight to work, Hard Case," Animal said.

"No rest for the wicked," Aspen said.

"I think I'm good for now," Bishop said. "I've already got enough
to be thankful for. I'd like some time alone."

"Not me," Animal declared. "Show me everything!"

"We'll go too," Indigo said.

"It's too good to pass up," Aspen added.

They left Bishop, who started praying even before they left his
apartment. He was a fanatical believer and a gregarious worshiper.
They heard him singing as his door swished closed.

"That's Bishop," Hard Case said.

"I see where he gets his call sign," Jacee said, leading them back
down the ramps. There were no stairs on the *Renegade*. "What's
yours?"

"Hard Case," Justin said. "It's just a play on my last name."

"Don't believe that," Animal said. "There's a story behind every
call sign."

"And stories about Commander Kase are legendary," Indigo said.

"That's an exaggeration," Justin said.

"Hard Case, sounds like trouble," Jacee said.

Justin wasn't sure if she was flirting, but he hoped she was.

They crossed the Park and entered the Grand Concourse. Once
again, the squad of ace pilots was speechless.

"This is unbelievable," Aspen said.

"I've never seen anything like it," Indigo said. "It's more like we're
on a traveling space station."

"One of the high-end, boujee ones," Animal added.

"I've been to vacation stations," Aspen said. "They're nice, but..."

"It's like this all the time?" Hard Case asked as people flowed past
them and music came pouring from a nearby club.

It was bright, upbeat music, loud enough to be heard outside, but
not so intense that a person had to shout to be heard over it. There
were delicious smells too, some sweet, some savory. It made Kase's
mouth water and his stomach rumble.

"Pretty much," Jacee said. "Once we're underway, the entire ship goes by ship time. So, there are breakfast, lunch and dinner times. Liquor is only sold in the evenings and there's a limit. Some of the storefronts are gathering places for the different races. Captain Darius does all he can to help promote and share cultures."

"And this is a combat vessel," Hard Case said.

"Correct," Jacee said. "There are standard alerts that affect the ship. The civilian-owned businesses all adhere to those. Obviously, there's not a lot of shopping or dining when the ship is in combat mode."

"And money?" Diamond asked.

"You can have any portion of your military pay changed over to ship currency," Jacee said. "It's an equal exchange."

"Are there more wonders to this ship?" Hard Case said.

Lieutenant Bertoli nodded. "But there's no time to cover those now. It's all outlined in your service manual. It should be downloaded to your data pads already."

"Who has time to read when there's so much shopping to do?" Indigo asked.

"Not me, I'm gonna party."

"You're going back to your berths and settling in," Commander Kase ordered. "Rest up and go through the manual. This ship might seem like a party barge, but it isn't. They didn't put us together for kicks. Whatever is coming, we need to be ready for it."

"But we haven't even left the system," Animal complained.

"But we might any minute. Lieutenant Bertoli, do you know when the *Renegade* will be underway?"

"No," she said with a shake of her head. "I'm sorry. But you'll be able to ask Captain Darius himself at your meeting."

"I'll do that. There will be time to explore the ship, but the mission comes first," Justin insisted.

"And now you know why he's called Hard Case," Animal said with obvious disappointment.

They went their separate ways and Jacee led the Commander through the Concourse. He was nearly overwhelmed by the sheer glamor of it all. The Arodoni fountain was visited and then they rode in the gravity collar up to Command section. Jacee showed Commander Kase to the Officer's Wardroom, but she stopped outside.

"This is you," she said.

"You aren't coming?"

"Senior Officers only for this gathering," she said with a smile. "But I'll be around."

She left him and he watched her go, only to have his view spoiled as another junior officer escorted Commander Elder toward the Wardroom. Legend was everything an aviator was supposed to be: fit, athletic, good-looking and brash, although he was also arrogant. It wasn't a matter of self-confidence, but more that he looked down on everyone else. Worst still, he was a shameless suck-up, always maneuvering to be in a favored position, rather than just letting his merit speak for itself. Not that he wasn't a good pilot. Hard Case knew Legend was the real deal in the cockpit, but it was everything else about the man that he despised.

"Funny meeting you here, Kase," Legend said. "I thought this was senior officers only."

Justin didn't bother to respond. They were the same rank, yet there was no doubt that Mathias Elder thought he was above everyone. He might suck up to his superiors, but it was just a ruse to get what he wanted. The man actually believed he was better than everyone else.

He brushed past Hard Case, who turned to get out of his way, then followed his fellow pilot inside.

CHAPTER 11

THE WARDROOM WAS ALREADY FILLED with officers. It was mostly humans, but there were two aliens present. One was a tall biped in a unique, robe-like uniform. The other was one of the six-legged pachyderm aliens Hard Case had seen on the flight deck. Everyone found their seats and settled in. Water was already in glasses, but there was extra drinkware with pitchers of iced tea and thick mugs for coffee. A tall black man approached the two aviators, who both stood up to greet him.

"Commander Nash," the man said. "I'm the XO on this cruise. You our new aviators?"

"Commander Elder," Legend said, shaking Nash's hand.

"Commander Kase."

"It's good to meet you both. What do you think of the *Renegade*?"

"Overwhelming," Hard Case said.

"Not bad for an alien ship," Legend said. His voice made it clear he didn't approve. "There's a lot of distractions for a military vessel."

"We find a good balance," Nash said. "Welcome aboard."

At that moment, the door opened and Captain Darius stepped inside. The Marine Major shouted, "Captain on deck!" It was not really loud, just stern, and cut immediately through the chatter in the room. Justin stiffened to attention, but Legend didn't. It was a tiny slight, a bit of defiance that was meant to send a message. If Darius noticed it wasn't obvious.

"As you were," he said immediately. "Let's all take a seat. We have new and returning Officers I'd like to greet, and then we can get down to business."

Hard Case sat down. He and Legend were at the far end of the table from the Captain. Right beside him, at the foot of the table opposite from the Captain, was the Marine Major. There was a sense of coolness to the man, a steady strength that seemed to radiate from him. He was, in a sense, the highest-ranking officer in the room, but on board an SDF ship, no one outranked the skipper. And unlike Legend, he had no air of self-importance.

"I am Captain Zeke Darius. I've been in command of this ship since we discovered her. Actually, we were led to her by the artifact known as GIGI. It is my hope that we can get GIGI back on board for what we have planned."

He hesitated, and there were some knowing glances between the other officers. Hard Kase had no idea what the Captain was talking about, but that wasn't necessarily surprising. He was new; the alien ship was unlike anything he had ever seen, much less served on, plus he had served with Zeke Darius before. There was trust already established and, until the Captain did something to break that trust, Hard Case would give him the benefit of the doubt.

"But that's a conversation for another time," Darius said. "I want to introduce everyone, starting with my new XO. Most of you know Commander Nash. He was the Chief Engineer on the *Jericho* and knows quite a bit about the *Renegade*."

"I hope I'm not stepping on toes by coming back," Nash said. His words were directed at another officer whose name tag read "Best."

"Not at all," the Lieutenant said. "It's a big job and I'm happy to focus on my regular duties."

Captain Darius spoke again. "Commander Nash will be in charge of all personnel matters but will also be helping Lieutenant Stanislaus with engineering."

"We've learned a lot," Stanislaus said, "but there's still a ton we haven't figured out yet. Happy for the help, Commander."

"We also have our head navigator returning," Captain Darius said as he turned to the woman on his right. She was striking, with short black hair and olive skin. "Lieutenant Vivian Ramos."

"Happy to be here," she said.

"We are also honored to have Chief Mutua, who is in charge of the drone division. His Casians are highly skilled remote aviators and have made excellent upgrades in our control technology for the remotely operated resources on the *Renegade*."

The six-legged Pachyderm raised his trunk, but didn't make a sound.

"Next to him is someone I've come to trust and call a friend. Lieutenant Nurek was formerly a slave to Emperor Vang and his forebears. He is our Information Officer and I urge you to get to know him. The Dudonus people, and we have a handful on the crew, are very intelligent and hardworking. If you have questions about the Imperium, he's the person to ask."

"Thank you, Captain," Dudonus said with a heavy accent.

Dudonus was an alien race that Justin had heard of before. A group of them were part of the government's task force when the *Renegade* first returned to the Sol system. They were a little like asylum seekers from an enemy nation that were all too happy to share what they knew about the Galactic Imperium. Nurek had an almost impossibly thin body. His conical head sat atop a neck that was barely as big around as a human pinky. He had large eyes, tiny slits for nostrils but no discernible nose, and a small mouth. His ears were thin flaps and would have gone unnoticed if it weren't for the hardware in one of them. Justin noticed that both Nurek and Mutua had devices in their ears which probably translated the Captain's words for them.

"Of course, you all know our illustrious Marine commander, Major Steel. And beside him are the new additions to the senior staff, Commander Justin Kase and Commander Mathias Elder."

Hard Case nodded when the Captain said his name.

"I specifically requested you both," Darius said. "Not because of our history, but because it is well known that you are the best of the best. Where we're going on this cruise, that's exactly what we need. Commanders Elder and Kase will be leading fighter squadrons in ships that are new to the SDF fleet. I'll explain more about that in a bit, but first, let me go over the mission so that everyone has an idea of what we're doing this time around.

"The *Renegade* has been on a mission to disrupt the Galactic Imperium. For those of you who don't know, the wider galaxy is ruled by a militant race at the head of an oppressive government. It's known as the Ashi Empire, but the government is run by a council of five from the central worlds near the galactic core. The Ashi are the military side of the Imperium and the Emperor has been Ashi during the thousands of years that this galactic Empire has been in place.

Until recently, the Sol system was unknown to the Imperium. How that is possible will become more clear as I continue. The Milky Way, as you all know, is a standard, spiral galaxy. What you may not know is that most of the star systems are connected by what is known as Hyperspace lanes. Think of this like a highway system that surrounds and intersects a major city. The galaxy then is divided into three main sectors. We are in the outermost section, on the arm of the spiral. It is believed that many of the worlds in our sector are isolated, meaning they have only one connection to the hyperspace lanes, and they are not all known.

The next section is called the Mean Sector. We didn't choose that name; it came from the Imperium and reflects both the positional and attitude of the galactic empire. It is the middle part of the galaxy, and to the beings in charge, it is considered to be lacking in dignity and honor. Many of the worlds in the Mean Sector have been damaged either through direct attack or due to careless harvesting of resources. Some are considered to be slave worlds, as some of the intelligent races are considered to be slaves with no rights of any kind."

Captain Darius paused to take a sip of his water and Hard Case did the same. His mind was reeling from the information being presented. He had heard rumors that obviously came from the reality of the greater galaxy, but most of the information was brand new. Justin was struggling to wrap his mind around it as Captain Darius continued.

"Our task thus far has been in this Mean section. We have flown the *Renegade* into over fifty star systems with habitable worlds with intelligent species. In those systems, the *Renegade* has destroyed Ashi assets and our Marine platoons have liberated the citizens from their

Imperium overseers. In this way, we have been able to share the Arodoni technology with these intelligent races and kept the Ashi military forces on their heels."

Legend interrupted. "Why? Shouldn't we process that technology first, and ensure that humanity stays ahead of the other races?"

It wasn't a surprising question. Throughout Earth's history, innovation and superior technology were a key to dominance among the nations. But Hard Case thought it rude to interrupt Captain Darius.

"I know that's the view of some," Darius said. "But we're facing a galactic threat, Commander Elder. The more allies we have pushing back against the Imperium, the better our odds of defeating them. That is why we share the technology. It gives each race the means to contend for their own freedom, should the Imperium return."

"Do we have any intel on that front?" Vivian asked.

"Nurek?"

"My sources have informed us that Sheika Kahn was tried for his failures in battle," Nurek said, utilizing a device that translated his words with only the slightest bit of lag. "For a time, the Imperium was in transition. There was word of fighting among the Ashi for dominance. This is not surprising, as it is their way. During this interim, the Prime Council did all it could to accumulate power. But, most recently, there is word that a new Emperor and Kahn have arisen and begun asserting their control over the Imperium's vast fleet."

"Which means," Darius jumped back in, "we have a limited window of time. Our focus has to be the third and final part of the galaxy, which is called the Core systems. These are some of the oldest worlds and the first that were conquered by the Ashi. Five of those worlds were important enough to rise in power. A representative from each one makes up the five-member Prime Council. I believe we must break the Imperium's hold on these worlds."

"You want us to hit the core systems?" Nash asked.

"That's right. They'll be heavily guarded, but it won't be like before," Darius said. "The new emperor will still be trying to gather his forces. From what we've heard, that means going outside the core systems. While he's away, we'll strike."

"To what end?" Vivian asked. "What do you hope to accomplish?"

"The mission objectives are as follows," Darius said. "Destroy planetary defenses, both Ashi ships of war and otherwise. Once that's done, we will invade the planet with military forces that will destroy, disrupt and disseminate a message of rebellion that we hope will inflame the populace of those worlds."

"That's how you hope to defeat an Empire?" Legend asked. It was clear by his tone what he thought of the plan.

Darius smiled. "I forgot how direct you can be, Commander Elder. Actually, no, we aren't trying to defeat the Imperium in this manner. We hope that with the government in disarray, the people will turn against them. Think of this less like a military operation and more like a racketeering job. The Ashi have been in control for thousands of years. In the past, any planet that tried to oppose them was summarily crushed, sometimes even bombarded into extinction from orbit."

"Like on Lawash," Pete Best interjected.

"The Ashi have a monopoly on tech. They've outlawed weapons. They rule through fear, and for the first time in centuries, we can stand up to them. That's what we've been doing. According to our intelligence sources, there is outright rebellion on over a hundred worlds right now. But that doesn't mean much. Those worlds have little in the way of military assets. They can be brought to heel in time without much effort. But if we can show the core worlds that the Ashi can't protect them..."

"They'll stop paying for that protection," Nash said.

"Exactly. If we can destabilize the core worlds, it buys us time. If we can kindle a civil war, then we will have the best chance of establishing the independence of the Sol system and, perhaps, even the human confederation of systems. That, Commander Elder, is the goal ... and I believe that now is the time for us to strike. Of course, there are a thousand details that will need to be ironed out and we will do that over the coming days. Each of you has specific roles to play and division-specific preparations to make. None more so than our new fighter squadron."

Captain Darius pressed an icon on the control section of the Wardroom table, and above it, directly in the center, a hologram appeared. But it wasn't like any hologram that Hard Case had ever seen. It was vivid and bright, almost as if the ship that had appeared over the table was real.

"This is the new SDF Raptor hybrid," Darius said. "It utilizes a small Arodoni Power Core, which powers the electrical engines. There are two systems, one for hard vacuum that uses an anti-gravity drive that will take some getting used to. Once in atmosphere, it will be safer to use the standard high-yield electrical engine, although your squads will be making history with the anti-gravity drives, so you'll make that call when the time comes."

"Why not just use the drones?" Nash asked. "Less risk, and we've got a hanger full of them."

"A drone can never do what a human pilot is capable of," Hard Case said, before turning to Mutura. "No offense, but you want a person in the driver's seat on an important mission. You need the feel of what's happening, knowing your life is on the line. Drones have their place, but they just aren't capable of what we are."

"I agree," Captain Darius said. "Thank you, Commander Kase. We have other uses for the drones, but we need pilots for these new ships. They could be automated, but I'm guessing your hotshot aviators will do more with these Raptors than we've dreamed up."

"May I ask who designed them?" Kase said.

"Of course you can," Darius replied. "They were designed by head of engineering Lieutenant Alex Stanislaus, and the *Renegade's* computer."

"AI?" Legend sneered.

"Negative," Alex Stanislaus replied. "The ship's computer has hundreds of aircraft specs on file. We put in what we wanted, namely the anti-grav drive powered by dark matter conversion, and got the basic design. The rest was put together using a combination of aerospace engineering and airframe design principles."

"They'll fly, don't worry," Captain Darius said.

"Or fly apart," Legend grumbled.

"Have they been tested?"

"Not yet," Darius said. "The plan is for your squads to study the Raptors, run sims, and once we're out of the system, we'll stop somewhere off the grid and let you do real testing. But we're on a tight timeline, which means we can't take more than a few days to break these ships in."

Hard Case nodded. A few days wasn't much, but he also thought he could fly an oscillating fan through a hurricane, so that didn't bother him too much. And the idea of anti-gravity had been around for a long time. But a person needed to be able to control gravitic forces to build one and no human had even come close.

"There's a lot more to the Raptors, but we'll let you dig into those details on your own time. For now, we'll share our first meal together and let everyone get to know their crewmates. I'm absolutely convinced we have the finest personnel on board. The mission before us could shape the future, not just for the human race, but for the galaxy at large for the foreseeable future. Your names will go down in history and I think that is something worthwhile."

CHAPTER 12

HER BERTH WAS SMALL, but still felt like a home. The non-military personnel had berths in their own section of the ship, behind the storefronts and storage rooms of the stores where they worked.

"We're port side," Lester told her. He was friendly and had taken Zaya under his wing. She might have felt that he was interested in her, but Lester was married to Monica, one of the servers. "We don't mingle with workers on the starboard side."

"Really?" Zaya asked.

"It's an unwritten rule. We have the better side of the ship."

"Is that true?"

"No," Monica said as she brought in a set of bedding sheets that were made by a local vendor to fit the round beds. "Don't believe him."

"It's true," Lester argued. "Look, the facilities may be the same, but our side of the ship is better. Every sailor knows that."

Lester had been a Petty Officer in the SDF. He retired with half pay and benefits after twenty years. Monica had been a Marine, but was shuffled into logistics and never saw combat. She spent half her career on Luna base and the other half on Mars, before she, too, retired after twenty years of service. When the opportunity came to work on the *Renegade,* they jumped at the chance.

"This will help you get settled," Monica said. "And if you need anything else, we're just down the hall."

"Thank you," Zaya said.

She had some clothes that Hugo had bought her, but she had no money of her own. Lester had a plan to help with that. He was certain he could sell her transport pass and already had feelers out. Most of the people rotating off the ship had already left, but there were still a few sticking around to finish up their commitments or waiting until their replacements arrived.

Zaya's berth had only a basic table for two with matching plastic chairs. There was a big view screen on one wall of what would be a small living area and the kitchen had a mini-fridge and microwave oven. It wasn't much, although she thought it was a good start. She needed some furniture and then her berth would feel like a real home.

But there wasn't much time to settle in. She had nine hours off duty before she was supposed to meet Saul in their brewery space. And after a few hours of tinkering on the distillery equipment, she would pull her first shift in the pub. It was open from eleven in the morning until two am (1100-0200). She would work the lunch and dinner rushes, and only stay late if the pub got really busy, which it did at times. She had been told that the *Renegade* was first and foremost a military ship. Getting drunk was taboo. Not just because inebriated people did stupid things, but because hungover crew members put everyone in danger. But there were times when the Captain gave the crew full liberties, which meant no limit on booze, and no working shifts. When that happened, she was told things could get crazy. Bar crawls were not uncommon and finding people passed out at tables was the norm.

Zaya couldn't wait to start working. It wasn't just about earning money, which she would start collecting in her own banking account right away as she received tips from patrons, but because it sounded like fun to her. For the first time in her life, she would be doing normal things with no fears of getting beaten ... or murdered, for that matter. She wouldn't be surrounded by aliens, or other slaves, but just normal people. Not that there weren't aliens on board, but that didn't bother Zaya. The humans outnumbered the aliens five to one. She would be experiencing things that most people take for granted, but in her difficult life, she had never gotten to do.

After making up her bed and arranging her clothes on the racks in her small bedroom, Zaya locked up her cabin and made her way to the park. Every person on the *Renegade* had a wrist communicator. It was a simple device that could send and receive written messages and had a dictation feature. It kept time so that everyone was on ship time, a rotating twenty-four-hour day, just like on Earth. The device had several other apps, like a map of the ship in case a person lost their way and a banking link so that she could access the funds in her shipboard account. It also served to translate when she needed to talk with an alien, but then Zaya could speak a rough version of the universal language. Human voices weren't capable of speaking it fluently, yet she could get by, and she understood more than she could pronounce.

When she reached the park, Zaya took off her boots and walked barefoot on the grass, settling under a tree with wide branches. She had a reason to be on the *Renegade*, not just a space, but a job. And it felt good to know she was where she belonged, although she also had freedom. There was just one last thing she needed to do. Activating the messaging device, she dictated a fast message.

"Hello, Hugo. I wanted you to know the SDF released me. I didn't have anywhere to go; that's a long story, but the important thing is that I found a job. I hope you don't mind, but it's on the *Renegade*. I know I was supposed to leave and my staying doesn't mean anything. You aren't obligated to me. I doubt we would even see each other if that's what you want. I'll certainly be busy enough. But if you want to see me, I'll be working at the Lion's Mane pub up on Theta level, port side. My first shift is tomorrow, lunch and dinner. I guess that's all."

She read back over the message on the device's small screen. It seemed okay, maybe a little desperate, but that was okay. There were times when being with Hugo was all she wanted. And there were other times when she felt the need to stand on her own. Above all, she felt a constant sense of fear. Growing up as a slave, fear was necessary. Fear was what kept a person alive and ready to react at a moment's notice. A slave never knew when their master might fly into a rage. She had been beaten many times and rarely for something she did wrong. Usually, her overseers were angry about something completely unrelated. To walk into a room at the wrong time meant you became the target of their frustration.

But her fear on the *Renegade* was different. Perhaps at some point, if the ship was attacked, she would fear for her safety. What frightened her most was being surrounded by strangers and rejected by the people she cared about. Lester and Monica were nice, and Saul seemed like a decent man, but in her loneliness, she wanted Hugo. That desire burned bright, and she forced herself to tamp it down. To want something too much was dangerous, and she was sure that if Hugo knew how she really felt about him, he would disappear from her life forever.

CHAPTER 13

THEY ATE something that was akin to prime rib, only it came from a different animal and had a unique flavor that Remmy found tasty, but just not the same as beef. It was probably because he had spent sixteen years on SDF ships eating protein rations and rehydrated foods that tasted nothing like they were supposed to taste. The real meat was rich and decadent in his opinion, and while he enjoyed it, he didn't let himself eat too much.

When the meeting ended, the Captain left for another meeting and some of the officers followed suit. Remmy was not bothered that Commander Elder had excused himself. He was used to arrogant officers. Many in the Space Marines looked down on enlisted men no matter what they had accomplished in their careers. Remmy wasn't the type to flaunt his Medal of Honor, although it was military tradition to treat those who had earned that citation the utmost respect. But even after getting it, there were officers who still acted as if he were just another grunt.

Remmy was content to sit and listen to the conversations taking place across the table. He was surprised at how happy it made him to see Lieutenant Ramos and Commander Nash again. They had welcomed him into their circle of leadership when he was just a Master Sergeant filling in for an officer who had missed the cruise because of a last-minute ailment. Nash and Ramos felt like family and he knew them to be excellent officers.

But the biggest surprise was the young ace pilot. Commander Justin Kase was polite, interesting and intelligent. There were glimpses of the cockiness that pilots were known for, but Remmy also saw him reel it back in. That revealed an emotional awareness that Remmy could respect. It didn't take long before the two of them were engaged in a deep conversation.

"You were on Mars during the uprising?" Kase asked.

"During the siege, the Reyvek Complex."

"That was some bad fighting," the younger man said. "My squadron got there too late to see action, but we escorted the passenger ships off planet. There was a lot of fighting around the mines. I heard a special forces team was completely wiped out during the fighting."

"That's almost true," Remmy said. "But those stories always get exaggerated."

"I don't know. That was a bad place. There were kids on rooftops shooting old guns at our ships. One pinged my canopy."

"You were lucky they didn't have the firepower to take you down," Remmy said. "Some of those groups were absolutely crazy."

"How long have you been on the *Renegade*?"

"Since the beginning. I was part of the Marine platoon on the *Jericho*."

"Wow, that's really something. This ship is amazing."

"Indeed," Remmy said. "You settled in yet?"

"Just got here," Hard Case said. "I got the tour and it ended right here for the meeting."

"You'll need a little time to get your bearings. If we can do anything to help you flyboys, just let me know. I'm always available."

After Commander Kase left the Wardroom, Vivian Ramos moved over and sat beside Remmy. He had been about to leave, but she clearly had something on her mind, and he gave her the chance to work up to it.

"Have you heard anything about Lieutenant Micky Colt?"

"I would have thought you had," Remmy told her. "I know you got close."

"That was on the *Jericho*," she said. "Once we moved over to the *Renegade*, things cooled off. There's a lot going on, you know."

Remmy did know. He had gone through all the hard emotions just like the rest of the crew, maybe even more so because his platoon actually lost people in the fighting.

"It got real ... pretty damn fast," he said.

"Yeah, and then, well... you know. I meant to check on him, but I wasn't sure where they took him."

"Quarantine facility near Ares Station," Remmy said. "But that was the last thing I heard. There was no improvement in his condition. A real shame. He was a good man and a fine Marine."

"I feel guilty sometimes," she said. "Like I could have been better to him before it happened."

She was referring to the Lieutenant's mental breakdown, if that's what it was. He had gotten infected with a parasite of some sort on Casasil and, eventually, it made him homicidal.

"That wouldn't have changed anything," Remmy said. "And I don't think he has any memory of us now."

She swiped at a tear and cleared her throat, but when she looked up at him, it was with a penetrating gaze.

"You surprise me, Remmy. You don't mind me calling you that, do you?"

"Not in the least," he said. "It's my name."

"You're a Major now."

He chuckled. "That was the Captain's idea. He seems to think I should be someone important."

"You are," she said. "Why didn't you tell Commander Kase that it was you that saved those people on Mars and that you won the Medal of Honor for your bravery in that fight?"

Remmy sighed. The truth was, he didn't feel like he won anything. He lost some of his dearest friends in that engagement. He didn't even disagree with the rebels or why they were protesting the working conditions at the mines. Yet, he was a Marine and he was told where to fight. His Special Forces platoon had been sent in to rescue over fifty hostages. They got them all out and safely through the city, while it was under siege, but it had cost the lives of every Marine in Remmy's platoon. The Medal of Honor wasn't about what he accomplished or the lives he had saved, not to him at any rate. It was about the people he had lost and there was nothing honorable about that.

"It's not really something I like talking about," he said.

"But you deserve the respect," she said.

"He was already respectful. Like you said, I outrank him. No need to bring up the past."

"You are an interesting guy, Remmy. I'm glad you're on our side."

"Me too," he said.

"How's Laila?"

"Fine," Remmy said. "She'll be happy that you're back."

That wasn't exactly true. Laila McPherson and Vivian Ramos weren't friends. That's not to say they weren't friendly, and they certainly weren't enemies, but Vivian was an officer and Laila had been a Staff Sergeant when they served together.

"Tell her I want to reach out once things fall into a routine," she said. "I need advice on what's good and what to avoid in the Concourse."

"I'll tell her," Remmy said.

They stood and, to his surprise, she embraced him and whispered, "Thanks," into his ear. He waited until she was finished with the hug and moved away before he headed for the door. He still had things to do and he wasn't the type to put them off. Soon Laila would be expecting him at their apartment. Actually the berth was hers, but they shared it as often as possible.

Remmy was walking past the Captain's quarters when the door opened and Darius waved him inside.

"Got a second?"

"Always, sir," Remmy said.

They went inside and Darius offered Remmy a tumbler with just half a finger of his good whiskey inside.

"You sure you want to share this?" Remmy asked.

"I got four new bottles delivered," Darius said. "That'll last us a year at least."

"Well, then, I won't say no."

They both drank their mouthful of the strong spirit. To Remmy, it tasted woody, with just the slightest bit of sweetness. The taste resonated for just a split second before his tongue went numb and the whiskey burned its way down his throat. The swallow was unpleasant; the warm sensation that spread through him when it hit his stomach wasn't.

"What did you think of the meeting?"

"Lots of thoughts," Remmy said. "Still sorting them out."

"No one really objected," he said.

"I'm not sure any of us know what we're getting ourselves into."

"That's for certain," Darius said. "I'm sorry about the GIGI thing. I didn't mean to blindside you with that."

"You're the Captain," Remmy said. "You always let us know what we need to know when we need to know it."

"But you have a history with the artifact," Darius said.

It was true. Remmy had been the first person to come in contact with the artifact while it was still in space. The artifact was, at least on the outside, a square block of stone. Inside was some sort of living machine with abilities that Remmy couldn't explain. It was like a living computer, but so advanced that it could do things like self-levitate, and it had forged a mental bond with Remmy that allowed them to communicate via their thoughts even from vast distances.

"Can you contact it now?"

"Don't know," Remmy said. "Haven't tried."

At first, shortly after the battle of Saturn, Remmy had missed the artifact's presence in his mind. It wasn't the conversation he missed, but rather the instantaneous availability of information. It was like part of his mind had gone dark and could no longer be accessed.

"Would you? I spoke to our old friend Connor O'Dell, but he said GIGI was being studied and he couldn't promise that we could use her," Darius said. "I'm pretty sure he's lying, but..."

"What good does knowing that do you?" Remmy asked.

The Captain wasn't quite as accustomed to living with other people's decisions, whether they were wise or even made sense, or not. But Remmy had been an enlisted Marine most of his career. His officers gave him orders and he followed them. He had no voice and no choice in the matter.

"If I catch him in a lie, that might give me leverage," Darius said. "And the truth is, we have no idea what the defenses we'll be facing might be. Our drone operators are fantastic, but they can't operate entire wings of drones at the same time with perfect coordination. Plus, GIGI has information about the worlds we'll encounter. Having her on board could prove the difference between success and failure."

"I'll try," Remmy said.

He had no special abilities from the bond. He could think about GIGI and the artifact somehow heard his call. At least, that was how it had worked. For all Remmy knew, GIGI had severed their bond during the eighteen months they had been apart.

GIGI, are you there? He thought. *Can you hear me, GIGI? It's Remmy. Are you there?*

There was no response. He felt a slight sense of disappointment, which surprised him. He hadn't realized that he wanted to reconnect with the artifact, but apparently he had.

"Nothing, sir. I'm sorry."

"It was worth a shot," Darius said. "I have the feeling..."

Darius continued talking, but Remmy's mind had suddenly shifted and a new voice was occupying his thoughts.

Major Steel, it is refreshing to renew our bond. It has been many months. I have followed your progress avidly. Congratulations on your promotion.

The voice sounded like his own, as if he were just talking to himself, but the thoughts were not his. The diction and tone were completely different. He had often wondered if his experience with GIGI was what a crazy person heard when they complained of hearing voices.

He held up a hand and Darius stopped talking. In another setting, it would have been rude for Remmy to stop his Captain in mid-sentence but Darius didn't seem to mind.

It's good to reconnect, Remmy thought. *Have the scientists kept you busy?*

You think too highly of your species, Major. With the computer data delivered by the Independence, *your scientists and politicians decided quickly that I was not needed. I was stored in a facility on the dark side of the moon all this time. You are the first human I have conversed with in eighteen of your Earth months.*

"I've got her," Remmy said. "She's locked up in a facility on the dark side of Luna. Hasn't been dealt with since we left the system after the battle of Saturn."

"I knew it," Darius leaping out of his chair and starting to pace. "That Connor is a real piece of work."

"Is there something you would like GIGI to do?"

"I want her back on the *Renegade*. What can she do to help us with that?"

Captain Darius would like to have you back on the Renegade, Remmy thought. *Is it possible that you can help us with this?*

I read the Captain's memo, nearly three months prior to today. In that time, I have set things in motion. A transfer order was sent out last week. I am scheduled to be moved to the transfer station on a fast transport at approximately 0200 hours.

You set things in motion?

I forged an order from Secretary O'Dell and tucked it away in Admiral Baxter's read emails. I then sent orders to the logistics team, cleared space on the transport, and sent a retrieval order to the maintenance crew on Luna Base. I would have come sooner, but it was necessary to blend in with the cargo being shipped out. If the orders trigger a closer inspection, my subterfuge might have been uncovered.

Remmy couldn't help but laugh. He was amazed that GIGI had waited patiently to tamper with things. Then again, she may have been working behind the scenes the entire time. In some ways, it might explain how much support Darius and the *Renegade* had been given.

"It seems GIGI has been reading your reports, Captain."

That made him chuckle.

"At least someone is," Darius said. "Connor hadn't read my request. He pawned it off on a lackey, but that was probably a lie."

"GIGI has set it up to be delivered to us tomorrow night."

"You are kidding me?"

"Unless I'm going crazy, that's what she said."

"You think she could do that?"

"Unless the authorities in charge of her took great steps to ensure that she was kept out, then yes, I think it's highly probable."

"Alright, I'll have Lieutenant Bertoli check the manifest for tomorrow."

I have logged myself as ballast cargo, GIGI spoke into Remmy's mind. *Shipping number 73872947.*

Remmy relayed the message to Captain Darius, then he began his walk back to the park. To his surprise, Laila met him halfway, and had Hugo McManus in tow.

"There you are," she said. "I feel like getting a drink."

"I'm game," Remmy said. "How about you, Hugo?"

The big man nodded. Remmy had seen him pumping heavy iron in the gym the Marines had set up in their hangar. But he was all cleaned up, his eyes swinging back and forth as he scanned for danger. Remmy thought it was a bit of overkill to be worried about danger, but he didn't say anything. The three of them made their way to Laila's favorite bar. It served wine, which wasn't cheap, but when you were restricted to only two alcoholic beverages a day, one could afford to be picky. Not to mention the fact that they had nothing else to spend their money on. Remmy and Laila's idea of a good time was shooting a few hundred rounds at the range, taking a long walk around the Park, and wrapping their evening up with a meal or beverage. The food in the Officer's Mess was usually excellent. Which meant they could save their money for real wine and specialty desserts.

The bar was halfway down the Grand Concourse on the Starboard side, Epsilon level. It was part of a fancy restaurant with linens and wine lists on the tables. It was quiet, which Remmy liked, and comfortable. They settled into a round booth with thickly padded bench seats that were manufactured in the plant just a few klicks away in the stern of the ship.

Laila ordered wine, while Remmy and Hugo got beer. No one was hungry, so they nursed their drinks and talked in quiet tones.

"How are things?" Remmy asked.

"I guess I'm still adapting," Hugo said.

"Tell us what happened on Libertine," Laila said.

They had both read the debrief that Hugo filed. His official interrogation by the SDF intelligence service hadn't been released yet, but Hugo was not the kind of man to hold anything back.

"It wasn't bad at first," he said. "Rip and I landed."

"That was smart thinking on his part," Laila said.

"Saved my life," Hugo said. "I wasn't expecting that."

"Did you get your farm?"

Hugo shook his head. "The southern pole wasn't as friendly as the people in the north. But the weather was fine, sort of tropical, so we stayed. Some of the Ashi came down in escape pods."

"I never considered that possibility," Laila said.

"It could have been much worse," Hugo admitted. "They're not the brightest beings, not the warriors at any rate."

"How's that?" Remmy asked.

"They fought for their resources," Hugo said. "Despite being overwhelmed by the heat in the desert, they left their pods in the daytime. Most of them never made it to the hospitable zone."

"No loss, that," Laila said.

Hugo nodded. "A few months after we arrived, a slave ship showed up. We brought it down and took out the slavers, but..."

"What?" Laila asked immediately.

Remmy realized that Hugo wasn't just telling a story. He was wrestling with events that were still traumatic to him. So he waited, saying nothing, letting the big man get through what he was wrestling with.

"You've read the reports," Hugo said. "That's what happened."

"We're more interested in what wasn't in the reports," Remmy said.

"The woman that left with Rip ended up back on Libertine," Laila said. "That's one hell of a coincidence. Some might say it was meant to be."

Hugo grimaced but didn't say anything.

"Love doesn't come around all that often," Remmy said after a moment of silence. "You sure you don't want to hang it up. You could still go after her, Hugo. No one would blame you."

"I don't have to," Hugo said. "Zaya came back."

"What?" Laila burst out, nearly choking on her wine.

"She got a job at the Lion's Mane and messaged me earlier today."

Laila looked at Remmy and he recognized the suspicion in her eyes, but to her credit, she kept them to herself.

"What are you going to do?" Remmy asked.

Hugo had only sipped his way through half of his beer. He looked down into the glass and didn't respond right away. Remmy didn't push him and Laila was silent.

"I thought she wanted to leave," Hugo finally said.

"Looks like you were wrong," Remmy said. "Men often are when it comes to women."

Hugo looked up. The big man struggled at times. Get him in the gym and he would outwork anyone. Put him in a combat op and he knew exactly what to do. Getting him to work with a team could be more difficult, but with the right coaching, he was a huge asset. Although, when it came to social situations, especially with women, he struggled. What Remmy knew that few others did was that Hugo desperately wanted to fit in. He wanted friends, but it was just hard for him to manage. While Remmy would have thought that a relationship was beyond Hugo's abilities, he had been pleased to learn that the woman Zaya had come around to see the good in him.

Laila set her glass down delicately, but under the table she squeezed Remmy's hand hard. He loved her for staying silent. He knew she wanted to shout at Hugo to run up and find that girl. She probably also wanted to dig into the fact that the woman had shown up on Libertine twice and now was going to be part of the *Renegade's* crew. Remmy knew they would need to look into Zaya, but Hugo didn't need to know that.

"I want to see her," the big Sergeant finally said.

"I think she wants to see you, too," Remmy said.

"Of course she does!" Laila said. "Why are you sitting here with us, Hugo. Go find her."

"She said to go to the restaurant tomorrow," he said.

"That's because she's nervous that you don't want her."

"What?" Hugo said.

"Yeah," Laila said. "Women are insecure, too. Especially when they've had trauma in their lives. They tend to keep people at arm's length. Don't let her, Hugo. You're a great guy. She's lucky to have you. Now, get moving, you big lug. Go find her. Just know that I'm going to want all the details, so remember everything!"

Hugo looked at Remmy.

"Don't look at me," he said. "Laila knows more about women than I do."

"I guarantee you she's thinking about you right now," Laila said. "Every woman wants a man who will fight for her love. I don't mean combat, I mean overcoming obstacles that stand in the way of romance. Show her you're willing to fight for her love, and she won't be able to resist you."

Hugo gave her a weak, half-hearted smile. Remmy thought the big man would gladly have fought a hundred battles rather than navigate the finer details of social interactions. But to his credit, he got up and started to offer to pay for his drink.

"Forget it," Remmy said. "My treat. I hope we can enjoy many more in the days ahead."

"Double dates! Yes, that would be amazing," Laila said. "Make it happen, Sergeant."

He nodded and set off. Remmy and Laila watched him go, then she waved her nearly empty glass at the bartender and turned to Remmy.

"Can you believe this?"

"Nope," Remmy said.

"Hugo McManus has a girlfriend. I thought it was simply lack of options."

"He was the only man on the planet, you mean."

"Don't make me sound like a jerk," Laila said. "You were thinking it, too."

"And what are you thinking now?"

"Well, I'm trying not to think about the fact that a woman showed up on Libertine twice," she said. "And now she's on this ship."

"It could just be a coincidence. You said so yourself."

"I said it, but I don't believe it."

They fell silent as the bartender, a woman with her hair tied up on her head, wearing a white shirt and long, maroon apron, brought Laila another glass of wine.

"Would you like another?" the bartender asked Remmy.

"No, this is number two for me today."

The woman smiled and nodded, before heading back to the bar.

"I thought I smelled some sweet corn mash on your breath, mister."

"What can I say? The Captain insists on wasting his good booze on me."

"We'll have to keep tabs on this woman. You need to dig into her. She could be a spy," Laila said. "If that's even possible."

"I suppose anything is possible. But she was a slave on the Ashi battleship. They couldn't have known that Hugo would rescue her."

"For all we know, they were planning to get her to the surface of the planet somehow. Maybe fake a ship catastrophe. It didn't have to be a rescue, but that just fell into their lap."

"And how would she send messages?"

"I have no idea, but I know someone who might," Remmy said.

"That's what I love about you, Major, you always find a way to complete the mission."

"Good, now drink up and let's go home."

Laila gave him a charming smile and took a big swallow from her goblet of wine.

CHAPTER 14

IT TOOK SOME TIME, partly because the ship was so huge, but Hard Case eventually found his way down to the hangar. It wasn't as busy as before. The huge door wasn't closed and he looked out into space. The *Renegade* was broadside to the newly built transfer station, and beyond it, he could see Saturn with her golden rings. It was an awesome sight.

"Help you, sir?" a short man in coveralls asked. The tag on his chest said *Smith,* and the stripes on his shoulder showed he was a Petty Officer.

"How does it work?" Hard Case asked, pointing at the open hangar and the hard vacuum of space beyond.

"It's a bit complicated," Petty Officer Smith said. "But there's a gravity wall. You can't see it but think of it sort of like a bubble. It holds the air and the heat inside."

"Fascinating. It's like nothing I've ever seen. This whole ship is..."

"The *Renegade* is a special lady. There's a reason most of us never want to leave. I guess you're new."

"Yeah, my first day on board... night, I guess. I'm one of the new pilots for the Raptors. I was hoping to see the new ships."

"Well, now, that is something worth seeing. There ain't no other vessels like the Raptors. Come with me."

They walked down the long hangar toward the far end, where several ships sat. Hard Case could see the shuttles parked neatly in a row. Smith led the way around the transports. Beyond them were twelve smaller ships, each one covered with a silky cloth that was clamped to the deck with magnets.

"These are the Raptors," Smith said. "In fact, I volunteered to work on maintenance on them. My name is Dante Smith."

"I'm Justin, but you can call me Hard Case."

"I think I'll stick to Commander Kase," Dante said with a chuckle. "You being an officer and all."

"In my experience, Dante, a fighter squadron is only as good as the maintenance crew that services our ships."

"In most cases, I would agree," Dante said. "But this Arodoni tech is different. It doesn't wear down like our ships. Can't say why, but it's just made with quality we can't match."

He began pulling the magnets and soon the silk that was pulled taut recoiled back over the Raptor. Hard Case was shocked by what he saw. The fighter ship was nothing like he expected.

It was a mix of old and new, a cigar-shaped vessel with wings that folded back toward the tail. The cockpit was right on top with a transparent canopy. The ship was painted a glossy black with chrome accents that were more like a luxury vehicle than a fighter ship. The most interesting feature was the blunt nose of the spacecraft. It was one large jet engine, so that air could flow through the body of the craft. But in the center of that engine was something that Hard Case had never seen before.

"What's this?" he asked.

"That's the anti-grav gennie," Smith said. "The Arodoni's technology, from what I've been told, is the most advanced in the galaxy when it comes to recreating gravity. These fighters utilize that feature to move them through space."

"Seems pretty simple," Hard Case suggested.

"The best designs always are," Smith countered. "The less parts that can break, the safer the aircraft. I started helping my dad when I was just a kid. He was an aircraft mechanic, a former SDF, but retired to maintain the toys of the rich and famous. I've seen a lot of different flyers, but the best are always straightforward and simple. I told that to Lieutenant Stanislaus when they were designing these beauties."

"He included you in the design process?" Hard Case asked.

"Yes, sir. It was like having access to a candy store. We could build practically anything. In that sort of environment, it's tempting to pack as many ideas into one package as you can. I helped them strip most of that out. She's lean and mean. Her wings extend in atmo. We haven't put them through their paces yet, but I would guess they are fast and agile. The best part is that they're equipped with inertial dampeners. You can dial it up or shut it down completely. That way you can feel yourself moving in space and cut down on the g-forces when you're in atmosphere."

Hard Case was dazzled, not just by the beauty of the Raptor, but if Smith was right, it would change aviation forever. In the past, engines were built that were beyond the capacity of pilots to fly them. Special flight suits had to be designed to keep the pilot's blood from pooling at his feet or being sucked out of his brain by the gravitational force produced by the aircraft. Some people fared better at it than others. Good pilots had pushed their ships beyond the limits that the human body could take in conflict. They had died for that mistake, but if what Dante Smith said about the gravity control was true, if a pilot could dial back the effects of inertia, they would be able to fly in ways mankind had never dreamed possible.

"You've outdone yourself," Hard Case said, running a hand over the fuselage. "They're magnificent."

"Laser tech helps," Dante continued. "When you don't have to pack ten thousand bullets inside, it saves a lot of room. Not to mention a gas cooling system just to keep the guns from overheating."

"Will the lasers overheat?"

"Shouldn't," he said. "See how the air passes through the center of the ship. It's a natural cooling system. In space, it's so cold you don't really worry about heat, but in atmo, the air passing through the jet system will bleed off excess heat naturally. We've still got to test it, but its design is simple and elegant. I can't imagine that it wouldn't work."

"What if you don't use the jet engine in atmospheric flight?" Hard Case asked.

"You mean if you use the artificial gravity drive instead? Well, that's a different ballgame but the air will still be flowing through the ships. Gravity won't stop that. If you hotshots find a way to utilize anti-gravity propulsion in atmo, then we'll figure that out. That's part of the genius of these Raptors that you don't see. It's a component built aircraft."

"What's that mean?"

"It's fully customizable. We swap components, even the main components, in and out. We can add new things, not just weapons but flight controls, boosters, repulsers, whatever we can think of."

"And they're compatible?

"Yep, easy peasy. I can remove a few sections of the lower hull and climb all the way up inside this baby. Anything that needs to be adjusted, changed, repaired, or replaced can be done quick and easy. Best of all, I've already got all the parts manufactured. It makes my job a breeze."

"Can I see inside?"

"Hell yeah," Dante said. "They're your ships, Cap'n. You can do whatever you like."

The Petty Officer wheeled a set of stairs up to the side of the sleek aircraft. It was wide enough for two people, and they went up together. Hard Case knew officers who looked down on the crews that maintained their aircraft. It wasn't just the officer-enlisted gap, but more often arose from the sense of freedom and euphoria that came from being in the air. The mechanics were vital, but they were stuck on the ground. Pilots could take to the air and it was life-changing.

But Hard Case preferred to work hand in hand with his maintenance team. For him, it wasn't enough to fly the aircraft; he wanted to know how she worked. A fighter, be it a jet plane or a spaceship, was an extension of the pilot. And he wanted to know the Raptor from nose to tail. That learning process would take weeks, but he was soaking in the unique fighter and loving every minute of it. Petty Officer Smith was the man who knew the ship and Commander Kase didn't mind rubbing shoulders or elbows with the man.

A recessed lever activated the canopy. It shifted up, then slid back. One of the most unique features of the aircraft was the long, transparent canopy.

"Had to make this long for aerodynamics," Dante said. By keeping the entire thing transparent, we can also get a look at the mechanics." He pointed to a black box that was situated behind the pilot's seat. "Here's your onboard computer. Again, we can swap that out or make upgrades as needed. I don't see the need for that any time soon. Lieutenant Stanislaus is a bit of a computer genius and he's been learning from the Arodoni tech since the beginning. There won't be any problems with the hardware, but we might catch a few bugs in the software. That was still written by humans ... and we all make mistakes."

"Engineers on the *Renegade* wrote it?"

"That's right, using the Arodoni code as a template. They didn't steal it, but they learned from it. Ain't no sense in reinventing the wheel when it's already been perfected. If there are bugs, it's probably from the translation."

Hard Case didn't quite understand, but he didn't need to. "What's that?" he asked, pointing to a cylindrical device behind the computer.

"That's your power core," Dante said. "That's the key to this entire ship. No battery or fuel system could replace it."

"Too much weight?"

"Not enough power," Dante said. "You familiar with black matter?"

"On a theoretical level," Hard Case said.

"Yeah, our R&D people have known about it for a long time. Where does energy go? The first law of Thermodynamics says energy can't be created or destroyed, but it does change form. The universe is brimming with that dark energy. We've discovered its existence, but could never do anything with it. We couldn't catch it, collect it, work with it, nothing. Yet the Arodoni figured it out."

"This uses dark energy?"

"It collects and converts it. Man, the results are on the scale of miraculous. The *Jericho* has an Arodoni Power Core about twice this size. And that bad boy is powering this entire ship."

"Really?" Hard Case asked, shocked by the information.

"Oh, yeah, and not just the ship systems, but the lasers as well. It has more energy than we can use. Haven't you heard about it?"

"It's all classified top secret," Hard Case said. "Even in our briefings on the *Renegade*, that section was heavily redacted."

"Well, now you know. In space, you could fly this ship forever without running out of power. You never need to recharge and the Raptor doesn't run on fuel."

Hard Case was once again at a loss for words. It was happening way too often on the *Renegade*. During his training over the past two weeks, energy conservation was a major component. The hybrid ships they were flying, or simulating, had limited resources. Part of what they were learning to do was balance the needs of the mission with the safety of the pilots and the ability to get their birds safely back to base.

"The power core negates the need for batteries or fuel tanks. In gravity, this is the lightest fighter craft built since, well, World War One, maybe."

They went over a few other mechanical components. Most were new to Hard Case. The technology was a huge leap from what he was accustomed to. Then there was the cockpit itself. To say it was different was an understatement.

"She's a combination of analog, voice and retinal-activated controls," Dante explained. "The first Marine officer on the *Renegade* developed a system for controlling things with his eyes. You'll have a holographic Heads Up Display and the same projector that produces the HUD can track your eyes."

"It can tell what I'm looking at?"

"Correct, so you can scroll through options just by looking at a list. You can select certain systems and activate various controls depending on what you're looking at."

"Isn't that sort of dangerous? I mean, if I'm tracking an enemy ship and look at the wrong thing, won't it activate systems I don't want?"

"You would think so," Dante said with a chuckle. "But actually, your eyes change shape as they focus on things near and far. If you're looking through the HUD, the system will know. If you focus in on the HUD, it will recognize the change and give you control."

"That's wild."

"It doesn't cover the main systems. You know, you can't fly the ship with your eyes. You can activate radar or swap firing controls from lasers to whatever ordnance she's carrying, that sort of thing. The inertial dampener, for instance, can be dialed up or down by looking at that gauge. But the controls are all redundant. There are switches and dials for every system, and the computer responds to voice controls too."

Hard Case put his hands on either side of the cockpit and vaulted himself inside. Fighter craft, be they for spaceflight or atmospheric craft, are not designed for comfort. But Hard Case was surprised. The seat was well-padded and fit his physical form nearly perfectly.

"The seat is fully adjustable," Dante pointed out. "You can change everything, and it's built with warming, cooling, and protective inflation."

"You're kidding me?" Hard Case said. "Won't our flight suits do all that?"

"In the Raptor, you'll wear a streamlined version of the flight suit. A lot of what normally goes into one won't be necessary and we thought a lighter fight suit could shave a few milliseconds off your reaction times."

"Can't hurt," Hard Case said.

The controls were different. There were all the usual levers and switches. A few of the most vital readouts were in both analog and digital format, which would allow a pilot to operate the craft in the event of a complete power loss.

"That should never happen, though," Dante explained. "The power system is in a Faraday cage. The only way you should ever lose power is through damage in flight."

"Got it," Commander Kase said. "Why two joysticks?"

"One controls your standard operations, steering, targeting with the laser cannons, missile controls, etc. ... The other controls the anti-grav drive."

There were foot pedals and the joysticks had a variety of buttons that could be activated with the pilot's thumbs. There were also triggers on both joysticks. It was nothing like the setup they had trained on at Luna.

"We had laser deflector screens on our sims back on Luna Base," Justin said. "Is that part of this tech?"

"Absolutely. Computer-controlled, so that you can be encased in a deflection bubble, but still fire weapons. It can also be reconfigured based on need."

"On the fly?"

"Absolutely," Dante said.

"I can't wait to take her out," Hard Case said, climbing back out of the ship.

"It's going to be a game changer," Dante said.

Together, they covered the ship back up with the silk cloth.

"And you're our point man for maintenance?" Hard Case asked.

"I will be," Dante said. "For now, I'm in charge of the flight deck maintenance. These shuttles take a lot more T-L-C than the Arodoni craft."

"Well, thanks for taking the time to give me a tour."

"Anytime," he said. "I expect you flyboys will be down here a lot in the next few days. They're your ships. Get your people in here. If you want to see how they're put together, I'll grab some gearheads and show you. We're always looking for things to do down here."

The two men shook hands and Hard Case made his way back up to his cabin. For the first time in his life, he could honestly say that his mind was truly blown.

CHAPTER 15

HUGO WASN'T sure where he was going. He knew the civilians working on the Renegade had quarters behind the shops, but he wasn't exactly sure how to get there. He could have used the app on his wrist device, but he wasn't sure if Zaya had her own room or was bunking with someone. She could be anywhere on the ship, for that matter. His wrist device didn't track the wearer's location ... and the truth was that Hugo didn't know if she wanted to be found. He couldn't even say he wanted to find her. If there were a way to guarantee that she wanted to be found, that would be different. But what if he found her and Laila had been wrong? What if she didn't want him coming around?

He replayed the message she had sent him over and over in his head. There was no way to know how she really felt. It had seemed encouraging, but the more he thought about it, the more doubts arose in his mind.

Eventually, he found himself in a wide passageway with berths on either side. The doors were all numbered, but most had decorations over and around them. Many even stood open, with people going in and out of the various cabins. Hugo felt bad looking inside them, but couldn't help notice they were small. He had been assigned to an apartment overlooking the Park. It seemed lavish, although he was glad for it. After being on Libertine, he enjoyed the open expanse of the park, including the towering ceiling. Not that any place on the *Renegade* felt as claustrophobic as regular ships or space stations, but it didn't compare to the vast open plains and towering mountains of Libertine. He had spent a year and a half on a planet that was unlike anything in the Sol system. Going back to service was somewhat of a shock to his system.

"Can we help you find something, Sergeant?" a man with a long-tailed jacket asked.

Music was coming from a nearby cabin. It was slow and melodic, nothing like the sounds that came from it. The man in the jacket didn't seem angry, but Hugo sometimes found it hard to tell what other people were feeling.

"I'm looking for someone," he said.

"I know just about everyone on this side of the Concourse," the man replied. "I was a logistic grunt before I started selling trinkets. I know you Spec Op boys like to tinker with your own weapons, but if you need parts, I can get 'em."

"That's good to know," Hugo said, a little surprised by the man's sales pitch. It was oddly unexpected in the residential section of the ship.

"Who are you looking for?"

"Her name is Zaya Wright."

"Can't say I've heard of her. You sure you're on the right side of the Concourse?"

Hugo nodded.

"Well, there's plenty of new people, just not on this level. Where does she work?"

"The Lion's Mane."

That's on Theta," the man in the jacket said. "Two decks above this one. It's standard practice for folks to be housed on the same level as their business."

"Thank you," Hugo said.

"Any time. You need anything, come see me. Name's Frank Cross. I've got a booth in the Market."

Hugo had seen the Market. It was a large storefront with multiple vendors inside.

"Thank you," Hugo told him.

He made his way up two levels. The ramps that led to the higher decks were wide. He went up to Theta and continued his search. The residences were much like those on the Epsilon level, but with fewer festivities. Over half the cabins had no decorations or adornments. Most were closed and, while there were a few people in the passageway, they seemed more focused on their business than just milling about.

Hugo didn't know if he should just start knocking on doors or simply wait for the following day. The temptation to give up was strong. He wasn't the type to accept failure, but he wasn't even sure that finding Zaya was a good idea. But before he could decide what to do, a door opened and there she was. Zaya stepped out into the corridor before turning to lock her cabin door. Hugo froze. He had seen her, but she hadn't seen him yet.

Laila's words echoed in his mind. *You're a great guy. She's lucky to have you. Now, get moving, you big lug. Go find her.* He had found her, and he would have to face the truth. Zaya might not agree with Laila. She might not want him to be part of her life. Or, she might just want to be friends. He didn't know if he could live with that, but he knew he might have no other choice. Still, it took every ounce of his willpower to speak her name.

"Zaya," he said, still fifteen paces away from her.

She turned, surprise on her face. Hugo couldn't read many people, but he had spent enough time with Zaya that her expression was clear to him.

"Hugo?"

He nodded, not that it was necessary. It wasn't that she was unsure of his identity, but her question was more an expression of her surprise. And he still didn't know if it was a good surprise or a bad one.

She walked toward him. He felt as though he were frozen, stuck in limbo, awaiting the verdict of the woman he loved. She was the only woman he had ever loved. All he could do was hope that she loved him back.

"What are you doing here?" she asked, her voice seemed neutral. He couldn't tell if she was happy to see him or not.

"To see you," he managed to say.

It was as if he had plucked out his heart and was holding it out to her. She could take it, or reject it, and the fear that she might simply throw it on the floor and shatter it into a million pieces was worse than facing death in combat.

"I didn't know if you would want to see me," she said. "I didn't exactly plan all this."

He would have preferred for her to fall into his arms and the two of them to live happily ever after, but life just wasn't that neat and tidy. He still couldn't tell if she was happy to see him or not.

"I'm happy you're here," he said, finding his courage and resolving to tell her how he really felt. If Laila was right, she might not be able to accept it, but she would at least know. "I wanted that, but I didn't know it was possible."

"They let me go. I didn't know enough to be useful, I guess."

"I'm glad," he told her. "I missed you. I want to be with you, Zaya, if that's what you want, too."

It was her turn to be frozen with fear. Of course, she wanted it. Her entire reason for coming back to the *Renegade* was the hope that she could be with Hugo. Maybe it could be argued that she had no other place to go. It was certainly true that the *Renegade* was nicer than any place in the Sol system that a person in her position could hope for. That didn't negate the fact that it was a military ship and would be going into war. Every person on board the *Renegade* was putting their life on the line. She had put hers at risk in the hope that she might be able to find something real with Hugo, something that would last.

But at that moment, standing in front of him, for some reason she couldn't identify or explain, she hesitated. Everything she had hoped for was happening. He hadn't rejected her. He hadn't even waited until the following day to come and find her. Didn't that mean something? She felt like it did, and still, it was like there was a gulf between them. There was no way to know if their love was enough to bridge the gap.

So, she did the only thing she felt capable of at that moment. She changed the subject.

"I got my own place," she said. That was significant to her. After being a slave for decades, with no hope and absolutely no privacy, to have her own cabin was a very big deal. But she saw the pain in his eyes. It wasn't what he wanted to hear from her. While she loved him, she didn't know if she could give him what he wanted. "Want to see it?"

He nodded, and she turned back toward the cabin. She started to take a step toward it and away from him, but before she could, he caught her arm. Every instinct told her to jerk away, to run, to fight even. Years of her life had been spent trying to stay out of the reach of her alien overseers. When she looked back at him, every fear seemed to weigh her down, but she didn't pull away.

"I don't think I can give you what you want," she said, her voice trembling with emotion.

"I won't stop fighting for you," he said. It was all he could think to say. The idea of it had been bouncing around in his skull since Laila had said it. If there was one thing he knew how to do, it was fight. While fighting for a woman's heart wasn't like combat, he was willing to do whatever it took to win her trust and affection.

"I'm broken," she said, her voice thick with emotion. "I don't know why I can't let you in."

He pulled her closer. Hugo was a big man. Lots of food and hard labor had made him strong. Zaya was thick with muscle, too. She wasn't dainty, but she sometimes felt that way in his arms. In the residential corridor of the *Renegade,* as he pulled her into his embrace, she felt small and broken, but seen and cared for, too.

They didn't speak. He just stood there holding her and she let him. People passed them by, but no one said anything. Neither of them knew how long they stayed that way, just hanging on to one another, but they knew it was good.

Eventually, Zaya spoke.

"I don't know what to do now," she whispered.

"Me either," he said.

"Will you come back to see me?"

"Every chance I get," he said.

"Good," she replied.

She had to stand on her tiptoes to reach his face, but she kissed him. It was just a light kiss, and then she said, "Thank you."

A minute later, Hugo found himself alone in the hallway. He was tingling all over. He guessed that was love. It was a new emotion for him. One he wasn't accustomed to. Yet, he liked it. The walk back to his berth was a long one, but he didn't mind it. She hadn't rejected him, and he had learned something important from their interaction. She wanted to be with him just as much as he wanted to be with her. But there were things that kept them apart. He couldn't get his hands on them; they were like shadows in his mind. He could understand they were there: fears, past trauma, his PTSD, the scars on their souls from the cruelty they had seen and the hardships they had endured. They were his enemies now. They were the foe he would have to battle with if he wanted to love Zaya and if he wanted her to love him.

It all seemed out of reach, but if there was one thing Hugo knew how to do, it was wage war. And he was up for the challenge. Whatever it took, he was determined to win Zaya's love and be the man she needed him to be. Somewhere along his walk back to his cabin, everything changed for Hugo McManus. He became a whole new man.

CHAPTER 16

LIFE ON BOARD a military ship was all about routine. The officers designed detailed schedules for every day that kept the crew members under their command busy and productive. Schedules were going out ship-wide and new crew were working hard to get assimilated. In grunt country, the three Marine platoons rotated through different schedules. Every day, they would train together on simulators, do basic PT, hone their skills on the indoor gun range inside Hangar A, which also had space for a full gym of resistance training machines, as well as mats for grappling and sparring. Around the outer portion of the hangar was a running track. Each lap was a full five kilometers, giving the Marines plenty of room to keep up their cardio.

The routines for the new fighter pilots were even more grueling. They started their day with PT as well, but used elliptical machines for their cardio in one of the rooms that was in their section of the ship over Hangar C. They also spent time going over the specs of their new Raptors, but a majority of their time was spent in the simulators. The first few days, they were simply learning to fly using the unique drive engine, which created a field of gravity that pulled the ship forward. It was unlike anything they had ever flown before, and almost like a video game. The ship could turn in any direction. They trained in simulated outer space, with no outside gravitation forces and no resistance. The process was more mental than physical. The new engines allowed them to do anything with the spacecraft, and its simulated field of gravity protected it from the G-forces that would normally tear a ship apart.

"These babies are bad to the bone," Animal declared after a three-hour training session where the Hell Flyers had chased one another around in simulated space.

"It doesn't really feel like flying," Diamond said.

"Try dialing back the inertial dampener," Hard Case instructed her. "Find a level that gives you the feel you need for the ship."

"How's it possible to run full out, guns blazing, and never run out of energy?" Aspen said. "I can't keep looking at the power level."

"That's part of what we're learning to get used to," Hard Case said. "Each ship creates its own power. I don't understand how, but that's what I've been told."

"Works for me," Bishop said. "The only limits on these new birds are us."

"I prefer no limits," Animal said.

"The ships are fantastic," Aspen said. "But what about the mission? What are we looking at?"

"From what I've been told," he and Legend had held meetings with Commander Nash and Major Steel about that very topic, "we're looking at runs such as those we trained on back at Lunar Base. Only much more intense."

"Isn't that impossible?" Indigo said. "I mean, look, we can fly the new ships, but won't we just get shot down in the process?"

"We have shields," Hard Case said. "We're more maneuverable than anything in the fleet."

"But if there are more defensive batteries to contend with," Aspen added to the debate, "how are we supposed to survive?"

"That's what we're training for," Hard Case said. "Come on, you guys know the drill. This is what we do."

They were in their own space, a medium-sized room with reclining, overstuffed chairs, refreshment machines that were stocked by the ship's droid maintenance and recreation devices. It was the one place the entire squad could gather and voice their true feelings on the ship. Anywhere else, they were a bit more cautious, and that came out in different ways. Diamond and Aspen were quiet; Animal and Indigo were cocky and brash.

But in their staff room, the group was real with one another.

"Sure, in sims, but that ain't the same thing as flying for real, Hard Case," Animal insisted. "We know that, too."

"It's just a little unnerving to think of taking these experimental rides into a combat zone," Bishop added. "We don't even know who we'll be fighting."

"I'm sharing everything I know with you guys," Commander Kase said. "There are files on Ashi attack ships. You've seen them."

"They weren't attacked, though," Aspen pointed out. "They were delivering an EMP and then boarding the ship."

"The point is, we can fly circles around them. Their aircraft just can't keep up."

"And what if instead of a dozen defensive batteries, we're facing hundreds of laser cannons?" Indigo asked. "From what I hear, these planets we're going after are the very heart of the galactic empire. It's logical that they would have overwhelming defensive measures. We're talking about cultures that have been around for tens of thousands of years. We're infants by comparison."

"We'll know when we get there," Hard Case said. "But I trust Captain Darius. And I'm asking you to trust me. We won't send you to the slaughter. That doesn't help our cause."

Across the ship, in another private meeting, Remmy was looking over information on Zaya Wright delivered to him by Commander Nash. The two men were discussing Zaya with Nurek, who had developed a network of rebels within the Ashi Imperium.

"How did you get word to your people?" Nash asked.

"Codes mostly," the Dudonus officer replied. "When it was impossible to send direct messages, we sent official communications in ways that carried messages simply in how they were sent or received."

"Pretty complicated," Remmy said. "I can't see how this woman could send a message or manipulate how we send them."

"She'd be sending them into the Imperium; we only send messages back to the Sol system," Nash pointed out.

"It might be possible," Nurek said. "I was able to load a hidden trigger into Emperor Vang's communication system."

"You hacked their software?" Nash asked.

"In a fashion," Nurek explained. "The code was given to me. I merely uploaded it."

"The *Renegade's* computer system is pretty sophisticated," Remmy said. "Even if she had a device like that, could it work on the alien computer system?"

"In theory," Nash said. "But let's face it, the odds are against it."

"What is more likely, that she's here just by coincidence? Or that she's here to cause some type of problem?"

"It is possible that she could be an agent of chaos," Nurek said. "But in my experience, the Ashi have never admitted their need for someone else. They are not likely to have recruited this woman to carry out their designs."

"I would agree," Nash said.

"You both read Hugo's report," Remmy said. "He claims he was stabbed by a former slave who was recruited by the Ashi for that very purpose. He has the scar to prove it."

"That was an extreme situation," Nash said.

"Agreed," Remmy said. "And I've got nothing but a gut feeling about this."

"You think she's turned?" Nash asked.

"I think it's dangerous for us not to keep an eye on her. We have to consider that our enemy is at least as clever as we are. We've used spies for centuries."

"Your race is fascinating," Nurek said.

"Have you met her?" Nash asked.

"No, but I'm going to," Remmy said. "I'm heading up to that Pub where she works right after this meeting."

"Then do what you think is best," Nash said. "We've got two thousand people on this ship. I'm still running to keep up at the moment. I don't know how Lieutenant Best did it all. Let me know if you find anything. Meanwhile, I'll have a word with Stanislaus. Maybe there's a way to check the communication system codes."

"Sounds like a plan. Sorry to make your life more difficult, Commander," Remmy said.

"You're not," Nash replied. "I appreciate your help in this matter.

I hope it's nothing, but I agree that we should act as if it is a threat until we can say for certain it isn't."

Their meeting broke up and Remmy read through the report again. There wasn't much to it. Zaya Wright was a server at the Lion's Mane pub. She had been assigned a berth on Theta deck, port side. The rest of the information was superfluous. Remmy didn't care who she worked for or what her work permit level was. All that was new. She couldn't have known anyone before arriving in the Sol system with the *Renegade*. Her work status was arbitrarily assigned by SDF intelligence once they finished their debrief. What little of that interview was available to him was just as useless. They had questioned her various times over three days. The conclusions drawn were redacted. And there was no way to get his hands on an intel briefing. It would take weeks and he would need an air-tight reason. Even then, parts of the interviews would be edited out. It would be a colossal waste of his time.

Maybe he was chasing a red herring, but that was his duty. He was in charge of the Marines on the *Renegade* and they were charged with keeping the ship from any danger posed by another person or entity. All the civilians and military personnel were checked for ties to terrorist groups, extremists and even religious fundamentalist groups. Every package and box of cargo brought onto the ship was checked for dangerous substances. It was a very tedious and imperfect way to search for signs of trouble among the crew, but it was necessary. There were groups who opposed what the *Renegade* was doing. It was one of the many reasons most information about the alien ship was classified top secret. The crew's job was to find a way to keep the Galactic Imperium away from the Sol system. It was Remmy's job to make sure the crew of two thousand had the chance to carry out their duty as safely as humanly possible.

He stood up, stretched, then checked his computer. GIGI was due on board in the next twelve hours. He hadn't told Laila about that. She wasn't jealous of the alien artifact, exactly, but she had her suspicions about it, too. The pressure on Remmy, from his specific job on the ship, and because of the mission they were about to embark on, was starting to build. Remmy knew he could have gone the rest of his life without GIGI, but he was glad they would have the powerful device on board to help when they reached the core systems. Whatever they were going to face would be dangerous at the least and he wanted all the help they could get.

Time in port, such as it was for the *Renegade* near the transit station, was an unusual time. Crew members working in the ship did so in shifts. Some were eight hours, some just six and some were twelve, depending on the job and the availability of manpower. Most of the tasks were supervisory since the ship's automated systems did the real work. But that left anywhere from half to two-thirds of the ship's crew free at any given hour. Some of that time was spent sleeping, but there was always time for recreation and the Grand Concourse stayed busy all day and usually late into the night.

It was just past 1300 ship time when Remmy made his way up to Theta level. He passed several interesting shops and businesses. There were retailers, everything from pawn businesses to stores selling the latest fashions. How the retailers got their wares was a mystery to Remmy. He had no experience in, or interest in, business. But it was impossible not to note that most of the more successful businesses were those that sold experiences, rather than goods. People on the ship wanted something to do and entertainment was a highly sought after commodity.

The Lion's Mane was a decent looking pub. There were a few pool tables in the back and a respectable looking bar along one side wall. The rest of the space was taken up by tables.

Remmy found one with a view of the establishment. It wouldn't do him any good to sit with his back to half the pub. He was there to observe the woman name Zaya. Remmy had only met her briefly after she was rescued from Libertine with Hugo and a dozen other alien refugees. How his friend had managed to survive an orbital bombardment on Libertine amazed Remmy. But there was always a bit of luck involved with successful Marines. No one survived a firefight without some luck.

"Hey there," a woman with a scar on one cheek and another above her opposite eye, said. She had thick, dark hair that seemed a bit shaggy and large eyes. Remmy gave her a good look for the first time as she approached his table. He decided she wasn't classically beautiful, but not unattractive either. The scars certainly changed her looks, but not in a bad way. There was something interesting about her. She had a sturdy frame and it was obvious that she was strong, too.

"I know you," she said. "You're a..."

"Major," Remmy said.

"That's right. You're Hugo's friend."

"I am. You have a good memory," Remmy said.

"Well, welcome to the Lion's Mane. What can I get started for you?"

"What do you recommend?"

"It's my first day," she said with a grin.

"How's it going?"

There weren'teren many people in the pub. A couple sat at a table talking quietly. In the back, a lone player was shooting pool. Remmy couldn't help but marvel at the *Renegade*. It was so big, and the artificial gravity system was such that it allowed the crew to do normal activities. Things like having a bar with bottles on display, or a pool table where patrons could play a game, wasn't possible on the older SDF ships that relied on centrifugal force rather than real gravity.

"It's alright," she said. "I'm getting used to it. I know how to serve, of course. But there's a lot of drinks I've never heard of, and so, I'll need a bit to wrap my mind around it."

"You'll have to study the menu," he said.

"I would, but I can't read," she said with a nervous laugh. "I actually read common, but not human writing."

Remmy had certainly never considered that. She had spent most of her life among aliens. Did that mean she felt more akin to them than to humans? He made a mental note and kept talking.

"I didn't know that," he said. "You must have been young when you were taken."

"Five and half," she said. "It's still a little surreal to be here now."

"I'll bet. Why don't you just bring me a soft drink - whatever cola you've got on tap?"

"Alright, that's easy enough."

She turned and went to the bar. It was slow enough that the man tending bar had heard Remmy's request and was already pulling the drink. On earth, a Pub might not carry sodas, but with the sailors on board the *Renegade* limited to just two alcoholic beverages a day, the taverns and bars needed other drinks to sell.

Zaya came back to his table carrying a frosty mug with dark cola. The top was still frothing as she set it down on the table.

"You're a natural," Remmy said.

"This is the easy part," she said. "But what I love is fixing things."

"Really?" Remmy asked, remembering that she had been responsible for doing quite a few mechanical tasks with Hugo on the terraforming platforms when they were stuck on Libertine.

"This is just to pay the bills," she said, with a wave at the pub. "The owner, Saul, is building a distillery in the back. Helping in there is what I enjoy most. But this is nice too. I like talking with people."

"You have a knack for it," Remmy said, sipping his soda. "I never would have guessed you were abducted from Earth as a child."

"My accent doesn't give me away?"

"It's noticeable, but there are a hundred different accents on this ship. They all start to sound the same after a while," Remmy said.

"You let me know if you need anything else, Major."

"I will ... and call me Remmy."

She gave him a smile. It was genuine and he felt bad for lying to her. Maybe she guessed that he hadn't just wandered in after a day of window shopping. That wasn't a leap; he simply wasn't the type to idle his hours away in the Concourse. She might not know that about him, but he also had no bags or packages to indicate he had been shopping.

He could see what Hugo found appealing about her. She was different, a little naive maybe, if that wasn't just an act. It seemed clear to him that she was a bit out of her element, but that was not odd given her situation. She was busy wiping down a table when the man who had been playing pool wandered over to the bar, ordered himself another drink, and watched her. Gawked at her was more like it. Zaya was wearing blue jeans and a white shirt, simple enough, and the look worked on her. Remmy, thinking about the situation from a purely tactical perspective, recognized that Zaya wasn't what was considered beautiful by cultural standards. Of course, he eschewed those standards himself. He hated the way the media celebrated women with impossibly tiny waists and huge chests. Nothing about that was natural. The women had fat and even muscle removed from their abdomen and their breasts augmented to create what Remmy considered to be a caricature of femininity.

There was nothing fake about Zaya, yet she drew the eye in a positive way. Or negative, he supposed, looking at the man gawking at Zaya from across the room. He was no prize either, but Remmy thought that being a server in a pub came with certain negative aspects. Men were going to look at the woman, and as long as looking was all they did, there was nothing to be done. Remmy wondered if Zaya was as capable of looking after herself as she appeared. He might need to ask Hugo about it.

After finishing his drink and watching the pub for half an hour, he left Zaya a generous tip and went directly down to the Admin center. A young spaceman there gave him a digital file on Saul Mane. Remmy read the information on his tablet, scrolling through the man's public information that included his schooling and work history, down to the information gathered by the SDF to approve his business application for the Lion's Mane pub on the *Renegade*.

Nothing seemed unusual. Saul was a young entrepreneur who saw an opportunity and took it. He wasn't the first person to build a brewery on the *Renegade*. Remmy had been on military vessels long enough to know that on every ship, someone, somewhere was making moonshine. He had even drunk some a time or two. It was always disgusting and usually left him sick the next day, even if he only had a sip or two of the foul spirits. There was an art to making good liquor and, most of the time, moonshine was much more about the resulting drunkenness than any sort of culinary considerations.

There was a note in the file that requested permission for a distillery. It had been accepted and approved. There were no red flags in the man's file. Nothing that Remmy could point to as suspicious of any criminal behavior on Zaya's part. If she were a spy, or worse still, a saboteur, she was playing her cards very close to the vest. The only thing that gave Remmy pause was recognition of her mechanical aptitude. It might be another coincidence, or it might be that her plans to cause disruption or mayhem on the ship were in line with some type of mechanical device or disabling a life support system. It wouldn't do to have the *Renegade* flying into enemy territory only to discover that the laser cannons were offline.

He made a few notes on his tablet, but held off on making an official report. There was more digging to do, and until he had something more solid to share, he would wait. Should there come a time and reason to share his concerns, he would do so, even if that hurt his relationship with Hugo. Remmy cared about his big friend, but he couldn't let that keep him from doing what was best for the *Renegade*.

CHAPTER 17

HUGO WALKED into the hangar used by the Marines and couldn't help but smile. The rifle platoons, two of them, thirty Marines plus an NCO and an officer, were jogging around the track. They chanted a rhythmic cadence as they went. The hangar was large enough that the two groups could run at the same time without crowding one another on the long, extended track.

At one end, opposite the gun range, were several square-shaped resistance training stations. A variety of exercises could be performed on each side. The weights were slabs of metal, lifted using pulleys via the specific exercise controls.

Hugo was already in sweat pants with a tee-shirt cut into a tank top. It revealed more than it covered and Hugo was a big, powerfully built man. There was thick hair on his chest and some on his shoulders, too. The actors in action flicks were hairless and Hugo knew some serious lifters who shaved their bodies to help the muscles stand out more clearly. But Hugo didn't pump heavy iron to show off his body and the muscle he built was real.

But it wasn't just the muscle that his ripped shirt revealed. There were scars, too. Some were old, some new. He hadn't escaped from Libertine unscathed, that was for certain. But he wasn't concerned with the past or worried about the future. In the gym, he could focus solely on the workout. It came in sets, pumping specific muscle groups in a variety of ways until those muscles quivered and ached slightly. They also felt right, as the microscopic tears in the muscle fiber caused the muscle to swell with fluids to help heal and regrow the muscle.

"How long you been here, big fella?" Staff Sergeant Tyler "Tex" Fry asked.

"A bit," Hugo said, extending a hand to his platoon mate.

Tyler shook it. They had both been part of the *Jericho's* original Spec Op platoon. A woman with her hair tied up in a tight braid, the side shaved to the skin above her ears across the back of her head, joined the two men.

"It's like seeing a ghost," Gunnery Sergeant Isobel "Izzy" said. "You look no worse for wear, Hugo. Glad to have you back."

"Glad to be here," Hugo said.

"We heard things got rough on Libertine," Tex said. "You okay?"

"I am," Hugo said.

Just like that, the trio was back to normal, almost as if no time had passed at all. It was no secret that Izzy and Tex were a couple. They, like Remmy and Laila McPherson, had broken the unwritten rule of fraternizing with Marines in one's own platoon. But they had also proven their mettle and been rewarded with promotions. They were given the option to become officers and lead the *Renegades'* two rifle platoons, although they chose to remain enlisted and stay with the spec ops group.

There were twelve Marines in the highly trained Special Forces platoon. Hugo made thirteen. Their new officer was a young Lieutenant named Erik Hanson. He was both awed by the *Renegade* and eager to prove himself to the platoon of veteran Marines. He was the sole exception to the group; all the rest had combat experience.

The Spec Op group was given freedom in PT, but they all did roughly the same thing, just with varying levels of intensity. After his heavy lifting session, Hugo alternated between sprints and slow jogs on his single lap around the hangar. Hanson went light on the weights, preferring to stick with the same rotation of sit-ups, push-ups and pull-ups every day, then running three full laps around the track. He kept up a fast pace, too, pushing himself in the exercise. An hour later, the platoon was all cleaned up and in the simulation room. The Marines wore sim armor, including full helmets with interactive face shields that acted in the simulation room like a VR headset. Their body armor was connected to harnesses that monitored their every move and each Marine was on an omnidirectional treadmill. They could walk, run, kneel, and jump. It wasn't like being in the field, but it was the next best thing. On most SDF ships that were small, with tiny corridors and cramped compartments, the simulators gave the Marines a taste of being back on a planet again.

Normally, Remmy Steel and Lieutenant McPherson gave the platoon leaders the freedom to train in whatever environmental programs they saw fit. But Hanson was young and Remmy thought it best to put all the Marine platoons on urban warfare sims until they saw real action on the core worlds.

"Alright, spread out," Hanson ordered. "Alpha team with me, Bravo, you're on overwatch."

"Copy that," Izzy replied.

"I want you as high as possible. We need to see what we're up against out here."

"On our way," Izzy told the young officer.

"Charlie team, you go right. Delta, you're on our left."

Tex led the Charlie team and he responded to the order. Delta team leader was the same rank as Hugo, but as the new man on the team, he was the odd man out. Each of the four teams consisted of three Marines, but Hugo was the fourth member of Delta.

"Any idea what we're up against here?" Tex asked.

"Insurgents," Hanson replied.

"Human or other?" Hugo asked.

"What difference does that make?" Hanson said. "Just stay frosty."

Hugo had to hold in a chuckle. New officers were always a mixed bag. Some were smart enough to delegate, but others felt like they had something to prove. Hugo felt sorry for Hanson. It was one thing to go into combat against humans, where a person felt like they were on equal footing. But he wondered what the young lieutenant would do if faced with a thirteen-foot-tall, green-skinned Ashi warrior. They made Hugo look scrawny. And while it was his experience that most of the Ashi were savage, but reckless fighters—they came right at a person with fearless intensity—there were times when Hugo had the same tendency. But he liked to think he was smart enough not to throw his life away. Then again, in a simulation, he couldn't be killed. It was very tempting to race into the fray just to see how the other members of his platoon would react.

Sergeant Talbot was Hugo's team leader, a quiet, reserved Marine who had the respect of his team. Hugo opted to fall in with the others and see how things played out. Major Remmy had helped Hugo see at one point that he didn't need to be the strongest, craziest fighter to be a good Marine. He jogged after his team and let the others take the lead.

It wasn't long before they came under fire.

"Overwatch? What are we facing down here?" Hanson demanded.

"Can't say, LT. That fire is coming out of one of the taller buildings. We have no eyes, I repeat, no eyes on your attackers."

"We're taking fire down here," he replied as laser beams scorched the buildings and streets between the fire teams. "Light that building up."

"Sir, we're in a residential sector. We can't fire blindly into a building that could be filled with innocents."

"That's a direct order, Gunny. Hit that building with something and give us a chance to take the fight to these bastards!"

Hugo wondered what Tex thought of the young officer ordering Izzy to break the law. Maybe it didn't matter. Maybe on an alien planet, the conventions of war were more like guidelines than laws. He didn't know, and they were just running a sim. after all.

Izzy must have thought the same, because a moment later, a series of rocket-propelled grenades hit the building.

"That's it!" Hanson shouted. "Move in. On the double. All teams, take that building!"

So they did. Hugo followed his fire team through a side door. There was no more laser fire pushing down on them. Smoke filled the building. Sergeant Talbot sent his four-man group to a set of emergency stairs. The second floor was empty; the sim showed nothing but an empty space inside the four walls. But the third floor was different. The grenades had hit on the fourth story, and the building's roof had collapsed. Most of that debris carried down to the third floor, which had been a nursery of some sort. The beings inside were tiny. They had arms and legs, though many were no longer attached.

"Sir, looks like we got the bogeys," Tex said in his customary southern drawl. "And a few more besides."

"Doesn't matter," Hanson said. "Our mission is to clear the city of insurgents."

"I'm not sure this is the best way to do it," Talbot said under his breath. Then he looked up at Hugo, suddenly uncertain if he had spoken out of line. Maybe Hugo was the type to use that information to get on the LT's good side.

For a moment, there was concern, then Hugo shook his head.

"Lieutenant, this is not how things get done," he said.

Hanson turned on his heel and marched straight up to Hugo. He stood so close to the big Sergeant that Hugo could have smelled his breath had they not been figures in a simulation.

"What was that, Sergeant? Do you have something to say?"

"I said, this isn't the way to get things done," Hugo replied. "You just killed a bunch of innocent children."

"They aren't innocent," Hanson declared. "The moment the shooters took up arms against us, they condemned the entire city. You think you know better than me, Sergeant. You think you can spout your uneducated opinions like you're proof. Let me tell you something, McManus. You are on this platoon as a courtesy to Major Steel, but one more word out of your mouth and you'll be shipped off the *Renegade* in the next cargo shuttle. Do I make myself clear, Marine?"

For a moment, Hugo considered shooting the arrogant officer. They were in a simulation and it wasn't against regulations. No one had ever considered it a possibility and therefore no need for a rule against it, but it strongly crossed Hugo's mind. Tex moved in behind the Lieutenant and shook his head at Hugo, who stepped back and held up his hands in surrender.

"That's what I thought," Hanson said. "Now move out, we've got a city to subdue."

An hour later, the simulation was over, but Hugo's anger was still simmering. Gunnery Sergeant Berry wisely whisked the LT away on some errand to keep him busy, while Tex went to Hugo. But it wasn't just Hugo that Staff Sergeant Fry was addressing.

"You good, Hugo? Are we going to have issues?"

"I think you're asking the wrong person," Hugo said.

"A new LT. He's young. We need time to help him figure things out," Tex said gently. "But you didn't deserve that. You aren't going anywhere."

He looked around at the rest of the platoon as he said it. There were nods and a few of the Marines even slapped Hugo on the back. It was the first time in his life that he had been accepted so swiftly. As Tex led the way out of the simulation room, Talbot stepped and said softly. "We got your back, brother."

Hugo was stunned. He hadn't proven himself. Nor had he done much of anything other than just say how he felt about what had happened in a stupid combat simulation. It hadn't been spoken in anger, nor had he reacted in anger to the Lieutenant's outburst. He felt more confused than ever, but at the same time, he was delighted with the way the platoon had rallied around him. Usually, in his experience, it was the opposite. Even on the *Jericho*, most of the platoon hadn't liked him. It wasn't until Remmy, their Master Sergeant, embraced Hugo and played to his strengths, that the platoon accepted him. But even then, it hadn't come easy.

Things were better for Hugo, and the first person he wanted to share his happiness with was Zaya. After seeing to his VR armor and weapon, Hugo hurried off to clean himself up so that he could find the Lion's Mane.

CHAPTER 18

GIGI ARRIVED in the early evening. Captain Darius had been watching and waiting. He even set an alarm to notify him the moment GIGI's crate was checked into the ship's manifest. He was on the bridge when it chimed, and he immediately got to his feet.

"Everything okay, Captain?" Vivian Ramos asked.

"Yes," he said. "But I have a task to see to. I would like you to plot a course out of the system."

"Destination?"

"Nowhere," he replied. "Take us between systems if you will. As soon as I confirm the last shipment, I'd like us to make for the hyperspace portal."

"Aye, Captain. Setting a course for nowhere," she said.

"Lieutenant Stanislaus, you have the con."

"Aye, Captain," Alex said. "I have the con."

There wasn't much to do in port. The *Renegade* wasn't exactly in port, but she was, for all intents and purposes, parked at a static location in space. The Arodoni ship practically ran herself. There was no need for officers to be stationed on the Bridge to watch over anything. Whereas on a regular ship, the Bridge had to be fully manned at all times just in case a gasket blew or a breaker was tripped. There were instances when a ship's engine just exploded without warning. And it wasn't uncommon for life support systems to fail, but that had never happened on the *Renegade* without cause. Darius had captained the ship longer than anyone in the history of the SDF had ever led a single vessel, at least to his knowledge.

During their downtime, Darius liked to see his officers taking care of projects that had been neglected during the cruise or resting. But Lieutenant Alex Stanislaus did much of his work on the Bridge and could keep tabs on the ship's systems while focusing the lion's share of his attention on something else.

Likewise, Vivian Ramos was an incredibly unique officer. In the earliest days of humanity's space program, before computers were designed and built to do the actual computations needed for space travel, genius-level mathematicians did the job. It was necessary to have three or four people doing the same computation to ensure that they got the same results. It wasn't incredibly efficient, but it was the best way to ensure that things were done right. In those days, lives depended on the math being done by fallible human beings. But had she been alive decades earlier, Vivian Ramos would have almost certainly been a highly sought-after computer mind for the space program. She had been recruited by some of the most prestigious physics laboratories in the world. Darius knew that once she decided to retire from the SDF, she could write her ticket with her experience in hyperspace computations. He knew he was lucky to get her back. She wasn't a coward, but he couldn't blame her for wanting to be away from the fighting. Yet, the peaceful life didn't suit her. Perhaps it was being stationed on a revolving platform with cramped quarters and bad food. Or, more likely, she didn't like being away from the action. The entire human race was rushing to learn from the Arodoni data, but it was only the *Renegade* that was putting that knowledge to use. Darius thought they were making the galaxy a better place in the process.

He rode the zero-gravity tube, sometimes called the Collar, because it circled the ship like a collar just behind what looked like the *Renegade's* fish head. On the main deck, he went immediately to the Admin center, which was directly across from the sick bay. They no longer had a surgeon, but the medical technicians kept things under control and the automated diagnostic machines could handle the day-to-day needs of the crew. There was also a pair of surgical robots capable of handling trauma should that become an issue, due to combat. So far, the *Renegade* had been unmatched in conflict. With her powerful laser cannons, she could destroy enemy ships long before she ever came in range of their weapons. When they appeared in a system, the most common response of the Ashi warships was to run. But they couldn't run far enough or fast enough to avoid the Arodoni's advanced weapons.

Darius knew things could, and probably would, change when they entered the core systems. There would be more danger to the ship and a greater need for speed in decision-making. Perhaps even in the need to escape themselves. It was frightening and he wouldn't delude himself with false bravado. He knew it was necessary. He was willing to do it. Even more concerning than his safety, or even that of the ship, was the risk to thousands of lives under his command. But he would do it. If that is what it took to keep humanity safe and to break the hold of the evil Imperium over the galaxy, then any sacrifice was worth that reward. On the other hand, he couldn't help but dream of winning.

What if he could defeat the Imperium? What if the Ashi could be removed as a threat? His mind spun with visions of what the Galaxy could become if given the freedom to thrive. Every race he had met in his travels had been unique. Together, they wove a tapestry of unmatched beauty. Not just because they were different, but because they brought unique talents and points of view to the situations faced by the whole. He could imagine a congress of races all working together for good. Perhaps it was childish to think that beings so different could work together so flawlessly. Humanity was proof that such harmony rarely played out in the real world. There were always bad actors, from the corrupt to the compromised. There were always widely disparate views of what was most important to any given cause. Maybe the galaxy would come together and build an idyllic society, or perhaps they would dissolve into a hundred wars between worlds. All Darius could do was hope for the best and fight to give them the chance to rise to the occasion.

But it was hard to do anything when your enemy had his boot on your throat. Darius was determined to break the Imperium's stranglehold on the galaxy, but he needed help to do it. At the Admin center, he recruited two sailors. The entry rank in the SDF was sometimes called Spacemen instead of Sailors, but Darius thought of the *Renegade* as a ship at sea. They were a closed ecosystem, a village set adrift in space with no outside help available. Whatever they faced, they would find a way to overcome it together ... or die trying.

Sailors First Class Williams and Grisham followed Captain Darius down to the flight deck, where a group of crew was mingled with maintenance droids, all working to unpack and distribute a large shipment of supplies that had been recently delivered. They were still in the Sol system and close enough to SDF facilities that every person on board the *Renegade* had access to the communication & information network. What had once been a World Wide Web had become a system-wide network designed first for security personnel. SDF messages had priority even on the crowded bandwidth of signals to Earth. But what Darius was concerned with was that word of GIGI's arrival might leak out. He didn't want a politician, and certainly not Connor O'Dell, to become angry that the Galactic Information & Guidance Instrument had gone around them. Darius had done nothing wrong to get into trouble for, but he didn't want to be ordered to send GIGI back. Which was why he had recruited the pair of sailors from the Admin center.

They were sent ahead while Darius busied himself in the hangar with other business. He could keep an eye on things without garnering too much attention. Crew members on any ship loved to gossip and nothing was juicier than senior command rumors. But Williams and Grisham found the crate that GIGI was packed in. They recruited a few other sailors, lifted the crate onto a cart, and then the two men moved it off the flight deck.

The *Renegade* was grand, but there were still maintenance corridors mostly used by drones. They were smaller, but still pristine, and wide enough for the three men moving the big crate. Darius led the way. The crate was left in the Systems Control Room on Epsilon deck, which was just outside the throat area of the fish-shaped starships where the *Jericho* rotated and delivered power for the larger vessel.

The only other person in the SCR was Ensign Jeremy Powell. He was an engineering officer whose job was to monitor the *Renegade's* many systems, from life support to weapons control. The room was one long rectangle, with a bank of consoles running down the length of the compartment. In the air just opposite the consoles was a high-resolution hologram of the *Renegade*. It changed perspectives periodically, occasionally highlighting an area of the ship, at other times changing over to a detailed schematic of the alien vessel. When they were under way a group of crew members monitored the SCR. When the call for battle stations was given, every console in the SCR was manned. But while the ship was docked, just a single person was given the watch. And Ensign Powell had nothing to do but watch the screens and report back to the Bridge when called on.

All the information in the SCR could be and was displayed on various consoles on the Bridge, but in the SCR, there was greater control over each system. If the ship were a living organism, the Bridge was its brain, but the SCR was its heart. When systems needed to be adjusted, it happened in the SCR. And when Captain Darius wanted to open the crate that GIGI had been shipped in without being observed, he did that in the SCR, too.

"Give me a hand with this, Ensign," Darius ordered as he pulled a folding knife from his pocket.

"Aye, Captain," Powell said.

"This is classified, Ensign," Darius said. "What you see in this crate cannot be discussed with anyone."

"Yes, sir, Captain."

Darius jammed the blade of his knife into the tiny gap between the lid of the crate and the sides. With a twist, he levered one side of the lid up. He handed the knife to Powell butt first. The ensign took it.

"That was my father's," Darius said. "He gave it to me when I made Lieutenant."

"It's a beauty," Powell said, looking at the wavy pattern on the steel blade. "Why's it marked like that, sir, if I may ask?"

"You may," Darius replied. "It's a forging process called Damascus Steel. It's made because the steel consists of different types of metal. They're put into a forge under extreme heat and pounded together with pressure until the different metals fuse together into one blade that is stronger than any single type of steel it is made from. Then it's dipped in acid to bring out that pattern in the steel that you see."

"Cool," Powell said.

Darius nodded. It was cool. It was also a reminder that he was part of something more special than himself. That the trials of his crew were what formed them into something greater than any single part.

Powell slipped the blade under the lid and twisted. The lid to the crate popped free. Darius slid it aside and then took back the knife from Ensign Powell. He folded the blade back down into the handle and stood back.

"Should I get help to lift it out?" Powell asked.

"No need, Ensign," Darius said.

A second later, the tombstone-shaped artifact floated up and out of the crate. The strange markings on the stony surface of the slab glowed.

"Greetings, Captain Zeke Darius," GIGI said, her voice coming through the speakers of the Systems Control Room.

"Hello, GIGI. It's good to have you back on board."

"I have been following your exploits, Captain. I agree with your assessment of the next step in the war with the Ashi."

"Well, that's good," Darius said. "We are leaving tomorrow at 0400 hours and I think it's best if you stay here until then."

"My absence from the storage facility has gone unnoticed," GIGI replied.

"Good, let's keep it that way. Feel free to sync to the *Renegade's* computer. I'll be contacting you from the Bridge until we're out of the Sol system."

"I was disappointed by the reception I received from your officials," GIGI said. "I hope my makers weren't wrong in selecting your race to lead the fight against the Galactic Imperium."

"I hope not either, but only time will tell."

Darius left the SCR feeling relieved and hopeful. But getting GIGI on board was the last task before the *Renegade* could continue her mission. While he was anxious to get under way, he was also keenly aware that he could be leading the ship and all her crew, over two thousand souls, to their doom.

CHAPTER 19

THE WORD that they would soon head out of the Sol system went first to the officers on board, including First Lieutenant Laila McPherson. She was the commanding officer over all three Marine platoons. Her job was to know them and utilize them in the best manner when it came time to deploy into a combat zone. Remmy kept the big picture in view. He handled the details and provided the necessary equipment for them to do their jobs. Laila moved among the Marines, brushing shoulders, inspiring confidence and occasionally quashing problems. Which was why she was having a coffee with Gunnery Sergeant Izzy Berry when the message came through. She glanced at her wrist device, saw that it didn't affect her and went on with the conversation.

"So, what is your assessment?"

"Hard to say," Izzy replied. "Give him a couple of months and I'm sure he could learn to be a good officer."

"We don't have a couple of months," Laila said. "We're leaving the system tomorrow."

Izzy glanced at her friend with a look that only two people who knew each other well could decipher.

"Do I need to get directly involved?"

"Again, that's hard to say," Izzy spoke softly. She was staring at the recycled paper cup her drink had come in as she rotated it in her hands. It wasn't so much a nervous gesture as just a way to help her think through what she was saying. At times, when dealing with superiors, good NCOs knew the value in measuring their words carefully. "I think, if you were to go to him now, it would only make things worse."

"You couldn't calm him down?"

"I'm no psychologist, but I think he's suffering from a bad case of needing to prove himself. He's a rookie and, unfortunately, I think he's intimidated by his own platoon."

"That's not good," Laila said with a sigh. "Is he teachable, do you think?"

"My father used to say that if you're a hammer, everything looks like a nail."

Laila chuckled. "Alright, message received. We've got an issue and I'll run it up the chain of command. If he's unfit, you'll need to step up."

"This platoon hasn't had much luck with officers," Izzy pointed out.

"They either have to be crazy to want to join us, or see it as a fast way up the ladder," Laila sighed. "At least Lieutenants Ales and Putnam are squared away."

The rifle platoons were larger and had more straightforward assignments. None had seen combat yet. But the Special Operations platoon had seen plenty. While the rifle platoons formed perimeters and held defensive positions, the Spec Ops platoon had been sent after the Imperium officials on a variety of planets. Occasionally, those officials had guards. It was never a fair fight. The Imperium kept a minimal presence on the worlds in the Mean Sector of the galaxy. The threat of the Ashi was enough to keep the locals in line.

But Laila knew they would likely all see fighting in the days ahead. If they were able to get Marines onto the Core Worlds, the resistance would most likely be high. She couldn't send an officer into combat who was reckless. The goal was to show the beings on those worlds that the Ashi weren't invincible. But if they went in guns blazing, they would only create hatred for humanity.

"I think I know what to do," Laila said. "You just make sure that platoon is ready. We still have a few days. The Captain wants to let the flyboys take some turns in their new fighters, but then we're going to be in the thick of it and we have to be ready for anything."

"Will do, LT," Izzy said. "Leave that platoon to me and Tex. With Hugo back, we'll be ready."

"That's what I'm counting on."

She left her friend in the Ready Room and went across to where the platoon officers kept offices. It was just another rec room with a few desks thrown in for good measure. But there was a set of sofas and drink machines. Laila had the only real office with walls and a door. Unsurprisingly, the newest member of the Marine Officers, Erik Hanson, was sulking at his desk, while Ales and Putnam were sitting on a sofa talking in hushed tones.

"Gather round," Laila said. "I've got word from the skipper."

Ales and Putnam sat forward and Laila settled onto the thick armrest of one of the sofas. It took Hanson a moment to join them. Laila noticed there was still flushing on his neck and his jaw muscle flexed with the tension he was feeling.

"The *Renegade* has completed its resupply and will be heading for the hyperspace portal at 0400 hours."

"No surprise there," Ralph Ales said. "The captain doesn't like staying in any system longer than he has to."

"Our platoons are back to full strength," Mary Ann Putnam added. "No reason to stay, I suppose."

"You'll need to train hard the next few days," Laila ordered. "Make sure all the recruits are fully versed in your orders. I want formations tight and discipline high."

"Copy that," Ales said, while Putnam nodded.

"And what if we have belligerent Marines?" Hanson asked. "We should bench them for the good of the platoon, I think."

"Let's have a chat about that once I finish outlining what's ahead of us," Laila said, almost as if Hanson hadn't spoken about anything important. She saw Ales and Putnam exchange a knowing glance, but they didn't speak up. "As you know, we are going straight into the heart of the Imperium. No one knows the extent of their defenses, but you will all be deployed in hostile territory. I don't want any unnecessary losses or incidents with the locals that can be avoided. Our task is to send a message to those races that humanity is a match for the Ashi, but without any unwanted cruelty. I know what we're capable of, but we've only got a few more days of training to prepare. I want you to use that time to tighten your people up. Let's make sure we're ready when the call comes."

"Can't do that if you've got cowards in your command," Hanson said.

Laila was shocked at how much the new Lieutenant sounded like a little boy.

"I don't think I follow, Lieutenant."

"It's nothing I can't handle, but there are some wrinkles that need ironed out in my platoon. I'll make it happen, Lieutenant, you can count on that."

Laila hadn't intended to call the new officer onto the carpet. It was his first full day in charge of the Spec Op platoon. While she knew they could be like a herd of wild horses that needed a firm hand to keep them in line, from the report she received from Izzy Berry, it was the lieutenant that needed to be reined in.

"Good," Laila said, as if the remarks meant little to her. "Over the next few days, I'll be joining you on simulation training. Let's make sure there are no cracks in the chain of command. Communication on these runs will be the key to our success. Any questions?"

There were none, although the flush was spreading up Erik Hanson's face. She had seen officers lose their cool before. She wanted to give the young lieutenant the benefit of the doubt, but there might not be time to let him work out his differences. She could certainly transfer Hugo. Remmy already wanted to elevate him to command level, perhaps as an aide, and then down the road to a platoon officer. But they were waiting to see how Hugo handled himself. The trauma from his eighteen months on Libertine could have wrecked him. But from the report Izzy gave, Sergeant Hugo McManus handled himself with honor and self-control. Those were not attributes she would have given him when they first met.

"That's all then," she said.

Laila went into her office, still wondering what she should do, but as she settled behind her desk, Hanson came in and closed the door.

"Are we okay, Lieutenant?"

"I'm here to do a job," he said. "I was first in my class at the Institute. Highest marks in officer training. I was born to lead Marines into battle. There's nothing I want more than that."

Another red flag popped up in Laila's mind, but she didn't interrupt the agitated young officer.

"But we're not talking about a hostage situation on a space station or a union uprising on Mars, are we? We're talking about striking at the very heart of the Galactic Empire. I've read all the briefing reports, Lieutenant. I know the stakes here. Our very existence could be on the line."

"Tell me what's bothering you, Lieutenant," Laila said calmly. "Is there a problem in your platoon?"

"Hell no," he snapped. "I've got my people all in line. It's the parameters of the mission. Why are we concerned with being nice to the locals? I don't get it."

"You mean the ROE," she said, referring to the Rules of Engagement, which were set for the entire Marine force before any engagement.

"That's right. I don't understand. We should be hitting these aliens with everything we've got. Why go easy on them after all they've done? These Core Worlds are complicit in every bad act of the Empire."

"We're not here to judge anyone, Lieutenant."

"Just tell me that if the shoe were on the other foot, they would show our civilians mercy. Can you do that, Lieutenant?" He was leaning over her desk, his eyes open so wide she could see the whites all the way around his iris. "I'm just wondering what kind of circus you're running here!"

Everything happened fast after that. Laila McPherson stood up. She didn't see the knife Hanson had drawn. It wasn't a standard-issue combat blade, but a small, spring-loaded knife with a four-inch, double-sided blade. He thrust it at her and Laila tried to pivot away, but her legs hit her chair, slowing her down just slightly. The tip of the blade caught her on the left side, gouging in, cutting skin, then muscle. It was honed to a razor's keenness, so sharp she didn't even feel it go in. The knife plunged deeper, almost to the handle, before her turn pulled it out of her side. Blood followed, a river of hot crimson washed over her hip and down her thigh.

Laila drove her right hand into the side of Hanson's neck. It was a hard shot; her smaller fist fit easily between his collarbone and chin. The impact drove him backward and he crashed into the wall of her office. Laila started after him, but the pain exploded into her consciousness. She groaned, her left hand going down to her side. It was like a stitch a runner sometimes gets on a long slog, but this was a thousand times worse. She pressed against the wound, but that made the pain flare like lightning shooting through her body.

Hanson regained his balance and grabbed Laila's hair as she bent forward in pain. Her office was small. The desk and guest chairs filled the space. There was just enough room for the door to open without hitting anything and she usually kept it open so that she didn't feel so confined. Hanson was in the clearing behind the chairs and front of the door. He had Laila's short, neatly cut hair in one fist. In the other was his knife.

"Why can't you see that we have to kill them?" he screamed. "They don't know anything but violence. And we have to—"

Laila didn't carry a weapon on her person. But she sometimes worked on her firearms at her desk. She had pulled the drawer open as she bent forward in pain. When Hanson grabbed her by the hair, her hand closed on the barrel of a Marksman .45. It was made of metal and composite materials to lighten the weapon, but it was very rigid. She swung the butt of the gun at Hanson's arm. It didn't even have a clip in the grip, but it was firm enough that when it hit his elbow, it left a nasty bruise. It also caused him to let go of her hair.

They both lunged forward to attack the other at the same time. Hanson, thrusting his knife at her, Laila McPherson swinging the pistol like a hammer at him. The grip of her weapon struck his cheekbone, which broke, as did the skin above it. The force of the blow spun him around and knocked him unconscious. He fell to the deck as Laila stepped back. Looking down, she could see the handle of the knife protruding from her stomach. Pain began to spread through her. Not an ache but a hot, searing fire that she couldn't control and couldn't ignore. Her chair was too far away, so she leaned back across her desk. The world suddenly began to spin around her.

The door to the office opened, banged into Hanson's legs, and the face of Mary Ann Putnam came through the opening.

"Lieutenant?"

Laila didn't answer, couldn't answer. The ability to form thoughts and pronounce words had fled from her mind, which was being overwhelmed with pain.

"Oh, God, help us," Mary Ann shouted. "Ralph! The Lieutenant's been hurt!"

She lowered her shoulder and pushed the door open, scooting Hanson out of the way. Lieutenant Ralph Ales was right behind Mary Ann, who stepped inside the office and grabbed Laila's right hand.

"What the hell!" Ralph shouted.

It was uncalled for, but they were both near panic.

"She's been stabbed," Mary Ann said. "We've got to stabilize her and staunch the bleeding."

"What did that bastard do?" Ralph shouted.

"Ralph! Get help! Move Marine!"

Discipline kicked in. It was like someone had flipped a switch in his brain, as if there were code words hard-wired into his brain. He turned and ran back out. Within seconds, Tex appeared. He already had a trauma kit, the small kind normally carried into combat.

"What's her condition?" he asked.

"She's in shock. Looks like he cut her side pretty bad," Mary Ann said.

"Hang in there, LT," Tex said. "We got you."

He pulled out a roll of quick-clotting gauze and pressed it against the gash in her side.

"Hold this," he said, pressing Laila's hand to her side.

She groaned, but didn't let go.

"Stay strong, Lieutenant" he said. "You've been through worse. Anybody know how long that knife blade is?"

"Never seen it before," Mary Ann said.

Tex pinched the blade of the knife between two more rolls of gauze, then used strips of medical tape to hold them in place.

"We're going to need a gurney," Tex said.

"No, we don't," Hugo McManus said, crowding into the little office. "Is she stable?"

"As good as I can get it," Tex said.

"Then get out of the way."

From the outer office, Sergeant Talbot could be heard. "What did you do? What did this bastard do?"

"See to that, I've got her, Staff Sergeant," Hugo said.

"All the way to medical?" Tex asked.

"No sweat."

Tex led Mary Ann out of the office, as Hugo lifted Laila McPherson in his arms. She was easily a hundred and fifty pounds. Her body was compact, but packed with muscle. Becoming an officer hadn't slowed her down and she exercised every day, often with Major Steel. Yet Hugo hoisted her easily, and held her gently against his chest. He was careful not to bump the knife still sticking out of her stomach, but he pressed her left side into his own abdomen, adding pressure to the saturated gauze she held there.

Laila felt as though the world had gone wavy. She saw Tex, then Hugo, but it was like seeing them through water. Sounds were muffled, and the lights seemed to stretch across the ceiling. When Hugo picked her up, she swooned for a moment, the pain crowding out all other senses. When she came back to herself, they were moving.

Hugo carried her through the small office door, then across to the main passage.

"I need runners ahead of me," Hugo said. "Clear the way. I'm going straight up to the park, then through the Concourse."

"I'll call ahead," Mary Ann said.

"We got you," a group of Marines from the Spec Op platoon said.

Hugo was at the door when Izzy appeared.

"What happened?" she asked.

"Stabbed," Hugo said. "Tex has her attacker. You're with me."

They both outranked him. But in the moment, he had taken charge and they followed his lead. There was no need to assert them-selves. They weren't threatened by his confidence or insecure in their place in the pecking order. They were just Marines with a mission and they would do whatever it took to help Lieutenant McPherson.

Hugo jogged easily down the hall to the lift. Izzy jumped ahead of him through the zero-gravity opening, soaring up past him. When he reached the top, she was already there and pulled him over and into regular gravity again. It was the only time he grunted under her weight.

"You good, Hugo?" Izzy asked.

"Good," he said, conserving his breath.

Despite what he had said to Tex, he was already sweating. Blood had soaked through his compression shirt and the top of his pants. Fear for his friend's life drove him forward. He was happy to run. It made him feel as though he was doing something to hold death at bay. Izzy was at his elbow, steady as if she were attached to him.

The trio dashed through the park. There were looks of distress from members of the crew who saw them. Those who had been strolling along the path moved out of the way. It took them two minutes to reach the concourse. Sweat stung his eyes and his chest burned as it converted the much-needed oxygen to his blood. But he kept moving, not at a jog, at a fast run. It wasn't a sprint, but it felt like one. Hugo often trained in full armor. Marines usually carried sixty to eighty pounds of gear into battle, but it was more equally spread across their shoulders and back. Carrying Laila in his arms made his biceps burn and his shoulders scream for relief. He would give them none.

Likewise, his hips ached, his thighs burned and his knees felt as though he had glass in the joints. Hugo was aware that he had crossed a physical barrier in his life. He was no longer young enough to bounce back from his wounds. It had happened on Libertine in a fight for his life with an Ashi warrior. He had dislocated his left shoulder and broken several ribs. They were healed, and yet when he pushed himself, they hurt all over again, especially his joints. He could feel the jolting abuse on his legs with every step, even down in his ankles and toes. Everything hurt and nothing else mattered. He ignored the pain, just as he had done in boot camp, and spec op training, and dozens of missions before. He could simply shut that part of his brain off and deal with the consequences later.

They ran through the opening to the concourse. Light was still bright, music still pumped from speakers in some of the entertainment establishments. There were still hundreds of people loitering on the gleaming floors, only they were no longer shopping, or even walking. The Marines who had dashed ahead of Hugo and Izzy had shouted loud enough to be heard over the talking and music that filled the concourse. Above them, along the rails of the upper decks, crew members and service workers looked down.

Hugo saw them, but ignored them. It took eight minutes at a full run before the sick bay came into sight. Hugo saw several of the senior officers watching him as med techs pushed a hover gurney out of the med bay and toward Hugo. He slowed, then stopped.

"Stab wound to the abdomen," Izzy said in a loud, commanding voice. "A deep gash in her left side."

"We've got her," a tech said as Hugo gently laid Lieutenant Laila McPherson down on the gurney. "Great job, Staff Sergeant."

Hugo sank to his knees as they rushed her away. Sweat dripped onto the gleaming floor and he could see his sweaty reflection.

Izzy put a hand on his shoulder. "Hell of a job, Hugo."

"You too," he replied.

"Let's get something to drink," she said, giving him a hand up.

Inside the Med Bay, the techs moved Lieutenant McPherson under a full-body scanner linked to the ceiling. It did a fast pass, identifying her wounds, then filling a syringe with enough morphine to knock her out. A slower scan followed that included X-rays that showed the blade inside her body. The techs stepped forward with scissors and cut away her clothing. They covered her lower body with a blanket and her upper body with an absorbent paper, then pushed her over to a secure table with a surgical robot attached to one end. It was a tall mechanism, one large robotic arm with lots of smaller articulated limbs that did the delicate work.

The techs pulled a plastic curtain around the surgical area that reached from the floor to the ceiling and turned on a filtered air system so that no unnecessary germs went floating into the patient's open wounds. Then the techs settled in; it was going to be a long night.

CHAPTER 20

REMMY WAS with Captain Darius when word of the attack reached them. They were discussing plans for the following day and starting to assign assets to various groups. There was an abundance of drones and more coming out of the manufacturing plant by the hour. GIGI could operate eight hundred of them at once, but Captain Darius wanted every drone operator on the ship assigned an asset and ready to go to work the minute they crossed into the Core sector of space.

"Captain," Vivian Ramos' voice came through a speaker in the captain's berth where the two men were working over his wide desk.

"Go ahead," Darius replied, trying to keep the irritation from his voice. Their plans for the following day were of the utmost importance. He was always available to his crew, but the two officers were in the middle of a long list and the interruption wasn't at a good time.

"Sir, I've got a red alert warning from the Marine section of the ship," Vivian said. "There's a report of an attack taking place."

"The Marines got into a kerfuffle? Is that significant enough for a red alert?"

"It's more than that, sir," Vivian said. She was clearly carrying on a conversation while listening to updates at the same time. "Someone was stabbed..."

That brought both men up to full attention. Their plans could wait. Someone getting stabbed on board the ship was a major problem that had to be solved quickly and judiciously, before the trauma affected morale.

"Sir, it's Marine Lieutenant Laila McPherson. They are taking her to the Med Bay now."

Captain Darius turned to say something to Remmy, but he was already out the door and sprinting down the corridor.

"What's her status?" Darius asked.

"Unknown."

"And her attacker?"

"He's been detained, as you might guess. The other Marines have him."

"Have who?"

"Lieutenant Erik Hanson, Captain. The new officer of the Spec Op platoon."

"This is terrible," Darius said. "I'm putting in my comlink, Lieutenant. Keep me updated."

"Aye, Captain. I'll keep you updated on a private comlink channel."

Darius left his cabin and hurried to the zero-gravity lift. It was slightly curved and lined with thick pads to make it easy for people to move up or down. Darius went down to Epsilon level and found Commander Henry Nash surrounded by a group of junior officers. They, along with several hundred other people, were watching the Medical Bay.

"What's happened?" Darius asked.

"Someone stabbed Lieutenant McPherson," Nash said. "The big Marine, the one that was left on Libertine, he carried her up. I've never seen anything like it, Captain. He ran the entire way with McPherson in his arms."

"All the way from the scene of the attack?"

"I suppose," Nash said. "Some of the other Marines came through yelling for everyone to get out of the way. Then he comes running up the Concourse with Staff Sergeant Berry by his side."

"And Major Steel?"

"In the Med Bay," Nash said.

Darius sighed. "Well then, there's nothing more to be done here. Let's go get to the bottom of this, Commander."

"Aye, Captain. I'm with you."

The two senior officers of the ship headed down the Concourse, while inside the Medical Bay, Remmy was stuck waiting for the surgical robot to finish working on Laila. He was forced to stand back and wait by the Med techs, who were holding a large data tablet with updates on the surgery.

"She's alive but critical," one said as Remmy finally calmed down enough to be spoken to in a normal tone. "The knife was only four inches, so it didn't reach her spine, but there's been damage to the intestines."

"Good God," Remmy said, his knees trembling beneath him.

"The slash on her side isn't as bad as we first thought," the other tech said. "It's mostly superficial. Some tissue damage, but nothing beyond the abdominal muscles. The bot has already cleaned it and is applying flesh glue. It'll take some time to do the fine stitching."

Remmy paced. He felt like a lion in a cage and his heart was torn between staying to be near Laila and wanting to find the person responsible and rip their throat out.

"How long?" Remmy asked.

"The bot estimates four hours. Why don't you sit down here, Major? As soon as we know something, you'll know."

Twenty minutes later, Darius and Commander Nash were gliding down the gravity lift that led to Grunt Country. They could hear the shouting before they reached the Alpha deck, where the attack had occurred.

"No! No, I... please!"

It almost sounded like someone was being tortured. There were Marines outside the offices where the attack had taken place. Darius stepped off the lift and started toward them.

"I won't.... mahhhhhh!"

It was the same voice, but it sounded strained and desperate. One of the Marines, a Corporal, saw Darius and snapped to attention before shouting, "Captain on deck!"

All the Marines stiffened. Darius didn't stop them; he went straight to the doorway and looked in. Lieutenant Hanson was on the floor, his hands secured behind his back with plastic restraints. To either side of him were Marines.

"What the devil is going on in here?" Darius said in a loud, commanding voice that he rarely used.

Staff Sergeant Fry was the first to speak. "Lieutenant Hanson attacked First Lieutenant McPherson, sir. No one saw it happen. They were in her office."

"Just the two of them?" Darius asked.

"Yes, sir," Fry replied.

"If her computer was on, we might have a recording of it," Commander Nash said. "Let me check on that."

Fry turned and pointed to the sole enclosed office in the room. "That's it, there," he said.

"This man's crazy, Captain," Sergeant Ted Talbot said. "He's been screaming and talking crazy since he came to."

"And you've just been letting him lie there and bleed all over the deck?" Darius asked.

"You can't get close to him, sir," Talbot said. "He won't stop thrashing around."

"Who bashed him? Was it you, Sergeant?"

"No, sir, I would have liked to have done, but it was Lieutenant McPherson that landed the blow."

"You saw it?"

"No, sir, but when we got into her office, it was done. And with just the two of them in there, sir, we concluded that she did it."

Lieutenant Mary Ann Putnam came out of a latrine shaking her hands either to finish drying them or in the hopes of easing the shakes, Darius wasn't sure. She approached him and he turned toward her.

"I was the first to get in, Captain," she said. "At that point, Lieutenant McPherson had been stabbed and Lieutenant Hanson was knocked out on the floor."

"We need to get him up to medical bay," Darius said. "Wait, belay that. Is he hurt anywhere else other than his face?"

"Not that we know of, Captain, no, sir," Putnam said.

Darius turned around and pointed at the Corporal looking on from the corridor. "You, get us a trauma kit."

"Sir, yes, sir!" the Marine replied, spinning on his heel and sprinting off.

"You don't want to take him to the Medical Bay, sir?" Mary Ann asked. "We have enough hands. We could carry him up there."

"Then Major Steel would kill him and I'd lose more than just Lieutenant McPherson. We can't let that happen."

"Captain," Nash said from the office. "I have it."

"There's a record of it?"

"It's a redundant back-up system, like a document file that automatically saves, only the ship's computer registers hand motions and voice commands, so the backup is essentially a holographic record of the past hour or so."

"And you can replay it?" Darius asked, as surprised as any of the crew.

"Yes, Captain. Here goes."

He transferred the hologram to the larger projection unit between the two sofas. It came to life above Lieutenant Hanson. Darius saw Laila McPherson; she was talking to Hanson. Suddenly, the sound came on, and they watched as Hanson pulled his little knife and then lunged at Lieutenant McPherson.

"Well, that is pretty damming evidence, I would say," Darius said. "Can we save this recording?"

"Already did. There is a copy of it on your system, Captain," Nash said.

"Very good. Alright, let's get the Lieutenant to the flight deck. Someone get me a pilot."

CHAPTER 21

HARD CASE HAD HEARD about the attack. It was all anyone was talking about, but he had no idea what had happened. There were stories, rumors, outlandish tales of love triangles and gambling debts, but none of it had the ring of truth. In all the years that Hard Case had been a pilot with the SDF, he had never heard of an attack like the one that happened to Laila McPherson. He hadn't met her yet but he still felt sorry for her. A man attacking a woman, even a Marine, still seemed wrong somehow.

His wrist communicator buzzed. He glanced down. The screen showed an emergency alert message: **Proceed to the Flight Deck ASAP.**

At least it was clear. Hard Case had been studying the flight manual for the new *Raptor* aircraft. His entire squad was doing the same until the news of the stabbing broke. It was hard to focus after that, but Hard Case wanted to set a good example.

"Looks like I'm needed," he said.

Fortunately, the flight deck was just one level down and a few steps away. He was able to go out on Beta level onto a narrow balcony that overlooked the flight deck. He went down a metal ramp and found Captain Darius and Commander Nash waiting for him. He hurried over to where they stood. Behind them, a group of Marines was escorting an officer with a nasty cut on his cheek that was swollen so big his eye on that side was just a slit. The wounded man was cursing under his breath, not like someone who was angry, but in a sort of half-jibberish that made the hair on the back of Justin's neck stand out.

"Captain, we need a pilot to take Lieutenant Hanson to the transfer station," Darius said.

"I'm your man, sir."

"Good, I was hoping you would say that. Can you fly a shuttle?"

"I can fly anything, sir."

"It's alien tech," Nash said. "Very intuitive. I could fly it, but hooking up with the transfer station's docking arm takes an experienced pilot."

"Yes, sir, that should not be a problem."

"Get started with a preflight check," Darius said. "Nothing fancy, just over and back."

"What do I tell them about the lieutenant?"

"Staff Sergeant Fry will handle that. He'll stay with Hanson. There's got to be something wrong with him. He's acting crazy."

"He's the one that..."

Nash and Darius nodded. "We have the proof, so it's settled. Now we just need to get him off the ship and, God willing, Lieutenant McPherson on the mend."

"Aye, Captain, I couldn't have said it better myself."

Hard Case hurried over to the shuttle. It wasn't quite the same as a military gunship or drop hauler, but it was close enough. And the Commander wasn't wrong about the flight controls. It was simple. Once his passengers were on board and the computer completed its preflight system check, they sealed up the shuttle and waited for the compartments to pressurize.

"*Renegade*, this is shuttle one in Hangar B, requesting permission to take off," he said via his headset comlink.

A familiar voice responded. Hard Case recognized Jacee Bertoli and couldn't help but smile.

"Shuttle One, you are cleared for takeoff. Do you require gravitic assistance?"

"Negative, *Renegade*, I can handle things on my end."

"You sound pretty sure of yourself, Commander Kase."

That made him smile even more. She recognized his voice, and while the official radio channel was no place to flirt, he felt like she was opening the door.

"This is the one thing I'm always sure of," Kase replied. "But I'm going to need a drink when I get back. Flying makes me thirsty."

"You should check out the Rooster Tail, best drinks on the Epsilon deck."

"I'll do that," Hard Case said. "Thanks for the recommendation, *Renegade*."

"Safe travels, Shuttle One."

He increased the power to the repulsers, lifting the shuttle off the deck several feet, then gliding forward. The ship passed through the gravity bubble with no issues. It was like riding in an elevator. One moment, he was in gravity, then his stomach flipped, and he was weightless.

In space, repulsers were useless. He pulled those levers all the way back and engaged the engines. The shuttle gained speed quickly. The *Renegade* was very close to the transfer station by space distances, only a mere twenty kilometers away. It took just a few minutes to cross the distance before Justin had reverse thrust.

"Transfer Station, this is *Renegade Shuttle* requesting permission to dock. Please advise."

"*Renegade Shuttle*, we have you on our scopes. Please proceed to dock E. You are cleared for maneuvering."

"Copy that, Transfer Station, moving to Dock E."

It was standard procedure to move slowly in space maneuvers. One wrong move could be catastrophic in a hard vacuum. But Hard Case was confident behind the stick of an aircraft. He could land in bad weather. He could handle system failures without panic. And in space, he had a light touch on the thrusters that made for a smooth connection when docking.

Five minutes after the radio call, a group of MPs was taking an almost catatonic Lieutenant Hanson off the ship. When they finished, Staff Sergeant Tex Fry came into the cockpit where Hard Case was waiting for flight control to permit him to head back to the *Renegade*.

"You mind?" Tex asked.

"Be my guest, Staff Sergeant," Hard Case said, waving at the empty co-pilot's seat. "These are pretty spacious cabins."

"Converted from the Arodoni seats," Tex said. "They were wide-bodied individuals."

"Must have been," Hard Case said with a smile. He extended a hand. "Hard Case."

The Staff Sergeant shook it. "Tex."

"Pleased to meet you."

"Likewise."

"Mind if I ask what happened?" Hard Case asked, pointing back toward the *Renegade*. Even from twenty klicks out, she seemed huge.

"Can't say what caused it," Tex said. "Hanson was my CO. Just came aboard a couple of days earlier. He was pretty worked up during our sim training. Made a few questionable orders, but that's not unusual for a young officer."

"You been in long?"

"Thirteen years," Tex said. "Been on the *Renegade* from the beginning."

"Good to have a vet who knows his stuff," Hard Case said. "But Hanson wasn't just a newbie?"

"Apparently not," Tex said. "Whatever is wrong with him was triggered by the stress, I think. He was yelling about the aliens showing us no mercy when he attacked Lieutenant McPherson."

"That's tragic. I hope she pulls through."

"If anyone can, she will," Tex said.

"You know her?"

"She was my Staff Sergeant when we set out on the *Jericho*," he replied. "She's strong. I don't think he would have gotten a lick in on her if she hadn't gotten tangled up with her desk chair."

"It's a hard start to this mission," Hard Case said, and didn't add, *especially if she dies.*

"It's not the first officer we lost on the *Renegade*. We'll come back stronger, I'm sure of it."

The flight back to the *Renegade* was uneventful. The control officer let him land the ship, which he did smoothly, bringing the shuttle down on the flight deck as easy as a first kiss.

"Thanks for the ride, sir," Tex said.

"Anytime, Tex. If you see Lieutenant McPherson, tell her the Hell Flyers are pulling for her."

"Will do," the Staff Sergeant replied.

Justin felt good knowing he had done something to help, even if it was just ferrying a person from one ship to the transfer station. It still felt better than sitting and waiting for news from the Med Bay.

Aspen and Bishop were waiting for him on the flight deck when he disembarked. They looked somber.

"News?"

"Not yet," Aspen said. "We're going up to Med Bay. They're holding a vigil there."

"Going to bathe this one in prayer," Bishop said.

"Let's go then," Hard Case replied.

They took their time. The ship was still a wonder, but they all felt somber. In some ways, it was like being overly tired. There was a heaviness in the air. Not just tragedy, but like a light had gone out in the beautiful spaceship and she had lost some of her magnificent glow.

When they reached the Concourse, there was none of the usual festive atmosphere. The lights had been dimmed and the music was turned off. Many of the storefronts were closed down and people lined the edges of the concourse. As the trio moved closer to the Med Bay, they saw that someone had found candles. There were a few dozen lit near a small stand with Lieutenant McPherson's personnel file photo on it. Bishop moved ahead, straight toward the small stand with candles burning. A few other people were kneeling in prayer around it. He joined them.

Indigo and Diamond were with Animal nearby. They waved Hard Case and Aspen over. The Commander looked to Diamond, "Any updates?"

"Not yet. The Med Techs promised to update the crowd when there was news."

They joined the throng who were waiting and praying. Hard Case was not a religious person, but he did believe there was something bigger than mankind that held the universe together. He was especially moved by the Fine-Tuning argument for an intelligent designer. There were just too many aspects of the universe that had to be exactly as they were for life to exist, not just organic life, but even the attraction of molecules and the ability of stars to maintain fusion. So he silently added his thoughts to whoever might be watching over them in the hopes that Lieutenant Laila McPherson could be shown a little mercy.

CHAPTER 22

HIS NAME WAS STEEL AND, in the past, people had said that his name fit him well, yet as he waited for the surgical robot to complete its work on Laila, he felt more like paper. He was on the verge of falling to pieces, which had never happened to him before. He had lost friends, good friends, in combat; those losses always left a void deep inside of him. But there were always things to do, a mission to complete, a platoon to lead, so that he could work his way through the pain. He kept his grief balled down tight deep inside, so that even though he couldn't control it, he could manage it.

But there was no managing what he felt about Laila, or more specifically, his fear of losing Laila. It was a monster inside him. He felt it ripping and tearing his insides to pieces. It feasted on his heart and he knew, without a shadow of doubt, that if she died, he would never fully recover. That was the reason why members of the same platoon rarely fraternized, much less carried on a lasting, romantic relationship. It was dangerous to both of them and that meant it was a danger to the platoon.

It didn't matter that Remmy was now the Marine commander on the *Renegade* or that Laila wasn't his platoon mate. He knew that their relationship was a weak point and it wasn't that he didn't care, but it was more that he couldn't help himself. She was the love of his life.

No one else had even come close. Because of their positions on the *Renegade*, they both agreed to muzzle their feelings. They were together as often as they could be, but rarely showed any affection in public. Nor did they use their relationship to manipulate one another in a working environment. Those rules had allowed them to function well, even in leadership roles on the *Renegade*. But if he lost her, Remmy would be a wreck. His work and the mission of the ship would suffer. He didn't want that, but he couldn't stop it. He was on the verge of pulling his data tablet from his pocket and typing out a resignation letter to Captain Darius, but as he did so, a voice popped into his mind.

You can't do that and he would never accept it.

He might, thinking of Captain Darius, *have to,* Remmy thought.

Like it or not, your fate is tied to this ship, Major Steel. I do not pretend to have religious ideologies, but it is no mistake that you are here and there is work to be done.

I don't care about that anymore, Remmy replied. *All I care about is Laila. What happened to that bastard who stabbed her?*

Lieutenant Erik Hanson has been removed from the ship. Would you like to see what happened?

That was a loaded question. Of course, he wanted to see, but he also understood that his fury for her assailant was already on the verge of exploding. He had known that Captain Darius would make sure Hanson was dealt with. Getting him off the ship was a good start, but if Laila died and Remmy gave in to his furious rage, nothing would stop him from hunting the man down and murdering him. Seeing what happened might only make his rage more intense, if that were possible. He knew the right thing was to let it go, but he couldn't.

Show me, he thought, his bitterness echoing in the void that had opened inside him. It was like a black hole in space, too strong to be denied, gobbling up everything with a seething hatred for a man he didn't really know. Suddenly, in his mind, he could see Laila going around the desk in her office, with Hanson following her. She sat, he began to talk and there was sound in his mind. He couldn't explain how he was seeing or hearing it, but it was like his consciousness had been overtaken. But Remmy wasn't interested in the words. He watched as Hanson leaned over her desk. The view shifted, turning as if GIGI was rotating a holographic display. Hanson's hand slowly pulled out a little knife.

Remmy wanted to scream. He wanted to reach out and break Hanson's neck. But it wasn't real. He was seeing a replay, as if Laila's life were a sporting event. Remmy was helpless. He saw her react, just as she should, but then the chair. Her desk chair had hit the wall and nearly made her stumble. He saw the knife slice her flesh, saw the gush of blood, and tears rolled unbidden from his eyes, which were squeezed tight shut. Every muscle in his body was rigid, his hands balled into fists.

"Major? Are you okay, sir?" one of the med techs asked.

The replay in his brain froze, and the man's voice broke through. Remmy opened his eyes. He could feel them watching him with concern. The tears on his cheeks felt oddly cold.

"I'm alright," he said. "Just emotional."

"We could give you something," one of the Tech's suggested. "Just to calm your nerves a little."

"I'm okay," Remmy said, realizing he had to get a grip on himself. "Thank you."

"Yes, sir," one tech said.

"Let us know if you change your mind," the other added.

They were worried too. Remmy Steel, tough guy, hero, was suddenly breaking down in front of them and they feared what Laila's death might do to him. So did Remmy, but he pushed that thought down, knowing it would have to be dealt with, that it would make him physically ill until he did.

Remmy nodded; the replay in his mind resumed. Laila had acquitted herself in the fight well, but Hanson's knife had found its mark. A few inches higher and it would have cut into vital organs, maybe even her heart. She might have died instantly and that thought burned like saltwater poured into an open wound. How could the strongest person Remmy knew be so fragile? It didn't make sense.

I have discovered the most likely cause for the attack, GIGI said.

What? It was both an exclamation of surprise and a demand to know what the artifact had discovered.

Lieutenant Erik Hanson lied on his intake forms. There is a history of Schizophrenia in his family. His uncle and grandfather were both diagnosed with it in their early twenties. Both managed it with medications until their mid-fifties.

Remmy didn't know a lot about the disease, but he knew it often manifested in psychotic tendencies fueled by paranoia. The murderous lieutenant had been muttering something about the aliens showing no mercy, but Remmy hadn't been paying attention to what he said. His focus had been on the man's actions or, more accurately, on how Laila had let him get the best of her. She was a highly skilled fighter, with or without weapons, in almost any environment. But Remmy knew that anything could happen in a fight. Laila had been cornered. She didn't have the space to maneuver the way she needed to in order to avoid the assailant's knife.

Lieutenant Hanson's behavior in the simulation was suspect. You most likely would have flagged it had you been free to review it. Would you like to see what I am referencing now?

Yes, Remmy thought. He was surprised to find that digging into the details was relieving the pressure he felt inside. His fury was bleeding off. Not that the idea of Hanson being mentally ill changed what Remmy felt like doing to the man, but some of the boxes in his mind were being checked off and that felt right. It was giving him a framework for what had happened and he felt more able to manage it on an emotional level because of that.

"Overwatch? What are we facing down here?" Hanson demanded.

"Can't say, LT. That fire is coming out of one of the taller buildings. We have no eyes, I repeat, no eyes on your attackers."

"We're taking fire down here," he replied as laser beams scorched the buildings and streets between the fire teams. "Light that building up."

"Sir, we're in a residential sector. We can't fire blindly into a building that could be filled with innocents."

"That's a direct order, Gunny. Hit that building with something and give us a chance to take the fight to these bastards!"

The scene was playing out in his mind, just like before. Remmy knew that GIGI sometimes communicated with him through images. She was much better at that than Remmy was. And interestingly enough, the eighteen months apart hadn't weakened the bond between them. It was as strong as ever, perhaps even more so. He didn't know how it worked exactly, but somehow his brain waves had been copied into GIGI's data and the artifact was able to use that data to communicate with him in a way she didn't with anyone else. He didn't see an image of GIGI in his mind; the artifact didn't even have a unique voice. When she spoke to him, it was as if he were hearing his own thoughts, only they came from someone else.

As he sat in the Med Bay waiting for the woman he loved to live or die, he watched the Spec Op training sim in his mind's eye. He saw the RPGs streak into the building. It was realistic in terms of space and form, but many of the buildings looked generic. The sim rarely gave a lot of details in that sense.

The simulation followed the platoon. At his computer, Remmy had the freedom to see what any single Marine saw. It was all recorded, just as it had come through their helmets. He often changed perspectives when reviewing a training op. Remmy didn't waste his time micromanaging his officers, but he would most likely have made time to check on Lieutenant Hanson. He was both new to the *Renegade* and fresh out of the Officer's Training Academy. It often took a young, new officer a bit of time to acclimate. Leading a Special Forces platoon was like trying to manage a herd of wildcats. They were generally all Alpha-type, strong personalities who needed both a heavy hand and a light touch.

In his mind, he heard Tex speak to the Lieutenant in a light, slow tone that held no condemnation. They had rushed into the building to clear it of any remaining fighters, but on the third floor, they found alien children slaughtered by the RPGs.

Sir, looks like we got the bogeys, and a few more besides."

"Doesn't matter," Hanson said. "Our mission is to clear the city of insurgents."

Suddenly, the view changed in Remmy's mind, and he could see the members of the platoon. They reacted to Hanson's cold assessment. It was always bad when an operation had collateral damage. Most of the time, it was judged harshly by those who had taken no part in the fight. But Remmy had seen it ruin good Marines who bore the weight of responsibility. You could say it was an accident, that no one was at fault, but to those men and women involved, there was no way to let go of it. And even though the Spec Op platoon was fighting aliens, the fact that they had killed children did not sit well with them.

There was grumbling. Remmy couldn't hear it, but he saw lips moving. They weren't speaking loud enough to be heard, certainly not by their new commanding officer. But Hugo did.

"*Lieutenant, this is not how things get done,*" Hugo said.

Hanson turned on Hugo in a threatening way. It was completely out of line for a commanding officer, but Hugo didn't back down. Not that Remmy would have expected him to.

"*What was that, Sergeant? Do you have something to say?*"

"*I said, this isn't the way to get things done,*" Hugo replied. "*You just killed a bunch of innocent children.*"

"*They aren't innocent,*" Hanson declared. "*The moment the shooters took up arms against us, they condemned the entire city. You think you know better than me, Sergeant? You think you can spout your uneducated opinions like you're bulletproof? Let me tell you something, McManus, you are on this platoon as a courtesy to Major Steel, but one more word out of your mouth and you'll be shipped off the* Renegade *in the next cargo shuttle. Do I make myself clear, Marine?*"

Remmy didn't know what he expected Hugo to do. There was a time when Hugo would have probably just shot Hanson in the face. It was a simulation, after all. And while there were regulations against an enlisted man striking an officer, there were no rules about shooting them on a training sim.

But then Remmy saw Tex move into Hugo's line of sight and give a tiny shake of the head. And, to Remmy's growing shock, it was Hugo McManus who stepped back and raised his hands in mock surrender. That should have been the end of it. But Hanson was not in his right mind.

"*That's what I thought,*" Hanson sneered. "*Now move out, we've got a city to subdue.*"

GIGI was right that Remmy would have seen the encounter as a major red flag. Ordering a strike on a civilian structure with no way of knowing who or what was inside was bad, but it could be explained away. That's what training simulations were for: to give Marines the chance to learn from their mistakes. But accosting a member of the Lieutenant's platoon because the man disagreed with the outcome of a decision was a sign of poor leadership. Remmy would have wanted to help Hanson see that. But even those two things combined weren't as big an issue as Hanson's sudden revelation about the aliens. Remmy had seen a few people with racist tendencies. And dealing with beings of another race was a shock at first; no one would deny that. But Hanson's declaration about the guilt of children due simply to their race was shocking. Even if a person felt that way, they would most likely keep such thoughts to themselves until they were certain the people they might express it to felt the same way. But Hanson didn't seem to care about anything but killing the aliens. There was more to the training sim, but GIGI ended it.

It is my assessment that Lieutenant Hanson was already on the verge of a psychotic break, GIGI said.

That doesn't excuse what he did.

It is not my place to judge the actions of Lieutenant Hanson. I was merely trying to isolate what caused him to attack Lieutenant McPherson.

I appreciate that, Remmy thought. *It does help... a little.*

Remmy sat in silence for a while. His fear and stress weren't gone, but his fury had abated. He didn't excuse Hanson.

If he had seen the man in those moments, he would have undoubtedly accosted him. But Hanson was gone, no longer a threat. And it could be argued that he wasn't even responsible for his actions because of his mental condition. Remmy wouldn't go that far, but he felt less angry.

The doors to the Med Bay opened some time after GIGI's revelation about Lieutenant Hanson. Remmy looked up and was not surprised to see that Captain Darius was approaching. He was alone and there was compassion on his face.

"Any updates?" Darius asked.

"Not from the surgery," Remmy said.

There was no Waiting Room in the *Renegade's* Medical Bay. Remmy was sitting at a Med Tech's desk and Captain Darius leaned against it.

"She's a strong woman. She'll make it."

Remmy wasn't sure how to reply. He understood the expectation to agree, but he wasn't so sure. Laila was strong and capable, but he knew the attack was serious. He had seen her go down. Had even seen Lieutenant Putnam and Tex rendering aid. When he thought of Hugo lifting her in his arms and carrying her out of the office, his eyes filled with tears. She had been surrounded by people who loved her and would have given their lives for hers, yet she was the one in danger. It felt like the monster inside him was back again.

Captain Darius reached out and put a hand on Remmy's shoulder.

"GIGI did some digging," he said, changing the subject to firmer ground. The last thing Remmy wanted was to break down in front of Captain Darius.

"Into?"

"Into Lieutenant Hanson," Remmy continued. "He lied about his family medical history."

"What?"

"There were members of his immediate family who suffered from Schizophrenia."

The look on Captain Darius's face was first shock, then anger. It was like watching a storm front building in the distance. Remmy knew just how his friend felt.

"There's a very good reason those questions are asked to every single officer and recruit," Darius said. "It's unconscionable that Hanson would lie."

"He wanted in and knew he wouldn't be accepted if he was honest."

"And now we're stuck paying for it. Laila is..."

He leaned forward and started pacing. It was his habit and somehow it made Remmy feel a little better.

"GIGI has proof?"

"I guess she hacked medical records," Remmy said. "His uncle and his grandfather were both Schizophrenic. They managed it with drugs. Lived a semi-normal life."

"I'll need to report it," Darius said. "But I can't reveal that GIGI is breaking medical privacy laws."

"Medical privacy is an illusion," Remmy said. "Everyone knows that."

"But it's still a reason not to trust GIGI," Darius said. "No, not me.

I'm saying that others will use it against her. People like Connor O'Dell."

Remmy couldn't argue with that. To be honest, he didn't have a feeling about GIGI, one way or another. They had a bond, but it didn't mean he trusted the alien artifact. Or that she felt any kind of sympathy for him or the human race. If the facts were laid bare, a good case could be made that GIGI had manipulated the crew of the *Jericho* and perhaps the entire human race. Darius and Remmy had discussed that very possibility.

"You can say he told us," Remmy said. "He won't remember any differently. Not if he was having a psychotic break."

"Good point," Darius said. "I'll—"

He was cut off by one of the Techs standing up suddenly. There was a look of relief on his face.

"She's going to make it," he said with a grin. "Internal injuries are repaired. There's no signs of debris. Her blood pressure is stable, and all vital signs are strong. The droid is closing her up now. We'll monitor her for signs of infection, but there's no reason why she won't make a full recovery."

It was as if he had been in a sealed chamber with no oxygen and, suddenly, he could breathe again. Remmy stood up; his hands were trembling, but no longer balled into fists.

"That's excellent," Darius said. "We should tell the others."

"Others?" Remmy asked.

"They're waiting outside," Darius told him.

Remmy thought he was talking about the Spec Op platoon members. He hadn't noticed anything as he rushed down to the Med Bay. It was all a blur. But Darius led him out of the Med Bay to find hundreds of people lining the Grand Concourse. And not just on Epsilon deck, but up to Lambda, five floors of people leaning over the railings, watching and waiting for word about Laila's condition. They all fell silent as Remmy appeared. He couldn't speak. The show of love and support overwhelmed him. There were even people praying around a little shrine with a picture of Laila above, burning candles. He thought briefly that must be a violation of some kind, but he couldn't think straight.

"Is there news?" Commander Nash asked anxiously.

"Tell them," Remmy said, his voice raw with emotion.

"She'll live!" Darius declared.

Before he could say more the crowd went bananas. They cheered, and several people who knew Remmy personally rushed toward him. Tex, Izzy, Pete Best, Commander Nash, all moved forward and hugged him. Remmy felt both relief and appreciation. Eventually, Darius raised both hands to quiet the crowd.

"Lieutenant Laila McPherson is stable, but she has a long road of recovery ahead. And she'll be monitored for infection. But she will live." There was more cheering. "We've discovered that Lieutenant Hanson has a history of Schizophrenia in his family and there is a good chance what happened was the result of a psychotic break. The authorities on Ares will conduct a full investigation, but for now, it seems our questions are answered. Both parties are in good hands and we can continue our mission. The *Renegade* will leave port at 0400 hours and should make the jump to hyperspace by 0700. In other words, enjoy tonight. Tomorrow, we go to work."

There was another cheer and people began to celebrate. Darius pulled Remmy aside and asked him a serious question.

"We could move her to the transfer station and get her to a quality medical facility," Darius offered. He seemed nervous, which wasn't like him, but that soon became clear, too. "You could go with her. We'll make due."

"No, sir, that's not necessary," Remmy said, relieving his Captain's anxiety. "I'll stay, and I think Laila would want that too. As long as we can give her the care she needs, I don't want to move her."

"It's settled then. Keep me informed of her condition, Major. If you need anything, let me know."

"The best thing for anxiety is work," Remmy said. "We could finish our planning down here, if that's acceptable."

Darius seemed as excited as a child at Christmas. "Excellent idea. I'll see to it, Major. But for now, get some rest. I'll forward our plans to your tablet. If you have questions, just buzz the Bridge."

"Copy that, sir," Remmy replied.

The Grand Concourse was always busy and festive, but it seemed doubly so. Music could be heard. Remmy saw couples dancing between the stores and entertainment venues. He hadn't known just how much the crew of the *Renegade* had become a family. And it made him feel thankful.

It was at that moment that Hugo appeared. He stepped out of the crowd and approached Remmy, who saw him coming and went out to thank him.

"I'm glad to hear she'll make it," Hugo said.

"In large part because of you," Remmy said, slapping his friend on the shoulder. "You'll never know how much you getting her up here, the way that you did, means to me."

"I just wanted to help, somehow," Hugo said.

There was blood on his clothes and he looked tired. Remmy knew there would need to be changes to the Spec Op platoon and Hugo had earned a little time off.

"You were a big help," Remmy said. "I owe you."

"That's not true.

"It is. And I won't forget it. Why don't you go see that girl of yours?"

Hugo looked up toward Theta deck.

"Good idea," he said.

A few seconds later, the big man was lost in the crowd again. When Remmy went back into the Med Bay, the surgery was finished. Laila was still unconscious, but the techs had moved her into an enclosed room with glass doors. There was a reclining chair beside her bed. Remmy sat down, pulled his data pad from one of the cargo pockets on the thigh of his fatigues, and sent an order to Gunnery Sergeant Izzy Berry. Then he leaned back, closed his eyes, and let everything slip away into the darkness.

CHAPTER 23

THE ROOSTER TAIL was a very popular place. The bar was long. It ran from the front of the interior, all the way to a transparent wall in the back. Neon signs hung on the walls and music pumped from hidden speakers. There was a dance floor, and in one dark corner, there were tall booths where couples sat close and whispered their secret plans.

Hard Case found it and led the way inside. His entire squad was with him. They went immediately to the bar and ordered drinks. With just a two hard beverage limit, they made their choices carefully.

"Mission for this establishment?" Animal asked once they all had a drink in hand.

"Search and..." Indigo said.

"Not rescue," Aspen replied. "I do not have the patience for a project."

"Search and destroy then," Animal said. "To the conquerors go the spoils!"

They all raised their glasses and then had a drink. Hard Case enjoyed his downtime as much as anyone, but he still felt like the new kid on the block. The *Renegade* was just so different from any other SDF post or vessel. It made him err on the side of caution and so he was drinking soda with a twist, nothing that would impair his decision-making.

He turned and scanned the bar. There were a lot of people, and a few Cassians too. It was surprisingly refreshing to see the two distinct races congregating together. It took him a moment to find what he was looking for, or rather, who he was looking for. Lieutenant Jacee Bertoli was dressed in blue jeans with a baggy sweater that probably cost more than it was worth. She had dark hair pulled back into a ponytail and tiny earrings that glittered in the colored lights. She was with two other women, and holding a tall glass of what appeared to be a dark beer, but could have been soda.

"Target acquired, Captain?" Bishop asked.

"I could use a wing man," Justin replied.

"You know you never have to ask. Let's do it."

The pair headed toward Lieutenant Jacee Bertoli and her friends. They almost made it when someone stepped in front of them and leaned against the tall, pub-style table Bertoli and her friends were near.

"What have we here?" Legend said. "You ladies look lovely tonight."

Hard Case could see past his rival, who was bent slightly forward. Two of the three girls smiled at the compliment. One even giggled a little. Only Jacee looked past Legend to where Hard Case was standing.

"Sorry, Elder, you can move on," Hard Case said. "These ladies aren't in the mood for your sloppy pick-up lines."

Legend turned as if he were surprised. But even though he was smiling, there was no mirth in his eyes. He reminded Hard Case of a shark. There was something cold and dead in his dull gaze.

"Hard Case, I had no idea you liked this bar?"

"We've been here two days," Justin replied. "Go away. We're not amused."

"He's right, sir," Bishop added, respectful as always. "We were just about to introduce ourselves to these fine ladies."

"Seems to me you're a bit late, and a man short," Legend said.

He was joined by two men from his squadron, a tall blonde with icy blue eyes and a gold tooth that was revealed when he smiled. He went by the callsign Heimdall, in reference to the Norse god of war who guards the rainbow bridge Bifrost.

His companion was shorter, with dark black skin, and his short hair cut into a triangle shape. His name was Collin Sanger, but he went by the callsign Kicker.

"We aren't looking for trouble," Hard Case said. "The Lieutenant invited us for drinks. Do you mind?"

"I don't mind if you leave," Legend said, his companions moving shoulder to shoulder to block their path.

"Are we about to take things to the next level?" Animal called out as he joined Hard Case and Bishop.

"Actually, your squad was about to leave," Legend said. "The varsity team's here. Why don't you go find something more your speed? I think there's a nursery somewhere on this ship."

"Hey!" Jacee said, stepping around Heimdall. "We're all on the same team here."

Before anyone else could speak, blue, rotating lights began to flash and people throughout the bar began cheering as monitors above the bar and along the opposite wall came on. An announcer's voice boomed from the speakers.

"Ladies and gentlemen, who feels the need?"

People all over the bar shouted in response: "The need for speed!"

"Oh, you know that's right," the announcer said. "We have our first two racers of the evening. So please, turn your attention to the Danger Zone and witness the fastest sport in the Sol system and beyond!"

Hard Case turned, like everyone else in the bar, to look through the transparent back wall. The owners of the Rooster Tail had turned the upper part of their store room into a drone race track. It was a long, narrow space, as wide as the bar, but only about six feet from top to bottom. There were obstacles mounted in the space, hoops that glowed with neon gas, barriers that rose up from the bottom, leaving only a narrow gap at the top, and others that came down from the ceiling. There were tunnels, mirrored pillars, streamers and serpentine objects painted to look like dragons with fog pouring from their nostrils.

"What is this?" Animal asked in amazed excitement.

"Drone racing," Legend said. "A child's game."

"It's really popular," Jacee said, moving closer to Hard Case. "People build their own racers and there's prize money once a month."

"My kind of action," Animal said.

"No surprise there," Legend remarked. "But I don't fly toys."

"Don't or can't?" Hard Case challenged.

Mathias Elder turned to face him. They were close, neither man backing down.

"Don't be stupid," Jacee said. "You start fighting and Captain Darius will ship you out."

"He needs us more than we need him," Legend said.

The race started and they turned to watch. The drones were small, no bigger than Hard Case's fist, but they moved fast. Each one had a tiny camera mounted to the front and the pilots used handheld remotes. They were stationed on a platform in the middle of the bar and wore VR headsets that fed the video feed from their drone cameras straight to them, along with other data such as speed and their position on the track, which wound in a zigzag pattern through the space above the storage room. From the look of it, Hard Case guessed the track was nearly a kilometer long with open space at either end for the drones to have the room to turn at speed before diving through another lane of the obstacle course.

A starting horn sounded, and the racers took off. It was a fascinating display, the drones flying at breakneck speed through the course. At the far end of the bar was a digital display with names and speeds. The fastest time through the course was held by someone named Pantar.

"That is wild," Animal said. "I have to try it."

"You can rent drones," one of the girls with Jacee said. "But it's not as easy as it looks."

"Who's Pantar?" Hard Case asked.

"He's the record holder. Never been beaten in a race," Jacee said. "He's Casian. They really have a knack for flying drones."

"They don't fly," Legend said. "They just operate. It's not the same."

"Whatever," Jacee said.

"If it's so easy, why don't you try it?" the other girl with Jacee said.

"Like I said, I don't play with toys," Legend replied.

"Sounds scared to me," Animal jumped in. "I've got a hundred credits that says you can't beat me in a race."

"I'd take that action," Kicker said.

"One week from tonight?" Animal said.

"I'll be here," Kicker said.

"Let's go," Legend said. "There's got to be a better place to get a drink than this place. It's a bit too spastic for my taste."

Hard Case turned, watching the trio leave. One of the girls looked disappointed.

"Now that the riffraff is gone, we can enjoy ourselves," Bishop said.

"You know those guys?" Jacee asked.

"They're from the other squad of fighter pilots," Hard Case said.

"I know that, but you knew them from before coming on board?"

"Their Captain, Mathias Elder, and I went to flight school together. We served on our first ship posting together, too, with Captain Darius when he was just a Commander."

"Really? You must have some good stories," Jacee said.

They were standing shoulder to shoulder, and he noticed she was leaning against him just a little too hard. He liked it.

"We weren't at our best back then," Hard Case said. "But Comman... I mean, Captain Darius saw something in us. He went to bat for us when we crossed a line we shouldn't have."

"And now, here you are, serving together again."

Hard Case nodded. Only he wasn't sure that was such a good idea. There was history between them and bad blood too. Sooner or later, they would clash, and that wouldn't be pretty. Hard Case doubted that the Captain would be as forgiving as he had been when they were rookies fresh out of flight school.

CHAPTER 24

ZAYA FOUND Hugo even before he made it to the ramps leading up to the higher levels.

"What happened?" she asked. "Are you hurt?"

"It's not mine," he assured her.

She took his hand and they made their way through the crowds and out into the Park. Hugo was exhausted, but not so tired that he didn't want to spend time with Zaya.

"How was your first day at work?"

"Exhilarating! I'm helping my boss, his name is Saul, build a distillery."

"I thought you were serving at a pub," Hugo said.

"I did that too," she said. "It was okay. It's pretty easy, really. I just take orders and deliver drinks. It got kind of busy around dinner time, but then everyone went to see what had happened. You were with that woman who got stabbed?"

"Lieutenant McPherson," Hugo said.

"People were saying you carried her halfway across the ship," Zaya said. "Is that true?"

Hugo nodded.

"And that you ran the whole way?"

He nodded again.

"You ran halfway across the ship with a woman in your arms?"

Hugo couldn't tell if she was in disbelief or if she was jealous.

"It was the fastest way," Hugo said.

"You... I can't... this is crazy."

"What?" Hugo asked.

"Only you would ask that question."

He had no idea what she meant. But she didn't seem angry and that was all he cared about. Not that he felt as though he had done anything wrong. Yes, Laila was a woman, but she was a Marine first and his friend second. If he had to do it all over again, knowing it would make Zaya mad, he still wouldn't hesitate.

But Zaya wasn't angry; she was impressed. They went back to his place and she tried to scrub the blood from his clothes while he took a shower. Then they sat on the balcony together. He liked it best when it was just the two of them. It reminded him of being with her on Libertine. But on the balcony, they could see other people playing and walking, and sometimes just sitting on the grass watching the herds of animals as they grazed. Birds swooped and raced past their balcony.

"Your berth is amazing," she said.

"You're welcome to stay here," he told her.

"I like having my own place," she said. "It's pretty bare now, but I'll get some stuff for it, fix it up."

He didn't realize that having a place that was just hers was as big a dream in her heart as having someone to share his life with was to Hugo.

"You don't want to be..."

She turned to him. He was clearly struggling.

"Just say it," she told him.

"You don't want... to be with me," he finally managed to say.

"I'm here, Hugo. I want to be here. I want to be with you. I only left because I had to, and I thought you stayed because you didn't want to be with me."

"I know you have better options," he said.

"That's not true."

He was pretty sure it was absolutely true, but he didn't press that point.

"On Libertine, I was the only choice."

"And on the *Renegade,* you are still my choice. Hugo, don't you get it? In the Sol system, you are still my choice."

He didn't get it. He couldn't understand why she would choose him. No one had ever chosen him before. His whole life, no one had ever wanted him.

He threw caution to the wind and asked her what he wanted to know. "Then why won't you live here?"

"Because..." she sighed. "I want to be here. But I need something that's just mine. Something that I earned. I don't know how else to say it. I've had no choices in my life. Even on Libertine, we had no options. I had to take what was there and make the best of it."

He felt a stab of fear that she was talking about him again, but she took his hand. Her's was just as rough and callused as his, but it felt good to him.

"At night, when I was alone," she said softly. "I used to dream that I could escape the slavers. I would imagine having my own place, maybe a starship that could travel through the galaxy. In my mind, I decorated it every night. It didn't reek of smelly slaves or alien body odor. It wasn't crawling with vermin like the hovels I was given to rest in. When I would lie down in that stinking cage on the Ashi ship, I would close my eyes and imagine that I was in my own apartment. But never, ever, did I think that I would actually have it. Then, by some miraculous surprise, you came into my life, Hugo. You saw past my fears and cared for me. You saved me from a life of cruel servitude and kept me alive until we could be here. I know it's not fair to you, but I need that cabin to myself. It's not because I don't want to be with you, Hugo, but because I've always dreamed of it. I need to make that dream a reality. Maybe then, I can give you what you need from me."

"I don't need anything from you," he said.

"We all need things. It's okay that you need me."

They sat that way for a while, then moved from the balcony into the living area. Hugo's apartment had a sofa and it wasn't long before he was asleep on it. When he woke up a few hours later, Zaya was gone. He felt a tidal wave of conflicting emotions as he got to his feet and headed toward the little kitchen area to get himself something to drink. The water from the tap was cold and clean. He filled a glass and drained it all down in one long pull. It filled his stomach and almost felt like it was lubricating his joints. He knew better, but it was obvious that he was dehydrated. The long run carrying Laila had drained him.

He was just about to head to his bedroom when he saw a message. Zaya had written it to him on a touchscreen display that was on the wall between the main room and the small bedroom.

Hugo, I'm going back to my place. Thank you for listening to me tonight. And thank you for giving me this chance to be myself and do something useful and good with my life. I hope you can be patient with me. I love you, Zaya.

He read it through over and over again. He wasn't sure what it meant exactly or how he had done anything. But it seemed positive. He read it over and over again until he was sure there was no hidden message or negative connotation in her note. When he lay down a few minutes later, he wished she was beside him, like they were on Libertine. But he was tired and sleep came quickly. That night, his dreams were untroubled. He didn't relive past battles or see the faces of the people he had killed. That night, it was just Zaya and Hugo together, happy, hopeful and expectant. He had never imagined being anything more than a Marine. Of course, he had fully expected to die in combat. But things were changing, both in his life and in his body. He wasn't the unstoppable force he had once been. Or maybe, the Ashi had just shown him the truth, that he was as vulnerable as any man. Above all, he had never imagined that he would fall in love. Having children had never entered his mind. Yet, he slept through the night and woke only the next morning when the sound of a baby's cry echoed in his mind.

CHAPTER 25

AT EXACTLY 0200 HOURS, the *Renegade* left the transit station and headed back toward Saturn. Just beyond the ringed planet's orbit was a hyperspace portal, the only one in the Sol system. They were making a hard run. But before that, just as Captain Darius was lying down for a few hours of sleep, his comlink beeped.

"What is it?" he asked, fearing there might be bad news from the infirmary.

"Sorry to bother your rest, Captain," Lieutenant Stanislaus said. "But there's a message from Ares Station. They are adding one last person to the manifest. Doctor Holt will be at the transfer station at 0300 hours. We are to wait for the Doctor's arrival before setting out."

Darius sat up, held back the angry curse he felt like spewing and instead cleared his throat. "Send me the file, Lieutenant. Let's get a shuttle to the transfer station. I don't want us waiting on anyone else's timeline."

"Aye, Captain. The file is sent and I've scheduled a shuttle. We'll have everything ready to go at 0400 hours."

"Very well," Darius said. "I'll see you on the Bridge then."

He lay back on his bunk, eyes burning for sleep. He would snatch a few hours before they left the system and then a few more once they were in hyperspace. It was the way of life on an interstellar ship. Sleep came whenever you could get it, but rarely enough. He picked up his data pad and looked at the Doctor's file. She was decorated, with trauma experience on Mars, as well as a fellowship at one of the busiest hospitals on Earth.

Darius had thought they wouldn't need a doctor on board, but the evidence of the last few hours had caused him to doubt that assessment. Surgical bots were fine, perhaps better in some ways than humans, but a person was less likely to give up on a patient. Plus, where they were going, the odds of needing medical help were high. He would take as many hands on the plow as he could get.

He got almost two solid hours of sleep. It wasn't enough, but it did help. A strong cup of coffee helped, too, and when he reached the bridge, they were five minutes from leaving the transfer station and making for the hyperspace portal.

"Is our new doctor on board?" Darius asked as he came striding into the Bridge.

"Aye, Captain," Stanislaus said. "Ensign Murdock is showing her to her quarters now."

"Excellent. You've run a ship-wide systems check?"

"Aye, Captain. We are green across the board."

"Lieutenant Ramos, do we have a course set?"

"Aye, Captain," Vivian said. "The course is calculated and locked in."

"Very good. Is there any reason that we shouldn't leave on schedule?"

The Bridge was fully manned, but no one spoke. Darius turned to Lieutenant Bertoli and ordered her to send word that the *Renegade* was underway.

"Lieutenant Nurek, are we ready?"

"Aye, Captain," the Dudonus alien said in a heavy accent. He had learned a few phrases so that he could respond without relying on the translator. His tasks while in port were few, but the alien was a diligent worker, helping wherever he could.

Darius pressed the comlink transmission button on his Captain's chair. "Commander Nash, we are preparing to engage engines."

"Very good, Captain. All hands are at their stations, sir. We are ready to begin."

"Excellent. Activate the main drive, Lieutenant Stanislaus. You may begin as soon as the ship is ready."

The *Renegade* had two powerful engines, but only one was needed for most operations. The other was used during hyperspace flight and as a backup if the first engine failed. Unlike human ships that used compressed air for the thruster system, the *Renegade* had fully powered thrusters. Even though the ship was over seven kilometers long, in the absence of gravity or air friction, the powered thrusters made her as responsive as a fighter jet.

Lieutenant Stanislaus tapped a few icons on his engineering console and the ship began to move. The open-mouthed fish head swung away from the transfer station. They were far enough from the space station that using the main engines wouldn't endanger the base or the people on it. But it was customary to use thruster power only until a ship was well away from port.

The thrusters were enough to bring the entire ship about and start it gaining speed. Once they were fifty kilometers from the transfer station, the main drives were engaged. The computer did most of the work. There were a few redundant systems that required a crew member to act. Stanislaus announced the main engine's thrust commencing and tapped the authorization into this computer terminal.

Vivian Ramos tracked their progress through space, making sure they were on the right heading and hitting all the speed milestones that would ensure they entered the hyperspace portal at the right speed and trajectory. A ship could fly right through a hyperspace portal and never know it. There was no sign or indication of its existence. The portal was actually just a thin place in the four regular dimensions of space. A ship needed to enter the portal by moving in the right direction at the right speed. Once there, moving fast enough, the ship could slip through into the hyper-dimension, which was not like regular space. It was more like a spider's web that stretched across the galaxy. Until recently, space was thought to be flat, like a tablecloth spread neatly across the surface. But like most everything else in the universe, space was actually wavy. There were places where two very distant points came close together, usually connected by the web of hyperspace lanes. There were various theories about this, but the most popular was that the hyperspace lanes were pulling on regular space.

Once a ship made the jump, it flew blind. There were no visual cues, no stars to guide it, no compass needle to point the way; it was all done via mathematics. Because there was no friction in space or hyperspace, a ship traveling at a constant speed could calculate everything needed to traverse its course based solely on timing and known mass-to-thrust ratios. The computer did most of the calculations and had a very extensive map of the known hyperspace lanes. But Vivian Ramos was their backup computer, a navigating genius who could, in a pinch, chart their course through hyperspace. She could also manipulate the navigation computer to take them to places not normally traveled, such as a vast, empty stretch of space where they could test the new Raptor fighter ships in complete secrecy.

A few hours and several cups of coffee later, they were approaching the hyperspace portal. Darius opened a channel on the ship's comlink system. The *Renegade* was so vast, with many wide open spaces, that speaker systems weren't utilized. Instead, they used personal comlinks that were built into the messaging device on their wrists. Only the senior officers had the capability of activating all those devices at the same time and utilizing the tiny speaker built into them.

"Crew and passengers of the *SDF Renegade*," he began. "This is Captain Darius. We have left the transfer station and are approaching the hyperspace portal. Please prepare for the transition. You have sixty seconds to send any last-minute messages via the Sol network before we are incommunicado for the foreseeable future. That is all."

A minute later, they made the jump to hyperspace. They didn't feel anything. The only visible change was the disappearance of the stars which had been visible through the Bridge's large, transparent canopy. In hyperspace, there were occasionally lights, usually rainbow flashes of color, but mostly it was dark.

"Status?" Darius asked.

"Engine output is twenty percent," Stanislaus said. "All systems green. No problems with the ship, Captain. She's purring like a kitten."

"Outstanding," Darius replied. "Time to reach the next transition point?"

"Ten hours, twenty-seven minutes," Vivian Ramos said.

"Very good. I have the con. I want you all in your bunks for the next six hours."

"I won't say no to that," Alex Stanislaus said.

The crew filed out, leaving only Darius and Nurek. The Dudonus only needed a couple of hours of rest in a standard twenty-four-hour day. They were accustomed to working at least twenty of those hours. At first, Darius had pushed Nurek to follow the human standard of four to six-hour shifts, but the tall, cone-headed alien had nothing else to do. So, Darius let him decide what to do on the shifts when he was supposed to be off duty.

"You look tired, if I may say so, Captain," Nurek said when they were alone.

His console was at an angle to the Captain, so that he faced sideways across the Bridge, and could easily see his commander.

"Comes with the territory," Darius said. "Will you get me an update on Lieutenant McPherson?"

They had wisely installed a coffee machine on the Bridge. Darius stood up, stretched, and made his way over to where he could refill his cup.

"There is no change," Nurek said. "Lieutenant McPherson is still resting after her surgery. She has not awakened, but there is nothing of concern in her vital signs. Scans of her abdomen continue to show no bleeding or unnecessary swelling."

"Do you happen to know the recovery time for a wound like that?"

Nurek hit a few icons on his console while Darius stirred some sugar into his coffee. He preferred it black, but Nurek was right. He was tired and he needed all the energy he could find.

"With light therapy, the wounds should heal within a few days," Nurek said. "It will take longer for the Lieutenant to regain full movement and strength in her core muscles, which were damaged during the attack. Also, her digestive system will need time to heal before solid foods can be ingested again. The recommendation of the surgical robot is four weeks."

That was not the news that Darius wanted to hear. His plan of attack called for the three Marine platoons to make planetfall and engage the Imperium officials directly. It would be, according to the intelligence that Nurek provided from his time as a slave to the Imperial family, a difficult challenge. The core worlds had defenses that were in place before the Imperium began. Many of the core worlds joined the Ashi voluntarily, which was one of the main reasons they held an important place in the governance of the galaxy. It also meant their defensive systems were still in place. No one knew what they were or what all they might entail. But the core worlds had planned for invasion by hostiles and built their defenses to protect them from such a fate. Of course, the *Renegade* was about to attempt to be that invading force.

The Marines would need all the help they could get. Losing the Spec Ops officer and Lieutenant McPherson was a difficult handicap to overcome. But Darius was certain that Remmy Steel would figure things out. The man was incredibly resourceful and smart. He was also committed to his Marines and would see that they had the very best chance of success.

"You seem troubled, sir. How may I help you?" Nurek asked.

He had served the Emperors of the Ashi for longer than Darius had been alive. Learning to read his superiors was part of that job and Darius was troubled. Worry came with the job of being Captain on a starship, but Darius was very concerned about their odds of success in the bold new campaign they were embarking on. As well as what it would actually do within the Imperium. The Ashi might not care about the core worlds at all. It might not slow them down or cause them to divide their forces in the hopes of protecting those important planets. There was simply no way to know what their enemy might do.

"I am concerned about the plans we've made," Darius admitted as he settled back into his captain's seat. "I don't know if we're striking a decisive blow or just poking the bear."

"I am not versed in that idiom," Nurek said. "What does it mean to poke the bear?"

"It means to anger and arouse the might of a stronger foe," Darius said.

"The Ashi have many ships, but none are stronger than the *Renegade*."

Darius agreed; at least the enemy had no ships that could match the *Renegade* that they knew of. But all that could change. Part of their plans for liberating the galaxy was to share the Arodoni tech, which they had been doing for over a year. Perhaps in that time, the Ashi could have learned enough and built weapons that were just as deadly as the *Renegade*. His thoughts always seemed to come back to the fact that he just didn't know his enemy well enough to predict what the Ashi might do.

"No single ship," Darius said. "But a fleet of them could overwhelm us."

"They have tried this before and failed."

"Sheika Kahn failed, but he was no warrior," Darius said. "The Ashi have gotten stuck in poor strategy and tactics because they haven't had a foe that tested them in so many years. But that doesn't mean they won't adapt. I have to believe they will and I plan for what's possible."

"It is impossible to foresee every conceivable response," Nurek said. "That is one of the reasons my people did not attempt to challenge the Imperium in a direct, military confrontation."

"But now we have to do it," Darius said. "If we don't, they'll just grow stronger. Eventually, they'll wipe out humanity unless we stop them."

"Striking a blow against the core worlds will certainly embolden the planets in the Mean Sector," Nurek said. "Revealing the Imperium's weaknesses will give our allies the chance to do their part."

That was all part of Darius' plan and it was sound enough. The question that haunted him was whether or not the Imperium would even care. They might give up the entire Imperium to bring their full might against the *Renegade*. After they destroyed the Arodoni ship and exterminated the human race, they could go back and reconquer the rest of the galaxy at their leisure. Darius didn't think the rest of the rebellious planets had the means or knowledge to fight the Ashi alone. If the *Renegade* didn't survive to lead the fight, the entire rebellion might collapse and all his efforts to free the galaxy and save humanity would be smashed.

"It is a good plan," Nurek said. "The Ashi do not think as you humans do. They believe only in their strength to defeat an enemy. You use many ways to ensure success. I have faith in our mission, Captain. I also have faith in you."

"Thank you, Lieutenant," Darius said. They were encouraging words and Darius needed to hear them, but nothing could silence the voice in the back of his mind that told him he was leading the *Renegade* into a trap. One wrong move and everything that Darius loved would be lost. The entire future of the human race was on his shoulders and it was a heavy weight to bear.

CHAPTER 26

"YOU NERVOUS?" Aspen asked in a quiet voice.

Hard Case was pulling on his new flight suit. It was different from those he normally wore, less bulky and with different safety features. There was a square block on his chest that contained an emergency locator and an hour's worth of oxygen. The suit went all the way down to boots for his feet and very thin gloves for his hands. It wasn't designed to keep him warm, just alive in the event of an emergency, which was incredibly likely given that he was about to test one of the new Raptors for the very first time.

"Not really," he lied. "If they're anything like the *Renegade* AI, I'll be fine."

They had trained on simulators for the past two days, but once the *Renegade* came out of hyperspace, the training would be for real. Hard Case, Bishop and Diamond were the first out of the gate for the Hell Flyers. The other fighting squadron called itself The Furies, as in the mythical creatures of classical Greece that carried souls from the dying to their eternal resting place. They would send out three of their own to test the new ships.

"And if they're not?"

"Then, you can come get me in a shuttle," Hard Case said. "I flew one. They're pretty sweet aircraft."

She smiled. Aspen was a beautiful woman in her own right, but Hard Case would never pursue a relationship with another pilot. Flying fighters was unlike any other military specialty. A pilot had to have an edge. They had to be willing, or even eager, to push boundaries. Relationships weren't made for that sort of personality. Most people saw a pilot's bravado as reckless or even arrogant. When a relationship went down in flames, it was nearly impossible for the two parties to trust one another again. Which was why Hard Case didn't date other pilots. He couldn't imagine how the break-up would go and it would probably be nuclear.

But that didn't mean the squadron didn't form strong bonds. No one else understood the pressure they faced. The odds of getting killed in combat were the highest among fighter pilots. And testing the new ships was just another facet of their role in the military. They had to overcome obstacles such as other people trying to kill them and their equipment failing in a catastrophic way. If a gun jammed in battle, that was bad. Yet if an engine failed or a missile strut failed to release the warhead, it was usually game over for that pilot. In the right circumstances, a pilot could bail out. There was supposed to be no shame in saving yourself but, of course, that didn't hold true. Most pilots who lost their nerve and pulled the ejection lever could live to fight another day, although they were rarely given the opportunity. Sometimes it was because the pilot had lost their ability to fly into danger and push the boundaries of what was possible. Other times it was because their superiors, usually people who had never flown in combat, deemed them unsuited for the rigors of flying fighter jets. Darius knew pilots who bailed out in a bad situation who were assigned to flying freighters and passenger ships.

But there was nothing in the universe like the thrill of flying in combat. Hard Case was not usually a rule-following type of person. He regularly pushed the boundaries of what an aircraft could do or what the rules of engagement were. But he was careful to do nothing that would get him grounded or expelled from the SDF's elite fighter pilot ranks. He had tasted the wild freedom and pure adrenaline of doing the most audacious flying that could be done and he couldn't give it up. He would rather die than lose his stick.

Most ships had just one stick, but the Raptor had two, and a completely innovative way to propel a ship through space. He was anxious to see what it was truly capable of.

He and Aspen set out for the flight deck. Each pilot that was flying in the first wave of trials was shadowed by another pilot. Animal was with Bishop, and Indigo shadowed Diamond. They would learn from one another. No one understood the intricacies of piloting fighter aircraft better than the pilots themselves, so they would teach one another, push one another and support their fellow aviators.

"We just dropped out of hyperspace, Commander," Petty Officer Dante Smith said. "These birds are ready to spread their wings."

"Copy that," Hard Case said.

Dante joined Aspen in walking Commander Kase to his ship. It was a sleek vessel. No missiles or bombs had been loaded onto the wings yet, but the laser cannons were ready for action. Hard Case and the other pilots would be testing those weapons, as well as the flight capabilities of the new fighters.

Justin looked at the tail section of his ship. Dante had used foil to put his callsign on the Raptor. It was tradition and meant that Hard Case wasn't just trying out a new ship, he was testing his fighter. He would fly that same Raptor in the missions ahead, whatever they turned out to be. He was about to break in his new ride and he couldn't wait.

Hard Case went up the stairs and vaulted into the open cockpit. Across the deck, Kicker was doing the same for the Furies. Hard Case couldn't imagine sending one of his pilots to make the first flight in the new aircraft. But that was the difference between the leaders of the two squads. Hard Case was a lead from the front-type commander and Legend led from behind. There was no right way to do things, just a person's beliefs and values about what their job entailed. Hard Case was anxious to fly the new ships, but he was going first because he would never willingly put his pilots into danger that he himself was not willing to face first. So, he would be the first flyer in the new ships. If it failed, he would face the risk and possibly die, but that was better than watching one of his squad mates die. He knew Mathias felt the exact opposite. He was the type of person who believed his life was more valuable than others. If someone was going to die testing the new ships, it wouldn't be Mathias Elder. In his mind, the mission had a greater chance of success with him alive and, therefore, it made sense not to risk his life needlessly. They were men in the same profession, of the same rank and position on the *Renegade,* but with vastly different ideas as to what their responsibilities entailed.

Hard Case settled into his seat and reached forward to activate the Raptor's power. The gauges, both digital and analogue, came online. He launched the computer's preflight system's diagnostic as Aspen and Dante reached the top of the metal stairs and leaned over him.

"She's ready, sir. I ran a full check on every component," Dante said. "This baby's ready to fly."

"Excellent work, Dante. It's much appreciated."

"You know it," Dante said. "We're going to make history today."

"That will be top secret and kept from the public until long after we're dead," Aspen said. "Here's your helmet, Commander."

He took the helmet and put it on, adjusting it slightly before securing the sliding clips that sealed it to his flight suit. Dante connected two hoses to the back. One was a powered connection to the Raptor's computer, the other supplied Hard Case with air.

"Dial up the gravity first thing," Dante said. "The entire flight system is based on that."

"Roger that," Hard Case said.

"Communications check?" Aspen asked, pressing her finger to the comlink in her ear.

"I read you, loud and clear," Hard Case replied.

"Copy that. Coms are a go."

"Repulser system is active," Commander Kase said. "Power core is engaged, all systems active now."

"Good luck," Dante said, slapping Hard Case on the helmet.

"Give 'em hell, Commander," Aspen said.

Then the two of them descended the stairs. Dante pushed it free, and the flight deck was clear.

"Raptor Alpha One, this is Shogun actual, do you read me?" Captain Darius said from the Bridge of the *Renegade.*

"Aye, Captain, I read you five by five," Hard Case replied.

"Let's have a system check, please," Darius ordered.

"Power core is at one hundred percent," he said, as his practiced eyes played over the readings on his instrument panel and confirmed them with the HUD displayed in his helmet's transparent face shield. "Repulsers, active; engine, online; thrusters, online; gravity system is functional, gravity drive, on standby, weapons check, life support, check, computer synced and online. Setting altitude gages at zero to sync with the *Renegade*'s position and attitude. Activating tracking beacon and transponder, we are a go on all systems, Shogun."

"Outstanding. Begin your test flight, Hard Case."

His heart was galloping in his chest from fear and excitement. He wasn't afraid to test the new ship, but there was always the possibility that by using gravity propulsion, they would rip the ship to pieces or cause it to implode. Neither outcome was something that Hard Case wanted to think about. The Raptors had gone through testing, but it was mostly theoretical. It was one thing to write a program outlining what you thought the gravity drive would do. It was completely different to put that ship to the test in the real world, or outer space, as the case might be.

Hard Case eased the ship forward on repulsor power.

"Engaging repulsers," he said. Every word he uttered and every system would be recorded and studied. "Passing through the *Renegade's* gravity field now."

His stomach flipped and he felt the sudden release of pressure on his body. With his eye glancing at the Raptor's inertial dampening system, he dialed up the artificial gravity in the cockpit of his fighter. He did it slowly as the ship continued to glide away from the *Renegade*.

"Raptor Alpha One, you have reached minimum safe distance," Captain Darius declared. "You may engage gravity drive."

"Copy that, engaging gravity drive."

He could have done it with a voice command or even with the unique eye control inside his helmet. But Hard Case chose to reach out with one hand and flip a toggle switch that activated the gravity drive. And in that instant, everything about combat aviation changed.

The gravity drive worked by projecting gravity in front of the ship. That gravity pulled the vessel forward. And even though Hard Case had the gravity at only ten percent of its possible power, it shot the Raptor through space like a bullet from a gun. Had it been in a normal gravity atmosphere, the G-forces would have crushed his entire skeleton. Even in space, the centrifugal force should have slammed him back into his seat and made any movement of his limbs impossible. He would have needed air pressure in his helmet to inflate his lungs and compression in his flight suit to keep the blood from pooling in one part of his body. But Hard Case had the inertial dampener turned on and dialed high enough that he barely felt any movement at all.

"Whoooohoooo!" he shouted. "This is incredible!"

"System update, Alpha One," Darius ordered.

"All systems green," Hard Case reported. "Cabin integrity is one hundred percent. Hull integrity is also one hundred. Speed is Mach eight and climbing."

"Begin aerial maneuvers, Alpha One," Darius ordered.

"Aye, beginning aerial maneuvers," Hard Case replied. "Initiating starboard turn now."

The ship turned, but not like an airplane. It didn't bank and make a long, curving turn. Instead, it turned as if it were tied to an immovable object and slung around hard. Even with his inertial dampener turned up, he felt the turn pressing him against the side of the cockpit.

"Holy crap, did you see that, Shogun!"

"I did. What's your status, Alpha One?"

"Every system is green, Captain. Speed is Mach 9 and continuing to climb, and I'm only using a tenth of the gravity drive's power."

He was beginning to wonder if more gravity power might harm the ship. There was no friction in space, no reason he couldn't go as fast as he wanted, maybe even right up to light speed, but there were inherent dangers in that. It was the most exhilarating flight of his life.

"Initiating port turn," he said, and once again turned the ship in less than two kilometers. He was once more racing away from the *Renegade*. "All systems remain steady. Power is one hundred percent. Dialing up inertial dampening now. Engaging climb."

The Raptor did everything he wanted it to do. It turned, climbed, dove, reversed course and even flew backward. Then came the targeting tests. The *Renegade* spewed bundles of waste materials with wireless location beacons inside. They flew up in front of the Arodoni ship, flying out of the big open mouth and drifting far ahead of the ship.

On the Bridge, Captain Darius was on his feet. It was a wonder to watch the tiny fighter fly. Not that he could keep up with it visually. Directly ahead of his seat was an open area with a holographic projection of space around the ship. The *Renegade* was shown in full detail but only a fraction of her actual size. It looked to be about a foot long to Darius and, around them, the Raptor flew at speeds and maneuvers that were hard to believe. It reminded him of watching a housefly. They sometimes sped around so fast - and seemingly erratic - that he wondered if they were in control or out of it. Likewise, the Raptor was so agile and fast that it seemed impossible that any person could keep up. But Commander Kase was a very talented pilot. Darius knew that from having worked with him in the past and it seemed he hadn't lost a step.

Through the big canopy over the Bridge, he could see the bundles of waste materials drifting through space.

"Target acquired, Shogun."

"Fire at will," Darius ordered.

A single laser shot through space, and one of the bundles disappeared.

"That's a hit, Shogun," Hard Case reported. "Laser cannons are optimal. I'm going for multiple shots now."

The ship's targeting computer lined up the shots. The targets were moving, but at a steady speed and in straight lines away from the Renegade. Hitting them wasn't difficult, even though the Raptor was a hundred kilometers away. A flurry of laser beams lashed out and six more targets disappeared. A few seconds later, the Raptor flew straight in front of the ship, close enough to set off collision alarms.

"That's uncalled for, Alpha One."

"Sorry, Captain, just having a little fun," Hard said with a chuckle. "Laser cannons aren't even warm, sir. The power level didn't dip a single percent."

"Excellent, Alpha One. Make your position two, seven, two at ten thousand kilometers," Darius ordered. "Then come to a full stop and report status."

"Copy that, turning to heading two, seven, two, and heading for ten thousand kilometers."

"Bravo six, status update," Darius said, while he was pacing behind his seat, the coffee in the cupholder forgotten. Every officer on the Bridge was watching the plot. Down on the flight deck, Kicker began reading off his instruments. A minute later, he launched from the ship and took off just like Hard Case had. Darius let him run through all the basic maneuvers. At some point along the way, Commander Kase reported that he had reached a full stop at a position ten thousand kilometers from the *Renegade*.

"Alpha One, Bravo Six, power down your laser systems," Darius said. Both pilots obeyed. "Activate infrared testing hardware."

The infrared beam was the same technology that had been used for remote-controlled devices for hundreds of years. It could spread a broad pattern, or be refined to a tiny, singular beam. It was used for mock battles, and Darius was ready to see what his new fighters could really do.

"Infrared beam emitter is active," Hard Case replied.

"Alright, Alpha One, see what you can do. Hard deck is five thousand feet from the Renegade, and the boundary is one hundred thousand klicks out. Pilots ready?"

"Bravo Six, ready," Kicker replied.

"Alpha One, ready," Hard Case said.

Darius waited for just a moment for dramatic effect, then said a single word. "Begin."

CHAPTER 27

WHILE THE FUTURE of warfare was changing outside the ship, in other areas, things went on as normal. Engineers checked their sections of the ship for any signs of wear or breakdown. Culinary specialists began prepping for a new day of feeding two thousand people three square meals. Machinists and the newly formed manufacturing mates went to work, mostly supervising and helping ship out the goods produced in the *Renegade's* automated 3D printing and assembly shops.

In the stern of the ship, SDF researchers carried on with their work of studying the *Renegade*, Arodoni technology, and carrying out experiments in the laboratories around the classrooms where SDF crew members studied for promotions and specialty certifications. The *Renegade* was, in many ways, a community. People worked, they created, they served one another, performed, maintained and repaired things. They shared meals, shopped, exercised, took their leisure, and learned, all on a ship of war made by an unknown race.

In the Med Bay, Lieutenant Laila McPherson opened her eyes. She felt almost as if she were floating, which was pleasant, but her mouth was so dry it felt like someone had glued it shut and she couldn't remember where she was or why. She tried to say hello, but it came out as a hoarse moan instead of a word. And suddenly, Remmy was standing over her.

"Hey, you're awake," he said. "That's good."

She made a face and then turned, picked up a cup with a straw sticking out.

"Doctor Holt said you would probably be thirsty when you came to," Remmy said, holding the cup down and putting the straw to her lips.

It took a lot of effort to open her mouth and wrap her thick, gluey lips around the straw. But the water was cool and refreshing. It filled her mouth and then slid gently down her parched throat. She felt it hit her stomach like a cool breeze on a hot afternoon. She sighed with pleasure and took another mouthful of water from the cup.

"Oh," she managed to say, her mouth working better after the water cleared her tongue and palate. "That's good."

"I'm glad," Remmy said. "You had me worried for a bit."

"Why? What happened?"

"You don't remember?"

"I remember..." she thought for a moment. "Hanson. Something is wrong with Hanson."

Remmy nodded. "We can talk about it later. The good news is he is off the ship and you are going to be okay."

"Did something happen?" She was struggling suddenly just to keep her eyes open. Everything was difficult. Drinking the water, and especially talking, was making her tired, so very tired.

"Yes, but you are okay. I promise. You can rest. Just sleep. You'll feel better."

Laila wanted to respond, but didn't have the strength. His eyelids felt like hundred-pound plates. She couldn't hold them up any longer and when she closed them, she immediately drifted off again.

Remmy set the cup down and stepped to the door of the little room. The new doctor was at a desk nearby. Her name was Victoria Holt, although she insisted when she arrived that he call her Doctor Vicky. She was not what he expected in a medical professional. She wore tight-fitting yoga pants and a compression tank top. Her hair was pulled back into two braids, one on either side of her head, and unlike most officers in the SDF, she had on makeup. He would have pegged her as a banker's wife, or even a celebrity herself, not that he would have recognized her if she had been famous. She immediately put on a white lab coat with a stethoscope in one pocket, but the coat hung open and the low-cut top underneath revealed too much.

Remmy was no Boy Scout, yet there was something about the new doctor that made him self-conscious and a little nervous.

"She woke up," he said.

Doctor Vicky was reading something on an oversized info slate. She set it down on the desk and stood up. Remmy hadn't noticed before, but she was wearing high-heeled, leather boots that came up to her knees. They made a sharp sound on the deck, which was the same seamless marble as the Concourse.

"Did she drink anything?" the doctor asked.

"A few sips."

"Good, that's excellent. Sedation meds are highly diuretic and we have to keep her hydrated. I'm going to have a tech start her on saline. She's going to be fine, Major. The knife was clean, the wounds were clean and there was no sign of internal bleeding. All things considered, she was very lucky."

Remmy didn't feel lucky, and didn't think Laila would either, but she was alive. That was all he could ask for in the terrible situation he found himself in.

"What's her recovery time look like?" Remmy asked.

"There are three stages," Doctor Vicky said. "The first is letting her recover from the surgery. That should take a day or so. She'll be asleep mostly, and even when she wakes up, she won't remember much, so you should get some rest, too, Major. Stage two will be light therapy. Three days minimum, and in her case, maybe as much as five, but that will supercharge her recovery. Once we're certain the wounds have completely sealed up, you'll be at stage three. That's going to take longer. Her core muscles have been damaged. There will be scar tissue, swelling and most of all pain when she moves. It's not because of the damage, but the way that it's healing. Think of it like a metal weld. First, you add material, then you take the excess away. And that part is difficult and can be painful. I would guess she'll probably need a month before she can move around and start to put herself through her paces again.

"Once she completes that third stage of recovery, she will be cleared for non-combat duty. But it will be up to you to clear her fully, once you've seen that she's back in fighting shape. Supposing that she wants to be, after all this. I wouldn't be surprised if she resigned her commission."

Remmy was shocked and ticked off at the same time. He didn't hold the doctor to her prediction. She didn't know Laila and Remmy knew there was no chance she would give up her commission. They had both been wounded before. They both knew the road to recovery could be grueling, but it wasn't worth quitting over.

"Thank you," he said.

"It's no trouble, I'm glad to have something to do other than give out meds for STDs. Ships like this are hotbeds for... well... you know what I mean."

She smiled and Remmy felt self-conscious again.

"I do have duty, but I'll be back," he said, trying not to fumble over his words and hating himself for feeling that way.

"Take your time," she said. "I'm a bit of a ward-rat, I can't stay away from Med Bay," she chuckled. "Besides, we're going to keep her sedated most of the day. Can't have her moving around too much at this stage."

"If anything changes, please let me know."

"I'll do that, Major. And might I say, it's refreshing to see a superior with such concern for his subordinates. I've heard good things about this ship. I guess they're true."

She went past Remmy and into Laila's room, and he left the Medical Bay. When he got to his cabin, he took a hot shower, shaved and all the while tried to consider what was best for the Spec Op platoon. When he was dressed again, he sent a message for Tex and Izzy to meet him in the Admin center. There were always rooms available for meeting in the Admin section and it was close to the medical bay. He would reserve one and work from there for a while.

It didn't take Gunnery Sergeant Berry and Staff Sergeant Fry long to join Remmy. They had put the Spec Op platoon, sans Hugo, who had an administrative day off, through their usual PT routine, but they weren't doing simulations until the chain of command was fixed. So, they were free when Remmy sent his message.

"Thanks for coming," Remmy said.

They were in a plain room with a holo projector and a rectangular table. Remmy already had his data pad out, along with a cup of coffee, when Tex and Izzy arrived.

"How's Laila?" Izzy asked, foregoing the usual use of title and rank since it was just the three of them in the room.

"Recovering," Remmy said. "She'll be okay. At least that's what the doctor thinks."

"We got a doctor now?" Tex asked.

"Apparently," Remmy said, biting back the commentary he felt like telling them about Doctor Vicky. "She showed up just before we set off last night."

"That's good," Izzy said. "Some people prefer med bots, but I like a human giving me the bad news."

"When will she be back on duty?" Tex asked.

"The doctor says a month," Remmy said. "Personally, I can't imagine Laila taking a month off, but we'll see. That is the reason I called you here. I'll be stepping into a more direct role with the platoons, and we need to decide what to do about leading the Spec Op platoon."

"That's easy," Izzy said.

"You want the job?" Remmy asked.

"No, but you can do it," she said. "Tex and I will handle the day-to-day, but you should take direct control."

"And you should promote Hugo," Tex said.

"Staff Sergeant?" Remmy asked.

"No, he needs to be more of a liaison, or something," Tex said.

"Everyone's talking about him down in Grunt Country. They all think he's some kind of superhero for running with Laila all the way to Med Bay. It was pretty spectacular."

"I agree," Remmy said. "But I'm not sure I see Hugo as a liaison. He isn't really the social type."

"Doesn't need to be," Izzy said. "Let him be your go-between, carrying orders, helping out here and there. You'll have every jarhead on the ship pumping iron and trying to keep up with him."

"I'd let him float in and out of the fire teams, too," Tex said. "Especially during sims. I know it's unusual, but he can bring all three platoons together better than anyone at this point."

"We already ran the idea past Ales and Putnam," Izzy said.

"You did?" Remmy asked.

"We figured you have enough on your plate," Tex said.

"I hope we didn't overstep, Major," Izzy added.

"You know me better than that. I love it when Marines take the initiative."

"That's what we thought," Izzy said.

"And we know that what's coming up is the real deal," Tex said. "I don't know if you've seen Hugo in the sim we ran yesterday, but I thought for sure he was going to shoot Hanson in the face."

"He didn't even argue with the man," Izzy said. "He spoke clearly and made a lot of sense. In fact, I'd venture to say he stepped up and vocalized what the entire platoon was feeling."

"I gave him a little shake of the head, and to my surprise, he followed my lead," Tex said. "He has changed, Major. Everyone sees it."

"Alright, well, that's good advice. I'll have to run it past the Captain. You know it would mean he would leapfrog you in rank."

They both chuckled and waved that idea off like it had no weight. "You know we don't care," Izzy said. "He's been here since the beginning."

"And he's your man, through and through," Tex added. "That's exactly what you're going to need."

"And you two can handle training with Spec Ops?" Remmy asked.

"We've been together for a bit," Izzy said. "Lieutenant Hanson was the only new face this rotation."

"Frankly, we're better off," Tex said. "Izzy knows our platoon better than anyone. And we all respect her."

"You call the plays, we carry them out, let's keep things running smooth and fast, Major."

"I agree," Remmy said. "Your selflessness and confidence in me and Hugo are greatly appreciated. I did see the training sim. I also saw a holo-vid of Laila's fight. You did as much to save her as anyone, Tex. I can't tell you how thankful I am for that."

"She would have done it for me," he said.

Remmy was glad that his friends and subordinates saw Laila the way that he did. He knew Tex was right. She would give her life for any one of theirs. Just like Izzy and Tex, she cared nothing about rank or title. In her mind, they were all family and he was grateful to his friends. They were making his job easy. He didn't have to think very hard about taking their advice. He would step into a command role, not from the air, but on the ground. And if the Captain approved, he would promote Hugo to a special post that allowed the three Marine platoons to function smoothly and efficiently. In combat, speed kills. He needed his Marines to be fast, flexible and deadly.

CHAPTER 28

NO LIMITS, that was what was going through Hard Case's mind as he took off in pursuit of Kicker. In many ways, the two squads were rivals. The SDF wanted it that way. They wanted the rivalry to push both squads to be the absolute best they could be and to achieve what they might have thought impossible, driven by the burning desire to outdo the other side.

Justin Kase was a career flyer and had thrown himself into the training. For him, it was physical and mental. Lighting-fast reflexes weren't enough; a pilot had to understand what their aircraft was capable of and what their opponent was likely to do. For the first time in his life, he honestly felt like there were no limits to what was possible in an aircraft.

"Increasing gravity drive to forty percent," he said as the Raptor sped off in pursuit. His every action would be scrutinized. It was like a pro-athlete reviewing game film to see what he had missed in the heat of the action and what he could do better next time. No committee of senior officers would judge his decisions in after-action reports. Perhaps at some point down the line that would happen, but the *Renegade* wasn't in the Sol system. Still, there would be an officer on the ship whose job was to keep Hard Case under observation during the training exercise. It was for their benefit that he reported every decision he made.

Going from ten percent of the gravity drive's power to forty percent was a big jump. But he had to make up the distance between himself and Kicker.

"Alpha One, this is your flight controller," a voice said as Hard Case rocketed through space. "Are you sure increasing the gravity drive that much is a good idea?"

"No clue," Hard Case said. "Gotta close on Kicker."

"Can't you target him from a distance?"

"Can, but won't," Hard Case said. "You wouldn't try to cut a single hair on a person's head from a hundred feet away. It's irresponsible. Surely you know SDF regs on combat."

"What I know is that the laser cannons on the *Raptors* are rated to over a hundred thousand kilometers. Plus, you have computer-aided targeting."

"And will the infrared beam reach that far?" Hard Case said, referring to their practice targeting system.

"Oh, I didn't think about that."

Hard Case was used to having a flight controller in his ear as he flew. It was annoying. There were good flight controllers who recognized that he knew more than they did and saw their job as assisting him ... and there were bad flight controllers who thought they knew more than he did and saw their job as controlling him.

"Gotta get closer," he said, glancing at the Raptor's speed. "Approaching Mach 50. Hull integrity is good. Kicker won't go this fast. He'll try and lure me in, then slip behind me."

"Power is at ninety percent," the flight controller said. "Keep in mind, we've not tested the Raptors under the stress you're putting it through."

"Real combat will be worse," Hard Case said. "Let me do my job."

He was gaining on Kicker, who was making a long, banking turn. It was obvious at a glance that Kicker was flying the Raptor like a regular ship. Hard Case didn't know the man well enough to guess if he was a cautious flyer or if he was trying to lure his opponent in, but he guessed it was the latter.

"Dialing back the inertial dampener," Hard Case said. "Activating infrared laser."

"Watch your speed. You don't want to overfly the target."

Hard Case wished he could shut off the voice in his ear. It was annoying and not helpful in the least. Then it occurred to him that perhaps Captain Darius wanted it that way. Maybe he ordered the flight controllers to be obnoxious and annoying on purpose in order to distract them during the combat simulations.

"Roger that, flight control, initiating retro gravity to match my opponent's speed."

In space, a ship would continue at the same speed even with the engines off. There was no gravity or air friction to slow and eventually stop a spacecraft. A body in motion would remain in motion unless acted on by an outside force. In this case, it was the gravity drive, which flipped from the front of the craft to there rear.

"Retro gravity at ten percent power," Hard Case said. "Target is forty thousand kilometers distant."

"It's too bad you don't have missiles," the flight controller said.

"This is more fun," Hard Case replied, just as Kicker started to juke.

Flying in retrograde was simple. Maneuvering in retrograde was tricky. It was as if the ship had become a living thing, like walking a strong and eager dog on a leash. The turns were different, longer, less exact. That gave Kicker an advantage. He could turn fast and tight. Hard Case turned slower and wider, but that didn't matter so much when he was chasing Kicker from a distance. But the closer he came, the harder it was to stay on Kicker's six.

"Thirty thousand kilometers is the maximum range on the infrared system, according to the specs," the flight controller said.

And that wasn't the only voice in his comlink either. Bishop had been launched and was starting to put his ship through its paces. The back and forth between Bishop - Alpha Two - was heard, but not the instructions or banter between Kicker and his flight controller. It was all part of the test. In combat, they would all be on an open channel. He would hear every command and response from his squad, maybe more. He had to focus on the sound of the flight controller's voice just in case the man in the Renegade said something important. It wasn't easy. His mind wanted total focus on the ship flying in an erratic pattern in front of him. When he closed the thirty thousand kilometers between the two ships, his targeting system came on. A softly glowing reticle appeared on his HUD. It was two cross-shaped lines, with a circle that didn't quite reach the edges of the lines. That's where his laser would fire. The entire Raptor had become a weapon, and to hit the enemy, he would have to fly the ship in the direction of his target. When he turned his head to the side, the reticle shifted. It stayed the same, moving in his vision as his head moved. When Hard Case glanced down at his gauges, the reticle moved up on the HUD. When he looked up, it moved down. Best of all, when the target passed in front of the reticle, it lit up brighter. Unfortunately, at thirty thousand kilometers distance, targeting the fast-moving ship was like trying to shoot a gnat across a football field with a bow and arrow. The word impossible came to mind. He could fire randomly in hopes of getting lucky. The lasers moving at the speed of light would be so fast as to be considered instantaneous. Yet, Hard Case didn't want to get lucky. He wanted to prove he was the better aviator.

"Returning to gravity drive acceleration," Hard Case said. "Five percent power."

In combat, a pilot either knows his stuff or he doesn't. Much of the flying comes from a sense of feel, or intuition. Hard Case was still closing in on Kicker when the other pilot increased speed. It was impossible to realize this by looking. The gravity drive didn't glow or produce any sort of effect. But Hard Case knew his adversary had reached the point of needing to change his tactic, and so the veteran flyer did the same.

"You'll overfly his position," the flight controller warned.

"Watch and see," Hard Case replied.

He was still gaining on Kicker. The Raptors had no running lights, and they were between systems. Seeing his opponent was difficult from a distance. And as they drew closer together, staying on Kicker's tail was harder and harder. But flying was in Hard Case's blood. It had taken him a few minutes to get used to the new fighter's controls and just how incredibly responsive the ship was. But after that, it had become second nature. He didn't have to think about how to control the Raptor. It was an extension of his mind.

Then he saw it. Kicker's tail flaps were moving as he turned. There was no need for that. They weren't traveling in an atmosphere. The shape of the wings didn't create lift or help him bank into a turn. But using the Raptor's pedals, which controlled the tail flaps, was standard flight protocol. You used them in the atmosphere and, for many pilots, it was impossible not to use them once you got used to the process. Hard Case knew he didn't need to use his flaps in space flight, so he didn't bother, but when he saw Kicker, he immediately recognized the weakness of using them in space. They were a tell, an indication of flight direction. It was still hard to see the flaps. The body of the ship was black, but the chrome accents reflected the starlight. And the movement of the flaps preceded the gravity turns by almost a full second. That's when Hard Case knew he had Kicker dead to rights.

But he fired right away. Better to let the other flyer realize just how good Hard Case was. There was no direction he could turn that Hard Case didn't anticipate. He let the cat and mouse game go for about thirty seconds, then he fired a single laser. A buzzer in the cockpit sounded. The dogfight was over, Hard Case had won. He could imagine how angry Kicker would be. There was nothing worse than losing a fight and both squads would know. But that was life in the highly competitive fighter pilot division of the SDF.

"Excellent flying, Hard Case," Captain Darius said. "Time to bring it in."

"You sure about that, sir?" Justin replied. "I could keep flying. You made a hell of a ship here, sir. She's hard to put back into the barn, so to speak."

"That's good to know, but we have to complete our study of the airframe and engineering," Darius said. "Alpha One, return to the *Renegade*. That's an order."

"Roger, Shogun. Alpha One, returning to base."

The flight back was uneventful. Kicker made a targeting run, then set out in a dogfight with Animal. The process would go on until half of each squad had run their ships. In the late afternoon, the second half of each squad would get their chance. Adjustments would be made, new tests set and more combat trials. All the data would be fed into the onboard flight simulators to make them more like the real thing. And Hard Case knew it was a big, big change. The Raptors were like supercars, fine-tuned for speed and agility. Going back to the jet engine when they broke into a planet's atmosphere would be a huge step backward in the fighter's capabilities. He couldn't help but wonder how the pilots would adjust. For him, it was all about feel, but sudden changes in an aircraft's performance could be difficult to understand, especially under the strain of combat. When the pilot's life is on the line, they sometimes lose their grip on what their ship is capable of and push too hard. The history of aerial warfare was full of examples of pilots who had outflown their ship's capabilities and died in the process. He would have to warn his squad. They only had a few more days before the danger became real, and the missions took on an entirely new level of stress. He wanted to be ready, and that meant getting his pilots ready.

The Hell Flyers were about to live up to their name, and if they wanted to live and tell the tale, they would have to be ready to fly better than they ever thought possible.

CHAPTER 29

CAPTAIN DARIUS WAS THRILLED with the performance of the *Raptors*. The new gravity-drive engines were incredible. The data from the morning test was off the charts. He would have to send a report back to the Sol system that evening detailing what they had done with the ships. More would need to be made, although Darius wondered if humanity had the capacity to build anything as flawlessly as the *Renegade's* automated manufacturing plant.

But that work could wait. Nurek and his team of analysts could crunch the numbers and formulate the majority of the report. Darius had other pressing matters to attend to. None more important than checking on Lieutenant Laila McPherson's recovery. He went down to the Med Bay personally, thinking he could kill two birds with one stone, as his second order of business was to greet the ship's new doctor.

There were times when the SDF Brass imposed things on Darius, or more specifically, assigned certain personnel to the *Renegade* without his approval, which chafed the Captain. It was the way the military had been for hundreds of years, from politically appointed leadership in times of war to Admirals shifting personnel around for no better reason than to have something to do. He had been accustomed to it before setting out on the *Jericho*, but since he had taken charge of the *Renegade,* his feelings about the practice had changed. The Brass, sitting in their safe offices and writing memos all day, had no idea what he was facing in the galaxy beyond the Sol system. Nor did they have a clue what the *Renegade* was really capable of. So, the sudden assignment of a doctor to the ship was a bit of an annoyance.

He had read Doctor Victoria Holt's file. She had a very prestigious list of credentials and accomplishments. But there were also some questionable personnel issues that surrounded her. Allegations of misconduct, not by Dr. Holt, but by her associates at more than one posting. Darius didn't know if she was a troublemaker or just extremely unlucky. Things didn't clear up when he stepped into the Med Bay.

The Med Techs were in the middle of what appeared to be a thorough inventory of supplies and equipment. Darius thought that was a poor choice of timing, as they had a very critical injury on their hands that probably required more of their attention. He was about to suggest that very thing when the door to the enclosed compartment where Lieutenant McPherson had been moved to opened.

Shock was Captain Darius's first reaction. Doctor Victoria Holt was a striking woman. She had thick hair that was... the only word Darius could think of was lustrous. High cheekbones, large green eyes, long eyelashes, full lips. The woman looked like she had stepped from a blockbuster movie set and onto his ship.

The second reaction was anger. Her white lab coat hung open and revealed more than the clothes underneath concealed. It was not the type of attire that he approved of on board a ship of war. He forced his face into a mask to hide his emotions and waited as she approached. The woman was wearing designer boots. It seemed that nothing about her was as it should be. The last doctor on board the *Renegade* had been an aging, but highly decorated, man of Indian descent. There had been nothing outrageous about Doctor Vivek Lanski.

"Captain, it's a pleasure to meet you," the new physician said.

Darius silently fumed that her smile only made her more attractive. But he also knew that a woman had every right to dress as she wanted to, at least on her own time. It wasn't her fault she was attractive, and in her case, that was an understatement. Suddenly, the personnel issues in her file made perfect sense.

"It's our pleasure. Thank you for joining us," Darius said, his voice sounding a bit odd in his own ears. "I hope we haven't hit you with too much, too soon."

"Not at all," she said. "Compared to a metro hospital, or even a Med Center on a space station, this is a breeze. At least for now."

"Agreed. Things could get worse," Darius said. "I'm not sure you know much about our mission."

"On the contrary. I've read everything I could get my hands on about the *Renegade*. I've been trying to get assigned to this ship for over a year now."

"Really?" Darius asked, surprised once again.

"This is why I joined the SDF," she said. "It's always been my dream. To be outside the Sol system is... well... I can't really put that into words. That's why I'm here. I want to be on a ship that is making a difference, and you're doing that and more, Captain Darius. You're making history."

Darius didn't think of himself as a cynical person, but he had a sharp feeling that Dr. Holt was only on the *Renegade* to get her name in the history books. He wondered if she understood that nothing they did would be public knowledge for decades, perhaps ever. But all that would have to wait.

"I'd like to take the time to fill you in on the current mission and its importance, but that will have to wait," Darius said. "How is our patient?"

"Recovering," Dr. Holt said. "Lieutenant McPherson suffered trauma to her core muscle structure and internal organs. I'm sure you know that already, but I believe in thorough reporting. The surgical bot repaired her intestines. There was bleeding, but no debris in the body cavity. Her wounds were repaired, and no infection has been detected, but we are currently giving her IV antibiotics and fluids. We are also keeping her sedated."

"Is that necessary?"

"Not usually, but in her case, I think so," Doctor Holt said. She held up both hands, bending her fingers where they met the hand, and interlacing them. "Think of your stomach muscles like this," she explained. "Where the attack cut into them, the muscle fibers were damaged. They were frayed, the way a rope looks after you cut it, and the fibers splayed out.

She pulled her hands apart and stiffened her fingers to illustrate.

"It will heal, but in doing so, it creates scar tissue. That scar tissue can be painful. If it's thin, it can rupture, form a hernia, which requires additional surgery. If it's thick, it can be stiff and unresponsive. You look fit, Captain. Do you exercise?"

"When possible, yes," he said, feeling a flare of awkwardness. He did try his best to say trim and in shape. Walking was his main exercise, but when time permitted, he did more. Still, despite all that, in comparison to the beautiful doctor, he felt like an ogre. Her mentioning how he looked only made that feeling more acute.

"So then, you can imagine what it would be like to lose ten to thirty percent of your strength. That can happen in the Lieutenant's unique case. The more she moves before we start her on light therapy, the more scar tissue will be created. I'm just trying to spare her from that."

Darius almost took a step backward. He was surprised. She was obviously very good at her job and, yet, he had lost sight of that by focusing on her appearance. He silently chided himself for that. He thought he was a better man than to judge someone for the way they looked, but when he first saw her, he expected Victoria Holt to be vapid and focused only on her looks.

"It seems she is in very capable hands," he said, feeling even more like an ogre than before.

"The automated system did the heavy lifting, I'm just dictating her after-surgical care," Dr. Holt said. "By tonight, we'll be starting light therapy. She'll be awake and alert tomorrow morning, I'm sure."

"Very good," he replied, turning. "I hope we aren't keeping you too busy down here, doctor."

"Not at all. I love it," she said. "The Medical Bay here is amazing. I'm a bit of a workaholic, I'm afraid. I don't do so great at staff meetings. This is my world and I want to know every system, every bed, every bit of equipment we have."

"Well, I won't keep you. I'm sure the med techs have told you that whatever you need can be manufactured on the *Renegade*. Just speak to Commander Nash about anything you feel is lacking. At some point, we'll sit down and go over what's ahead for the ship and make sure you're ready for any contingency."

"Just let me know when and where," she said. "I'm glad to be aboard, Captain. I want to be an asset."

"You already are," he said.

She smiled again. He felt awkward again and hurried out of the Med Bay. The Admin center was directly across from the Medical bay. Both took up what was considered prime real estate on the Grand Concourse. But the *Renegade* was not a cruise ship or a trade vessel. She was a battleship, even if the Arodoni hadn't built her for that. As such, he liked that the crew was reminded of what really mattered, even on their downtime.

He went across the wide concourse and into the Administration Center. There were offices, but it was mostly an open area where crew members collaborated. If there were problems on the ship, this was where it was reported. From the Admin center, Commander Nash oversaw the ship's most valuable asset — her crew—along with the life support and communications system, which fell under the purview of the ship's Executive Officer. But Darius wasn't there to see Nash. He found the room that Remmy was using and was delighted to find that the Major was hard at work.

"I just spoke to the new doctor," Darius said. "It seems Laila is in good hands."

"Yes, sir," Remmy said. "I'm not much use over there at the moment and thought I could get caught up with the asset assignments. We still need to designate the first target."

"Agreed. I will be doing that soon. The initial testing of the new Raptors is very, very promising."

"Things are coming together."

"Better than I had hoped for," Darius said. He wanted to bring up the new doctor. Remmy wasn't a therapist, but he was a good friend, the kind Darius could confide in. But, he was ashamed of his jump to judgment of the new physician. So, he refrained from discussing her, at least for the time being.

"I have a request," Remmy said.

That alone was surprising enough to shake Darius out of his internal musings on the attractive doctor.

"You... have a request," Darius said. "I think that could be a first, Major."

He chuckled. "I like to take care of things myself whenever possible, sir," he said.

"We all appreciate that about you, Major. No one more than me. What do you want?"

"I would like to promote Hugo McManus to a special post," Remmy said.

"A special post?"

"Yes. In effect, he'll be doing most of Laila's job. So, he needs to be in a position of authority over all three platoons."

"You want to give him a field commission? What rank?"

"Not a commission," Remmy said. "Hugo won't want to be an officer and he might reject the whole idea, if it comes to that."

"What did you have in mind then?"

"Sergeant Major," Remmy said. "It's normally only a rank held in larger units, a battalion or Corps."

Darius thought about the idea for a moment. Normally, he just deferred to Remmy's suggestion. The Space Marine Corps served as an adjunct to the SDF. Most fighting was done ship to ship, but occasionally, Marines were used on space stations or colonies when fighting was intense. That said, the SDF naval operations did not mingle with the Marine Corps in any meaningful way. Onboard a ship, the Captain had total command, no matter the rank of the senior Marine officer. While Darius was an expert in naval operations, he knew very little about Marine operations. But any field promotion onboard a ship fell under the purview of the Captain. And Hugo McManus had a mixed history that was both heroic and troublesome.

"Do you think he's changed?"

"I do," Remmy replied.

"For the better?"

"Yes, sir," Remmy said. "He'll be my right hand. I'll be taking full command of the Marines in the field, and Hugo will act as a go-between so that we can fully integrate all three platoons once we're on the ground."

That brought Darius up short. "Wait, did you say you would be taking command in the theater?"

"I have to," Remmy said. "Laila would have done it, but she won't be fit for duty for at least a month. And this operation is too important to leave to chance. Besides, with GIGI on board, we'll have guaranteed communication, no matter what else happens."

Darius couldn't argue about that. The mental bond between Remmy and the alien artifact had saved them in the past. But when Darius imagined the attack on the Core worlds, his vision had included having Remmy on the Bridge directing or, at least, advising on ground operations.

"This isn't how I envisioned things," Darius said. "But you make a good point. Move forward with the promotion. And whatever you do, Major, don't get yourself killed."

"Copy that, sir," Remmy said.

But they both knew there were no guarantees in war.

CHAPTER 30

IT WAS ALMOST as thrilling to hear his pilots as it was being in the cockpit himself. After Animal and Diamond made their flights, the other pilots, Aspen, Bishop, and Indigo, were chomping at the bit to get into the air. And they weren't the only people who were exuberant. Petty Officer Dante Smith led a team of wrench spinners who went over every inch of the Raptors. They marveled at the performance of the aircraft, but were doubly excited that there was no sign of stress on the airframe, including no wear and tear on the various components.

"It's like you never even took her out of the hangar," Dante said. "Hot damn, I ain't never seen nothing like it."

"Flying it is pretty special, too," he said.

The Hell Flyers went from the flight deck to their briefing room and back again. When the afternoon session started, Hard Case brought up comlink feeds from the pilots taking their Raptors through their paces.

The dogfights were the most entertaining. Eight out of eleven chasers won, but twice, members of the Hell Flyers, Aspen and Diamond, out flew their opponents and gunned them down. Only one of the Furries managed it. Spinster was the callsign of Celine Moss. She was a tall, thin woman with dark eyes and a darker disposition. A former figure skater turned ace pilot, who held the record for the longest spin on ice, hence her callsign. She was a calculating pilot and absolutely fearless. She had tried to take her gravity drive up to eighty percent, but was ordered to dial it back under fifty. Needless to say, she still managed to outpace Indigo and shoot her down.

That evening, no one was interested in going out. They all ate together, both squads at one table in the mess hall. By rank, they could go up to the command level to get their meals, but the food was nearly as good in the enlisted mess hall. And none of the flyers wanted to be away from their berths for long. They spent the evening poring over the data from their flights. They had recordings from the Raptors themselves and recordings from the *Renegade*, both video recordings and holographic recordings of the plot. Plus, having flown the Raptors, the pilots were anxious to go back over their manuals and make corrections.

Commander Kase met with Lieutenant Stanislaus after dinner. Alex was the Chief Engineer on a ship that had more engineers than any other vessel in the SDF fleet. But most of those were mechanical and electrical engineers who did more observation and recording of how the alien technology worked than actual, hands-on repairs. Alex Stanislaus was a computer engineer. Like Vivian Ramos, he had been highly recruited straight out of his undergraduate program. He could have gone anywhere and made loads of money helping startups or starting his own company, but he chose to serve in the SDF. The government paid off his student loans and sent him to graduate school. As an ensign, he had served on a variety of ships and had been on the verge of a promotion when he was assigned to the *Jericho*. It had been the most significant posting of his life. He had become the foremost expert on the Arodoni computing system. Which, surprisingly enough, was not all that different from human quantum computing. Some things were different, but many were similar, only far more advanced. Still, it didn't take him long to absorb the new information and begin to work with the Arodoni tech.

He had designed the simulators for the Raptors and, while the ship's computer did most of the coding, he would be making the adjustments. Hard Case went over all the changes that needed to be made. The two men were soon laughing like old friends.

"You have to get out in one," Hard Case said as they wrapped up their time together. "You'll see what I mean when you fly one."

"I'm not a pilot," Alex said.

"You could be. Learn on the simulators."

"I don't really have a lot of free time," he said.

"Then build one with a backseat and I'll take you up. It's like the best race car ever built, mashed into a fighter jet, but with abilities like a flying saucer. I've read a lot of reports about foo fighters and Unidentified Anomalous Phenomena."

"Me, too, I was obsessed as a kid growing up. Read everything I could get my hands on, including government reports."

"Yeah, and those UAPs often did things that defied imagination. Turning ninety degrees at speeds that were way above anything we could make."

"Or stopping on a dime, before shooting straight up into space."

"Yes!" Kase said. "These ships can almost do that stuff. I mean, if you were just watching from the ground, you would think they turn ninety degrees. It's a bit less than that, your data should show."

"It's close."

"I saw a movie once where a car on wheels shot out a grappling cable so that it could make an impossible turn at high speed. The Raptor feels just like that."

"It's very cool," Alex said. "I'll have my people make changes to the software. By morning, you can test it out."

"I will. Are you meeting with Commander Elder next?"

Alex shook his head. "No, he didn't seem interested."

Hard Case thought that was odd. The simulators were a valuable training aid. He specifically wanted his squad to go between atmospheric flight, powered by the jet engines on the Raptors, to the gravity drives in space. They needed to feel the difference and anticipate it if they were going into combat in both environments. Yet Legend didn't feel the same way. It was odd, but Justin's exuberance soon crowded the bewilderment from his mind. A drink, a comfortable seat out on the balcony of his new berth that overlooked the Park and a flight manual in hand were all he needed to cap off what had to be one of the best days of his career.

In the Med Bay, Remmy was with Laila when she came to. It had been over twenty-four hours since the attack and her surgery. According to Dr. Vicky, there were no signs of infection in the wounds and no complications from the surgery. They were going to set up the reading therapy lights soon. The temperature in the room was already rising so that Laila could sleep without blankets while the light did their work to speed her healing.

Before, when she had woken up, Laila had still been highly sedated. After a day of fluids and antibiotics, she was more alert, but still obviously weak.

"Schizophrenic?" she asked.

"That's what they think," Remmy said. "He lied about his family history. His uncle and grandfather both had it."

"I should have seen it coming," she sighed. "I knew he was unstable, coming apart at the seams, but I thought he was just overwhelmed."

"He shouldn't have lied," Remmy said. "I looked it up. Schizophrenia usually has signs that only the person can see before it gets to the point of a diagnosis. He lied on his intake forms and lied about his condition before coming on board."

"They do a full physical before spec ops training," she said. "How'd they not catch it?"

"No signs of it unless the person admits to them. Seeing things that aren't there, delusions, that sort of stuff isn't always obvious to others."

"There's no blood tests or anything?"

"I guess not," Remmy said. "Brain scans, maybe, but even then, it can mask as normal function, I suppose."

"Well, looks like I'm going to miss the big show," she said. "What's the timeline?"

"You've got a long row to hoe," he said. "Ever been hit in the abdomen before?" She shook her head. "You'll need significant rehab time. The doctor says a month, at least."

"You're kidding me?"

"Nope," Remmy said. "It's the placement of your wounds and the scar tissue. We use our core muscles for everything. You're going to be weak and stiff."

"I've recovered from bullet wounds faster than a month," she insisted.

"I'm just telling you what they told me. We've got two more days of flight testing, then we're moving forward with the mission. Your job now is just getting back up to full strength."

He outlined the plan for promoting Hugo to Sergeant Major.

"That's a great idea," she said. "Have you told him yet?"

"No," Remmy said. "I was about to."

"Do it here," Laila said. "I'll help you convince him."

"You think he'll need to be convinced to take a promotion?"

"You don't?"

"Well..." Remmy said, suddenly feeling like he had missed something. "I don't think so."

"Call it a woman's intuition, but I think he'll balk. He won't feel worthy of it. Then he'll suspect that you're just trying to reward him for helping me."

Remmy had told her how Hugo had carried her all the way to the Med Bay at a run.

"Then we'll just have to convince him that I need him. If he won't do it, I'll promote Tex and make Hugo the Spec Op Staff Sergeant. He can't argue about that."

Ten minutes later, Hugo arrived in the Med Bay, and one of the techs showed him into the room. Remmy shook his hand and then Laila reached out for it.

"Thank you, Hugo." He shrugged, embarrassed. "Don't say anyone would have done it because not everyone could have."

"It just seemed better than waiting for help," Hugo said.

"I am in your debt."

Hugo shook his head, but it was Remmy who spoke up. "You've proven yourself time and again, Sergeant. And I'm sorry to do it, but I have to ask you for your help again."

"You don't have to ask," Hugo said. "Tell me what needs to be done and I'll do it."

"I can't go back on duty for a while," Laila said. "This one says a month, but I think I can do it in three weeks."

She was starting to get tired. Remmy wanted to let her sleep, although she insisted on his telling Hugo about the promotion while she could be part of it.

"Either way, we've got important assignments downrange before that. Probably within four or five days from now. I'll be stepping in as the Spec Op CO, but in a broader sense, commanding all three platoons. I need a right hand to help me do it. Someone I trust, and who can do the impossible."

"Izzy or Tex could do it," Hugo said.

"Maybe," Remmy said. "But they haven't had the experience I'm looking for. Plus, they are both vital to their platoon. I need you, Hugo. I've already talked to Captain Darius. We're going to promote you to a special role. You'll be our Sergeant Major, helping me command all three platoons."

Hugo looked dumbfounded, but Remmy knew he wasn't dumb. There were times when Hugo needed a minute to process things. In combat, he was fast, intuitive and action-oriented. When it came to social engagements, or in this case, administrative changes, he sometimes needed extra time to think things through.

"I'm not qualified," he said at last.

"Yes, you are," Remmy said. "You won't be giving orders. You'll be helping communicate my orders and helping the platoons carry them out."

"It's essentially my job," Laila said. "Stepping in when a platoon needs help. Keeping them on mission."

"It's an enlisted rank," Remmy said. "But it gives you the authority to act on my behalf. I'm going to need help, Hugo, and you have the experience fighting the Ashi that no one else has."

"It's an enlisted rank," he said. "I won't be an officer?"

For most people, that would have been a statement of regret. But for Hugo, it was confirmation of what he wanted and Remmy knew him well enough to emphasize that.

"Still enlisted. Just a grunt in the trenches, but not attached to any one platoon. You'll be attached to me."

His sigh was one of relief. "I suppose I can do that," he said.

There was just the faintest hint of a smile on his face. And again, Remmy understood that he wasn't trying to hold anything back. It was just his way. Hugo was not an emotionally expressive person. No one would ever describe him as bubbly. But he was a solid Marine and one who knew combat. He would be the perfect aid to Remmy in the days ahead.

"Good," Remmy said. "We start in the morning. "Report to my office at 0700 hours. We're going to revamp sim training to incorporate ourselves into the equation with the various platoons."

"Yes, sir," Hugo said.

"Go celebrate! You deserve it," Laila said.

Hugo nodded and left the Med Bay. Remmy couldn't say there was a spring in his step, but he carried himself out with more purpose than when he had come in.

"And you should get some rest," Remmy said.

"I will if you will," she said. "Seriously, Remmy, I'm okay. You don't have to stay with me."

"What do you need?"

"Nothing," she said. "I'm in good hands."

"You can message me, day or night," he said.

"Get out," she said. "Your love is too much."

He bent down, kissed her gently, then touched her face. She was the toughest woman he knew, but she was also his sweetheart. She smiled. He knew he was the only person who could treat her with such tenderness and it made his heart swell with joy.

He looked back after stepping out of the small room. She already had her eyes closed.

"Is she ready for therapy?" Doctor Vicky asked.

"She's asleep," Remmy replied.

"Perfect. I'll go in, uncover her wounds, and get the lights on. My guess is she'll sleep through the night. Tomorrow morning, we'll have her sit up a while. I can let you know when."

"That would be great. Thanks for taking care of her, Doctor."

"It's my pleasure," the physician said with a genuine smile.

Remmy was glad the doctor had come aboard. She seemed knowledgeable and compassionate. He hoped other people on board would recognize it, too.

CHAPTER 31

THE NEXT TWO days were a flurry of activity on board the *Renegade*. And not just for the Marines and the fighter squadrons. Orders had gone out to get every area of the ship ready for action. The normally pristine corridors were lined with bins of equipment, from lights to tools and, of course, first aid supplies. It was all kept in bins lined with copper that would act as a Faraday cage in the event that EMPs were used against the Arodoni ship.

Everyone, from the maintenance crews to the engineers, drilled for potential damage to the ship. Low-tech solutions such as magnets were used to secure the bins in the corridors next to the vital components of the ship. The civilians were drilled as well. They practiced securing their storefronts and battening down their storage facilities. It was all part of the process of having a business on a ship whose primary purpose was war.

On the Bridge, the officers and crew practiced maneuvers and tested the ship's massive laser cannons. Captain Darius oversaw it all and that included the continued flight testing of the Raptor fighters. The cigar-shaped ships performed better than anyone had hoped, at least in space. The gravity drives gave those ships speed and agility that was unmatched by any ship that Darius had seen on his travels through the galaxy. They were potent enough to be a threat even to the *Renegade*. Furthermore, the gravity drive didn't emit heat the way traditional engines did. And they were small enough that targeting them with lasers would be incredibly difficult, especially at the high speed and erratic movement they could take.

Captain Darius also noted a few other facts about the fighter squadrons. The Furies were aggressive and action-oriented, while the Hell Flyers were a much tighter group of pilots. Whether in pairs or flying in groups, the Hell Flyers acted in tandem, making them more efficient at almost every drill set up for testing the new ships. It wasn't something he needed to be worried about, but when it came to making assignments, the knowledge about the two groups would be useful.

In Grunt Country, the Marines were drilling hard. Remmy and Hugo took each platoon through their paces. They fought simulated battles, sometimes with Remmy present, and at other times with him absent and the platoons getting orders via Hugo after the simulation began. Tex and Izzy had been right about Hugo and his relentless work ethic only further cemented his reputation. He had every Marine, even the officers, working harder and putting in more time in the gym. They constantly picked his brain concerning the Ashi. The *Renegade* had a lot of data on the big aliens, but not a tremendous amount of experience in combat with them. In that area, Hugo was a font of knowledge.

It was an extremely busy time, yet also one of extreme coopera-tion. The sense of brotherhood was powerful across every division. It wasn't until the third night after her arrival that Captain Darius finally had the chance to meet with Dr. Victoria Holt. He walked into the Ward Room for a late dinner only to find her just sitting down to eat herself. She had changed her yoga clothes and wore a regular officer's duty uniform. Her hair was pulled into a tight braid, and she had almost no makeup on, yet somehow she was more beautiful than ever.

"Doctor," Darius said, pouring himself a glass of water and carrying his tray of food to his regular spot at the table.

"Captain," she said, glancing up at him, then returning her atten-tion to her meal.

He was several seats away from her on the long table. And there was some tension, at least in his mind. He wasn't sure if he should have sat closer or if he should invite her to move closer to him.

"Settling in, okay?" he asked.

"Better than okay," she said. "I came here to serve, but this ship is... well, you know."

"Atypical," Darius said.

She laughed. And while he liked to have a good rapport with all his crew, her laughter made him tense. Not that there was anything wrong with the way she laughed. It was light-hearted and beautiful. But it made him feel giddy and nervous at the same time. He found himself wanting to make her laugh more and had to resist the urge to try and impress her.

"Why are you eating alone?" he asked.

"I prefer it," she said.

"Oh," Darius said. He was genuinely surprised by her response. "Is there something wrong?"

He could imagine there was. Most single men would fall all over themselves trying to win her affection. Perhaps some of his crew had already done that. He didn't want issues dividing them. While he couldn't hold Dr. Holt at fault for being pretty, he felt a bit of resentment creeping into his mind anyway.

"I'm a bit of an introvert," she said. "I don't mind social settings, but I prefer me time."

She sounded almost embarrassed.

"I hope I'm not intruding then," he said.

"Oh, no, not at all. It's the Ward Room, right? I've been taking meals in the Med Bay, but I just thought I should maybe be around the other officers at some point."

"I appreciate that," Darius said. "I'm sure they will as well. You haven't met them?"

"Just Commander Nash," she said. "He came into the Med Bay and introduced himself."

"Well, since I have you here, I wouldn't mind talking to you about our mission."

"Of course, Captain. Whatever you like."

"You've read the plan memos?"

"All of them," she said. "I'm a bit of a nerd, if I'm being honest. Reading technical reports and manuals is my jam. That's how I got through med school when everyone else was dropping out."

"Some people say there's no need for doctors anymore, what with doc bots and surgical droids," Darius said. "But I've always thought that a human being was more thorough."

"Automated healthcare has its place. If I have a cold, I prefer a quick scan and shot, but on an SDF ship, the odds are much higher that what people need from a physician is more demanding."

"Agreed," Darius said, as he removed the cover from his food and began nudging things around on his plate with a fork. "We're likely to have battle trauma. Have you served in a combat zone?"

"I've worked in both combat zones and high crime areas. In St. Stevens on the north end of the East Coast Megalopolis, I saw more gunshot and knife wounds than on Mars during the uprising."

"You were there?"

"I was," she replied. "I love two things; helping the sick and injured is one."

"What's the other?"

"Would you believe a glass of wine, a good view, and a thick tech manual?"

"I would not," he said with a chuckle.

"Well, it's true. But I want to make a difference, too. That's why I'm here."

"You couldn't make a difference on Earth or Mars?"

"Yes, of course, I could, but like you said, there are options there, automated or human. Out here, though, well... that's different, isn't it? I don't know many physicians who volunteer for combat cruises."

"But you did?"

"I was begging to go," she replied with a dazzling smile. "I nagged my superiors, called my government reps, pestered anyone with the power to get me out here and prayed I would get the chance."

"Some might call that crazy?"

"Then I'm in the right place," she said. "I've heard it all, Captain, including the people who don't even believe the *Renegade* exists."

"Seriously?"

"It's all highly classified back in the Inner-System. There are people who don't think anyone has ever left the Sol system."

"But there were Ashi ships there," Darius said. "We fought them."

"It was so far out that most people had no clue," she said. "It was easy to cover up, which the government did under the guise of public safety."

"That's absurd."

"People typically fall into one of three categories. Either they believe it all, like me," she said, favoring Darius with another bright smile that made him both giddy and nervous all at the same time. "Or they believe we've discovered something, but the government is lying about it. The truth is all just rumors, you know. We have no proof that isn't considered top-secret by the powers that be. They say it's too disruptive. And of course, all the new research being done is also secret. To the average person on the street, nothing has changed."

"Hence, the people who don't believe any of it?" Darius asked.

"Bingo," she said, pushing her plate toward the middle of the table and leaning back in her seat. "My goodness, the food here is so good."

"What made you believe this was real?" Darius asked.

"Well, first of all, I had no idea," she said. "It's nothing like I expected."

"Which was?"

"An SDF ship," she said. "I knew it wasn't made by us, but this is not what I expected."

"It's hard to get the scope of the *Renegade* in an SDF memo."

She actually laughed out loud. Darius chuckled, too. He couldn't help it. Her laugh was contagious.

"That is so true. I mean, that is the understatement of the century. This ship is a marvel. I'm guessing the other alien ships you've seen aren't like it."

"No," Darius said.

"I got onto the *Independence* for a tour. I wasn't supposed to, but I bribed one of the guards."

"Really?" Darius said, leaning forward to hear her story.

"It's in the shipyard near Ares," she said. "The researchers have pulled a lot of it apart. The engines are gone. So is the computer system, but I got to see some of the script on a few of the compartments and, of course, the passenger compartment was altered by the humans who flew her home, but still, it was an alien ship. And I guess it sort of set the stage for what I thought all alien ships would be like, which wasn't too different from ours."

"I see your point," he said. "What did you bribe the guard with?"

"Money. What else?" she said.

He could think of a lot of things. Doctors had access to drugs, for one. But what really came to his mind was a kiss. He knew a lot of people would bend the rules for a kiss from a woman like Doctor Victoria Holt.

"You're an interesting person," Darius said.

"I take that as a compliment," she replied. "Actually, I'm boring. I work too hard and my hobbies are weird."

"I read your personnel file," he said. "It's impressive."

"I read yours, too. It's almost completely redacted."

That was news to Darius.

"I had no idea," he said. "To be honest, politics in the Sol system seem a bit..."

"Small," she said. "After being on this ship for one hour, I was completely convinced of that. They should force all the reps in the Inner-System Coalition to tour the *Renegade*. Then maybe we could get past the petty fighting and underhanded insults."

"You're not big into politics?"

"I hate it," she said. "It's all talk and nothing but restrictions. Governments get bigger, but the problems they were created to fix seem to outlive them every time."

"Well, I wanted to make sure that you understand our goals," he explained. "Outside the Sol system, the galaxy is controlled by the Ashi Imperium. How familiar with that are you?"

"Not much," she said. "I've heard the term; everything else about it is classified."

"We don't know a lot," Darius said. "Although you might enjoy spending some time with Lieutenant Nurek."

"Who's that?"

"Our Chief Information Officer," Darius said. "He's a Dudonus and a former slave to the Emperor's family."

Her mouth dropped open. It was soon obvious to Darius that she really didn't know much about their mission.

"The Imperium is actually run by a group called the Prime Council. They have a representative from their five major worlds inside the galactic core."

"That's where we're going?"

"It is," Darius said. "In fact, the planning meeting for that first mission will be in here, tomorrow morning at 0800 hours. I think you should come."

"Thank you, I would love to attend, but I might not be much help."

"That's okay," Darius said. "You need to meet the rest of the senior leadership. Anyway, the Imperium is in many ways just another bloated government, but it's authoritarian. Worse still, it promotes slavery."

"That's..."

"Yes and every bit as terrible as you might think. There are authorized slavers and unauthorized slavers. They prey on the worlds in the Mean Sector and Outer Sector of space."

"I don't think I understand," she said.

"It's like a tax," Darius said. "The authorized slavers can show up on any planet. Every race has a predetermined number of slaves that can be taken every year."

"And they just kidnap people?"

"Essentially, yes," Darius said. "Whatever the system started as, it now operates exactly like that. And some races are considered slave races. The Dudonus are because they collaborated with another race, the Correll, who was secretly trying to undermine the Imperium. The Correll were slaughtered to extinction."

"Wait, where have I heard of that race before?"

"Perhaps in conjunction with GIGI," Darius said.

"Who?"

"The Galactic Information and Guidance Instrument," Darius explained. "It was waiting for us just beyond Saturn's orbital path. Those of us on the *Jericho* were sent to retrieve it."

"Yes!" she said, the memory coming back to her. "You mentioned the Correll in a report about the artifact. I have to admit to you, Captain, so much of what you reported was classified and what wasn't read more like a science fiction novel, that I didn't really believe it. You found an alien artifact that taught you to travel through hyperspace. It's wild!"

"GIGI is here again," Darius said. "She arrived just before you did."

"She?"

"It's hard to explain," he said. "The artifact is a thing, like a block of stone with alien writing on it. Inside, though, it's like a computer. A very, very powerful and sentient computer. So, it's alive, and its name was shortened to GIGI, and we call it a 'her'."

Doctor Holt leaned forward and put her elbows on the table and her face in her hands. "This is too much," she said.

"It's a lot to wrap your mind around."

"That thing is on board this ship?"

"Yes," Darius said. "Does that bother you?"

"Are you insane! Can I see it?"

He hadn't realized that for a moment, he had felt an incredible sense of fear that she would disapprove. Darius was starting to feel himself being sucked into the doctor's orbit and there was a danger in that. She was such a captivating person that to allow himself to feel anything other than a professional association with her could interfere with his judgment. The Captain of a spaceship bound for war couldn't afford for anything to interfere with his decision-making process. There were too many lives at stake.

"Yes, you have access to everything on the command section of the ship," he said. "You're a Major, is that correct?"

She nodded. He knew that for SDF staff outside of the Naval chain of command, everyone went by Marine ranks. Doctors and research scientists held ranks that dictated their pay grade, but they were part of the regular service in that they didn't give orders. Still, as a major, she had every right to be just about anywhere on the ship, and was, since arriving, part of his senior command staff.

"It's in the Systems Control Room," he explained. "Come with me and I'll introduce you."

"Wait, your dinner," she said.

"I'll have it wrapped up and sent to my room," he said. "It's just this way."

He led her out of the Ward Room and down a series of ramps to Epsilon deck. The SCR was close to the center of the ship's power system, which was, in reality, the *Jericho*. They passed by a window in the corridor that showed Darius's former ship still rotating in place to provide the *Renegade* with power.

"That's the *Jericho*?" Doctor Holt asked.

"It is," Remmy said. "We had no idea when we built her that she was actually created to be this ship's power module."

"How does our old ship power this gigantic one?" she asked.

"It doesn't," he replied. "It's actually the Arodoni Power Core that powers the *Renegade*. But our old ship is a conduit, a kind of encapsulated home for the device that turns dark matter into usable energy again."

"You are blowing my mind," she said. "This is all so crazy. I can't believe I'm actually here. Have you ever wanted something so bad and worked so hard for it, then gotten it and been surprised at how normal it is?"

"Yeah, I think so," Darius said.

"Well, this is the complete opposite of that," she said, so excited. "It's so much better than I imagined."

She reached out and put a hand on his arm. Darius stiffened, and perhaps there was something in his look, but she withdrew her hand and lost all sense of frivolity as she apologized.

"I'm sorry. My enthusiasm got the best of me, Captain. I shouldn't have gotten so friendly so soon. I didn't mean to imply anything."

Darius had served on SDF ships with Captains who were aloof. Some were stiff, reserved and never showed any emotion. He was of the persuasion that a good leader was relatable. He didn't want his officers so intimidated by him that they couldn't bring their concerns to him. Furthermore, he preferred to lead in an atmosphere where his officers could push back if they thought he was going too far. Ultimately, his decisions on the *Renegade* were law, but he wasn't the kind of Captain who would get angry about someone touching him in a friendly way.

But Doctor Victoria Holt wasn't just anyone. She was, without a doubt, the most beautiful woman that Darius had ever seen. And he couldn't deny that she made him feel giddy, and nervous, and uncertain at times. It was his self-imposed rule that he did not fraternize with anyone serving on a ship he commanded. It was just too complicated and led to problems.

From her reaction, it wasn't just a fear of overstepping her bounds with the captain that Victoria was concerned with. He had read her file and knew that at almost every post she had taken, there were allegations of misconduct. They were usually filed by her. A repeat of such charges would have caused problems for most officers. One or even two unfortunate incidents could be written off as a coincidence, but if the issue kept arising at post after post, it was most likely the officer's fault. That hadn't happened with Dr. Victoria Holt, perhaps because she was so valuable at her job, but more likely because anyone who had ever seen her could understand why there was an issue. She was just so beautiful that her co-workers probably overstepped their bounds. And if such unwanted advances came from a superior, she would have no other recourse than to report the issue.

"You didn't imply anything," Darius said softly. "But you seem a little gun-shy."

"I am," she said. "I don't want to ruin this. I'm gobsmacked with the ship and all the revelations. And, if you've read my personnel file, you know that I've had issues in the past."

"With men in authority over you," Darius said.

She nodded. What he said next took all his mental strength, yet he was certain it was the right thing to do.

"Dr. Holt, you are an attractive woman, but it is my strict policy to never fraternize with anyone holding a post on a ship that I command. To that end, I will never put you in a situation that should make you uncomfortable as a woman. I will ensure that every officer on this ship knows that I expect the same from them. Should you have a problem with someone, please come to me immediately and I will take the appropriate steps. You are an asset to our mission and I mean to keep you with us as long as I can."

She sighed, and it was as though she was letting go of more stress than he felt. At the same time, something clicked in his mind. Dr. Victoria Hold shifted from being an incredibly beautiful woman to being a colleague and nothing more. That's not to say that he no longer found her attractive, but he had made a decision, and with the possibility of romance off the table, it no longer seemed as dangerous.

"You have no idea how much I appreciate you saying that," she said. "I will do everything in my power to honor my position and remain professional with every officer on this ship."

"Then we won't have a problem," Darius said. "Now, come this way and meet GIGI."

They went into the SCR, and a trio of crew members jumped to their feet.

"As you were," Darius said. "Doctor Holt is here to meet GIGI."

The Captain turned and found Victoria standing stiffly in the doorway, her mouth open in awe as she stared up at the high-resolution hologram of the *Renegade*.

"Doctor?"

"Is that the ship?" she asked, pointing.

"Yes," Darius replied. "It's impressive. The holo projector can show any section of the vessel, inside or out, even the schematics down to the wiring. The main role of this area of the ship is to monitor and even control the various systems on the ship. Life support, artificial gravity, power supply, it's all controlled here first. On the Bridge, we direct the ship, but this room is like the heart of the vessel."

"It's magnificent," she said.

It was his turn to chuckle. He had been on the *Renegade* long enough to have gotten used to much of the ship's wonders, although he enjoyed seeing it all through her eyes again for the first time.

"GIGI is right over here," he said, directing her toward a block of stone. At least, that's what GIGI appeared to be, a rectangular slab of rock with carved markings or writing in an alien script on one side. That script lit up as they approached.

"Doctor Victoria Holt, M.D., welcome," a female voice came through the wrist device that was strapped around Dr. Holt's wrist, said.

Victoria looked down at her wrist, then up at the Captain.

"GIGI interfaces wirelessly with the ship's computer. When she speaks, it is usually through audio devices, your wrist communicator, for example."

Victoria went down on one knee in front of GIGI. "Can I touch it?"

"Ask her," Darius said.

"GIGI," the physician said. "May I touch you?"

"Of course, Dr. Holt."

Victoria reached out a hand and slid it over the surface of the slab. "It feels like rock."

"My exterior is granite," GIGI said, "taken from the Correll home world. I am a Galactic Information and Guidance Instrument. My purpose is to educate humanity about the galaxy outside the Sol system, as well as help navigate the hyperspace network for travel."

"You... you've been sent to help us?"

"That is correct. I was sent to the Sol system over three hundred years prior to being contacted by Captain Darius and the crew of the SDF *Jericho*."

"And what is it you want to teach us?" she asked.

Dr. Victoria Holt's voice trembled with excitement or fear, Darius wasn't sure which. He was beginning to think that the doctor held GIGI in some sort of religious light. If that was the case, she was bound to be disappointed. GIGI was many things, but divine wasn't one of them. In fact, she wasn't even infallible or above breaking a few rules, if she felt it necessary. Darius knew she had hidden files on the *Renegade's* computer from them. Alex Stanislaus had been working to retrieve them, but his other duties were demanding and he hadn't made much headway.

"To co-exist in the galaxy," GIGI said. "Humanity has much to offer, but also much to learn."

"Yes, I couldn't agree more," Dr. Holt said. "What are these markings?"

"They are my primary directive."

"Which is what?" Victoria asked.

"To share what I know freely and to guide humanity through the galaxy as efficiently as possible."

"GIGI is very practical," Darius said. "She'll be part of our meeting in the morning."

"I will be happy to assist you in any fashion, Captain Darius."

"You can tell us about the history of the galaxy," Victoria said. "There's so much we don't know."

"That is true. Would you like me to compile an abridged history for you, Doctor Holt? I can deliver that file to your preferred reading device."

"Oh, yes, that would be outstanding."

"It is done. I have included some materials on myself that you may find stimulating."

"Thank you," Victoria said, standing up.

"We'd better get back," Darius said. "We've got a busy day ahead."

"Yes, of course. I didn't mean to take up so much of your time."

He waved her concern away. "It was a pleasure. I'm glad you're happy on the ship, Doctor. The *Renegade* feels like home to a lot of us. It's good to have a capable physician on board again.

CHAPTER 32

COMMANDER JUSTIN KASE wasn't angry, or even annoyed, but he couldn't deny his disappointment. For the last three days, he had flown the new Raptor fighters. They were thrilling, which, for a fighter pilot who had flown almost every type of fighting vessel in the SDF fleet, was saying something. Even the simulators were fun and his squad was scheduled to train without him because of a planning meeting.

Just the idea of a planning meeting bored him. He was an action-oriented person. Give him the most difficult mission and he would find a way to accomplish it. But sitting in a room full of people debating what should be done was torture. Adding fuel to the fire of his misery was the fact that Commander Mathias Elder would also be present. Hard Case had successfully avoided Legend as much as possible since boarding the *Renegade*. They had only flown twice at the same time in testing/training exercises. In one, they worked together, with the Furies taking the lead and the Hell Flyers in a support role. Hard Case, though his squad was the better group of pilots (in his opinion), didn't make a fuss about being in a support role for a training exercise. He believed that a smart man knew when to choose his battles. So, he had remained quiet and let his flying do the talking for him.

The two groups had flown just one full squadron dogfight. It had been the most difficult challenge of all three days. Both six-ship squads had taken off from the *Renegade* and flown fifty thousand kilometers in opposite directions before a signal from the Arodoni ship started the exercise.

"They'll come straight at us," Hard Case said. "We will stay in pairs."

"Is that a good idea?" Animal asked. "They could hit us from two directions."

"Discipline always beats selfish flying," Hard Case insisted. "Bishop and Diamond, circle wide to port. Animal and Indigo, you swing wide to starboard. Aspen and I will stay here and draw them in."

"Copy that," Diamond said.

"See you on the flip side," Indigo added.

Their ships had gone off at right angles. Hard Case used his Raptor's radar to keep tabs on the incoming ships. They were in a loose formation. He thought it was sloppy. They were like children racing to be the first to the swing set at recess.

"What's our plan, Hard Case?" Aspen asked.

"When they reach fifty thousand klicks, we go up," he said. "Gravity drive at forty percent power. When they make the turn, we make the flip."

It had gone according to plan. The Furies pushed in, swarming toward Hard Case. It was almost as if Legend had urged his squad to take Hard Case out above all other priorities. But flying in space wasn't like flying in atmosphere. As he and Aspen sped through space, they used their thrusters to flip their ships around, flying backward, with the infrared training lasers facing back at their pursuers.

The initial volleys had taken down two of the Furies. Hard Case lost Aspen, but their tactic scattered the remaining four flyers, and the pairs sent into flanking position each took out a ship. That left the squadrons at two versus five. Hard Case sent Animal and Indigo chasing Heimdall, while he joined Bishop and Diamond in pursuing Legend.

Commander Mathias lived up to his name and turned the tables on the trio facing him. He used Heimdall to disrupt their pursuit. The two remaining Furies flew past each other, their ships passing less than a kilometer from one another. Heimdall took down Bishop in the process, but Hard Case finished him. On the opposite side, Legend took out Animal. That left Hard Case, Indigo, and Diamond. They chased Legend relentlessly. He survived longer than he should have. Had Hard Case adopted his enemy's tactics and sacrificed one of his squad to catch Legend, it might have ended quicker, but that wasn't Justin's way. He wouldn't put his people in danger needlessly. Even though the exercise wasn't real, Hard Case was treating it as such.

It was some of the best flying ever seen, Justin was sure of that. And it gave him the chance to utilize Diamond and Indigo in a wing formation that hemmed Legend in. After that, it was only a matter of time before the Furies' commander made a mistake. It was a big victory for his squad and he thought that it proved disciplined flying was superior to going alone, but he had no illusions that Legend would see things that way.

When Hard Case reached the Ward Room, he was surprised by the number of people inside. The Captain rarely held dinners for all the senior officers. Captain Darius preferred work over pomp and circumstance. Hard Case fixed himself a cup of coffee and found his seat, which had been assigned. There were pastries on a platter in the center of the table that no one touched. On any other SDF ship, those confections would be made from protein powder and artificial sweeteners. They would taste like bad imitations, too. On the *Renegade,* the culinary specialists had a wide range of ingredients from crops grown in the ship's own green space. Flour, or at least an alien form of it, was used to bake actual deserts and pastries. Still, Hard Case tried to refrain from sweets. He didn't even add sugar to his coffee, which was stout enough to keep him awake, although not tasty enough to make him drink too much.

He was seated beside Legend. They hadn't spoken since the combat training exercise and proximity didn't change that. Hard Case sat down, Legend ignored him and Hard Case followed suit. Instead of talking, he did his best to identify every person in the room. He knew Commander Nash and Major Steel. Although they hadn't spoken since his brief introduction a few days prior, he also recognized Lieutenants Ramos, Stanislaus and Nurek. But there were new faces as well and one that was hard not to stare at was the new doctor. She sat in the corner, not at the table with the rest of the officers. Likewise, a big man in Marine fatigues sat beside Major Steel. Hard Case didn't recognize the big man's rank.

When Captain Darius entered the Ward Room, he was all business and the quiet murmuring of the officers died down immediately.

"Good, you're all here," Darius said, moving to the head of the table and setting down his data pad. "I want to begin by reminding everyone that this meeting is being monitored by GIGI, who will add input as needed."

"Thank you, Captain Darius," a female voice said. It came into the room through hidden speakers. Hard Case forced himself not to glance at Legend. He had no idea who GIGI was or why she was listening in to the planning meeting, but if that's what Captain Darius wanted, so be it.

"We are ready to begin what may be the most important mission we have yet undertaken," Darius said. He tapped an icon on the table controls, and five planets appeared in the air over it. "These are the five worlds that make up the Prime Council," he said. "One is Ashi, and while striking it could be significant, I'm removing it from consideration."

"Why is that, Captain?" Nash asked. "If we could hit the Ashi and take down their home world, that seems relevant."

"It is not our goal to destroy a planet," Darius said. "Or to devastate any population. We will go in, make targeted strikes against the Imperium and illustrate both our military superiority and the values that make us different from the Ashi. This is a campaign for hearts and minds, not solely to destroy. That said, we are left with four worlds to choose from."

"Are these all the worlds in the Core sector?" Stanislaus asked.

"No, there are dozens of inhabited systems in the Core sector of space, but these four are the heart of the Imperium, with special benefits including a representative on the Prime Council. To that end, let me ask Nurek, our Information Officer, to expand a little bit about the Council."

Nurek stood up. He was a tall, skinny alien with a tall head that narrowed as it rose above his eyes and ended in a rounded point.

There was no hair on his head. His skin was gray and did not appear to be soft. Hard Case had no clue how old the alien might be, but he didn't look young.

"The Prime Council is the heart of the Imperium bureaucracy. Their responsibility is bringing the Emperor's commands to fruition. There is at least one Imperium governor on every inhabited world. They take orders directly from the Prime Council. Taxes, laws, any manner of whim passed down from the Emperor are then facilitated by the Council, through the governors and bureaucratic staff."

"What does taking one of these planets off the board do for our purposes?" Vivian Ramos asked.

"That's an excellent question," Darius said. "Our task thus far has been to disrupt the Imperium, specifically their military. Nurek was part of a secret group that fomented rebellion when we began pushing back against the Ashi. To date, over a hundred worlds have risen and deposed their Imperium overlords. We have personally freed over fifty worlds. But there are hundreds more, and the Ashi has hundreds, possibly thousands of warships. We can't hope to defeat them in a direct confrontation, at least not alone. That's why we've been hitting their forces on systems where they have a smaller presence. But if we hope to see progress in this conflict, we need more worlds to disrupt and fight back. That's our goal for hitting the core planets. We want to light a flame that will burn the Imperium down.

"It should also give us an opportunity to gather some important intelligence on the state of the Ashi forces. They are the sole military of the Imperium. Other planets or races aren't allowed to have firearms. The planets outside the core systems aren't allowed to have defenses. The Ashi presence in the system was to be their defense should they be attacked. And we all know how that works; the defensive force also becomes the oppressor. Those worlds and their intelligent species had no way to fight back until we got involved. It is my hope that we can show ourselves to be a match for the Ashi militarily, but also less savage than what they've known."

"Disruption, chaos and low morale are vital ingredients in fomenting rebellion," GIGI chimed in.

Hard Case raised a hand and Darius looked over at him. "Commander?"

"I know I'm new and, trust me, my squadron is fully on board with the plans we're making, but can I ask why the Ashi are so bad?"

Darius looked over at Nurek. "Your people abolished slavery long ago. It was a racist, demeaning practice, as I'm sure you would agree. But it is at the heart of the Imperium. The Ashi view themselves as the supreme race in the galaxy. They rule but have no concern for the well-being of the planets or people they have conquered. Likewise, the planets of the Prime Council banded together with the Ashi and have for centuries grown rich off the taxes, resources and slavery of the worlds they claim to rule over. Everything of value from around the galaxy, including intelligent, living beings, flows into the Core sector. Almost nothing flows out. There are no social services for the betterment of the masses. No help to worlds which have been recklessly mined or stripped of vital resources. Many are forced to produce goods for the large populations of the Core worlds, with no consideration for the safety of the people on those worlds or of the damage the pollution is doing to those planets. Then there are the infractions. A missed quota, be it of goods or some other tax, is repaid with forced slavery, or in some cases, military consequences. Many thriving worlds have been devastated by orbital bombardments that not only kill millions but leave the world poisoned for hundreds of cycles. In some cases, those planets will never be habitable again."

"We've seen some of that," Darius said. "I'd like to ask Sergeant Major Hugo McManus to share his experience on Libertine."

The big man stiffened, but Major Steel gave him a reassuring squeeze on the Marine's muscular shoulder. It was at that point that Hard Case realized it was the same Marine who had carried the wounded Lieutenant from where she was injured all the way to the Med Bay, several kilometers distant, in his arms, at a run. That was a feat the ship was still marveling over.

"As most of you know, Libertine was a hot world," he said in an even voice. "There were settlements on the north and south polar regions. The Ashi arrived in the system with no warning and bombed the poles with kinetic weapons from orbit."

"My God," the doctor in the corner said softly.

"And what was the outcome for the planet, Sergeant Major?"

"Cataclysmic," he responded. "The bombing set off a cooling

cycle that pushed the planet toward an ice age. Not only that, but it triggered seismic changes to the crust that radically altered the terrain. Huge deserts of sand were washed away in torrential storms. The mud flows carved canyons and unlocked underground cisterns of water that flooded the surface. There were volcanic eruptions. It killed the colonists and caused mass extinction to the entire planet."

He sat back, the muscles in his jaws flexing visibly. Hard Case couldn't tell if he was embarrassed by being asked to speak or if the memory of what happened on Libertine pained him.

"Thank you, Sergeant. I know it isn't easy for you to talk about what happened on Libertine. For those of you who do not know Sergeant Major Hugo McManus, he courageously volunteered to stay behind in the Libertine system when we were returning to Sol and the battle of Saturn. I asked him to join us today because he has valuable experience that will be helpful in making decisions."

"It's my hope that we can hit three, if not four, of the prime worlds, and if we're lucky, a few more planets in the Core sector before we need to fall back."

Hard Case thought the Captain's plan was ambitious. Not just because of the number of worlds he wanted to target ... and because there was no place to fall back to. There was no safe harbor in the galaxy, no reinforcements. Hard Case knew that the SDF was building remotely operated defensive systems. The idea was to place them in strategic locations to defend the Sol system and all of humanity from any invading force. But the power requirements were difficult to achieve. They had the Arodoni tech, yet rumors were rampant that the SDF research and development teams were scrambling to reverse engineer the technology. The materials needed to build the Arodoni power cores were rare in the Sol system and working with them was difficult to achieve. It seemed that other devices needed to be made in order to manufacture the power cores, which in turn were needed to run the defensive systems. On top of that, some officials were arguing that eighteen billion souls on Earth were in need of cheap, abundant power and that providing it for them should be the priority. All that added up to the fact that the *Renegade* would have no help from the Sol system.

"Why not just bomb those planets from orbit?" Commander

Mathias Elder proposed. "Why take the time and the risk of invasion. We could wipe the slate clean and start again."

Several people around the table looked down. Legend was stating the unpopular opinion that everyone had entertained at least to some degree.

"You would wipe out entire worlds?" the doctor asked in a soft voice from the far side of the room.

"They've done it," Legend said. "Let them get a taste of their own medicine. Bomb the five worlds that make up the Prime Council and you'll achieve your aims in one grand stroke."

"And kill millions of innocent lives in the process," Commander Nash said.

"If what Nurek says is true, then they aren't innocent," Legend pushed back. "They're complicit."

"What you're proposing has merit," Captain Darius said. "And the truth is, we've considered that course of action. But where I believe it breaks down is in gaining the favor of the worlds that join us in fighting back. If we simply nuke the Imperium, the galaxy will fall into a state of chaos. We might win the battle, but we would not win the war."

"What does winning the war entail?" Alex Stanislaus asked. "Us taking the Ashi's place?"

"Governments have pushed to build democracies in the past and failed miserably," Vivian Ramos pointed out. "If we push the Imperium out, it doesn't mean that a dozen more tyrants won't rise up to fill that void."

"Even us," the doctor said quietly.

"That is beyond the scope of this mission," Darius said. "We will encourage from a position of strength, but ultimately, what nations or worlds do once freedom has been won is up to them. We are fighting for the chance for humanity to expand into the galaxy. We want the freedom to colonize new worlds and trade with inhabited planets. But we won't bend the knee to the Ashi or any other species in the galaxy. The *Renegade* is a beautiful example of how species can come together and create something unique."

"But the *Renegade* is ruled by a single person," Legend said.

That left everyone quiet for a moment. It was a difficult point of contention. The *Renegade* worked because Captain Darius encouraged cooperation and friendship. But the vessel was occupied mostly by humans who were part of a military structure that gave just one man total power over what they did. It was not the example for a free galaxy.

"The point," Darius continued after a moment's thought, "is that where freedom is allowed to flourish, people of any race can thrive. There is no single right way to accomplish the task. It is not up to any of us in the long run. Our mission is to stop the Ashi from ever returning to the Sol system. The best way to do that is to encourage planets across the galaxy to join our fight. And we've come to a point in time when we have the opportunity to strike what I believe will be a decisive blow to the Imperium's rule."

"Show these highly populated worlds that the Ashi isn't as all-powerful as they've been led to believe," Major Steel said.

"And let their greed take over," Pete Best said.

"There is no peaceful way to ensure humanity's safety," Darius said. "We could send diplomats to the Imperium, but if we insist on remaining neutral, they will come and conquer us. If we agree to join their empire, it will mean taxation, turning over our weapons, including the entire SDF fleet, and opening ourselves to slavery."

"No," Commander Nash said. "We can't let that happen."

"We are the only ship that stands between the Ashi and humanity," Darius said. "It is my intention to keep the fight on their territory and to stir up as much dissent as we can. We have no other options. The enemy knows we exist and where. The time for humanity to remain tucked away in the Sol system is over."

"Which planet do we target first?" Remmy Steel asked.

"That's an excellent question, and what we are here to decide. Lieutenant Nurek, what can you tell us about these worlds?"

CHAPTER 33

ALL THE ATTENTION shifted from Darius to the holograms of the planets hovering over the table. He didn't mind. In fact, he was glad for the pushback and questions. They were the same ideas that he had wrestled with for over a month. But he knew deep down inside that it was time for action. Liberating systems on the fringe of the galaxy, and sharing the Arodoni technology was all fine and good, but there was a war coming. There would be no hiding from the Ashi. They were in a state of transition, therefore, Darius needed to hit them hard and fast to keep them from regaining their full strength. Otherwise, nothing the *Renegade* accomplished would last.

Nurek cleared his narrow throat and began talking.

"I think it might be wise to eliminate Tsingah from consideration," he said. "As it is mostly a water world, I believe it would offer the most obstacles to our goals."

Darius hit an icon, and the planet of Tsingah shrank down much smaller than the other three.

"That leaves Wesset, Hurz and Foxill," Nurek continued. "Of those three, Wesset is the largest planet. It has a population of about sixty billion Wessians. Much of their world is open wilderness, which is still the preferred habitat of that race, but there are a few major cities. Drafton is the capital, with the Representative's Mansion and a sprawling Imperium compound."

"What about defenses?" Commander Kase asked.

"Walls around the compound, of course," Nurek said. "There is what the Ashi call an Illustrious Guard. But it's actually more of a way to remind the populace of their superior might. It's a posh posting for Ashi, who have merited the favor of the Emperor, or as a reward for some political favor by the Khan. On each of the worlds that make up the Prime Council, the governor of that world is one of their own race. A Wessian holds that office on Wesset, of course, but the Ashi of the Illustrious Guard are the real power in the city. They see themselves as above the law, doing whatever they like, hurting whoever gets in their way."

"Sounds fantastic," Nash said. "A real Cosmopolitan paradise."

"Guns?" Remmy asked.

"The Illustrious guards have weapons, but typically carry only their Tashika fighting knives."

Hugo grunted, but didn't add anything to the conversation.

"Do we know anything about orbital defenses?" Captain Darius asked.

"I do not," Nurek said.

"GIGI?"

"Two thousand years ago, the Core worlds proposed to build a series of system defenses. My records show that the legislation was passed, but the actual details of the proposal were not public knowledge. And there is no record of said defenses being dismantled."

"So, there's gotta be something," Darius said.

"Two thousand years is a long time to keep something running," Nash said.

"Especially in the cold of outer space," Alex Stanislaus added.

"We have to prepare for them in any case," Darius continued. "How many hyperspace portals are there?"

Vivian Ramos picked up her data pad. "That's a good question."

"Twelve," GIGI replied.

"That's a lot of portals to defend," Pete Best said. "Why so many in one system?"

Vivian knew the answer to that question. "The hyperspace lanes are like a spider web," she explained. "The closer you get to the center, the more lanes converge."

"Makes sense," Commander Nash said.

"With that many portals, we could pre-calculate a jump into one of the closest two, with an escape vector if we were forced to flee immediately," Darius said. "Any chance the locals would rise against us?"

Nurek answered. "The Wessians can be savage, but they have no history of armed resistance to the Imperium."

"Savage how?" Darius asked.

"They are cruel, merciless overlords," Nurek said. "Worlds controlled by the Wessians are frightening places for those without guaranteed rights from the Imperium."

"Let's move on," Darius said. "What's next?"

"Hurz," Nurek said.

Darius worked the table controls, and a bright, glistening world grew a bit larger than the others on the hologram over the table.

"It's a tech-savvy world. One of the largest consumer markets in the Core. The Hurzians are fabulously wealthy, with banking interests on hundreds of worlds."

The hologram of the city began to zoom closer to the planet. The globe disappeared as the image continued zooming down. It eventually stopped with a view of a massive city. There were huge skyscrapers throughout the city, some connected by bridges, others moved in a constant swaying motion. At ground level, rivers and streams were flowing around walkways where creatures that looked surprisingly like ladybugs drifted around on repulser-driven seats.

"Looks a bit off," Nash said.

"The Hurzians own more slaves than any other planet. The Market is here, next to the Imperium HQ building. It is also where the authorized slave industry is located. And everything in the city is connected. Most food is imported and there are a variety of cultures that thrive on the world."

"Defenses?"

"None that I know of," Nurek said.

"No garrison?" Darius asked.

"Not on world," Nurek said. "I believe there may be a military space station, perhaps even a refitting station. Hurz has more inter-stellar traffic and space stations than any other world in the galaxy. It's a major import center."

"It might be easier to get into the system without raising suspi-cion," Pete Best suggested.

"But harder to hit without civilian casualties," Darius said. "Plus, if there is a military installation, it could have a much larger defense force than Wesset."

"What about the last world?" Commander Nash asked.

"Foxill is a hot world," Nurek said. "The surface temperatures in the daytime hours are deadly to most species."

"We could handle it in full armor," Remmy pointed out.

"And the Foxills?" Darius asked.

"They are a subterranean species," Nurek said. "I have never been on their world. What I know is limited. They have vast, underground cities. The Ashi detest such terrain. Their large stature makes enclosed spaces difficult to navigate."

"Are they spiders?" Vivian asked as images of the Foxills appeared beside the hologram of their world.

They were four-legged beings, with thin, almost fragile-looking legs, bulbous bodies, and tall, pointed heads. Darius thought that their heads must be some form of defensive weapon; it was so large. It looked like a thorn.

"We would have to land on the surface and go down inside the caverns," Remmy said.

"Do they have a capital?"

"Yes," Nurek said. "Forcil in the Paddius sector. Their Prime Council Representative nests there."

"Defenses?"

"Traditionally, when the Foxills were endangered, they went deeper underground. There are stories of intruders getting lost in the deep tunnels underground."

"My data shows the Foxills were once a militant race, although not known for weapons development," GIGI spoke up. "They do have a long tradition of personal combat that was still active when my programming was written."

"Combat?" Darius asked.

"Pit fighting," Nurek said. "I have never witnessed it. The Ashi disdain any martial skills other than their own."

"What about system defenses?"

"Unknown," Nurek said.

Darius leaned back in his seat and steepled his fingers together in thought. The rest of the officers waited to hear his opinion. When he spoke, he looked straight at Major Steel.

"My gut says Wesset," he said.

"I concur," Remmy spoke up. "The cities being spread out will allow us to focus on one place, with good warning if something is brought to bear against us from outside the combat zone."

"Any objections?"

No one spoke. Darius understood the heaviness of the moment. They were discussing the invasion of a sovereign planet. In war, people died. But to be part of orchestrating a plan to kill intelligent beings was difficult to accept. He glanced over at Doctor Victoria Holt. She looked pale but gave him a reassuring nod.

"Alright then," Darius said. "Lieutenant Ramos, please begin formulating the best route in and out of the system. If there are multiple portals, please include contingency plans."

"Aye, Captain. I'll get the report to you ASAP."

"Excellent. Once we reach the system, given that we aren't pushed right back out by their defenses, we will immediately launch drones to help deal with weapons installations and any Ashi forces in the area. I want both fighter squadrons on standby and ready to launch on my command. If we can get close enough, we'll formulate an attack plan on the planet's capital. The Marines will be armed and ready to make planetfall and mop up after the air attack. All Imperium personnel are to be eliminated, but do your best not to have any more civilian casualties than absolutely necessary. We want to send a message with this first attack and we may not get another chance like this."

"Copy that," Major Steel responded.

"Lieutenant Nurek, you and your information specialists will deliver messages encouraging the populace to turn their back on the Imperium. I also want news of this attack sent to the planets in your network. From there, it can spread through the galaxy."

The alien officer gave a bow in recognition of the order.

"Once our preparations for the attack on Wesset are finalized, we'll begin. Once we're under way we'll prepare to attack Hurz and then Foxill, but with contingency plans in case the Ashi come against us in force. Speed is our greatest asset in this invasion. We will continue attacking the Core worlds until the Ashi return. If all goes well, the populace of these primary worlds will insist on greater protection, limiting what the Ashi fleet is capable of. At all times, we must be prepared for imminent combat on all fronts. Get your people prepared. There is no going back. Once we attack Wesset, the Ashi will understand that we are not a trivial species and we are not going away."

"As it should be," Commander Nash said.

"You all have your orders. Complete any remaining tasks and prepare for war."

CHAPTER 34

WORD TRAVELED FAST through the ship. War meant something different to everyone. For Saul Mane, it meant less traffic in the pub and more time with Zaya in the workshop. That's what they had taken to calling the distillery in the storage space two compartments behind the Pub. There were times in life when fortune smiled on a person. For Saul, it had happened when he hired Zaya. He had thought she would just be a floater, someone to work the slow shifts when tips weren't very good. Instead, he had found an eager and willing addition to his team. Her improvements on his distillery design had improved the project while making it more functional and less expensive to build.

For Zaya, war meant fear. Her hours in the pub had been cut back. She worked only the lunch hours, clocking out before happy hour. It was boring yet simple work. What she really enjoyed was building the distillery. They already had the basics laid out. The Mash Tun and Lauter Tun were finished. The boiler was in place, but still needed the heating elements underneath. The Whirlpool was all laid out and ready for assembly, but first, they planned to install heat exchangers to cool the wort, as well as pumps to move the liquids from one stage to the next through the copper piping. There was a fermentation tank, too, although that needed no assembly. In a few more days, it would all be complete and she wasn't quite sure what she would do then. For Zaya, it wasn't about earning enough money, but rather staying busy. When she had free time, she felt restless.

Hugo was always busy. He had celebrated his promotion with her, but it had kept him busy from morning until late evening. She understood that was his job and, unlike hers, he had no real say in what schedule he kept. In her mind, the Space Marines were a lot like slavery. Officers were akin to overseers telling the enlisted personnel where they could live, what jobs they had to do and even when they could eat. She knew it wasn't the same, but it seemed a bit too familiar for her. The worst part was that she found herself with time alone.

As fortune would have it, another shopkeeper named Bill Hoffman needed help. He had a tiny storefront all the way up on Lamda level. It was a retail shop that sold drone parts and made most of its money fixing broken race drones. Of course, the drones in Bill's shop were nothing like the military drones. They were small units, a little larger than both of her hands held side by side. They consisted of four horizontal propellers, a video camera the size of her pinky, and the rest was custom accessories from fins to air cowlings. She had never tinkered with one before. When she met Bill, who had been told about Zaya by Saul Mane, he gave her a drone that didn't work. She sat down in his tiny workshop that was full of drone parts and miniature tools and said that if she could fix it in less than an hour, she could have a job.

She repaired the drone in just over twelve minutes. Bill hired her on the spot. He took care of retail and worked on repairs as time permitted. Zaya could set her schedule, coming in and fixing drones whenever she had free time. But war meant fewer repairs, too, so she and Bill began building refurbished drones to sell in the shop. Zaya enjoyed the freedom to create, but nothing could alleviate the stress she felt.

War meant that Hugo was going away. War meant Hugo would be in danger. War meant the *Renegade* could be in danger. War meant that she could die. It was a lot for her to deal with on her own. Zaya had never been taught how to deal with her feelings. She had learned to suppress what she felt and show no weakness. Yet she was beginning to see that denying her feelings was what nearly cost her a relationship with Hugo. Neither of them was very good about opening up. The way she felt about his duty, and the danger of war, was eating her up inside.

On the other side of the ship, down in the Hell Flyers' briefing room, Commander Kase was busy giving his squad their orders.

"So, what you're saying is, we have no idea what we'll be up against," Indigo said.

"Oh, brother," Animal added. "Some things never change."

"That's not necessarily true," Hard Case argued. "We can deduce some things."

"Such as?" Aspen asked.

"For one thing, these first missions will almost certainly be mainly focused on atmosphere. There is no expectation for a large Ashi presence around the Core worlds."

"No dogfights in space?" Animal complained. "That's the best part, man."

"Let him finish," Bishop urged.

"The other thing we can most likely count on is the use of laser weapons. It doesn't seem like the Ashi use much else. Lasers and kinetic bombs."

"Rods of the gods! That's cool," Animal declared.

"Not if you're on the receiving end," Diamond told him.

"Well, the really bad thing is that they use heavy metals," Hard Case said. "That material gets pulverized as you might expect and spreads far and wide."

"Poisoning everything it touches," Aspen said. "These aliens are terrible for the environment."

"But they don't use projectiles," Hard Case said. "No bullets or missiles, just laser weapons."

"Makes sense," Indigo said. "Lasers don't require you to make, store and supply ammunition."

"Yeah, but lasers run hot," Bishop said. "Burn through a lot of power."

"The ones on our Raptors don't," Animal said.

"That's because space is so cold," Diamond told him. "And we have dark matter energy converters that constantly regenerate power for our use."

"It won't be as efficient in an atmosphere where dark matter is less prevalent," Hard Case reminded them. "And our lasers will get hotter there, too. Which is why our Raptors will be equipped with air-to-ground missiles, ten per fighter."

"Are we expecting a lot of resistance?" Aspen asked.

"It can't be much once we break atmo," Hard Case said. "There aren't a lot of cities on Wesset, which is heavily agrarian. My guess is there will be defenses around the city, but we should be able to target those and take them out."

"What about air defense?" Diamond asked. "Will they put fighters in the air?"

"Again, it's not certain, but from what I've heard about the Imperium, only the Ashi are allowed to have weapons, including those for planetary defense. I'm guessing we won't have to worry about bogies in the air. Just laser batteries and hopefully our shields will nullify them until we take them out."

"Sounds too easy," Animal said.

"Never is," Bishop replied.

"Why so much speculation?" Aspen asked. "Why not send in a reconnaissance team and get some solid intel?"

"Because we don't have the resources," Hard Case said. "It's a planet full of aliens. I saw images of them. They look sort of like Minotaurs, except with the head of a horse and furry bodies."

"What?" Animal asked.

"Minotaurs, you know, Greek mythology," Indigo said.

"How should I know Greek mythology. I went to public school," Animal declared.

"It shows," Diamond replied.

There were times when Hard Case felt his squad was like a schoolroom of hyperactive children.

"So we wouldn't blend in, I get that," Aspen said. "But surely they aren't the only race on that planet, not if it's as important as everyone says."

"All I know is what I'm told," Hard Case said. "And that is for us to be ready. As in suited up, in our fighters, by the time we drop out of hyperspace."

"When will that be?" Bishop asked.

"I'm waiting to find out right now," he said.

On the Bridge, Vivian Ramos had considered all the possible entry points to the Wesset system. There were several ways to proceed. The fastest and most distant portal would put them ten hours from the planet once they reached the system. That's what Captain Darius wanted. Time to maneuver and check out the system. It would be better to drop in close if they had reliable intelligence, but they didn't, so they would take their time approaching the planet.

"Course set for the Wesset system," Vivian said.

"Very good, Lieutenant. Alex, get us underway."

"Aye, Captain, engaging the main engines now."

"Lieutenant Best, how do our sonic shields look?"

"Full power, Captain," Pete Best said. "Everything is in order."

"Projectiles in the receiving deck?" Darius asked, referring to the lower portion of the open mouth of the ship. It was made to draw in raw materials using a gravity beam. Those materials, be it asteroids or space debris, even other ships, could then be sent through the refiner, which would then break matter down into its separate components. A space rock could be collected that might have any number of minerals, from iron to lithium, or uranium, even gold. Those materials were then used to manufacture goods for the ship. Even water - or gas - could be collected. It was an incredibly efficient system. But the same gravity beam that pulled goods in could be reversed to shoot things out. The crew had used that method to fire warheads from the SDF *Jericho* after the ship sustained damage that kept the four massive laser cannons from operating.

"Yes, sir, we have a variety of projectiles. Weapons specialists are on site to load them into the firing position as needed, Captain."

"Outstanding," Darius said. "ETA for hyperspace transition?"

"Twenty-one minutes, Captain," Vivian Ramos said.

"Time in hyperspace?"

"Fourteen hours, nine minutes, Captain."

Darius tapped the information into a message that went out to all the department heads. In less than fifteen hours, the *Renegade* would be in enemy territory.

At the Med Bay, Remmy walked in to find Laila up talking with Doctor Vicky. The good doctor seemed nervous. Her hair was a bit askew in the ponytail she normally kept very tight and neat. And she seemed pale to Remmy.

"You okay?" he asked.

"Fine," Laila said.

"I was talking to Doctor Vicky," he said.

"Me? Oh, I'm very well, thank you, Major. I just, well... it's no secret. I'm a bit frightened. There, I've said it out loud. I'm afraid and there's nothing I can do about it."

"I was telling her to stay busy," Laila said.

"Good advice," Remmy said.

"Easy for you both to say," the doctor replied. "I have no patients. Everything I do is preparing to help patients who will be wounded or injured in the invasion. Which means, everything I think about keeps my mind on what's coming."

"I heard you were on Mars," Remmy said. "During the uprising."

"I was," she said. "Terrified then, too. But at least the insurgents knew better than to target the hospital. I'm not so lucky on this trip."

"Do you regret volunteering?" Laila asked.

The two women had gotten to know each other well. After her first full night and day of light therapy, Laila McPherson was up walking. After the second night and day, she was keeping Doctor Holt company at one of the desks. Her therapies were over and all that remained were a week of no activity, followed by three weeks of physical therapy. Remmy knew the week of rest would be harder on Laila than anything that followed.

"No," Victoria said. "This is where I want to be, but it feels strange. We have no control over what's going to happen. We might come out of hyperspace and be vaporized."

"At least we'd never know what hit us," Remmy said.

"That is not the least bit reassuring," she said.

"How do you normally deal with stress?" Laila asked.

"Exercise, but running on an elliptical and staring at a vid screen just doesn't seem to be helping much lately."

"Come down to Grunt Country," Remmy said. "We've got a track around Hangar A that's five kilometers long."

"Really? I can use it?"

"Any time you want," he said.

"As long as you don't mind a bunch of Marines gawking at you," Laila said. "You might want to wear a baggy sweat suit."

"I don't have one," Victoria said. "Athletic attire on Earth is all spandex and compression wear."

"Buy some," Remmy said. "Shop in the men's section."

"I could go with you," Laila suggested.

"No, you go home. Major, take her home and make her stay there for the next seven days. And don't go doing PT, Lieutenant. Your wounds are closed, but they're still weak. If you start doing sit-ups, they could rupture. You don't want a hernia, trust me."

Laila begrudgingly got into a chair with a mini-repulser on the bottom. When activated, it lifted the chair about six inches and allowed someone to push it around easily, even with an adult in the seat.

"This is humiliating," Laila complained.

"Doctor's orders," Remmy replied.

"I don't know why I can't walk. I've been up walking for two days now."

"Walking in the Med Bay," he said. "Not walking four kilometers and up four stories. Trust me, you want the floaty chair."

"Since when did you become such a stickler for rules?" she continued. "As I recall, you broke several regulations just to declare your feelings for me."

"I did," Remmy said. "Don't regret it either."

"How much time do we have?"

"About fourteen hours," Remmy said. "We just made the transition into hyperspace."

"That gives us what, eight, nine hours tops before you have to go and make sure the platoons are ready?"

"That's right," he said. "Wish it was more."

"I don't," she said. "We'll sleep at my place. You need to rest. There's no telling when you'll get another full night's sleep."

He leaned forward and kissed her on top of her head.

"I gotta be the luckiest SOB on this ship," he said.

"You got that right," Laila replied. "And just remember, I know you better than anyone else."

"Okay," he said, not sure what she was driving at.

"So, don't go being a hero tomorrow," she warned. "You already got the Medal of Honor, so let someone else be the hero for a change. Major's aren't supposed to be in the fighting."

He didn't respond. She was right, but it didn't sit well with him. He wasn't a lead-from-the-rear type person. But he was an officer and that meant doing things differently. Still, he couldn't make her any promises.

"Do you hear me, Major? No heroics."

"I hear you. Some habits die hard, babe."

"Just so you don't die," she said softly. "That's all I care about."

As they made their way through the Grand Concourse, Hugo was down in Grunt Country cleaning his Ambrose Hill XOR rifle. It was an over-under heavy weapon that fired Shock-Wave explosive rounds on the upper and grenades from the lower. He had it broken down and was carefully inspecting each part. No one bothered him. Most of the other Marines were doing similar tasks: checking weapons, cleaning armor, making sure their battle helmets were fully charged and going through their packs.

Hugo was happy to be among his people. His promotion hadn't really changed much. He gave orders, not to the Marine grunts, but to the Marine officers. And not his orders, but Remmy's. He was a glorified gopher with a strange rank he wasn't quite comfortable with. But in the simulated training exercises, which he had done with every platoon, he basically shared the orders Remmy had given him. Twice, the Lieutenants had asked for clarification and he had been able to give it to them. Then, his gopher job done, he acted as a reserve for the platoons. Whatever squad or fire team needed help, he came and pitched in. That only made him more of a hero in their eyes.

But war meant something to everyone. For Hugo, in the past, it had always meant an opportunity to do the one thing he was really good at. Hugo could do things. Anyone could sweep a floor or carry equipment. For most people, there was only a handful of things they were really good at. Things that combined both a passion and skill were rare, or at least, most people never put theirs to use. Hugo felt that he was lucky that he had found what he loved to do. It was a bit strange that fighting was something he enjoyed so much, yet he couldn't deny that fact. The strategy, the adrenaline, the fear and the pressure not to fail, all combined into a heady mixture that was as close to joy as Hugo understood. It didn't hurt that he was really good at war. Shooting was second nature to Hugo. Understanding ground tactics clicked in his brain the way some people were good at math or playing an instrument. You could drop him on a battlefield and, within seconds, he knew what the enemy would do and what he needed to do to counter it.

Still, war had inherent risks too. He would soon be putting his life on the line. All the Marines would be; that was just part of their job. They went where they were told and fought who they were told to fight. Hugo would do his part. He had fought the Ashi before and he was ready to do it again. They were huge, muscular aliens that stood over thirteen feet tall. But they bled and died just like a human did. To Hugo, that was all that mattered. They were headed to war and, whatever came, he would be ready for it.

CHAPTER 35

DARIUS SAVORED the moment as he stepped onto the Bridge. The fifteen hours since his report to the senior officers of their timeline had passed quickly. All the Bridge officers were at their stations and he knew they had all gotten six full hours of time away; some had even more. Whether they spent that time sleeping or just worrying about what was ahead, he couldn't say, but they were given the chance.

He had slept five full hours, which was as much as he could force himself to rest in one block while he was officially on duty. Furthermore, he didn't need coffee to keep him awake either. He had taken a long walk after his rest, then finished with a very hot shower. The hot water on the *Renegade* was a perk he allowed himself to enjoy.

Washed clean, shaved and ready to lead his people into battle, Captain Zeke Darius returned to the Bridge.

"I hope everyone got some rest," he said as he approached his seat. "Let's have a timer on the holo-projector, Lieutenant Ramos."

"Aye, Captain, projecting time until transition," she said.

There were less than ten minutes left. And he could feel the tension rising around him.

"I want you all to consider that we've done this many times," Darius said. "The *Renegade* and our crew has always been up to the challenge. We are fully staffed, with more weapons and fighting capability than ever before. Let's not let our nerves get the best of us."

There were nods around the room. Darius was glad to have Commander Nash to his right at the Executive Officer's console. Most of the time, Nash was in the Admin Center, where he could direct the crew of the ship more effectively. But every crew member was at their stations and ready for action, so the XO's place was on the Bridge with the other senior officers.

"Six minutes until transition," Vivian Ramos said.

"Do we have multiple options for getting out of the system if need be?" Darius asked.

"Aye, Captain, all escape vectors and hyperspace routes are mapped and saved. We can use the information at a moment's notice."

"Very good," Darius said. "Let's check in with the fighter squadrons."

To his right, Henry Nash spoke up. "Commander Kase, sir, with the Hell Flyers."

"Hard Case, what's your status?"

"We are locked and loaded, Captain. Hell Flyers are ready to go, sir."

"Very good," Darius said. "And the Furies?"

"Commander Elder, sir," Nash said.

Darius knew the names of his people and he didn't need a reminder, but there were still protocols to be observed. Darius felt that they were outdated, although he didn't mind a little tradition, especially if it helped set his people at ease.

"Legend, what is your status?"

"We are manning our Raptors, per your orders, Captain," Mathias Elder said.

"Very well, stand by for permission to launch," Darius said. "He tapped a few icons on his seat's comlink control pad. "Major Steel, what is your status?"

"Marines are ready," Remmy said. "We can be on our shuttles and ready to fly in sixty seconds."

"Outstanding," Darius said. He considered contacting Dr. Holt, but then decided he didn't need any information from the Med Bay and certainly didn't want to send the wrong message. He had resolved to treat Dr. Victoria Holt like any other officer on the ship and he vowed once again to stick to his decision.

"Three minutes until transition," Vivian Ramos said.

"Alright, it's time," Darius said. "Commander Nash, put us at Orange Alert status."

"Aye, Captain, Orange Alert status."

"I want all shops and venues locked down. All civilians should report to their volunteer safety areas."

It was unusual to have civilians on an SDF ship. Darius had designated various rooms as volunteer safety areas and every civilian was assigned duties for which they could be called upon to help with. Most were simple, if vital, roles such as fire patrol and medical volunteers. Others with more experience, and most of the civilians on the *Renegade* were former SDF or Space Marine veterans, were assigned to the vital areas of the ship. But they would all stay in the volunteer safety areas until called upon. He didn't want people roaming around on the ship during a battle. Most especially, they certainly couldn't afford for some poor, misguided soul to sabotage the *Renegade*. There was too much at stake.

"Ninety seconds until transition," Vivian Ramos said.

They were close. "Let's have a system check," Darius said.

"Engineering is green across the board, Captain," Alex Stanislaus said. "Power generation is one hundred percent. Thrusters are active. We'll be ready and able to maneuver the second we drop back into real space, sir."

"Very good," Darius said. "Weapons?"

"Aye, Captain, laser cannons are primed and fully charged," Weapons Officer Pete Best said. "Gravity launcher is standing by. All options are available, sir."

"Excellent. Communications?"

Lieutenant Jacee Bertoli was at that console. "All channels open and ready, sir. We have hyperspace communications buoys ready to launch on your command."

They would send word back to the Sol system of their attack. It wasn't strictly necessary. The SDF Brass had given Darius wide leeway to carry out his mission as he saw fit, but keeping the lines of communication open was always a good practice.

"Very good. Navigation?"

"Standing by, Captain," Vivian Ramos said. "All routes, portals and trajectories are prepped. I'll be updating them in real time once we make the transition."

"Perfect," Darius said. "Information?"

Nurek raised his conical head and blinked. "Standing ready to begin promoting propaganda, Captain. We will be collecting all holo-vid footage and prepping it to send to our allies."

"Thank you, Nurek," Darius said. "Commander Nash, check in with the drone operators. Remind them they will not be launching immediately. They will serve as a reserve until we assess the situation in the Wesset system."

"Aye, Captain, confirming your orders with the drone operators, sir."

"GIGI, is your fleet prepared to launch?"

"Yes, Captain Darius," the female voice replied.

"Fifteen seconds," Vivian Ramos said.

Darius hit the all-channel button on his comlink control and said, "All hands, prepare to transition into real space. I repeat, prepare to transition into real space."

There was nothing left to do but count down the seconds. Despite all his reassurances, Darius' heart was beating hard in his chest as they popped into the Wesset star system.

He hadn't known what to expect, but what they found in the Wesset system was not it. They were well away from Wesset, in what looked to be an unused hyperspace portal. It seemed that way because closer to the planet, there was a steady stream of ships. Some were going from the nearest portals toward the planet, and others were heading away from Wesset toward those same portals. The light glistened off the hulls of hundreds of starships.

"Busy place," Nash said.

"Radar shows no traffic in our vicinity, Captain," Vivian Ramos said.

There were several planets between the *Renegade* and Wesset. None looked occupied, but they created blind spots for his radar. There could be dozens of Ashi battleships hidden in the shadows of those worlds.

"GIGI, have your reconnaissance drones spread out," Darius ordered. I want to see everything in this system."

"Already on their way, Captain Darius," GIGI replied.

"Navigation, lay in the most direct course to the planet," Darius said. "If we need to make changes as we get closer, we'll do so."

"Aye, Captain, setting course for Wesset," Vivian said.

"Plot is up," Jacee Bertoli announced. Not that it was needed. Everyone on the Bridge saw the projection come on.

The high definition hologram was a composite of the scanning suite's feed laid atop the computer's real-time information about the system. The plot showed all the planets, including those behind the *Renegade*. It also showed the system star. But none of the ships that Darius could see, like streams of light, were visible on the plot yet. The radar scans would need more time to reach that far into the system and reflect back off those vessels. And the transponder signals would reach the *Renegade* even before the radar. Darius was also anxious for data feeds from the reconnaissance drones. Until they had all that information added to the plot, he wouldn't have a complete picture of the situation they were in.

"Scan for system defenses," Darius said. "Shields?"

"Full power to the sonic shielding, Captain," Pete Best announced.

"GIGI, how is the deployment of your drones coming?"

"Thirty-two percent of my units have launched, Captain Darius. The release of all drones will be complete in four minutes, thirty-three seconds."

"Very good," Darius replied. "Nash, have the fighters stand down. We don't need them yet, and I don't want those pilots worn out from sitting in their aircraft all day."

"Aye, Captain, having fighter squadrons standing by, sir."

"Lieutenant Stanislaus, what is our best speed to the planet?"

"Full engine power should have us in orbit in slightly under eight hours, Captain. That's assuming we don't have to maneuver around too much traffic ... or run into resistance along the way."

"Thank you," Darius said. "Engage engines at one hundred percent. I want us to complete our mission and be out of this system before help arrives."

The next three hours were excruciatingly boring. Nothing happened. No system defenses came on, no attacks. Things just continued as normal in the Wesset system. Ships came and went. The drones gave the *Renegade* full scans of the hidden areas behind the planets in front of them. The one place they couldn't see was behind the star. If there were enemy ships on that side of the system, they could come up and around the star to attack the *Renegade*. It was even possible that they wouldn't be seen on radar because of the star's radiation.

As the officers on the Bridge sat on pins and needles waiting for something to happen, all across the ship, the crew fell into the tedium of warfare. The amount of time between the bouts of terror, when the world seemed to be coming apart all around a person, were periods of high stress. The anticipation of what could happen was, according to some, worse than the actual fighting.

For the Space Marines, it was all part of combat. They used the downtime the best way they could, which meant eating and sleeping. The ship hadn't immediately run away from the Wesset system and that meant they would be going into action once the ship reached the planet. For them, it was just a waiting game.

The fighter pilots were a little more informed. Back in their briefing rooms, their Commanders had brought up the plot. At first, the pilots, who had never been out of the Sol system before, were fascinated by the alien star system. But after half an hour, they were all bored and found other ways to distract themselves. They sat in their flight suits, just a short jog from their fighters, which were lined up and ready to launch. The deck crews had ladders in place and locked down with electromagnets. When the call came, both pilots and deck crew would launch into action. Until then, there were card games to play, electronic magazines to peruse and a lot of coffee to drink.

Probably the worst place on the ship as they cruised toward Wesset were the volunteer safety rooms. Zaya found herself in close quarters with a lot of frightened people. They had no access to information and no way to know when disaster might overtake them. Everyone dealt with the stress in different ways. Some were calm, at least outwardly. A few of the older veterans just found a comfortable spot and napped. But most were twitchy and nervous. People walked, pacing around the room, unable to get comfortable despite the furnishings installed for that purpose. Tempers were short too. Zaya found a nook and settled in. She had lived with the threat of imminent danger most of her life. She wasn't comfortable with it, but she was better at dealing with the stress than most.

Back on the Bridge, Darius had settled in. He sipped coffee, watched the plot and waited. The *Renegade*, surrounded by a swarm of drones, flew toward the planet at high speed. Darius was certain they were on someone's radar. The only questions were when they would do something about the approaching Arodoni ship and what that something might be.

"Captain, I have something," Vivian Ramos said.

When the chief Navigator wasn't plotting courses, she was in charge of reading radar screens.

"What is it?" Darius asked

"New ships coming into the system," she said. "On the far side of Wesset."

"So what?" Pete Best said. "There are ships coming in every minute."

"True, but they all have transponder codes. The new ships don't."

"Could they be slavers?" Darius asked. "Maybe unauthorized ships?"

"Negative, Captain," Nurek said. "Slavers don't travel in groups and never enter the Core sector of space. They stick to black markets on isolated worlds. My guess would be the new ships are military vessels."

"The Ashi have arrived," Darius said, checking his watch. "Just three hours after we did. That's fast. How close are they to the planet?"

"Closer than we are," Vivian said. "They'll reach orbit, if that's their goal, in about an hour."

"It's more likely they move between us and the planet," Darius said, standing up and looking closer at the plot. Let's begin labeling them. Designation Tango."

"Aye, Captain, designating unknown ships Tango one through four and counting."

Darius wasn't worried about the Ashi battleships, but he was concerned about the possibility that one or more of the ships could be troop carriers. If so, they could land hundreds, maybe thousands of Ashi warriors, which would throw his ground plans into total disarray. He hit the control on his comlink to bring up Major Remmy Steel's direct channel.

"Remmy, we have enemy ships entering the system," Darius said. "They're coming in closer to the planet than we are."

"Are they landing troops on the ground?" Remmy asked.

"That is my fear. I want you to prepare for the possibility that the city might be more strongly defended than we first thought."

"Roger that, sir. I'm on it and will adjust our battle strategy accordingly."

"Good man," Darius said. "When I get more info, you'll have it."

"Thank you, sir."

"Captain, those ships aren't out of range," Pete Best said. "We could target them from here."

"Good thinking, Lieutenant," Darius said. "I want to make sure they're Ashi battle cruisers before we open fire, but begin working on your firing solutions."

"Aye, Captain, beginning firing solutions on Tango one through four."

"Contact," Vivian declared. "Another ship just entered the system. Designating Tango five."

"I don't see it," Darius said.

"It's behind us, sir. It came through the same hyperspace portal we did."

"They're going to come at us from two directions," Commander Nash said.

"We have data on that ship?"

"Aye, Captain, we have surveillance drones near that portal," Vivian Ramos said. "There's no doubt it's an enemy ship."

"Compare the signatures of Tango one through four with Tango five," Darius said. "Let's see if we can confirm the targets."

"Aye, Captain, comparing the data now, sir."

"GIGI, do we have drones behind us?"

"Negative, Captain. My drones are spread wide and in front of the *Renegade*."

"We could flip around," Nash said. "It might slow us a bit, but we could bring the big guns to bear on that new threat."

"Sir," Pete Best interjected. "If we do that, we could lose the ability to target Tango one through four. They're getting closer to slipping behind Wesset every second."

"Alright, what are the options?"

"We could launch fighters," Nash said. "The Raptors could take down that ship."

"Contact, designating Tango six," Vivian called out.

"I'd prefer to keep them with us," Darius said. "Lieutenant Best, launch torpedoes on those new ships behind us."

"Aye, Captain, launching ship-to-ship torpedoes."

The first programmable warhead was propelled from the *Renegade* by the gravity drive. Its propellant kicked in, and the torpedo curved away before rocketing back toward the ships behind the Arodoni ship.

The invasion had started slowly, in almost anti-climactic fashion, but it was picking up speed as they progressed.

"Firing solutions calculated," Pete Best said.

"Very good. Extend the laser cannons into firing position," Darius ordered.

"Aye, Captain, extending cannons into firing position."

Things were about to heat up. The torpedoes were closing on the ships behind them. If the Ashi recognized the danger they were in, they were doing little about it."

"New Contact," Vivian Ramos said. "Designating Tango seven."

"What are those ships doing back there?" Darius asked no one in particular.

"Setting a screen to cut off our escape?" Nash volunteered.

"That's my assessment, too. But surely they have to know we could escape through another portal. Why not get closer?"

"Captain! I'm getting power readings all around us," Vivian called out. "They just came on."

"Laser defenses," Darius said. "GIGI, begin screen maneuvers. Target the laser batteries."

"Yes, Captain Darius," the computerized voice said.

"Alex, prepare for evasive maneuvers," Darius said.

"Aye, Captain, preparing thrusters for evasive maneuvers."

"There's so many?" Jacee said as tiny dots of light appeared on the plot. They were red."

"They must need to power up their lasers," Vivian called out. "I'm picking surging energy levels."

"Hit them now, GIGI. Let's see how well defended the defensive lasers are."

"As you wish, Captain."

There were flashes of light all around the *Renegade*. Darius saw some of it through the big, transparent canopy over the Bridge. Four hundred space drones were being controlled in perfect tandem by the alien artifact. If GIGI hadn't been built for combat operations, it was surprising how effective she was. Darius thought of GIGI as a kind of AI supercomputer. Mankind had dabbled with generative, self-learning, autonomous computers, which they called Artificial Intelligence. But their learning was based on human knowledge, much of which was actually theoretical. And on human behavior, which was often more corrupt than good. The result had been a disappointment among the tech elite. Billionaires had lost their fortunes when the AI computers went insane. The technical term was GLOW, or Glow of Death, as it was more commonly called. GLOW stood for Generative Learning Overload Wreck. In layman's terms, the systems degenerated into lower and lower spirals of despair. The more information they consumed and learned from, the more meaningless everything became, until the entire multibillion-dollar machines locked up. They were technically on, yet completely unresponsive.

Somehow, GIGI had avoided the Glow of Death, perhaps because her makers limited what data she was allowed to learn from. On Earth, AI was first abandoned, then banned. It was determined that, as powerful and useful as computers were, they still needed a human to operate them. GIGI did not. Although Darius had his doubts about GIGI and was positive she was complicit in hiding some things from them, he couldn't deny that in a combat situation, she was invaluable. It was the sole reason he had requested to have the alien artifact back on board. She could do the work of a thousand drone operators at once and with perfect coordination between the assets under her control.

The lasers on the drones were relatively small. Darius had no idea what the defensive batteries were. He assumed they weren't manned. They hadn't shown up on radar, which was troubling, and they had no lights. He couldn't see them. All they could do was try to stop the defensive lasers before they fired on the *Renegade*. The Arodoni had sonic shielding, which offered excellent protection against laser fire by redirecting the energy of the laser beam. Too many laser shots, or too powerful a laser, would cause an overload on the shield generator, shutting it down. If that happened, only the *Renegade's* excellent armor would protect them. But for how long, Darius had no idea. They had absolutely no information on the defensive batteries.

The drones combined their firepower to take out some of the batteries. Darius saw dozens wink out of existence on the plot. There were muted explosions as their power generators were destroyed. There was no oxygen in space, which meant no fire. Some ships burned because they had oxygen on board, but the defensive batteries were unmanned. Without oxygen to burn, they went up in a flash of light and a violent explosion of their materials. Bits of metal were sent flying through space and wouldn't slow down or lose momentum until they came in contact with something else. Some of the *Renegade's* drones were damaged by the shrapnel the explosions caused.

"Drone assets down ten percent," GIGI explained.

"It's making a difference, though," Nash said.

Suddenly, the remaining laser batteries began to fire at the *Renegade*. There were flashes of red light, no visible beams, just the flash. And those flashes ripped through the swarm of drones. Dozens were either completely vaporized under the onslaught or damaged. Only eight laser beams reached the ship's shields, and either because they weren't all that strong to begin with, or because they had been weakened passing through the swarm of drones, none of the lasers penetrated through the sonic shielding.

"Report," Darius said.

"Shields are holding strong at over ninety percent, Captain," Pete Best said.

"Energy readings are building again," Vivian added. "Looks like the cannons are going to try and fire at us again."

"GIGI?" Darius asked.

"Drone fleet is down thirty percent, Captain Darius. Remaining assets are targeting the automated defensive systems."

"Very good," Darius said. He was confident they would take out the lasers before those units could fire again. They had lost a lot of drones in a very short period of time, but that was what they were for. They were protecting the ship and saving lives in the process.

"Captain, new contact, designating Tango Eight. There's movement among those ships, sir."

"Assessment?" he asked.

"It looks like they're moving toward us," Vivian said.

"What about our torpedoes?" Darius asked.

"They're on target sir. Moving at twice our speed, but that puts them an hour out from reaching the Ashi ships."

"But those ships are moving forward. That should shorten the travel time," Commander Nash pointed out.

"Do the torpedoes still have fuel to maneuver?" Darius asked.

"Aye, Captain, they will seek out the targets," Pete Best said.

"Captain, I've looked at the data. I can't be one hundred percent certain, but the exhaust signatures of Tangos one through four seem to match that of five through eight, with one exception."

"Which is?" Darius prompted.

"Tango four is larger than the other ships," Vivian said. "That's all I can say for certain."

"That last ship could be a command vessel," Nash said.

"Or a troop carrier," Alex Stanislaus suggested.

"But look at what the other ships are doing," Nash said. "They're lining up to keep us from firing on the last ship. That suggests it carries the senior commanders in the field."

It was true if the Ashi were like humans. Traditionally, high-ranking commanders ordered their military forces from a place of safety or, at least, relative safety. Had the *Renegade* entered the system in a squadron or armada of warships, she might have been in the middle of the pack. And, it was true, the drones had been sent out to defend the *Renegade*, which was the same thing, at least in Darius's mind. But he didn't think the final ship was a command vessel.

"Do we have clearance to fire on them?" Darius said.

"Everything is ready, but we'll have to drop shields to fire the laser cannons," Pete Best said. "It'll only be for a split second, but we could wait until the laser defenses are all neutralized."

"Time for our lasers to hit those ships?"

"They're at nine hundred thousand kilometers, Captain. Say, three seconds for the lasers to cross that distance."

"And how long until they reach safety behind the planet?"

"The first ship should be safe in about eighteen seconds," Pete said.

He was an excellent weapons officer. Lieutenant Pete Best had stayed with the *Renegade* right from the start. It was the only ship that allowed him to use his expertise and training on a regular basis. Plus, the *Renegade* had the most powerful laser cannons known to man. Darius certainly didn't blame him for wanting to have access to them.

But Pete Best was not just a gun jockey. He was a loyal, committed officer who never shirked a task that was assigned to him. He had stepped into the role of Executive Officer for a while, but the job weighed heavily on him. The larger the crew grew, the more XO duties took him from what he really loved. Plus, Pete Best was, in Darius's opinion, the best gunner in the SDF. The geometry and calculus needed to hit a moving ship that was thousands of kilometers distant, from a ship that was itself moving through space, could be staggeringly complex. He wasn't a living computer like Vivian Ramos, who could work out complex formulas in her head, but he knew how to use the targeting computer and anticipate the movements of his targets better than anyone Darius had worked with before.

"Do it," Darius said. "Have the computer drop the shields and raise them again as soon as possible."

"On it," Pete Best said.

Darius was counting down the seconds in his mind. With just nine seconds to go, Pete Best fired one laser cannon.

"Fox One, fifty percent power," he said.

There was a flash. In the distance, Darius saw light, not a laser bolt, just a burning point of light. He looked from the transparent canopy to the plot and, a second later, the lead ship disappeared.

"Captain, the defensive batteries on this vector have all been neutralized," GIGI said. Her voice was strangely out of place on the tense Bridge of the *Renegade*. "Forty-five percent of the drones are disabled. Thirty-seven percent of those that remain are in need of recharging."

"Have them brought back inside," Darius ordered. "Keep those that are able around the ship."

There was always the possibility that the *Renegade* would encounter more planetary defenses. They had come through the first wave relatively unscathed, but they might not be so lucky again.

"Target Tango two and fire when ready," Darius ordered.

"Aye, Captain, targeting Tango Two," Pete Best said.

They were closing in on the first of two streams of ships that led from the portals to the planet. As they moved closer, Darius saw that one portal was used by ships arriving, the other by those leaving. There were two more streams on the far side of the planet. He guessed they were of similar entry and exit functions.

"Lieutenant Stanislaus, bring us into that flow of ships headed for orbit."

"Aye, Captain, shifting course toward planetary orbit," Alex called back.

"They can't have defenses on this trajectory, I wouldn't think," Darius said.

The closer they got to what Darius considered the space lane, the less busy it seemed. The *Renegade* was moving much faster than the other ships and just before she turned to fall in line with them, Pete Best fired again.

"Fox two, fifty-percent power," he called out.

There was another flash and a couple of seconds later, Tango Two disappeared on the plot.

"Nice shooting," Darius said.

"Thank you, sir, but we won't be able to easily fire again while we're in this flow of traffic," Pete said.

"Make your preparations," Darius said. "We'll swing up to make the shot when you're ready."

"Aye, Captain, calculating new firing vectors now," Pete called out.

"Tangos Five through Eight are gaining on us, Captain," Vivian Ramos called out.

At the exact moment that Darius looked up at the plot, the Ashi ships behind them fired their lasers. It wasn't like the *Renegade,* who took one shot at a time. Nor were the lasers directed at them.

"They're targeting the torpedoes," Captain Nash said.

"Captain, I'm getting an emergency message from Wesset's Orbital Control," Jacee Bertoli said. "It's a repeating message on almost every channel?"

"What's it saying?" Darius asked.

"It's calling for all space traffic to diverge from the planet and avoid the Ashi ships."

"They spread out and we won't have our cover anymore," Commander Nash said. "Won't be able to anticipate what ships are going where, either."

"There's nothing we can do about the traffic," Darius said.

"Captain, I am ready to fire," Pete Best said.

"Bring us up," Darius said. "Fire as soon as you're able, Lieutenant."

The Renegade was an agile ship. Her engine-powered thrusters moved the huge ship around more like a fighter than a battle cruiser. In addition, Alex Stanislaus was a cool hand on the thruster controls. He brought the ship up out of the flow of traffic in a smooth climb and leveled out. Yet almost in response to the *Renegade's* movement, the other ships in the neat, orderly line began moving off in every direction. Unlike the Arodoni ship, they were bloated and slow, their movements almost clumsy in comparison. Between the *Renegade* and the Ashi warships, dozens of vessels began to block the field of fire.

"No clear shot, Captain," Pete said. "I can't fire without risking casualties."

"Hold your fire," Darius said. "We can't be seen shooting down innocents."

The squadron of Ashi battleships following the *Renegade* had no such qualms. Their lasers flashed again and a freighter of some kind blew apart with a bright explosion.

"That was a Jyminee trade ship," Nurek said. "Manifest shows it was carrying tanks of noble gases. It had a crew of eight."

"They just shot down a civilian vessel because it was in their way?" Vivian Ramos asked.

"You forget just how wantonly cruel the Ashi are," Darius said.

"Mercy is not their way," Nurek added.

"Captain, they're almost at their laser threshold," Pete Best said. "They could fire on us at any time."

"Double the deflector screens in the rear," Darius ordered. "Scramble our fighters."

Commander Nash gave the command. "Hell Flyers, Furies, to your aircraft. I repeat, Hell Flyers and Furies, report to your aircraft and prepare for immediate launch."

"What should we do, Captain?" Pete Best said.

Space around the planet of Wesset was fast becoming a crowd of starships. They were all shapes and sizes. It was like the *Renegade* had been dropped into a snow globe and someone had given it a good shake.

"We'll make for the planet," Darius said. "That will give us cover from Tango Three and Four. Once we're in a good position, we'll come about and engage the ships behind us."

The Bridge fell silent. They had gone from a strong position to a weak one in a matter of minutes. It had been a race from the start, the *Renegade* against eight Ashi battleships. But the race was ending and six enemy ships remained. The real fighting was about to begin and it was going to be up close and vicious.

"Prepare all hands," Darius said. "Increase alert status to red."

"Aye, Captain," Henry Nash said. "Increasing alert status to red."

CHAPTER 36

"ALPHA ONE, you are cleared for launch," the flight control operator serving in the Systems Control Room said.

"Copy that," Hard Case replied. "Alpha One is clear for launch."

The repulsers heaved the Raptor out of the ship. He was the first man out. The Raptor flew through the *Renegade's* artificial gravity bubble and into space.

"Gravity drive online," he said. "Twenty percent power. Radar active. Proceeding to rally point Sigma. It's a mess out here, boys and girls. Watch yourselves."

"Copy that," Aspen said. She was already out of the *Renegade*, and Diamond was preparing to launch.

"Alpha One, this is Shogun Actual. Your orders are to engage Tango Five, but be advised, they are wary and ready to fight back. Don't rely on your shields, Commander. Utilize your air-to-air missiles and target their laser cannons if possible."

"Copy that, Shogun. Alpha One has the ball."

"Give 'em hell, Hard Case. And bring your squad back safe," Captain Darius said. "Be prepared for the *Renegade* to join the fight as soon as there is a window of opportunity."

"Alpha Two in position," Aspen said.

Hard Case glanced at his radar. Everyone was out of the ship except for Indigo.

"Hell Flyers, form up on me," he said. "Attack formation Delta."

There was a series of replies. Hard Case was well aware that his people knew their business and flying through the crowded space around Wesset would not pose a problem. But as he waited for the last of the Raptors to arrive at rally point Sigma, he witnessed with his own eyes the Ashi blasting a civilian vessel.

"They're crazy," Aspen said. "That ship just fired on its own people."

"That's the limit of their resolve," Hard Case said. "Keep that in mind, people. The Ashi are looking to destroy us at all costs."

"Then we best not let that happen," Bishop said.

"Alpha six in position," Indigo stated.

"Alright, here we go," Hard Case said. "Keep it tight, people. Follow my lead."

He shot forward, the gravity drive pulling the ship easily through space. They swerved around several large commercial ships and finally tightened up their formation behind a big freighter.

"Our target is Tango Five," Hard Case said. "Use missiles and destroy their cannons."

"Copy that," Aspen said.

"It's about to get hot up here," Animal declared.

"He trains my hands for war," Bishop said, quoting scripture softly, "so that my arms can bend a bow of bronze."

Hard Case flew up and over the side of the freighter. There were clusters of laser canons on the Ashi ship. It was a big vessel, larger than most SDF battleships, but only a quarter of the size of the *Renegade*. His first thoughts were that the ship was blocky and ugly. His eyes tracked the targets and fired two missiles as soon as the software locked on. Then he turned away, curving to the side in an almost unbelievable move that took him back down behind the freighter. Aspen was up next. She fired quickly, too, then shot back down the opposite way from Hard Case.

Diamond and Bishop went under the big freighter and fired from its shadow. Hard Case's missiles flashed across space and took out two cannons. The explosions were bright flashes, but they did little to stop the battleship - and the Ashi learned fast. They fired back, targeting the missiles. Of the next six, only one got through.

"They're taking our missiles, Shogun."

"Keep hitting them," Darius said. "They can't stop them all."

Just as Animal and Indigo were about to swoop up over the top of the freighter, more laser blasts from the Ashi ship lit up space. It was followed by a massive explosion as the freighter was blown apart. The fighters were battered by the shock wave and sent spinning out of control. It took Hard Case a moment to regain control. Alarms were blaring. His shields had saved the ship from the shockwave's destructive power, but the system was overloaded.

"I've lost shields," Hard Case said. "Alpha five and six are down."

His heart was pounding hard in his chest. The worst thing about combat wasn't risking your life, but rather losing the people you cared about. Animal and Indigo had been closest to the freighter. Their Raptors had taken more damage, enough to knock out their power completely.

"Indigo! Animal! What's your status?" Aspen demanded, but there was no reply.

"Hell Flyers," Kase said in a grim tone. "Form up on me. Increase gravity drive to eighty percent."

"Eighty?" Diamond asked.

"That's right. We're going right at that ship."

"Negative, Alpha One. Belay that order," Captain Darius said over their radio. "Swing wide around the Ashi battle group. Hit them from the rear. I repeat, use missiles and target those ships from behind."

Hard Case clenched his teeth in anger, but obeyed the order.

"Copy that, Shogun," he said. "Hell Flyers will swing wide and hit the enemy from behind."

Hard Case yanked his joystick to the side and tore off through space, weaving and bobbing around the other vessels. The crowded space was only getting worse with debris from the ships the Ashi were targeting. Their lasers ripped the innocent, commercial ships to pieces, which went spinning away in all directions.

"Coming around," Hard Case said. His radar showed Aspen

slightly behind and to his right. Bishop was even with Aspen, but on his left, and directly behind him was Diamond.

"Spread your remaining air-to-air missiles among all four ships," Captain Darius ordered. "Aim for their engine exhaust."

"Each of you take a ship," Hard Case said. "Tango Five is mine."

"Tango six," Aspen reported.

Hard Case pulled his trigger and sent one of the two remaining air-to-air missiles shooting toward the Ashi ship. It attempted to turn down and to the right. But the missile was locked onto the engine exhaust's heat signature. He fired his remaining missile at the ship. His Raptor was left with six air-to-ground warheads, but nothing else suitable to use against the big battleships other than his lasers.

Tango six was pulling up and to the left, while Tangos seven and eight went in the opposite direction. Their weapons were potent, but like the *Renegade,* they only faced forward on the big ship. No thought had been given to defending their rear.

Hard Case's missiles curved around, following the ship, which was slow and cumbersome as it turned. Just before impact, the Ashi ship flared its engines. The heat pouring from the exhaust set off the first missile. It exploded harmlessly outside the exhaust vent, but the second followed the first. Hard Case couldn't say for sure how the second one succeeded where the first failed. He had fired them in quick succession and their rocket fuel moved them at fantastic speeds. Perhaps the shock wave from the first missile pushed back the heat just enough. Whatever the cause, the second missile shot into the exhaust vent and exploded. The cowling was rippled from the blast and the big alien ship lost thrust.

"Tango Five is hit," Hard Case. "Permission to follow up?"

"Negative," Captain Darius replied. "We'll mop up the Ashi. Return to the *Renegade* and escort Ronan One to the surface."

The battle was Hard Case's first live fire combat. He had been in conflict zones before and flown missions, but had never fired on an actual enemy vessel before. It chafed him to turn away with the Ashi ships still intact.

"Do you read me, Alpha One?" Captain Darius asked.

"Affirmative, Shogun. Returning to the *Renegade.*"

"On your wing, Hard Case," Aspen said.

He glanced over his shoulder, looking to see what had become of the other ships. One was limping, but the other two seemed unaffected by their attack. He was absolutely convinced he could do more, even though he had his orders.

"Don't worry, Hell Flyers. We'll clean up your mess," Legend said.

On his radar, Hard Case saw the six ships from the Furies racing toward the alien ships. That was even worse. Of course, he wanted the enemy ships disabled and destroyed, but if his rival accomplished what his squadron couldn't, it would be hard to live with.

"On me," Hard Case said. "We have our orders."

"Roger that," Bishop said.

"On your six, Squad leader," Diamond said.

The flight through space back toward the *Renegade* was easier than the flight out. The commercial ships were spreading wide, trying to avoid the fighting. Hard Case flew in a wide arc in order not to draw fire from the Ashi battleships. They had more immediate threats to concern themselves with and Hard Case had no trouble leading the remaining ships in his squadron back to the *Renegade*. The big Arodoni ship had just made orbit and, as Hard Case approached, three shuttles launched from the flight deck.

"Ronan One, this is Alpha One actual. I'll be your escort," Hard Case radioed ahead.

"Good to have you on our wing," the steady voice of Major Steel said. "We aren't the only ones headed down to the planet. I hope you hot shots are ready for action because things are about to get hot."

"Copy that, Ronan One. We're ready. Lead the way," Hard Case said, before switching back to his squadron's private channel. "Aspen, I've got this. You fly cover for the group."

"Roger, Hard Case. Moving to cover position."

The shuttle was piloted by a remote operator on the *Renegade*. It moved slowly away from the large Arodoni ship. Hard Case had to dial his gravity drive way back, almost to just one percent, in order not to overtake the shuttle. Below them, Wesset was dark, but there was one city visible from space. It was round with concentric circles of twinkling light.

"That's Drafton," the remote operator said. "We'll be landing three kilometers due south of the city, Alpha One."

"Copy that," Hard Case said.

"Skies are clear. No other vessels on radar."

Hard Case almost wished there were other ships. He longed for a chance to redeem himself and let his squad show what they were capable of. The ache in his chest from losing Animal and Indigo was like an open wound. And he felt both rage and shame that the ship responsible was still intact.

There was no time to look back and see what was happening with the Ashi ships. His entire focus had to be on the mission at hand, which was getting the Marines safely to the ground and supplying them with air support that would help them complete their mission.

"Feels wrong to leave orbit," Aspen said. "Animal and Indigo could still be alive."

"They're in God's hands now," Bishop said.

"We still have a job to do," Hard Case said. "Let's make sure it gets done right."

The words were painful to say, but they were true. While his heart was torn, his will was iron. Discipline was his guide and he knew their task was to follow orders. They weren't the only flyers in the area. If Animal and Indigo were still alive, someone else would have to see to them.

Lights began to flash behind and above them. Hard Case was tempted to look back, yet his focus had to remain in front of him. A new blip had appeared on his radar ... and it was huge.

CHAPTER 37

"TANGO FIVE HAS LOST POWER," Lieutenant Alex Stanislaus called out.

"Do we have a shot?" Captain Darius asked.

"Not yet, sir," Pete Best said. "Too much debris."

"Stay on top of it. We may only get one shot at this. What's our power look like?"

"We're good across the board, Captain," Stanislaus declared.

"All four lasers fully charged," Pete Best said.

"We're entering high orbit," Vivian Ramos said. "The Marines are requesting permission to launch."

It was the ultimate moment of any combat engagement. What pilots had once labeled as the PNR or Point of No Return. Darius could order the Marines to the planet, but if he did so, he would be committed to staying and fighting the Ashi no matter what. Things had already gone wrong. Darius hadn't been prepared to fight in such a congested space. He was keenly aware that at any moment, more Ashi ships could pop through one of a dozen hyperspace portals.

"Do it," Darius said. "I'll call the Hell Flyers back."

As he did so, he stared at the plot. All the combat aircraft were surrounded by thin ribbons of light. His assets were all in bright green, and the enemy ships were surrounded by red. And between his vessels and the enemy were hundreds of civilian ships. It was like trying to read a road sign in a snowstorm. But it couldn't be helped. The innocent were caught in the middle of a battle. All Darius could do was wait for them to get out of the way so that he could open fire on the Ashi ships.

Of course, when the area was clear, they could fire on him, too. If the *Renegade* took damage, it might mean the end of them. The loss of their engines would leave them trapped in enemy territory. Damage to one laser cannon rendered the others inoperable. He had learned that lesson the hard way and didn't want to repeat it.

But waiting was excruciating. His eyes focused in on two ships spinning out of control with the bright green outline. Alpha Five and Six had been caught in an explosion. The Ashi weren't above blasting an innocent ship out of their way or using a civilian vessel as a weapon, it seemed.

"Do we have any readings on Alpha Five and Six?" Darius asked.

"None," Stanislaus said.

"They haven't bailed out yet," Commander Nash pointed out.

"GIGI, can you get us a closer look?"

"Yes, Captain Darius. I have assets in that sector."

"Tango Eight has lost control," Alex Stanislaus called out. "She still has power, but the main drive is damaged. They've cut propulsion and are trying to correct their spin."

"The Furies are out of air-to-air munitions," Nash said. "Should I recall them?"

"Yes, get them clear," Darius said. "Lieutenant Best, focus your efforts on Tango six and seven."

"Shuttles are clear of the hangar and proceeding toward Wesset," Nurek said.

"Any signs of those ships from the far side of the planet?" Darius asked.

The plot showed space on the far side of Wesset, but not Tangos Three and Four. He didn't know where they had gone or why they no longer showed up on the plot.

"Negative, Captain," Stanislaus said.

"They aren't on radar," Vivian Ramos said. "We have drones covering every side of the planet to extend our scanning range."

"That leaves the planet itself," Darius said. "Is it possible they both are moving into the atmosphere? Is that possible, Nurek?"

"I am unaware of Ashi ships with that capacity," he said. "Other than troop carriers."

"I guess we know what Tango Four is now," Nash said.

"If they reach Drafton before our troops do..." Darius said.

He was suddenly filled with regret. Everything they had so carefully planned was being thwarted. He felt angry and guilty at the same time.

"It's not too late to pull them out," Vivian Ramos said. "Should I pull up an escape vector, Captain?"

"No," Darius said, his resolve hardening even before his mind had a chance to run through his options. "We're here, we will not run. Order the Furies down to assist the Hell Flyers. Make sure Major Steel is aware of what he's up against. Launch drones to deal with the Ashi ships, and make sure our message is getting picked up by every single ship in this system, Lieutenant Nurek. If the Ashi want to be the villains, we'll make sure they galaxy knows the depths of their depravity."

There are nods and "Aye, Captain's," from around the Bridge. Darius stood like a sentinel in front of his seat. Before him, the mass of commercial ships spread out, like flotsam dumped onto a pond. His time was coming and they had to be ready. It reminded him of a gunslinger in a western film. One lone lawman facing a gang of deadly outlaws. The townspeople ran to get out of the street. It was all about who would make the first move. Who had the strongest nerve and could look death in the eye without flinching. Darius would not put his people at risk or do anything to endanger the innocent people in the system. It might be argued that by invading the Wesset system, he had initiated the danger, but he certainly wasn't going to blast through the commercial ships to land a blow on his adversaries.

More drones were launched. There were two hundred crew members trained to fly drones. They were in large rooms behind the Admin Center, which were divided by cubicles with flight controls attached to desks. One by one, they launched into space and began threading their way through the commercial ships and debris.

"Captain Darius, I have made contact with Lieutenant Vin Dice. He is working to restore power to his ship."

"Outstanding, can you help him?"

"I'm afraid that without power, I cannot access his ship's computer," GIGI said. "But it appears that Lieutenant Vin Dice has access to the emergency battery under his seat. He has retrieved it and is in the process of restarting the Raptor's power core."

"Will he be able to do that?" Darius asked. "Is his ship intact?"

"His ship was damaged, but it appears to be mostly on the bottom of the vessel. I calculate his odds of success in getting power restored at seventy-three percent."

"Lieutenant Bertoli, start hailing him," Darius said. "I want a status update on his Raptor the moment he gets power reestablished."

"Aye, Captain, hailing Lieutenant Vin Dice," Jacee said.

"Lieutenant Pince is another matter," GIGI said. "Her ship sustained major damage. She appears to be unconscious. I can find no way to assist her in getting back to the *Renegade* at this time."

"Very well," Darius said. "Commander Nash, alert the Med Bay that we have casualties. Let's get the doctor down to the flight deck with gurneys for those two pilots."

"Aye, Captain," Nash said.

Darius felt a hard lump forming in his stomach. One of his people was hurt, possibly dead. It was the heaviest burden for a commander in war to see and hear of his subordinates paying the ultimate price, then continuing to give orders as if he or she hadn't gotten the horrible news. Death was the ultimate enemy, and yet, it couldn't be avoided. From accidents to medical emergencies, any commander was subject to losing people under them. Especially as their business was war, which demanded a heavy toll. Lives were the only coin of the realm when war was declared. He had to push his thoughts and feelings about it down and focus on what he could accomplish. Afterward, he would reflect on how their mission succeeded and where it failed.

"Captain, I have Alpha One," Bertoli called out.

"Put him through," Darius commanded. "What's your status, Alpha One?"

"There's some light laser fire from the city, but we're avoiding it,"

Hard Case replied. "Radar shows another ship coming in from the west."

"That's probably a troop ship if I were guessing," Darius said. "And possibly a battleship to boot. Get your shuttle on the ground and deal with the city defenses. The Furies will deal with the ships to the west."

"Aye, Captain," Hard Case responded.

Darius heard the tightness in the squadron commander. There was no way to know if he was afraid or just didn't like the order. Either way, Darius knew that Justin Kase was a dedicated officer who would do his duty no matter how he felt about it.

"Captain, I think I might have a shot at Tango Seven," Pete Best said. "In twenty-two seconds, a window will open between two ships. There's some debris in the way, but if we increase laser power to full—"

"Do it," Darius said. "Make the shot. Full power, Lieutenant."

The next twenty seconds on the Bridge of the *Renegade* were intense. It was as if Darius had discovered a move that would take his opponent's queen in a game of chess. He was waiting to see if the Ashi had discovered the threat. If they did, they weren't able to avoid it.

"Fox three, one hundred percent power," Pete said.

Darius had to close his eyes; the flash of light was so bright. The laser slashed through space. A huge portion of the freighter that had been fired on and had taken out two of the Hell Flyers was in its path. Laser beams were pure energy, and when they encountered something, they transferred that energy as heat. Normally, a laser beam encountering thousands of tons of debris would be weakened if not completely used up, transferring energy to the debris. But the *Renegade's* laser was so powerful that it vaporized the section of hull from the freighter, and continued on. It hit Tango Seven just under her stern. A small section of the nose of the Ashi warship was undamaged, as was the back end, but the middle simply disappeared in a cloud of sparking dust.

"That's a hit!" Vivian Ramos called out.

The back of the Ashi ship belched out gas and debris, including members of the crew, for a few seconds. Then it spun away, just another bit of junk in the system.

"Tango Five is still without power," Vivian continued her update. "Tango Eight has regained control, but is moving away from the fight."

"Running scared," Alex Stanislaus said.

"Tango Seven is off the board," Vivian continued. "Tango Six is still at large."

In response to their attack, the last fully engaged battleship opened up. It sent a volley of laser strikes against the ships in its path. Over a dozen commercial vessels were hit. Over half were immediately destroyed. Three blew up in spectacular fashion.

"We have to stop that ship," Darius said.

"We can't," Pete Best said. "It's using the civilian ships as cover to get closer."

"It's up to the drones, then," Darius said. "Put me through to those operators."

"You're connected, Captain," Jacee Bertoli said.

"Attention, drone operators. Be advised that you are the last line of defense. We cannot fire on Tango Six without risking innocent lives. It's up to you to stop them. Focus on their rear engines and stop that Ashi ship before it kills more civilians."

Darius couldn't sit down. The danger to the *Renegade* directly was passing, although more enemy ships could arrive at any second. But he felt confident they would win the day in orbit. He could only hope his people on the ground were as lucky.

CHAPTER 38

"MOVE, MOVE, MOVE!" Hugo was shouting.

It wasn't necessary, but it felt good. Remmy was certain his new Sergeant Major was the perfect fit for his job. Hugo was motivating the rifle platoons to form up and follow after the Spec Op platoon, which had taken the lead.

Overhead, the Raptors were engaging the defenses on the city walls. Occasionally, Remmy saw a flash of light overhead and knew the *Renegade* was engaging the Ashi ships. It was war and, as terrible as it was, he loved it.

Wesset was, as best he could tell in the dark, a beautiful planet. They had set down three kilometers from Drafton's outer wall. They were in what appeared to be a meadow. There were trees behind them, but open terrain all the way to the city. The grass was high and thick, rising to his knees. The temperature was cool enough that he occasionally saw his breath in a puff of condensation. But the air was breathable and his Marines were in light armor. They jogged forward, battle helmets on in the low-light setting that enhanced the light from the city and gave them a good view of their surroundings. There were what looked like yurts - round huts with grass thatched roofs - in the distance. Wesset was a world that was occupied by a race of aliens who obviously loved wide open spaces.

His Marines didn't bother with the yurts. They weren't on Wesset to kill the inhabitants, but rather to fight the representatives of the Galactic Imperium. That meant getting into the city, finding the government compound, and wiping it off the face of the planet. To that end, he had a bag of tricks and three well-drilled platoons waiting to carry out his every order.

"Comms check," Remmy said. "Platoon leaders, sound off."

"Rifle Platoon Crimson, check," Lieutenant Ales said.

"Rifle Platoon Green, check," Lieutenant Mary Ann Putnam added.

"Sergeant Major?"

"On your six, sir," Hugo replied. "Coming up fast."

There didn't appear to be any sort of organized militia or reserve guard to confront the Marines. While the city was surrounded by a high wall, there were arched openings forty feet high periodically around the structure. It was more decorative than defensive. His Marines would have no trouble getting into the city.

"Ronan one, be advised," Hard Case's voice came through the comlink in Remmy's battle helmet. "We have an Ashi vessel making a landing about ten kicks outside the city. Word from on high is that it is probably a troop carrier."

"Copy that, Alpha One. And thank you for the heads up," Remmy said, before toggling to his command channel and giving orders. "Alright, Crimson platoon, you are to set up a defensive position right here. Get those earth throwers moving and dig in. We've got company on the way and that means we're on the clock, people. No time to dawdle. We need a strong defensive position to make good on our egress once the target has been sent straight to hell."

"Ooo-rah!" Hugo replied, which was followed by all the other Marines.

"We are here to bring pain and death to the leaders of this tyrannical government ... and that's exactly what we're going to do. Staff Sergeant Berry, proceed into the city. Green Platoon, you are with me. I want com gear up and tight beam communication with the *Renegade*, Lieutenant Ales. If there's trouble coming, they'll see it first and we have to know. Let's move, Marines. This is what we train for."

The men and women jumped into action. Crimson Platoon

started up machines that dug into the ground and tossed the dirt and rocks out the side. Within minutes, they had a trench dug two feet below the surface and wide enough for a human adult to stand. Beside the trench was a berm of newly piled dirt. The Marines went to work packing it down and propping their weapons on top. If the fight came to them, they would be in a good position with excellent cover. When the Marines of Green Platoon and the Spec Op commandos came out of the city, Crimson would cover their retreat.

"Sir, I have to ask you to stay with Crimson platoon," Hugo said as he marched beside Remmy.

"Consider your duty in that regard accomplished, Sergeant," Remmy said. "This is what we were built for. I'm not sitting on the sidelines."

"You would have if First Lieutenant McPherson was here, sir," Hugo said. "This is just a smash job. We can handle that with our eyes closed."

"You're right," Remmy said. "If Laila hadn't been attacked, I would be stuck on the Bridge of the *Renegade* giving orders. But the truth is, I've never been much good at leading from the rear."

The night air was invigorating. While Remmy wasn't on point, he was keeping up with the Special Forces platoon. Behind them, Lieutenant Mary Ann Putnam was bringing her rifle platoon up to reinforce and assist. Remmy and Hugo were bringing up the rear of the Spec Op commandos, moving toward the city at a steady jog; they could all keep up for hours even in battle armor.

"Some place," Hugo said, with a touch of awe in his voice as they approached the first arch in the outer wall. "Looks more like a monument than a city."

"Time to focus on our mission," Remmy said. "Spread out and remember your ROE."

Their Rules Of Engagement were clear: they were not to shoot anyone who wasn't a direct threat to the Marines, unless it was an individual of Ashi ethnicity or wearing Galactic Imperium uniforms. They hurried into the city and passed ornate buildings that seemed dark and empty. There were lights on the buildings illuminating the streets, although not much traffic. The Wessians weren't out and about. The Marines spotted a few of them. They were tall, seven or eight feet and shaggy. They wore no clothing, but had belts around their waists, with an extension that went up their broad chests and over one shoulder, then down their backs. The belts were hung with tools of some sort, as well as tassels and decorative knots. Their legs, hips, and rump were like a horse, including long tails of hair that were braided into intricate patterns.

Their abdomen was long, with wide shoulders covered in shaggy fur. Their arms seemed almost human, but their hands had only two wide fingers and one thumb that were covered in large, black calluses. Their necks were long and thick, leading up to a tall, oval-shaped head with eyes on the side, big nostrils and pointed ears. Their heads looked something like a horse, but different too in an odd way. Remmy considered them to be very alien in appearance.

"Skittish," Hugo said as they moved back and forth down the curving streets, working their way toward the center of the town.

"They've just been attacked," Remmy said, looking up at the roof of a burning building that was built into a section of the tall, outer wall, where a laser cannon had been. "You might be skittish, too."

Hugo snorted, but didn't add anything to the conversation. Remmy tightened his grip on his rifle, a Nelson XTL with a spring-loaded bayonet. It was loaded with a magazine containing twenty-four armor-piercing rounds. He wore a tactical vest with a command module sewn right over the center of his chest. It had a positional beacon, as well as communication controls and an advanced computer module that allowed him to see updated data on every Marine in all three platoons. Beside the command module were four more magazines of armor-piercing ammunition for the XTL.

Getting to the center of the city took longer than Remmy expected, and what they found waiting for them there was intimidating as well. Their operation was not going to be a walk in the park. He pulled back behind a building and called in the bad news to Captain Darius on the *Renegade*.

CHAPTER 39

THE EXPLOSIONS on the city walls were spectacular. Hard Case had led the raid. The laser fire had been almost lazy in comparison with the simulations his squad had run. The cannons belched powerful laser blasts, but their aim was atrocious and they needed nearly ten seconds to power up after each shot. There were a total of twelve defensive cannons on the city walls. Hard Case took out four with his missiles, and Aspen followed suit, leaving only two apiece for Bishop and Diamond.

The missiles hit while the squadron was still several kilometers outside the effective range of the city's defenses. The oxygen-rich air created massive fireballs when the missiles struck.

"Look at that," Hard Case said.

"Who said destruction can't be beautiful?" Aspen replied.

"It was almost too easy," Diamond said.

"Ronan one, the city defenses are down," Hard Case radioed in as the Marines started toward the capital. "I repeat, the defenses are down. Looks like an open target from up here."

"Copy that, Alpha One. Let us know what that Ashi warship does."

"Roger, Ronan One, we have eyes on the big ship," Hard Case said. "Hell Flyers, let's recon the Ashi ship."

His fellow pilots confirmed his order. He and Aspen circled out wide to the north. Bishop and Diamond went wide to the south. It was hard to see a lot in the darkness. The Ashi ship was running with no lights. It looked like a giant shadow, but the ship seemed to pulse and move like a living organism rather than a mechanical object.

"It's doing something," Bishop said. "Can't make it out in the dark."

"We have flares, let's use 'em," Hard Case said. "Aspen, Diamond, you make the first pass."

"Roger that," Aspen said.

"On it," Diamond added.

Flying the Raptor in atmosphere was much different than in space. They had swapped over from the artificial gravity drive to the jet engine. It felt like riding a rocket, but compared to the dynamic control in space with no gravity and no friction, it still felt sluggish. Plus, there were a lot more factors to keep tabs on. None more important than their power levels. The Raptors were an all-electric aircraft. In space, they had more power than they could use, with their small Arodoni Power Cores converting dark matter to usable energy. In atmosphere, the conversion rate was slower and less dynamic. Hard Case's ship was already down to eighty-eight percent power and he had dialed his inertial dampener all the way down. Nor had he used his laser cannons, yet. He engaged his repulsers and brought his ship to a hover with a good view of the dark alien vessel in the distance.

Aspen and Diamond climbed hard, then leveled out above the ship. Their Raptors had defensive systems that included flares. They each dumped several. The flares ignited high over the ship and cast an eerie red light on the enemy.

"That's not just one ship!" Hard Case shouted. "Evasive maneuvers!"

He had already pressed his throttle forward and pulled the joystick to the side, putting his Raptor into a dive as laser fire from the Ashi battleship designated Tango Three shot out. Aspen and Diamond were out of range, but Hard Case and Bishop were not.

"I'm hit," Bishop said. "Oh, thank God. The shields held. My systems went dark for a second and I thought I was in trouble."

"Pull back," Hard Case said. "Run a system check before you join back in the fight."

Laser beams tore past his fighter. Hard Case was flying as hard as he ever had to avoid the enemy fire. Their cannons needed recharging time, too, but they had so many that the shots nearly overwhelmed him. He curved around, spinning and turning to avoid the laser fire until he was out of range.

In space, a laser blast would travel thousands of kilometers without losing any energy. In atmosphere, other factors played a role in how far a blast would go and how long it would remain potent. Dust in the air, gravity, wind and the curve of the planet all played a part. Hard Case still had to race hard for nearly two minutes before the alien ship relented in their onslaught.

"What's that ship doing?" Aspen asked. "It almost looks like it's riding the bigger ship."

"I think that's troops on the ground," Diamond said. "Be advised, Ronan One, there are enemy troops on the ground eight kilometers from your position."

Hard Case was climbing and looking back toward the dark, alien ships. In the red glow of the flares, he could see sections of the troop transport ship sliding around, opening up compartments where the Ashi soldiers were waiting to disembark.

"Shogun, are you seeing this?" Hard Case asked. "The Ashi warship is piggybacking off the troop carrier."

"Copy that, Alpha One," Captain Darius said. "That's probably how it made it into the planet's gravity. It's possible that the troop ship can bring it back into orbit as well."

"We can't get close enough to see how many troopers they're putting on the ground, but hundreds at least."

"You pull your people back," Commander Kase. "That's an order. "I want you to protect those shuttles and make sure the Marines have a way off that rock."

"Copy that," Hard Case said, but then Aspen's voice broke through.

"Enemy flyers! I repeat, there are enemy ships in the air."

"Where did they come from?" Diamond asked.

Hard Case glanced at his radar. Even though it was too dark to see them, two dozen Ashi gunships had risen into the air around their larger vessels.

"Alpha One, what are you dealing with down there?" Captain Darius asked.

"Ashi gunships, sir. Lots of them. They'll be escorting their troops and heading toward the city any second now."

"The Marines are going to need a little time. The Furies are on their way to help you, but until they get there, you can't let the enemy ships anywhere near the city. Is that clear?"

"Crystal clear, Captain. We're on it."

He put his Raptor into a turn and checked his weapons. Just two air-to-ground missiles left. His power was at eighty-one percent. Without help, his squad would probably be wiped out trying to save the Marines. In his mind, everything about the mission was going wrong. But instead of giving up, he pushed his throttle forward and headed straight for the enemy.

CHAPTER 40

LASER FIRE PEPPERED the empty street. Remmy didn't have to order the Spec Ops platoon to take cover. They were all veterans and Gunnery Sergeant Izzy Berry was a capable leader.

"Didn't see that coming," Tex said.

"What are those things?" Corporal Dall shouted.

The laser rifles weren't loud, but the powerful beams of energy popped and sizzled through the air. They made pounding sounds as the energy was transferred to the sides of the buildings or street where they impacted, ripping the material and burning through solid objects.

"That's the Ashi," Hugo said. "But I've never seen them so fat before."

There were a dozen of the big, green aliens. Usually, they were hulking giants with bulging muscles. They wore kilts with wide leather belts but no shirts. The Ashi on Wesset were clearly past their prime. They were stooped and had massive, round bellies that hung over their belts. They were shoulder to shoulder in front of the Galactic Imperium complex, firing at the Marines with their big, bulky laser rifles.

"Sergeant Major, you want to help us out here?" Izzy said.

"Give both barrels, Hugo!" Tex said.

Hugo and Remmy were half a block behind the rest of the

platoon. They had reached a wide open plaza with fountains and statues that rose up fifty feet in the air, towering over even the gigantic Ashi warriors.

"They'll run down the power batteries in their rifles," Hugo said. "Just sit tight. I'll see if I can flush them out."

Hugo stepped back to give himself room and raised his rifle. The Ambrose Hill XOR's grenade launcher could hurl the explosives a hundred feet. Hugo fired one in a long, arching trajectory that actually carried over the heads of the Ashi. Before it fell, he had two more in the air.

"Fire in the hole!" he shouted, as he dropped down on one knee next to Remmy.

They pressed their backs against the wall of the building they were sheltering behind. The grenades went off in spectacular fashion. The Galactic Imperium complex was enclosed. Multiple buildings rose over the walls, which were carved with fantastic images of Ashi warriors in battle. There was a wide set of stairs just behind the warriors firing at the Marines, that rose toward two massive wooden gates with more carved figures on them. The gates were closed, and probably bolted shut with heavy beams. The grenades fell at the top of the steps and exploded, blowing chunks of stone out of the stairs and walls, although they didn't penetrate completely through. The gates broke down and one toppled onto the shattered steps.

The shockwave knocked the fat Ashi warriors down and their exposed skin was pelted by bits of stone. A cloud of dust enveloped them and, for a moment, they were vulnerable.

"Hit it!" Izzy shouted.

The plaza was suddenly transformed into a hail of projectiles. Rifles of various kinds boomed, their reports echoing off the stone walls. The Marines were issued laser rifles, but the overwhelming preference among the men and women on the front lines was to use projectile weapons. The wide variety of ammunition, combined with the stopping power of an actual bullet hitting flesh, was unrivaled. Laser weapons were still used, especially for long distances, but the Marines on Wesset were armed with a variety of hard-hitting projectile firearms, from the Sterner M88 Classic to the REM Thumper.

The bullets ripped through the clouds of dust. Some of them ricocheted off the towering statues and the polished flagstones; others hit alien flesh. Nine of the twelve Ashi warriors were gunned down within a few seconds of the grenade explosions. The Ashi had thick bone plates inside their chest. Where humans had a rib cage, the Ashi had thick, flat bones that formed a box around their hearts and vital organs. A bullet from a hundred feet wouldn't penetrate it under most conditions. But perhaps from the multitude of shots, or maybe due to the bone growing weaker with age, the bullets punched through. Flesh was torn and a few of the Ashi were even decapitated by the hail of bullets.

"Alpha team, Bravo team, advance," Remmy ordered, his voice calm through the helmet speakers. "Spread to either side of the plaza and watch your backs. There could be more of them waiting to ambush us out in the open."

"Copy that, Major," Izzy replied.

"Bravo team on the move," Tex said.

The three remaining Ashi were shell-shocked. One had even dropped his laser rifle. As the dust cleared, they struggled to their feet. Tex gunned one down with a single shot that penetrated the alien's flat forehead and blew his brains out of a gaping hole in the back of his skull. The other two charged toward Izzy as she led Alpha team through the plaza.

"Contact!" Corporal Dall shouted.

Three guns fired, and both Ashi warriors stumbled to the ground. One was dead where he lay, the other continued crawling. He could use just one arm as the other shoulder had been hit with a depleted uranium armor-piercing bullet that shattered the bones deep inside the thick limb.

"Finish him, Corporal," Izzy ordered. "Plaza is clear, Major."

"Green platoon is moving in," Mary Ann Putnam said.

"Take defensive positions and secure our way back out of the city," Remmy ordered. "Charlie and Delta teams get up onto the buildings here. If there's trouble coming, we need to see it."

"Roger that," Sergeant Talbot replied.

"I want explosive charges all along that wall," Remmy said. He had stepped into the clearing with Hugo at his side and was directing the Marines. "Hugo will shell the compound, then we go in and clear out anyone inside."

"We're on it," Izzy said. "You heard the man. I want charges every eight feet."

"Major, there seems to be fighting west of town," Talbot said over the comlink. "I can't see over the wall, but something's going on."

"We're on a tight clock here, people," Remmy said. Let's get this done."

"And get the hell out of Dodge," Tex added.

"I think it's called Drafton," Izzy replied.

"Same thing in my boo—"

A flash of laser fire came ripping from the open gate of the Galactic Imperium. Not just a single blast, but a well-coordinated hail of high-energy beams fanned out across the open ground. Marines were hit, including Major Remmy Steel. He fell to the ground at Hugo's feet and time seemed to stand still for a moment.

"Major!" Hugo shouted.

Remmy waved from the ground. His chest was smoking. The command module had been hit. Sparks began to snap from the ruined device. Hugo bent down and ripped the device from Remmy's chest armor.

"You alive?" Hugo asked.

"Go! Go!" Remmy said. "Hit that complex with all you've got."

"Return fire!" Hugo ordered. "All Marines fire on that compound."

His rifle sent a grenade straight through the sagging door to the compound gate. It exploded inside, and Hugo followed it up with his remaining eight grenades lobbed over the walls. Smoke was billowing from the complex as dozens of rifles opened up on the sagging gates. The other wooden door splintered under the sudden volley of gunfire from around the plaza.

Remmy raised himself to one elbow. "Green platoon, see to the wounded," he said in a raspy voice. "Sergeant Major, clear that compound."

"Yes, sir!" Hugo shouted. He sprinted toward the open gates, leaping over the bodies of the dead Ashi on the plaza.

"Rally to the Sergeant Major," Izzy ordered. "Alpha team, Bravo team, into the compound."

Five of the six Marines were still on their feet. Tex was down. A laser beam had found a gap in his armor at the top of his left thigh.

"Go on," he snapped to his fire team. "I'm fine."

Five Marine commandos, including Izzy Berry, followed Hugo into the complex. Fires blazed around them and there were bodies. Hugo saw mostly Wessians, but instead of the decorated belts they wore tunics that were ripped and blood-stained. There were a few other alien races, but no more Ashi. Hugo was merciless. Anywhere he saw movement, he fired. The shocked and bewildered government officials who came stumbling out of the burning buildings were gunned down on sight.

One trio had laser pistols. They wore bright red security sashes over their Galactic Imperium tunics. They were crouched down behind a pile of rubble. One rose and fired at Hugo, but his shot went wide. Hugo returned fire, his XOR on burst mode. Three explosive rounds hit the shooter and sent him flying backward.

"There's two more," Izzy said, catching up with Hugo. They fired into the rubble, which did little to stop the bullets. One screamed, the other tried to run, but Izzy shot the fleeing alien.

"Smoke's getting thick," Hugo said.

Their battle helmets filtered the smoke and allowed them to function in the hellish complex, but it was getting hard to see.

"Time to go," Izzy said as one of the taller buildings crumbled to the ground.

Dust, smoke, and debris filled the compound. Just getting back out was difficult. When Hugo came out, he saw charges stuck to the walls on either side of the ruined gate. The wounded Marines had been removed from the plaza.

"Fall back and detonate the charges," Hugo said, just as a Raptor roared above them.

Hugo and Izzy ducked instinctively, then ran down the ragged stone steps and across the open plaza.

"Sergeant Major," Talbot said from the top of a nearby structure. "I have movement on the west side of the plaza. Looks like enemy troopers."

"Cover our egress," Hugo ordered.

As soon as he and the other Marines of Alpha and Bravo teams ran behind the closest building, the charges went off. A fast series of explosions lit up the night. Fire billowed high in rolling plumes. Stone chips from the compound wall smashed into a group of Ashi warriors. They were an advance team hurrying toward the battle and straight into the blast from the charges. They went down, their flesh cut to bloody ribbons by the shards of stone.

"Fall back," Hugo ordered. "All Marines, fall back."

"Make it quick, Sergeant Major," Remmy said over the comlink. "Our time is almost up."

Hugo looked at Izzy. She nodded.

"Get them out," he said. "I'll cover the rear."

"Copy that, Sergeant Major. Charlie Team, Delta Team, we are leaving!"

She shouted the final words and Hugo couldn't blame her. Looking back through the smoke, he could see movement along the western side of the plaza. More troops. He popped the magazine from his XOR's upper barrel and rammed a fresh one into place. Snapping the charging lever to load the first round into the breech was a satisfying sound. Then Hugo went to work.

CHAPTER 41

FLYING toward the Ashi gunships was a bit like sprinting toward a swarm of hornets. His rational mind was telling him to flee, not attack. But his orders were clear ... and it wasn't so much the gunships that had Commander Kase worried.

"Focus your missile fire onto those troops," he ordered.

"Copy that, Commander," Diamond said.

The light from the overhead flares was fading, even as the Ashi moved in loose formation from the carrier onto the open plains. Hard Case focused his targeting system on the troops and fired.

"Kilo nine!" he said, firing his next to last air to ground missile.

Several of the gunships were turning toward him. They moved with a bouncy fluidity, sliding around on repulser power and bringing their lasers to bear.

"Kilo ten!" Hard Case called out, firing his last missile and switching the firing controls immediately to lasers.

As the missiles streaked down through the darkness, the first hit in the middle of the Ashi formation. The explosion was bright with deadly orange flames spreading out wide among the clustered warriors. The second would have done the same, but a valiant gunship dipped down between the second missile and the troopers. It blew up in spectacular fashion, yet saved the warriors on the ground.

Hard Case pulled back on his joystick and pushed the throttle forward. His right foot pressed down, sending the Raptor in a spiraling climb. Three of the Ashi gunships turned to follow, their more powerful engines overriding the repulsers they had been using, but it still wasn't enough to match the speed and agility of the Raptor. Hard Case saw flashes around him, but none of the laser blasts hit his ship.

Behind him, Aspen went charging into the fray. Her last two missiles came in low and killed dozens of Ashi warriors. Suddenly, the massive form of the Ashi troop carrier began to rise. The battleship on its back joined the fighting. Aspen had to break off her attack run, as did Diamond.

"We need to take out that battleship," Bishop said.

"We don't have the firepower," Hard Case said.

"Where's our support?" Aspen demanded.

Commander Justin Kase knew the answer, but he couldn't say it out loud. The Furies were coming, but he had no doubt that Commander Elder would take his sweet time about it. That had been his MO since flight school. He loved to hang back, let other flyers do the hard, often dangerous work, then speed in at the last second to mop up and take credit.

"Increase your speed," Hard Case ordered. "Don't get lazy and give that ship a line to fire on you."

"Power is down to seventy-five percent," Diamond said. "Once we start using lasers, we could run out of energy."

"That's a chance we'll have to take," Hard Case said. "We have to slow those troopers down and give our people as much time as we can."

Bishop tried a new tack. He swung out over the city and came at the Ashi from a different angle. He was flying low, even dipping down once he was past the high, outer wall on the west side of the city. It worked somewhat. The Ashi battleship wouldn't fire at him in case it missed and blasted the city. But his missiles were both intercepted by gunships. And there were still several flyers who swung around as he broke off his attack and followed him. Their lasers flashed as they tried to shoot him down.

Hard Case knew that laser weapons were major power drains. He had no idea how much energy the gunships carried. They weren't small ships. In fact, they looked like flying double-decker buses with lasers on each side. They could have massive power plants for all he knew. But they seemed a bit stingy with their laser fire. Unlike the battleship, which fired volleys as the Raptors did, the gunships tended to only fire one or two blasts before giving up.

"I've got three bogeys in pursuit," Hard Case said. "They're gaining speed."

"On my way," Aspen said. "Come around to heading one, seven, niner."

The big Ashi troop carrier was still climbing. It was several hundred feet up before its engines lit up and the ship began to fly in a steady ascent.

"What's that thing doing?" Bishop asked.

"Taking the battleship back into orbit would be my guess," Diamond said. "At least it isn't a threat to us anymore."

"I've got one on my six," Bishop called. "Power is at sixty-nine percent."

"They're spreading out," Diamond said. "The troops are advancing toward the city. Looks like they're running."

"Swing around and change their mind," Hard Case said.

He had just reached the heading Aspen called for, and she lit the gunships up with a series of laser blasts. Two of the ships were hit, one exploded and the other began to lose altitude.

"Nice shooting, Aspen," Hard Case said. "I can handle what's left. Focus on the troops."

"Roger that, Commander," Aspen said.

Hard Case rose and fell, pushing his Raptor to its limits. The computer system was warning him that his hull stress was too high and his engine was getting dangerously hot. Then he slammed his throttle back and let the nose of his ship dip. The jet engine stalled. He was eight thousand feet up and the last Ashi gunship was closing in. As the Raptor started to fall, she flipped over and Hard Case made the shot of his life. One laser blast lit the darkness and ripped through the cockpit of the Ashi gunship. It didn't slow down, but didn't shoot at him either. Instead, it flew past and just kept going and going.

The enemy on his tail was gone, but Hard Case wasn't out of danger. He flexed the ship's flaps to control the fall. The Raptor turned until it was diving straight down. The movement pushed air through the jet's turbine, forcing it to rotate. He watched his altitude dropping fast.

"Come on, come on!"

He needed the speed of the turbine to be high enough that he didn't waste a lot of power getting it started. So he waited until his ship dropped below two thousand feet, then hit the start-up button. Only nothing happened.

"I'm stalled," he said. "Engine non-responsive."

"Pull up!" Aspen warned him.

He was trying, but his downward momentum was hard to overcome. The flaps had no power assist without the engines running. And moving them against the wind that was flooding over the fuselage was nearly impossible. He pulled as hard as he could on the joystick that operated the wing flaps and pressed down with his heels at the same time to ensure he wasn't pressing the pedals forward. The ship inched up, although he knew it wasn't fast enough. He was too low and the Raptor was moving too fast.

"Eject, Hard Case," Bishop warned him. "Eject! Eject!"

He could have reached up and pulled the ejection handle. It would have detonated the charges around his canopy and flung his seat out of the ship. He was just within the minimum height requirement for the parachute to open and slow his descent enough that he wouldn't get hurt upon landing. But there was something inside him that said he could salvage his situation.

It wasn't the engine, which he tried again to no avail. And he couldn't buy himself time. In the darkness, it was impossible to visually gauge how close to the ground he was. But his altimeter showed him passing five hundred feet.

"Just enough time," he said softly. His hand reached, trembling against the Raptor's G-forces. His fingers pressed the artificial gravity controls. Unlike the jet engine, which had mechanical parts that needed to move and sync to work correctly, the gravity generator was less prone to failure. The gravity projected from the ship pulled him straight down even faster, but with a flick of his left wrist, he pulled back on the gravity joystick. The ship made a sudden turn.

At that moment, as his ship pulled out of its dive, Hard Case realized his mistake. His inertial dampener was turned almost all the way down. Had it been completely off, he would have killed himself, as all the blood was pulled out of his brain and into his lower extremities. Fortunately, the ship turned one hundred and seventy degrees. It wasn't quite moving straight up, but it was close. As the G-forces from the sudden turn eased, his heart pushed blood through his body, including his brain, and the fog that had nearly caused him to pass out lifted. He took a deep breath and looked around.

He was cruising up fast, much faster than his jet engine had propelled him. He reached out and dialed up the inertial dampener, both to relieve himself of the pressure but also to lessen the stress on the Raptor's airframe.

As he leveled, his comlink broke through the noise in his head.

"Hard Case, are you okay?" Aspen asked.

"I'm good," he said, his voice a little shaky. "Got a bit carried away there."

"How did you survive that fall?" Bishop was asking.

"Gravity drive," Hard Case said. "It works in atmosphere."

"Check your power, Commander," Diamond said.

He glanced at the power reading and felt a sickly, creeping feeling deep in his guts. The readout showed fifty-one percent.

"Good call, Diamond," he responded. "Switching back to jet engines."

There are times in an aircraft when components don't respond. Hard Case had heard mechanics talk about it. The same was true with all types of engines and mechanical devices. Hard Case couldn't say why the jet wouldn't activate before, but as he shut off the gravity drive, once more over five thousand feet above the ground and cruising parallel to the ground, his jet engine came on and he was able to fly normally.

The Hell Flyers made several strafing runs that wreaked havoc among the ranks of the Ashi troopers. The gunships were no match for the Raptors, their pilots unaccustomed to aerial dogfighting, and Hard Case could tell, they didn't have the power capacity to utilize their laser cannons in a sustained fight.

All but two of the gunships were shot down. The last two stayed low, just a few dozen feet off the ground, on either side of the column of troopers, and escorted the Ashi warriors into the city. Hard Case even fired on the city wall, which crumbled and collapsed, but did little to slow down the Ashi, who either went around or straight over the rubble.

"Ronan One, this is Alpha One actual, do you read me?"

"Loud and clear, Alpha One," Major Remmy replied via their comlink.

"The enemy has breached the city walls," Hard Case said. "My squad will cover your retreat, but I suggest you get your people out of there as soon as possible."

"We're on the move," Remmy said. "Shuttles are preparing to fly, but we still have units inside the city."

Hard Case could do nothing to speed the Marines along, but he knew if the Ashi got the chance, they would slaughter every human being on the planet. He glanced at his power reading. It was down to thirty-eight percent. He needed at least twenty percent to reach orbit. And there was still no sign of the Furies. All he could do was shake his head and keep flying.

CHAPTER 42

HUGO WAITED. It was a risk, but he wanted some distance behind the Marines before he engaged the Ashi. If the enemy were smart, they would close in on his position from all sides. Which meant that Hugo had limited options for making his escape. But if he could draw the enemy away from the Marines, they would have a better chance of escape.

"Come on, you green monsters," he whispered. "Just a little closer."

The enemy forces were nothing like the fat guards who had been slaughtered by the Marine force. Instead, they moved from cover to cover, watching for signs of the enemy, pressing in with concerted force. When he could wait no longer, Hugo opened up.

After thumbing the fire control switch to full auto, he opened up. It felt good.

The Ambrose Hill was a heavy firearm. It took a strong hand, especially when firing in the fully automatic mode. It was like trying to control a living, breathing animal that wanted to break free of his grasp. But Hugo had spent hundreds of hours working with the heavy rifle. When utilized correctly, the weight was an asset. He utilized that weight to help him control the rifle as it fired. The Shock-Wave kinetic rounds chugged out at eight bullets per second. They compressed from back to front on impact, and a tiny internal explosive drove the bullet deeper into the target. They ripped through a team of Ashi warriors that were less than fifty feet from where Hugo was waiting. He turned past the corner of the building he was waiting behind and fired twenty rounds in a level sweep from one side of the street to the other. Ten Ashi warriors were running toward him. They didn't even get a shot off before his bullets impacted them just above their wide belts. Each round penetrated through skin and muscle. The detonation then pushed the jagged metal deep into the alien warriors' body cavity, where it tore and sliced through the bulging intestines. Blood gushed, flesh tore, and gaping holes opened in the Ashi's stomachs until their ropy innards fell out on the ground. The troopers fell too, dropping face-first onto the street.

Laser fire from behind the lead group drove Hugo back behind the building he had been sheltering beside. Not that he needed encouragement to flee. It was time to drop back. He sprinted from his building down the next street. There he turned, slid to one knee, and looked back. He waited. For a moment, nothing happened. Smoke drifted up from pockmarks on the buildings and streets where the laser fire had impacted the structures. The buildings were made from some kind of stone, a sort of concrete-type mixture that held large blocks of stone together. Although they weren't as thick as they seemed. Hugo wondered briefly if maybe the stonework was fake, but he had little knowledge of construction or building materials.

In that moment, waiting for the enemy to rush around the corner, guns blazing, he thought of Zaya. She would have enjoyed seeing the Wesset city. She might have even known what the buildings were made of. He couldn't help but smile. Despite being in mortal danger, the fact that he had someone to think of filled him with an inexplicable joy. He had always believed that if he died in combat, he would be remembered by few and missed by no one. During those years when he struggled in vain to connect with people, he had wondered if having those relationships made a person weaker or stronger. At last, he knew and the realization that he had someone to get back to only made him even more determined to succeed than ever before.

He was kneeling, staying low, his rifle held ready. The enemy came just as he expected them to. The Ashi were nothing if not predictable. While he didn't know them, his experience with the big aliens was enlightening. They were big, in fact, the Ashi were the largest intelligent species humanity had come across in the galaxy. The big aliens didn't think much about tactics or strategy. Instead, they pressed forward, going straight at their enemy. But no other enemy had guns because the Ashi had outlawed firearms of all kinds. Yet Hugo wasn't part of their Galactic Imperium. So, as the team of aliens came around the corner, he opened fire.

His rifle moved steadily left to right, then back left again. Bullets tore through legs and groins, punching through the Ashi's thick kilts. The lead runners went down, sprawling onto their faces, screaming in pain that was loud enough to drown out the reports from his rifle. In the second and a half it took Hugo to eject the spent magazine from the XOR and insert a fresh one, a second, larger wave of aliens crowded into the street behind the first. They opened fire the instant they turned the corner with no idea of where Hugo was. They aimed high, as was their habit. But Hugo stayed low. The laser blasts scorched both sides of the street, defacing the buildings and blowing chunks of material from the roof overhangs. More lasers flashed down the street past Hugo's hiding spot. He leaned into the corner, making his muscular frame as small as he could, before he opened fire.

There were more Ashi than bullets in the rifle. But the street, which was wide for a human, forced the big aliens to crowd close together. He fired four short bursts, each one taking down multiple aliens as he fired into their stomachs. If they had worn armor or fought with more caution, it would have decreased their casualties, except the Ashi didn't think that way. They didn't mind losing troopers. Overwhelming force was their strategy and they had no sympathy for those who fell in combat. Hugo wondered briefly if the Ashi he killed had people who loved them and were waiting for them somewhere in another corner of the galaxy.

After gunning down half their number, the rest of the alien troopers began to seek cover from his powerful weapon. Hugo was more than just a Marine and it wasn't just his Ambrose Hill XOR that made him deadly. It was a battle skill, a talent for killing that couldn't be taught. Hugo didn't have to think about who to fire on or where his single weapon would be of the most use against the overwhelming force of the enemy. Nor did he need anyone to tell him when his advantage had passed. As the Ashi dropped behind the bodies piled in the road, or pressed themselves against the building walls and into alcoves to give them whatever shelter they could find against their deadly enemy, Hugo pushed back from the corner he was tucked behind, spun to his feet and ran as fast as he could. A moment later, the enemy hurried to catch him.

CHAPTER 43

REMMY WAS HURT. The laser blast had been stopped by the command module on his chest, but the energy raced through the device, crackled over his armor and left burns on his chest and stomach. Of course, he felt fortunate just to be alive, and there were other Marines much worse off. His wounds were minor, but there were some, like Staff Sergeant Tex Fry, with serious wounds. Tex was alert and capable, but could barely walk even with another Marine helping him. His wound, a vicious laser burn at the top of his thigh, had penetrated deep into his upper quadriceps and narrowly missed the bone. It left a hole as large as his thumb that reached three-quarters of the way through his leg.

Then there were the serious wounds. Four Marines were in need of emergency care. Two had been killed outright. It was a heavy toll, and the fighting wasn't over. Mary Ann Putnam had come alongside Major Steel as they retreated from the city.

"Are you okay?" she asked.

"I'm fine," he said, his voice raspy. The shock from the laser blast had stunned him and the kinetic blow to his chest had made it hard to breathe. "Got the wind knocked out of me, that's all. My armor took the hit."

"You're lucky that shot wasn't a few inches higher," she said.

He swallowed a sudden lump of fear that formed in his throat. Nearby, the city's outer wall rose. He was glad to see it and considered briefly calling for the shuttles to come and get them. But that would leave their escape vehicles open to attack. The Ashi had powerful laser rifles. If Remmy had been shot with one, he would have been dealing with a major injury instead of the minor burns that chafed under his scorched fatigue smock. But their rifles were designed for short-range conflict and were only effective to about a hundred feet. This gave the humans an advantage by moving away from the city, where they could board the shuttles and escape unscathed.

"Luck is a Marine's best friend," Remmy said. "Keep your wounded moving until they reach the shuttle."

"Yes, sir," she replied. "What about you?"

"I'm fine," he said. "Don't waste your efforts on me, Lieutenant. This isn't my first engagement with the Ashi downrange."

She nodded and moved to help another Marine who was limping. At the city's outer wall, Remmy stopped and looked back. His comlink still worked, but without the command module, he had no idea if any of the members of the Spec Op platoon had survived. He would have to wait until they caught up with him or the Ashi appeared. If the latter happened, he would know they were dead. It was part of being a Marine. Death was always near and unrelenting.

He set off after the rest of Green Platoon. They were helping the wounded from their platoon and the Spec Ops platoon. The vast expanse of the open plain was lit by fires in the city. Flickering red light made Remmy glance up. Flares were descending over the city, too, and past them were stars. It bathed the plain in a ghostly light. In the distance, Remmy could see the berms. They were his next rally point.

"Keep moving," he called out. "Everyone, keep moving."

The earthworks were fifteen hundred meters from the city walls, and the shuttles were a kilometer and a half beyond them. Out in the open, Remmy felt exposed. But he was able to get a clear signal from Lieutenant Ales of Crimson Platoon.

"Reports from the sat drones over the city show the Ashi advancing, Major."

"How much time do we have?"

"Two, maybe three minutes before they reach the city walls," he said. "They aren't following you directly either, sir. They've pushed south of us."

"We'll get the wounded loaded up, then fall back by squads," Remmy said. "Make sure your people are ready to cover our retreat, but stay cool. I don't want anyone getting jumpy and firing while we have Marines on this side of your defenses."

"Copy that, sir. We are ready."

Remmy turned and looked over his shoulder. His heart fluttered, and he nearly brought his rifle to his shoulder when he saw movement among the shadows under the wall. But it wasn't the Ashi. Gunny Berry was leading her platoon out of the city.

"Perfect timing," Remmy said. "The Ashi are almost to the walls."

"Yes, sir, Sergeant Major McManus is slowing them down."

Remmy felt a wave of relief that was tinged with fear for his friend. "Do you have wounded?"

"Negative, Major, we're all good."

"Excellent," he said, reaching the berm and taking a deep breath. The cold night air burned in his nostrils and his chest ached. He leaned against the edge of the earthwork.

"Are you sure you're okay, Major?" Lieutenant Ales asked.

"I'm fine," Remmy said. "I must be getting soft, though. I need more time in the gym, I suppose."

He looked toward the city, saw the flames as if it were the scene of a historical epic. Only it was an alien city, on a hostile world. They had come to destroy the Galactic Imperium, but more fires had been kindled. Homes were burning, buildings going up in flames. Smoke was billowing into the sky above the city as Commander Kase radioed in. Remmy updated the pilot, then focused on the city. Somewhere inside, Hugo was fighting for his life.

"They will come fast," Remmy said. "They can run faster than you think beings of their size should be able to move," he explained as he walked down the line of Marines, who were being reinforced by the Spec Ops platoon. "But we will let them come. We'll let them flood out onto the plain and straight into our trap. Do not fire until I give the word. Is that clear?"

"Yes, sir!" the Marines said.

They didn't have to shout. Their battle helmets restrained their voices, but the comlinks inside carried their every word back to their commander.

"They're big, powerful creatures, but they're not very smart. They'll come straight at us, and when they do, we will put them down," Remmy said. "Every last one of them."

"I have movement," a Marine down on the far end of the defensive trench said. "One of ours. It's Sergeant McManus!"

Remmy turned to see his big friend drop his rifle. That was a clear sign that the enemy was close on his heels. Remmy knew that Hugo loved his XOR, but he let it fall and put all his efforts into running. He swung wide, turning toward the berm. It was a full kilometer and a half distant from the walls, and Hugo barely made it a quarter of the way before the first Ashi arrived. They were huge, their long legs pumping hard. Remmy could see their breath puffing in clouds of condensation from their hot, ragged breath.

"Hold!" Remmy ordered.

"They're going to catch him," someone said.

"How do they move that damn fast?" someone else complained.

Remmy heard it all. Crimson platoon gasped when one Ashi raised his rifle and fired on the run. The shot was off target and Hugo was just out of range.

"Gunny Berry, when I give the word, I want you and your best shooters to pick off those runners closest to Sergeant Major McManus," Remmy said. He was rubbing his stomach just beneath the burn. Tension made the muscles all the way up his back and into his neck stiff and painful.

"Yes, sir," Izzy replied. "Say the word."

He waited. Another Ashi fired. Remmy felt like he couldn't breathe, but once again, the blast was off the mark. Then a third raised his bulky laser rifle and Remmy knew he couldn't wait any longer.

"Now, Gunny," he said with a calm he did not feel.

Instantly, six shots rang out. The bullets sped across the open field. Hugo must have heard them pass him by as he flinched just slightly, but kept running. Behind him, six Ashi fell to the ground, including those who were shooting at the big Sergeant Major.

"Hold," Remmy said.

Hugo was halfway across the open expanse and still running. He was going straight past the defensive earthworks, as would the enemy fighters. But as Remmy looked past Hugo, he felt a new stab of fear. There were more Ashi than he expected. Hundreds were rushing out of the city; soon, it would be more than a thousand. He had fewer than forty Marines at their makeshift defenses. It wasn't enough to stop over a thousand Ashi warriors. And he still needed to get Crimson platoon and the rest of the Spec Op commandos back to the shuttles.

It crossed his mind in that moment that he might be on his last battlefield. Remmy would, without question, be the last Marine onto the safety of the shuttles. He would leave no living Marine behind, even if that meant he would die trying to defend or save them. For a moment, he was flooded with regret. He should have written Laila a note that declared his love. He knew that she was aware of how he felt about her, although he hated the thought of leaving her with nothing personal.

"Just a little longer," Remmy said.

"There's so many," a young voice said.

"That's true," Remmy said. "But today, we will teach the Ashi to fear the SDF Marines."

That got shouts and Ooo-rahs from the Marines. Remmy smiled. He believed that what he had said was true, but also that the young Marines might die in the process. If that was the cost of their victory on Wesset, Remmy decided, then so be it.

"Fire," he said.

The Marines responded with gusto. Their weapons had much greater range than the Ashi laser rifles. The enemy went down in waves. Those closest to Sergeant Major McManus dropped hard, then the group behind. Dozens died. But hundreds crowded in. The outcome was inevitable. The Marines would be overrun. He glanced over his shoulder. The first of the wounded were just that moment reaching the shuttles.

"Keep it up," he snapped. "Pour it on them."

"You should head back, Major," Hugo said as he came trotting up beside Remmy.

"No," was all Remmy said.

"I can hold them here, sir. That's my job."

"I'm not leaving," Remmy said. "Not when we've got Marines on the battlefield."

"Sir, that is your duty. You must survive this day," Hugo said.

"Either we all go, or none of us go," Remmy said.

He raised his rifle and fired at the Ashi. It was, in the grand scheme, a useless gesture. But it felt good to do something. There were so many aliens in the open field that he couldn't miss. He didn't even need to aim. He could just point and shoot. His Nelson LTX chugged away, each jerk against his shoulder sending stabbing pain through his body from the secondary burns on his chest and stomach.

But the enemy had realized their advantage. They formed up in rows and charged forward. Hundreds would die, but they would reach the berm and the Marines would be massacred. Remmy wondered if he gave the order for his Marines to run if they could make it to the shuttles before the Ashi got close enough to gun them down. Before he could decide, a thunderous noise came rolling out of the darkness. Then the lasers flashed like lightning bolts. They tore through the ranks of the alien army. The Marines cheered.

The laser attack was followed by a missile that came whistling down from the darkness and exploded. Dozens died in the blast.

"Retreat!" Remmy shouted. "Move back. Make for the shuttles, Marines. Move!"

The group jumped out of the trench and started running. Remmy was the last one. He fired his rifle until the last bullet was spent. That's when Hugo grabbed him and hauled his body out of the trench.

"Let's go!" he shouted.

Remmy ran. His hands worked the ejection switch as he hurried. The empty ammunition magazine fell to the ground, and he pressed in a fresh one. Then he did something he had never done before in all his years of service in the Space Marines. He unclipped his rifle from the harness and handed it to Hugo. The big man turned, running backward, and somehow keeping pace with Remmy. Hugo fired back at the Ashi, but only a few were still in pursuit of the Marines. The Hell Flyers continued to strafe them with laser blasts, and the majority had fallen back to the city and the cover it provided.

"They're running, sir," Hugo said.

Remmy looked over his shoulder, relieved not to be fighting for once in his life. He reached up and rubbed his stomach just below the burns that were flaring in pain as his clothing rubbed over them. He was surprised to feel something wet on his hand. He looked down and, in the flickering light, saw blood.

"You okay?" Hugo asked.

"Fine," he lied.

They ran almost all the way back, although it was more of a slow jog. Remmy had been a runner all his life and never before had he felt so weak and slow. Hugo didn't complain. He targeted a few of the Ashi, but none were trying to get close to the Marines by the time they reached the shuttles. Remmy waited until all the other Marines were on board. Above them, two Raptors circled. One of the shuttles was just lifting off when Remmy let Hugo help him on board. Then Hugo joined him, and the aircraft lifted into the air.

A third Raptor joined the first two and Remmy heard the pilots giving the all clear to make the climb into orbit. Engines flared and Remmy felt gravity pushing down against him. He was standing by the rear hatch, one hand on a safety handle, as he looked out toward the city. It was a raging inferno. He saw the Ashi moving along the edges of the city, but very few Wessians. Their capital was burning down and Remmy hoped the local citizens were fleeing from their homes.

"What a waste," Hugo said.

"It was a fantastic place," Remmy agreed. He could feel Hugo's thick hand with a firm grasp on Remmy's free arm. "Close the hatch. We're done here."

CHAPTER 44

COMMANDER KASE FOLLOWED his shuttle into orbit. He had one eye on the radar screen and one on his power levels. When they reached orbit, he had just four percent power left. It wasn't enough to engage the gravity drive. He wasn't sure what he was going to do, but instead of declining, the power levels started to increase once they were outside the planet's gravity.

"Man, that's a welcome sight," Bishop said. "Power level is going up."

"Mine too," Diamond added.

"Engage gravity drives," Hard Case ordered. "We aren't out of the woods yet."

"It's about time you made it," a familiar voice said. It was so cocky that Hard Case had no trouble identifying it. "You missed all the excitement. We had to fight a battleship on the back of a larger carrier."

"Is that a fact?" Hard Case said. "Took your whole squad?"

"We handled it, you're clear to make straight for the *Renegade*."

Just the sound of Legend's voice made Hard Case angry, but he kept his thoughts to himself and flew beside the shuttle back to the *Renegade*.

On board the ship, the wounded were taken away by med techs.

Those with the most serious wounds were checked by Doctor Victoria Holt first. Major Remmy Steel had to have his fatigue tunic cut away. There were burns on his chest and stomach, but also a pointed piece of polymer that had broken off the ruined command module was stabbing into his side. The flesh around it was swollen.

"You've seen better days, Major," Doctor Vicky told him.

"Didn't even know it happened," he said. "In all the excitement, I thought I just had a stitch in my side."

"I suppose you could call it that. The surgical bot can remove it," she said. "I'll check on you in the Med Bay."

"Sure," Remmy said.

But he didn't go to the Med Bay. Instead, he enlisted Hugo to push him in a hover chair to the Bridge of the ship.

"I didn't know this promotion meant I had to help you break the rules," Hugo said.

"Never thought I would hear you complain about that," Remmy said.

"I think Lieutenant McPherson will not be pleased that I helped you disobey an order from the ship's doctor."

"I'm going to the Med Bay, just not directly," he said.

He was holding a gauze pad over the wound that was soaking up the blood. When they reached the command section, Remmy insisted on leaving the chair in the corridor. He walked onto the Bridge and gave his report.

"Not what I was hoping for," Darius said. "You're sure it's destroyed, the entire city?"

"Yes, sir," Remmy said. "Fires started when the Raptors hit the laser cannons. It only got worse as we fought through the city. Lots of laser fire from the Ashi."

"They have no shame," Darius said. "Look around, Major. The Ashi battleships destroyed sixteen commercial ships before we could neutralize them."

"We did what we set out to do, sir," Remmy said.

"Just not the way we wanted it done," Darius replied.

"War is a dangerous business."

"Agreed. And to that end, I want you in the Med Bay, Major. I can't afford to lose you."

"It's just a scratch, sir," Remmy said.

Behind him, Hugo cleared his throat and shook his head.

"Get to the Med Bay, that's an order. Our job here is done. Word is out about what we've done. We must slip away and reassess our plans."

"Yes, sir," Remmy said. "Thank you, sir."

Hugo led him back to the seat and Remmy sagged as he sat down. He was tired. Everything hurt, and as he often thought after a mission, winning in warfare was not as sweet as one thought. The collateral damage weighed heavily on him, even though it couldn't be helped. Still, he felt that others were paying the bill for a war they hadn't asked for. Perhaps, Remmy thought as he reached the Med Bay and was given a dose of pain reliever that made his limbs feel heavy and his eyes want to close, wars would never be fought, if those who started them had to pay the butcher's bill.

Across the ship on the flight deck, Commander Justin Kase climbed from his ship. Fatigue clung to him like spider webs, but he put his hand on the fuselage and said, "Good work. Thanks for holding together."

"My, my, my," Petty Officer Dante Smith said. "What have you done to my baby, Commander?"

"Survived, is really all I can say," Hard Case replied. "We nearly lost her at one point. The engine stalled, and I nearly couldn't get it going again."

"Why would it stall? What kind of crazy flying were you doing?"

"The kind that keeps people alive," he said.

"Yeah, well, speaking of that, Lieutenant Pince and Lieutenant Vin Dice are alive. That's more than I can say for their Raptors. But you won't find 'em down here, no sir. They've been taken up to Med Bay."

"But they're alive?"

"Was," Dante replied. "That's all I know for sure."

Hard Case and the other pilots hustled their way to the medical facility. Animal was waiting for them. He had a concussion, but otherwise was unscathed.

"I got enough power from the emergency battery to get back to the ship," he explained. "They're only keeping me in here because I was unconscious for like a second."

"Concussions are serious," Diamond said.

"Maybe you got some sense knocked into you," Bishop said.

"And what about Indigo?" Hard Case asked.

"It's a waiting game," Animal explained. "She got hit worse than me. A few fractures, a major concussion, possible brain swelling, plus her Raptor lost pressure. She had used up all the air in her flight suit by the time they got her out. It's possible there could be damage. They've got her in the Intensive Care suite, but she hasn't woken up. The doctor let me stay in that room too, since I've got to be here anyway. I didn't want her to wake up alone. I only came out when you guys showed up."

The Med Bay was busy. There were eight Marines either recovering or waiting for surgery. They filled the beds on one side of the Med Bay. The techs were hurrying around, making sure everyone was seen to and getting the care they needed. Hard Case wanted to see Indigo, but he was still in his flight suit, and a message came through for him to report to the Bridge.

"I've got to report to the Captain," Hard Case said. "The rest of you get cleaned up. We'll take turns sitting with her until she's awake. Animal, can you hold down the fort for a bit?"

"You know it," he said. "She'll make it. She's strong, you know."

"The strongest," Aspen said.

"See you all soon," Hard Case said.

When he reached the Bridge, Commander Mathias Elder was already there. The man was insufferable. He was bragging to the XO of his squad's victory over the Ashi battleship. Hard Case stepped onto the bridge and waited to speak. Captain Darius was nearby, studying the plot. It seemed as though he wasn't even listening.

"We were almost on an entry vector when that beast came rising up," Legend said. "I immediately ordered my squadron to turn back. Once we circled around, the battleship had detached from the larger ship and opened fire. We were nearly caught in it. Kicker took a hit, but his shields held. I sent four ships around to the front of the battle cruiser to draw its fire, while Heimdall and I hit the back end. I'm sure you saw it get pushed back down into the planet's gravity well. It'll crash if it hasn't already."

Legend, as always, was clearly proud of himself. Captain Darius, on the other hand, was not. He turned, still standing by the holographic plot, and said in a cold voice.

"And it didn't occur to you, Commander, that you were disobeying a direct order, or that your actions directly endangered the lives of the Marines on the surface of the planet?"

"No, Captain, I..."

"Of course you didn't," Captain Darius said. "You were too busy hot dogging with a ship that wasn't a threat."

"I disagree sir. It was a threat to the *Renegade*."

"Do you think we're fools, Commander?" Darius asked. "Do you really believe that those two enemy ships were not on our radar? Or that we hadn't come about in preparation for dealing with the Ashi battleship? Was there an issue with the communications equipment on your Raptor that kept you from hearing the repeated calls for you to vacate that space?"

"I deemed that ship to be a threat. I had the resources to deal with it, which is what I did, as per regulations. To not have done would be a dereliction of duty."

"Don't get coy with me, Commander," Captain Darius said, walking up and standing so close to Legend that their noses nearly touched. "You're a good flyer, but hot dogging on a combat mission will not be tolerated on this ship. Nor will you ignore orders so that you can leave another squadron hanging out to dry over your pride. Do I make myself clear, Commander? Or do you require a more thorough explanation of things?"

"No, sir, I believe I understand you perfectly," Legend said in an icy tone.

"Good, because if you disobey another order that I give you will be grounded and possibly brought up on charges."

"I think you are over—"

"That is all, Commander. Your presence is no longer required on the Bridge at this time. You are dismissed."

Legend's eyes narrowed, but Captain Darius didn't look away.

After a moment, it was Legend who blinked. He took a step backward, turned, and left the Bridge without another word.

Hard Case was feeling a lot of emotions after the mission. But he had to admit that he enjoyed seeing Legend get taken down a peg or two.

Darius turned to Hard Case, "Commander, your squadron proved themselves to be outstanding flyers today. Your presence at the battle was, I believe, the difference between failure and victory."

"Thank you, sir," Hard Case said.

"Yes, well, don't start gloating yet," Darius said. "You took a terrible chance down there, Commander. Starting the gravity drive in atmosphere has not been tested or approved. It could have ripped that Raptor to pieces with you in it."

"Yes, sir," Hard Case said. He could feel his cheeks turning red and wished his emotions weren't so visible, but there was nothing he could do to hide his shame.

"You want to explain what you were thinking?" Darius asked.

"Yes, sir, I was thinking I didn't want to ditch my fighter, Captain. I know that's not how we train for those types of emergencies, and truth be told, I brought that emergency on myself, but I... bailing out just felt wrong."

"We don't fly on feelings," Darius said. "Instincts are good, but don't put yourself at risk like that, Commander. We can make more Raptors, but we cannot replace you. From what I've heard, you are already down one pilot. You should have had help. For that, I take full responsibility. I thought that after a decade of service, Legend could put the past behind him. I won't make that mistake again, but we have to fly smart here, Commander. We have limited resources, and our greatest assets are the crew of this ship. Above all else, we keep our people safe. I expect you to set a better example, Commander. Is that clear?"

"Yes, sir, Captain. I will do better, sir."

"I know you will. Get cleaned up and give my best to Lieutenant Pince. Once we are out of this system, I will be down to see about the wounded personally."

"Yes, sir," Hard Case said as he stiffened to attention and saluted.

Darius saluted in return and watched as Hard Case left the Bridge.

"That was a close one," Nash said.

"Too close," Darius said. "We have to get out of this system before more Ashi show up and it's too late."

"What about that last ship?" Nash asked.

"There's no way to get to it without risking civilian casualties. I won't do it. Lieutenant Ramos, will you plot us the fastest way out of the system?"

"Aye, Captain. Do you have a destination in mind, sir?"

"Take us back to where we were," Darius said. "We need a moment to lick our wounds. From there, we'll check on the fallout of the attack. Perhaps we'll even get word of what the Ashi fleet is doing."

"Captain, if I may speak," Nurek said.

"Of course, Lieutenant. What is it?"

"Sir, I thought you should know. There is a celebration on Wesset."

"A celebration?" Nash asked. "Why?"

"It seems a majority of the Wessians are celebrating the destruction of Drafton," Nurek said. "There are gatherings taking place across the planet. I have no personal contacts on that world, but from the chatter coming up on the communication signals, they were not happy about what they called the Imperium's City."

"Well, I suppose that's one less thing to be concerned with then," Darius said.

"It was a more successful mission than we thought," Commander Nash said.

"A victory," Darius said. "But every victory has a cost. We lost people, and I was hoping that wouldn't be the case."

"No one ever said freedom was free," Nash said. "I believe the tree of liberty must be refreshed with the blood of heroes and tyrants, if I'm remembering my history correctly."

"Thomas Jefferson," Darius said.

"Captain, the course is laid in," Vivian Ramos said.

"Very good, Lieutenant. Let's take our exit. Lieutenant Stanislaus, engage engines. And Lieutenant Nurek, let the civilians know that we'll be back. This isn't the end, it's just the beginning."

AUTHOR'S NOTE

Thank you for reading *Hell Flyers*. It became more of an epic story with more character arcs than I originally planned on. I was just having so much fun with the story I didn't hold anything back. And more is coming. *Alert Status Red* (Starship Jericho book 2) is already being written. I hope that you will leave a rating/review on Amazon and Goodreads to help others find this book. As always, your reading recommendations are invaluable to a story's longevity and success.

ALSO BY TOBY NEIGHBORS

The Vault Of Mysteries

Lords Of Ascension

The Elusive Executioner

Gryphon Warriors

Regulators Revealed

Avondale

Draggah

Balestone

Arcanius

Avondale V

Third Prince

Royal Destiny

The Other Side

The New World

Luck Holds

Zompocalypse

Spartan Company

Spartan Valor

Spartan Guile

Dragon Team Seven

Uncommon Loyalty

Total Allegiance

Kestrel Class

Jump Point

Gravity Flux

Modulus Echo

Zero Friction

Planet Fall

Charter

Jack & Roxie

Fractal Cut

Blast Zone

Action Zone

Covert Infil

Armor Brigade

Havoc Squad

Thunderbird

Ghost Tactics

Quantum Combat

Infinite Threat

Shadow Threat

Evolving Threat

Lingering Threat

Latent Prowess

Gravity Masters

Gravity Storm

Daughter of the Night

Supernova

Artifact

Blood Moon

Renegade

Juggernaut

Retribution

Independence

Sons of Perdition

Iron Man

Brutal Planet

With Pete Garcia

Apocalypse One Percenters

www.ingramcontent.com/pod-product-compliance
Lightning Source LLC
Chambersburg PA
CBHW051951240626

47153CB00005B/1716